I0551933

The Return of Hitler

Anonymous

1

Books by Anonymous –

The Book With No Name
The Eye of the Moon
The Devil's Graveyard
The Book of Death
The Red Mohawk
Sanchez: A Christmas Carol
The Plot to Kill the Pope
The Day It Rained Blood
The Greatest Trick the Devil Ever Pulled
Showdown With the Devil
Killing the Elite
The Return of Hitler

"This is the best plan I have ever come up with," – Adolf Hitler

One

B Movie Hell – Three years ago

One of the highlights of Silvio Mellencamp's day was his mid-morning jacuzzi. It was a great way to relax with a cigar, a glass of cognac and a beautiful young woman for company. The beautiful young woman in question was Jasmine, his favourite of all the prostitutes that worked in his brothel, the Beaver Palace. Jasmine had creamy brown skin and long dark hair, and she gave the best blowjob Mellencamp had ever known. And he'd known a great many. For her part, Jasmine enjoyed sucking him off and rimming him in the jacuzzi because she said it made her feel like the servant who did the same thing to Prince Akeem in the movie, *Coming To America*.

But while Jasmine had a similar figure to the servant in the movie, Silvio Mellencamp looked nothing like Eddie Murphy's Prince Akeem. Mellencamp was a sweaty, bald, overweight, hairy, middle-aged white man in his fifties with a dyed black goatee. In spite of his lack of physical appeal, he had sex with at least one beautiful young woman every day. None came close to Jasmine though. She was the only one who could make him wriggle and squeal like a ticklish hyena.

After Jasmine completed her early morning jacuzzi tasks, she climbed out of the bubbling bath and started drying off with one of Mellencamp's towels. While he ogled her naked form as she rubbed herself down with the towel, he picked up a remote and switched on the TV that hung on the wall of his oversized private bathroom. Jasmine's favourite old show, *The A-Team* was on. Mellencamp thought the show was dumb, but he was willing to let Jasmine watch it while he watched her dry off. In the current episode, Mr T's character, B.A. Baracus had just been hit over the head and knocked unconscious by one of his friends so they could get him onto an aeroplane.

'You know, they shouldn't keep knocking him out like that,' said Jasmine, while bending over and drying her feet.

'He doesn't like flying,' Mellencamp reminded her, his eyes firmly glued to her perfectly formed ass. 'They have to knock him out otherwise they'd never get him on the plane.'

'I know that,' Jasmine replied. 'But yesterday they drugged his cheeseburger again, and the day before that they hit him over the head. It can't be good for him. He'll end up with terrible brain damage.'

5

Mellencamp took a long puff on his cigar. 'It's just a TV show,' he reminded her.

'Yes, I know,' said Jasmine, 'but it can't be doing Mr T any good can it? All those drugged cheeseburgers and bangs on the head will destroy his acting career eventually.'

'The cheeseburgers aren't really drugged. He's acting, remember?'

'They keep injecting him with stuff too, and gassing him. No wonder he's always so angry.'

Mellencamp rolled his eyes. 'Could you turn around a second?' he asked her.

Jasmine turned to face him. He looked her up and down. *That body, so sexy.* He could feel another boner coming on already.

'What's up?' she asked him.

'Same thing that's always up when I look at you,' said Mellencamp, grinning. 'Why don't you slide back into the water with me. It's still warm.'

Before Jasmine could respond to his irresistible request, there was a knock at the door.

'Come in,' Mellencamp called out.

One of the other women who worked at the Beaver Palace pushed the door open and stepped inside. Her name was Baby, and she had a bright blue birthmark on her left cheek. She was wearing a pair of white jeans and a pink T-shirt. She was very timid, which appealed to a number of the brothel's creepier customers. The name Baby had been given to her because she looked a little like Jennifer Grey from *Dirty Dancing*.

'Hi Baby,' said Jasmine.

'Hi Jas.'

'Wanna hop into the bath with me and Jasmine?' Mellencamp asked her.

'I'd love to,' Baby replied. 'But I've been sent here to get Jasmine.'

Mellencamp picked up his glass of cognac. 'What for?' he asked, before taking a sip.

'Clarisse says there's a couple of guys downstairs who have requested a threesome with Jasmine. They're offering a thousand bucks for it.'

Mellencamp put his drink back down on the side of the bath and looked over at Jasmine. 'What are you waiting for?' he asked. 'That's a thousand bucks. And a hundred of it will be yours. Get going.'

'I'm still wet,' said Jasmine. 'You'll have to give me a minute, Baby.'

6

'Go down there as you are,' said Mellencamp. 'Give them guys a surprise by turning up naked. They'll love it. It'll be the quickest hundred bucks you've ever earned.'

'Okay. Can you tell me how The A-Team ends later?'

'I'll tell you now,' said Mellencamp. 'They'll get locked in a cave by the bad guys but they'll build a tank out of paperclips and sausage meat, then they'll bust out, scare the bad guys into surrendering, and the show will end without anyone getting shot.'

'Oh, that's okay then,' said Jasmine. 'I've already seen this one.'

'Come here,' said Mellencamp, dragging himself across the jacuzzi towards Jasmine. 'Give us a kiss before you go.'

Jasmine wrapped her towel around her head, then leaned down to give Mellencamp a kiss. He grabbed the back of her head and slid his tongue into her mouth. The slobbery kiss went on for about ten seconds. When it ended, Mellencamp slapped her on the ass and sent her on her way.

Jasmine left her clothes behind and followed Baby out into the corridor. 'Are there really two guys?' she asked once the door was shut behind them.

'Yeah,' Baby replied. 'One's a big hunk, the other is kind of strange-looking.'

'Strange-looking?'

'Yeah. He's wearing a gimp mask and a flasher's coat.'

'And what's strange about him?'

Baby hesitated. 'Oh, he just seemed a bit weird to me. It's hard to explain.'

Halfway along the corridor they took a turn and headed down a set of stairs to the ground floor.

'They're probably regulars,' said Jasmine.

'I don't think so,' said Baby. 'Even Clarisse has never seen them before.'

They eventually arrived on the lower ground floor where most of the private rooms were situated. Baby pointed down a corridor that was lined with yellow carpet and orange walls. 'They're in room fourteen,' she said. 'Do you want me to come in and introduce you to them?'

'Nah, it's okay. I'll be fine. It makes a nice change to get out of Silvio's room and earn some money this early in the day.'

Baby glanced down at Jasmine's naked body. 'Are you really not going to put anything on before you go in?' she asked. Jasmine seemed to be naked more than anyone in the brothel, even when it wasn't necessary, or even appropriate.

7

'What's the point?' Jasmine said with a shrug. 'Anything I put on will be coming straight off again.'

'I guess so,' said Baby. 'Have fun. I'll see you later.'

The two women went their separate ways. Jasmine headed along the corridor to room 14. There was plenty of sex going on in some of the other rooms already, judging by the sounds filtering out into the corridor. A client was being whipped in room 8 by Chardonnay, who was calling him a sissy bitch at the same time. Room 11 was party to some very loud grunting. Jasmine recognised the grunts. They belonged to one of the local cops. When she arrived outside room 14, there was already a "DO NOT DISTURB" sign hanging from the doorknob. She twisted the knob and walked in. The first thing she saw was a tall, handsome man with short, dark hair and piercing green eyes sitting on the king-size bed in the middle of the room. He was wearing an expensive black suit with a white shirt and shiny black shoes. He stood up when he saw her enter.

'Hi, I'm Jasmine,' she said, kicking the door shut behind her. 'Pleased to meet you. I heard there were two of you.'

'My friend is in the bathroom,' the man said, approaching her.

'What should I call you?'

'You may call me Herman.'

Jasmine reached up and unfurled the towel that was wrapped around her head. She tossed it to her newest customer. 'Here you go, Herman. I just dried my ass with that,' she said, seductively. 'Feel free to sniff it.'

Herman dropped the towel to the floor without even considering having a whiff of it. Baby had told Jasmine one of the customers was weird. Well, this guy was *definitely* weird. Nothing like the usual customers.

'Lie face-down on the bed,' he said. 'And close your eyes. Pretend to be dead.'

Jasmine was unfazed by the request because it didn't even register in the top thousand weirdest things she'd been asked to do in the Beaver Palace. She climbed onto the bed and stretched out on it, pressing her face into one of the pillows. Herman sat down on the edge of the bed and placed his hand on her ass.

'You have wonderful skin,' he said, squeezing some cheek. 'Just what we're looking for.'

'Awesome,' said Jasmine, closing her eyes. 'What did you want to do?'

'Hey, I said play dead.'

'Oh, right.' Jasmine closed her eyes and let her mouth fall open a little, doing her best impression of a dead hooker.

8

'Ready,' Herman called out.

The door to the en-suite bathroom opened and a second man entered the bedroom. Jasmine couldn't see him on account of her face being buried in the pillow. 'Hello, Jasmine,' the man said, his voice creepy and *very* unsexy. 'You can turn over now.'

Jasmine didn't move.

'I said you can turn over now.'

'I thought I was playing dead?'

'Not anymore. Over please, on your back. Let me get a good look at you.'

Jasmine rolled over onto her back and finally got a look at the second man. He was wearing a leather gimp mask and a long brown coat.

'Nice mask,' Jasmine said.

The man didn't respond. For a few seconds he was transfixed by her nakedness, his eyes running up and down her body like he'd never seen a naked woman before.

'Close your eyes,' said Herman.

'Who? Me or him?' Jasmine asked.

'You.'

Jasmine closed her eyes.

'Have you ever seen The A-Team?' the masked man asked.

'I was just watching it upstairs.'

'Good. We're doing an A-Team role play game. My friend here will play Hannibal, I'll be Murdoch, and you can be B.A.'

'B.A? Really?'

'Yes. In our game, Hannibal and Murdoch need to get B.A on a plane, so we're going to pretend to drug you, okay?'

'Okay, *fool.*'

'Good, now stay still and keep your eyes closed.'

After some shuffling around, Jasmine felt one of the men press a handkerchief over her mouth and nose. It smelt strange, like garlic infused with balls. Jasmine played her part in the game. Instead of struggling, she inhaled the toxic stench, and within a short space of time she was unconscious.

'That was easy enough,' said the man in the gimp mask as he ran his hands over Jasmine's body, helping himself to a free grope. 'Look at this, Herman. She's even better in the flesh.'

'She is definitely better than all the women we killed in London.'

'Pick her up. Let's get her out of here.'

Herman slid his hands under Jasmine's body and lifted her off the bed like she weighed nothing, then he slung her over his shoulder.

'Wow, what an ass that is,' said the masked man, gawping at Jasmine's derriere.

'We're wasting time,' Herman reminded him. 'You said we shouldn't loiter here in case someone comes in.'

'You're absolutely correct.'

The masked man pulled back one of the sleeves on his coat, revealing a chunky silver watch on his wrist. He pressed a button on the top of the watch, then he and his friend Herman vanished in a haze of blue smoke, taking Jasmine with them.

Two

Despair - Population 17,000 - Present day.

For the third day running, Carson glared at Debbie as she entered the store. He said nothing because he couldn't say anything, but she knew what that glare meant. He was pissed because she was late again. Debbie smiled, said "good morning" and strolled into the back of the store. She took off her jacket and hung it up in the cloakroom next to Louise's. Then came the dreaded look in the cloakroom mirror. She looked the way she felt. Hungover. Her eyes were glazed, her skin a greyer shade of its usual pale, and her peach-coloured hair looked windswept even though it wasn't. She took a few deep breaths and gave herself the usual pep talk: she could survive another eight-hour shift. Eight hours of sitting at a checkout scanning items and loyalty cards and answering the dumbest, most mundane questions in the history of checkouts.

Pep talk over, she put on her "fake enthusiasm" face and walked back onto the shop floor. Carson Drummond's supermarket (imaginatively titled, "Drummond's") was the biggest store in the town of Despair. The main reason for its success was that it doubled up as a hardware store. Half the store was dedicated to groceries, the other half to step ladders, planks of wood, drills, lawnmowers, all kinds of random crap. Hardware crap was big business in Despair.

The digital clock on the wall behind the checkouts showed the time as 7:37 a.m. The customers at that time of morning tended to be the handymen on their way to work, and *the oldies*, their grey hair and saggy skin looking sallow and washed-out under the fluorescent lights. The sound of their shuffling feet made Debbie's hangover worse. She felt like an extra in a low-budget movie with a title like *Early Morning Shopping of the Living Dead*. She eased into her seat on checkout number two, her usual office. Louise was already up and running on checkout number one.

While she waited for her first customer, Debbie fidgeted around in her ill-fitting brown and white checked dress that didn't quite come down to her knees. It was the same uniform Louise was wearing, but Louise was slimmer, not hungover, and had the top three buttons of her dress undone. The uniform looked better on her, as if it had been designed with her in mind. Louise was a pony-tailed blonde who could have been a cheerleader if she'd been blessed with smaller butt cheeks.

11

'Wassup, Deb,' said Louise, chewing on some gum. 'Any news on your sister?'

'Nothing,' Debbie replied.

'How long has it been now?'

'Three and a half days.'

'Shit. You must be going nuts right now, huh?'

'It's hard to think about anything else. Doing braindead work in here doesn't help much either.'

'Yeah, I'll bet. Morning, Ruth.'

Ruth Bucket, a hunched-over old lady in her eighties, was pushing her trolley around the store aimlessly as she tended to do. But upon hearing Louise wish her a good morning, she quit browsing the cereals and headed for the checkout. She wheeled her trolley up to Louise's unit, ready to do some talking. *Unlucky, Louise.*

Debbie turned away and looked aimlessly around the store rather than risk getting caught up in Ruth's inane banter. In spite of the old biddy being perfectly pleasant, Debbie just wasn't in the mood to listen to her tell the same old stories about her dead husband.

While casting her eye around the store, Debbie caught sight of the magazine stand. Front and centre was the local newspaper, "The Daily Rag". It had a photo of Debbie's sister Glenda on the front, along with two other similarly aged women. The pictures were accompanied by the headline, "SOMEONE MUST KNOW SOMETHING.".

Debbie looked away. Someone somewhere definitely did know something. That much was fucking obvious. But no one was saying anything. Glenda was the most recent of the three women to go missing. According to a movie Debbie had seen, if you don't find a missing person within the first forty-eight hours, you're probably not going to find them at all. That stupid phrase had been going round in her head for the last week and a half. She scanned the store for something else to focus on, something that didn't have her sister's face on it.

There were several customers wandering around in the aisles. An old fart named Art, a plasterer named Rick, and a tall, handsome fella who didn't look familiar. Debbie assessed the situation. Art was carrying a basket, but he was only on aisle three. Rick was pushing a trolley full of hardware stuff but was heading for the liquor section. The tall guy also had a trolley, but he didn't seem to know his way around the store. If she had to put money on it, she'd bet on Rick being first to her checkout, with a load of nails and screws, and maybe some gloves and a bottle of gin.

As luck would have it, the tall, handsome stranger got to her first. He looked like a Dan, or a Chad. Rugged, maybe thirty years old, good

12

head of dark hair, and a set of biceps to phone home about. He was wearing black jeans and a matching T-shirt, untucked. Style, good looks and muscles. Debbie greeted him with a semi-genuine smile.

'Morning, sir.'

'Good morning,' he said, without making eye contact. His trolley was full of toilet rolls and packs of batteries. He started unloading it all on the checkout's conveyor belt, scooping up twenty packs of batteries at a time in his huge hands before eventually moving on to the packs of toilet roll. At the bottom of his trolley he had a couple of porn mags and a large box of tissues. *"Jeez, that's disappointing,"* Debbie thought inconsequentially. No one *ever* bought porno mags early in the morning. And good looking guys *never* bought porn. It gave his credibility a knock.

It took about three minutes to scan all his items through the till. Mister "Big Hands" was a good packer though. He made no small talk whatsoever, which was often the way for men who bought porn. And he didn't fuck around when it came to packing. This guy was efficient. He packed like a woman, or a man with OCD.

'That'll be two hundred and eighty-six dollars and forty cents,' Debbie informed him after she'd rung everything up.

Mr Big Hands pulled a wallet from his back pocket and hooked out a credit card. He stuck it into the card reader and typed in his PIN.

CARD DECLINED.

Debbie hated it when a stranger's card got declined. There was always a chance of an argument. Local folks were embarrassed when it happened to them. Strangers were *sometimes* embarrassed, but more often than not, they were agitated.

'Sorry, sir,' she said, forcing a smile. 'That card has been declined. Do you have another?'

'Declined?'

'Yes.' Debbie pulled the card from the reader. 'Maybe it's expired?' she ventured quickly, checking the date on the card. The expiry date was fine. The card was valid for another two years. She was just about to hand the card back when she noticed the name on it.

Fuck.

Double fuck!

Debbie's blood ran cold. This was no time to panic though. She took a silent breath, fixed a small smile on her face, and looked back up at Mr Big Hands. 'Just give it a minute,' she said. 'My card reader is being a bit temperamental this morning.' While keeping up her fake smile she calmly reached under the till and pressed the silent alarm.

13

Her customer didn't move, but Debbie could see his eyes darting. She had to keep him in the store until the cops showed up. Because the name on the card, embossed in silver letters, was *Glenda Dallas*. Debbie's sister.

Debbie tried to think of something to say to stall him. Something that wasn't, *"What the fuck have you done with my sister?"* or, *"How the fuck do you know her PIN number?"*

Three

It had been a good start to the day. By seven forty-five, Officer Harry Teasle and his rookie sidekick, Chet Preston, had already dealt with two situations. An early trip to the house of Agnes Fender had seen them solve the case of her missing cat within twenty minutes of her phoning it in. Solving it was probably a generous way of putting things, seeing as how the cat just showed up while they were taking a description of it. That had been followed by a domestic emergency call from Old Man Cartwright, who couldn't get the remote to work on his TV. New batteries were installed, and Cartwright was a happy man again. With those two cases wrapped up inside less than an hour, Harry and Chet were back in the car and heading to the local donut store for breakfast.

When Chet first joined the force as a fresh-faced twenty-two-year-old, he wasn't a fan of donuts, or coffee. Harry, a veteran at age forty-nine, had soon shown him the benefits of the "policeman's diet." The only way to stay awake and keep your energy levels up when fighting crime in the town of Despair was to load up on sugar, carbs, and coffee.

They were less than a minute away from the donut store when the radio crackled into life again. The voice of Beverly, the switchboard operator at the station, came through, garbled and too loud as usual.

'Anyone near Drummond's?'

Chet had both hands on the wheel so Harry reached down and picked up the radio receiver. He pressed a red button on the side and spoke into it. 'This is Harry, what's up, Bev?'

'Hi Harry. I'm not sure what it is exactly, but someone's hit the emergency alarm at Drummond's. Can you get there ASAP? Could be another shoplifter.'

'Okay, Bev, we've got it. We're a minute away.' He replaced the receiver and slapped Chet's hand away from the control box to stop him using the siren.

Chet groaned. 'Why don't we ever use the siren when it's a crime?'

'Hey, if it's a shoplifter let's not let 'em know we're coming.'

Chet rolled his eyes.

'Don't roll your eyes.'

Chet rolled his eyes again but then hit the gas. Tyres screeched, red lights were jumped, other drivers were flipped the bird. This was big time. Tuesday morning crime. Thieves in Drummond's. A chance to cuff somebody and slam them against the side of the car. Potentially a better rush than strawberry donuts and sprinkles.

'I wonder who it is this time?' Harry asked.

'I bet it's a false alarm.'

15

'I'm not taking that bet.'

Chet thought for a second then said, 'I bet you five bucks it's Tina who hit the alarm.'

'I'll take *that* bet,' said Harry. 'And you can pay up now because Tina don't work Tuesdays.'

'Goddammit.'

Drummond's came into view on the side of the road up ahead. Nothing looked out of the ordinary. Chet swung a hard right turn onto the store's forecourt and screeched to a halt outside the front entrance. He killed the engine, and the race to be first out of the car was on. Harry had his door open before the car even hit the forecourt, and his feet were on the ground before Chet pulled the key from the ignition.

Half a mile away, a police siren rang out to signify that backup was on the way.

'See, *they're* using the siren!' Chet complained.

Harry ignored him. He rushed up to the automatic doors at the front of the store. The doors parted, splitting the store's name into DRUM and MOND'S. Harry marched on through, his hand hovering by the gun on his hip. He spotted the perp right away. A stranger from out of town. Big fucker too. Standing at Debbie's till. Debbie glanced over at Harry and threw eyes at her customer. Harry knew the score. *Mr Big fucker, if you've shoplifted, you're going down.*

'Morning, folks. What's going on here?' Harry asked. He headed towards Debbie's till, but spoke like he was addressing everyone. Chet hung back, covering the exit and checking his reflection in the glass doors.

'This man's card isn't working,' said Debbie. 'We've tried it a bunch of times and I've even rebooted the card machine. Could you take a look at it?'

Take a look at it? Bank card not working? Harry was disappointed to say the least. He'd been hoping to wrestle a shoplifter to the ground. People loved seeing him throw down on shoplifters. And he loved it too. All was not lost though because there was a stranger involved in this situation. And strangers did strange things.

Debbie held out the bank card. She was still doing weird eye exercises too, glancing at the card, then over at the customer. Harry took the card and looked up at Mr Big Fucker.

'What's your name, son?'

No reply.

'Okay,' Harry glanced down at the card Debbie had handed him. The name on the card was Miss Glenda Dallas. It took a second for the information to sink in. Glenda was a missing person, one of three young

16

women who had recently vanished. *Fucking hell, a lead on a missing person case.* Harry took a moment to control his excitement, then he slipped the card into the breast pocket on his shirt. 'I'll take this from here,' he assured Debbie.

Chet was still loitering by the doors, and running his hands through his mop of blonde hair in the hope of catching the eye of Louise on the other checkout. Harry cleared his throat.

'Chet, look lively, we gotta code seventeen.'

'Seventeen?' Chet hissed. 'Are you serious?'

'Of course I'm serious.' Harry unholstered his gun and wrapped both hands around it as he pointed it at Mr Big Fucker. 'Okay, Mister, hands in the air!'

Chet drew his own piece and scampered over to the checkout to back up his partner. He took up his hard man stance, feet half a yard apart, knees bent, gun pointed at the perp.

'What's the deal here, Harry?' Chet asked, the anxiety in his voice clear to everyone.

Harry kept his eyes on the target but replied through the corner of his mouth. 'Stolen bank card, belongs to Glenda Dallas.'

Chet's breath hitched, and his grip on the gun tightened. *'No way!'*

'HANDS IN THE AIR!' Harry repeated, louder this time. Through his peripheral vision, he noticed everyone in the store had stopped shopping and was eagerly watching the situation unfold. This was rock star territory if he didn't fuck it up. Local legend. Front page of the Daily Rag. Maybe even a medal?

But the Big Fucker ignored Harry's request to raise his hands. With a crowd of people gathering outside as well, Harry and Chet had to get the situation under control. For the next ten seconds there was a lot of shouting of things like, *"Put your hands in the air! Hit the floor! You're under arrest! Don't make me shoot you!"* and just about every other cliché that Harry and Chet could come out with.

Big fucker ignored them all. *The bastard.*

'LAST CHANCE!' Harry yelled. 'HANDS IN THE AIR, OR I'LL SHOOT! I SWEAR TO GOD ALMIGHTY, I'LL SHOOT YOU WHERE YOU STAND!'

Mr Big Fucker finally responded, but not in the way Harry or Chet hoped. He reached around the back of his jeans and pulled out a big, heavy-duty handgun that had been hidden behind his untucked black T-shirt. To Harry, the whole thing happened in slow motion. He saw it, but just like in a bad dream, he was paralysed, unable to react. The big fucker lifted his piece, his eyes lasered in on Harry, his target.

Chet fired first, God bless him. Damn near deafened Harry. Set off a ringing in his ears that could only be drowned out by firing his own gun. The checkout girls ducked for cover. Customers screamed.

The Big Fucker staggered back as a bullet hit him in the shoulder. Another hit him in the chest. It hindered him from firing back, but it wasn't enough to put him down. He regained his composure quickly and fired back like a pro.

BANG!

BANG!

Chet and Harry, donut-and-coffee-loving cops who served their community well, both landed on the floor in stupid poses, dumb looks on their faces, and bullet holes in their foreheads.

Big fucker put his gun away and carried on with his business, oblivious to the dumbfounded stares of everyone else in the store. He wheeled his trolley full of batteries, porn, tissues, and toilet roll out through the automatic doors without bothering to make another attempt to pay for any of it.

The second cop car was already waiting for him outside. Two cops had taken cover behind it, guns pointed at him, yelling shit.

Mr Big Fucker was bored of cops yelling at him. Cops were an irritation, there to be swatted away like flies, if you liked swatting your flies away by shooting them in the forehead. He let go of the trolley and pulled out his gun again with the intention of executing the two cops. The pair of them stopped yelling and ducked down out of sight behind their car. But unbeknown to Mr Big Fucker their job was done. They had distracted him, diverted his attention from another threat. It wasn't what they had intended, more a stroke of luck really. Mr Big Fucker never saw the third cop sneak up behind him.

BZZZZZ!

Lights out. Big Fucker seized up. His brain shut down. His knees folded. He knocked into his trolley on his way down, pushing it away. Then he hit the ground. Hard.

'JOSIE! YOU GOT HIM!'

Josie Rockford, a young, black, female trainee cop, stood over the fallen gunman, her eyes bulging, her mouth gasping in air like a young man seeing tits for the first time. Being a trainee cop, Josie wasn't permitted to carry a firearm yet. But she sure knew how to tase the fuck out of someone. The big, gun-toting, cop-killing psycho never saw her sneak up behind him, *thank God.* Her heart was knocking on her rib cage, asking to be let out for a quick scream.

Captain Jim Hockley, one of the two cops hiding behind the squad car, poked his head up and got a look at what had happened. Hockley

18

was in his late fifties with thin legs, a fat gut, and a full head of thick grey hair. He rushed over to the fallen gunman and slapped some cuffs on him.

'You're a goddamn hero, Josie,' he said, breathing a sigh of enormous relief.

Josie was still hanging onto her taser like it was glued to her hands. 'Who is this guy anyway?' she asked.

Hockley rifled through the man's pockets and pulled out a leather wallet. He flicked through some of the cards inside it, then looked up at Josie. 'This guy's got loads of different ID's,' he muttered. 'Whoever he is, he's bad news.'

Four

Riccardo Almeda chewed relentlessly on his gum as he stared through the two-way mirror into the interrogation room. On the other side of the mirror, a tall man with short dark hair was sitting behind a rectangular table in the middle of the room.

'This is the man?' said Almeda. 'The one who killed Harry and Chet?'

'That's him.'

'And we think he's got something to do with the three missing women?'

The man Almeda was talking to was Alan Jones, a senior detective with white hair who'd been around a long time, certainly long enough to remember all six of the murders that had taken place in the last twenty years. Jones was standing a step behind Almeda, ready to go in and start the interrogation.

'He's definitely the man we're looking for,' said Jones. 'That asshole is responsible for fucking up our murder rate and our missing persons rate.'

Almeda stepped away from the mirror and looked Jones in the eye. 'Let's go rough him up then.'

Jones grabbed Almeda's arm before he had a chance to move for the door. 'We can't mess this one up. If you leave so much as a scratch on him, you could blow this case completely. This asshole could walk. I don't know about you, but I don't wanna tell Harry's wife the guy walked because we didn't follow protocol. You just know them new lawyers in town will be working their witchcraft to keep this man from seeing justice. And don't give Judge Dickhead any excuse to call a mistrial.'

Almeda spat his gum into his hand then flicked it across the room into a wastepaper bin for three points. The score did nothing to ease his frustration. He tugged at his thick, black hair, almost pulling a chunk out. 'You're right. Fuck it, you're right. That pisses me off. Fucking lawyers and judges. I hope this piece of shit isn't one of those fucking cult people. If he is, this is a waste of time for sure.'

'You finished? Got it out of your system? Good. This has gotta go by the book.'

'Yeah, let's do it.'

Jones checked his appearance in the slight reflection offered by the two-way mirror. He had on a light blue suit. It looked smart. Not as smart as the grey one he usually wore, but he looked authoritative. Almeda, his younger, olive-skinned colleague, was more casual, wearing brown

20

pants and a black waistcoat over a white shirt. The two of them looked like they meant business.

Jones turned the door knob and entered the interrogation room, with Almeda following a step behind. Jones pulled up a chair and sat down opposite the man who had killed two of his colleagues that morning. Almeda perched his chunky ass on the edge of the table and leaned across to speak to the suspect.

'Would you like a lawyer?'

No reply. The suspect stared straight ahead, not blinking.

'Okay, mister,' Almeda continued. 'Let me put it another way. If you do not want a lawyer present during this interrogation, then say nothing.'

No reply again. *Perfect.*

'Okay, suit yourself. Are you gonna tell us your name?'

No reply.

'We found seven different ID's in your wallet. Were any of them you?'

Still no reply.

'In that case, for the rest of this interview we will refer to you as John Doe. Understand? Nod your head if you understand?'

The man sitting in the plastic chair on the other side of the table did not reply or nod his head.

Jones moved into John Doe's eye line. 'Two dead cops gets you the needle, mister,' he said, clicking his fingers in front of the other man's face. 'Lucky for you, you've got a bargaining chip. You're in possession of a credit card belonging to a young woman who's recently been reported missing, the third girl in six weeks. If you tell us where she is, and where the others are, you just might get a prison sentence instead. Would you like that?'

Still no answer. The guy showed no signs of nerves, no signs of anything at all in fact. He still wasn't blinking either. There was blood speckled on his neck and his T-shirt. Blood from Chet and Harry.

'Listen, fuckface,' said Almeda. 'We can do this the old fashioned way if you want? We can beat it out of you.'

A knock at the door broke the tension. The door opened, and in walked a tall, smartly dressed, blonde lady in her thirties with round spectacles. Her name was Sarah Kiam and she was a DNA specialist. 'Alan, can I have a word with you?' she asked.

Jones looked around. 'Have you got a DNA match for this guy yet?'

'Kind of,' Kiam replied, her fingers drumming against a blue cardboard folder she was holding. 'Can we discuss it outside?'

21

Jones kicked his chair back and stood up. 'Okay.'

Almeda eyeballed the suspect for another few seconds, then he slid off the table and joined Jones on the other side of the door to see what Kiam had for them.

Sarah Kiam was fidgety, unable to keep her hands still. If she wasn't touching her hair, she was adjusting her glasses, blouse, or skirt. It was unusual to see her like that. She was normally super cool.

'What have you got?' Jones asked her.

For some reason, Kiam wasn't happy being in the room on the other side of the two-way mirror. She stepped out into the corridor and headed for an empty room on the other side. Jones locked the door on the interrogation room, then he and Almeda joined Kiam in the small square office on the other side of the corridor. It had a table and four chairs in it.

'Sit, please,' said Kiam, closing the door.

Jones and Almeda ignored the chairs, instead perching themselves on the edge of the table.

'You're going to think I'm crazy,' said Kiam, still fidgeting, like she was playing an invisible harp with her free hand. 'But I want you to look at something.'

Alan Jones held out his hand, expecting Kiam to hand him her folder. 'What is it?'

Kiam didn't offer him the folder. 'That guy you're interrogating, the cop killer, his DNA doesn't match anything on our records,' she said.

'Really?' said Jones. 'Then what *have* you got?'

'His DNA was flagged up as something highly unusual. You see…' she paused and took a breath, 'it's a perfect match for something on a database for historical unsolved cases. It's a kind of an anomaly this database, like something that's normally only used in training exercises, stupid things like that.'

'Just spit it out,' Almeda groaned. 'Come on, our guy is sitting in there laughing at us. Any second now one of those fucking lawyers from Brailsford's could show up and get him out of here.'

Kiam swallowed hard. 'Okay, look, don't shoot the messenger, okay.'

'Does his name match with any of those ID's in his wallet?' Jones asked.

Kiam shook her head. 'His DNA matches with the semen found on a silk shawl that belonged to Catherine Eddowes.'

'Who?' said Almeda, more confused than before.

'Catherine Eddowes?' said Jones, straightening up. '*The* Catherine Eddowes?'

22

'Who's Catherine Eddowes?' Almeda asked.

'That can't be right,' said Jones. He snatched Kiam's folder from her.

'Who the fuck is Catherine Eddowes?' Almeda repeated, louder than before.

Jones placed the folder down on the table and started flicking through the paperwork inside it. He answered Almeda without looking up. 'Catherine Eddowes was the fourth victim of Jack the Ripper.'

Almeda stood up, irritation etched into his face like he thought he was being made fun of. 'That's bullshit!'

'It's true,' said Kiam, wincing like she expected a barrage of abuse. 'I'm sure it's just a mistake or something, but that's what the records brought up.' She pointed across the corridor. 'That guy in there, his DNA is an exact match for Jack the Ripper.'

'That guy in there isn't two hundred years old,' said Almeda.

'He ain't even forty,' Jones added.

'I'm sorry,' said Kiam. 'I know it's ridiculous, but that's what came up. I've checked it a bunch of times. I feel stupid coming here telling you about it, but I can't go hiding it from you, can I?'

Almeda stormed past her and headed for the door. 'Let's go ask him if he's Jack the Ripper,' he said, pulling the door open.

Jones closed the folder and slapped it against Kiam's shoulder. 'This is good work, Sarah. I appreciate this.'

'Thanks.'

'Don't go anywhere. I might need you again in a minute.'

Almeda charged back across the corridor into the room with the two-way mirror. His attempts to burst into the interrogation room on the other side of the mirror were thwarted by a locked door. Jones strolled casually over to him, key in hand. He unlocked the door and allowed Almeda to barge in first. But when the two detectives entered the room, John Doe, or whoever the hell he *really* was, was not there. His chair was empty.

'Where'd he go?' Jones asked.

Almeda stormed back out into the corridor and yelled as loud as he could. 'WHO'S MOVED MY SUSPECT?'

As was becoming the norm, he received no answer, only the sound of his own voice echoing around the corridor.

Eventually, an overweight, middle-aged male officer with thick brown hair appeared at the end of the corridor. His name was Lyle O'Malley, and he was known to be an irritable prick.

'WHAT'S ALL THE YELLING ABOUT?' he shouted at Almeda.

'SOMEONE'S MOVED MY SUSPECT!'

23

'Wasn't me.'

Jones joined them in the corridor. He looked pale and shaken. 'What the hell has happened?' he muttered. 'I locked that door when we left him.'

'You could check the security camera footage?' Sarah Kiam suggested.

Jones and Almeda exchanged a quick look, then bolted for the stairs that led up to the security office on the floor above. Almeda, the fitter and faster of the two, made it to the top of the stairs ten steps ahead of Jones.

The only person in the security office was Bobby Mahomes, a fat guy in standard blue uniform. He had thinning red hair, man-boobs and serious body odour. He was sitting at a desk in front of a bank of monitors, eating a sandwich that reeked of garlic. Almeda got a good waft of it as he stormed in. Mahomes, on seeing Almeda's agitated face, sat up straight.

'Wassup fella?' he asked, as he put his sandwich down and tried to surreptitiously wipe some mayonnaise from his chin.

Jones, still out of breath and clutching his chest, walked in and answered the question. 'We need to see the footage from the main interrogation room for the last ten minutes.'

'You got it.'

Despite his slovenly appearance, Mahomes was actually very competent at his job. He calmly tapped away on his greasy keyboard and eventually brought up some footage on one of the monitors in front of him. 'Here ya go,' he said, pointing at it. 'Is this what you're after?'

'That's it,' said Almeda, moving in closer and getting a waft of garlic and sweat. Jones moved around to Mahomes's other side where the garlic was less prominent.

The footage on the monitor showed the two detectives quizzing their suspect just a few minutes earlier.

'Skip forward to what happens after we leave the room,' said Almeda.

Mahomes fast-forwarded the footage up to the moment when Jones and Almeda left the room, then he hit PLAY again. Almost immediately the answer to the mystery of the missing suspect played out in front of them. John Doe simply vanished into thin air.

'What the fuck was that?' said Almeda.

'Did he just disappear?' said Jones. 'Or did the camera feed cut out?'

'He did disappear,' said Mahomes as he rewound the footage. 'Isn't that weird?'

24

'Of course it's weird,' said Almeda, slapping Mahomes on the shoulder.

'Play it again at half speed,' said Jones.

Mahomes did as he was told, and the three men watched the screen intently. Just before the moment the suspect disappeared, a second man appeared out of nowhere just behind him. A few frames later both men vanished.

'Okay, go back and pause it,' said Almeda. 'I wanna see who the other guy was.'

'You're not gonna see who it was,' said Mahomes. 'He was wearing a balaclava. Look.' He rewound and then paused the footage on the appearance of the second man, who was wearing cargo pants and a black sweater with patches on the sleeves. And just as Mahomes had said, he was wearing a balaclava.

'Who the fuck is that?' said Almeda, chewing his fist in frustration. 'And how the fuck did he do that? What the fuck is going on? I mean, how is that possible?'

'Maybe it's a trick?' said Mahomes, clearly unbothered by men appearing and disappearing from locked interrogation rooms. He picked up his sandwich again and took a big bite.

'We've lost our fucking suspect,' said Almeda, stepping away and rubbing his forehead. 'What the fuck just happened here?'

'Above my pay grade,' Mahomes said, chewing away contentedly on his sandwich.

'That's true,' Almeda agreed. 'It's above *all* our pay grades.' He whispered in Jones's ear. 'Who the hell do we call about this? The FBI?'

Jones shook his head. 'Nah, this is way beyond the FBI. If that was really Jack the Ripper, and he vanished into thin air with a man in a balaclava, then this goes right to the top, to the people we've never heard of, who don't exist.'

'What are you talking about?' Almeda asked.

'I'm not sure. I kind of lost track of where I was going with that. But I guess what I was kind of saying is we really need to escalate this to someone very high up.'

'Well yeah, but who?'

Jones thought for a moment, then snapped his fingers. 'I know!' he said, wagging his finger at nothing in particular. 'There's a number in the Captain's Filofax. It's the lady who oversaw the investigation on Blue Corn Island after that day when it rained blood there.'

Almeda raised a curious eyebrow. 'You mean Alexis Calhoon? The church people are gonna go nuts about this.'

'The church people aren't going to know about it,' Jones reminded him. 'This is a police case, remember. Don't give out any information about this to anyone. Those fucking lawyers will do us if they hear about any of this.'

Almeda nodded at the door. 'Let's go make the call.'

Five

<u>Downtown, Washington</u>

The Dive Bomb was moderately busy for a week night. Aaron walked in and surveyed the scene. There were two guys playing pool at a table in the corner. A couple of drunk women with beers in hand were dancing nearby to some background rap music. The rest of the bar area was made up of people sitting at tables, chatting, laughing, and having a good time. A few fat guys were drinking at the bar. Aaron's eyes darted back and forth for a few more seconds before he found what he was looking for - a young blonde hottie sitting on a stool at the bar, smiling at Cam the bartender, who was making her a cocktail. Aaron kept his eyes on her. She was an unfamiliar face in a locals bar. *Please let her be on her own or just with a couple of girlfriends.* Aaron checked out all of the tables and could see no group of newbies.

The woman paid for her drink but remained seated at the bar, all on her lonesome. Aaron inwardly fist-pumped. He was just this girl's type. Truth be told, he was every girl's type, even though some of them would never admit it. He was in his early twenties with killer good looks. He had a good head of brown hair, just messy enough to be both endearing and sexy. And he looked handsome as fuck in his skinny jeans, white T-shirt, and expensive red leather jacket. He breezed on over, picked up an empty stool and plonked it down next to the blonde. 'Hi there,' he said.

The blonde looked at him and smiled. She had gleaming white teeth, and on top of that she had a super healthy tan and a red crop top that drew attention to a toned stomach and a fantastic pair of knockers. There was nothing about this chick Aaron didn't like. He glanced down at her legs. Blue jeans, cut off at the knee. Toned legs, great thighs. She was definitely his number one girl for the night.

He gestured towards her drink. 'Those cocktails are lethal, you know,' he said with his well-practiced lopsided grin

She giggled, then sucked up some of her drink through a straw, but she said nothing. Hopefully she was nervous. Another great attribute.

'You can't be alone here, surely?' said Aaron, grinning. 'You're way too pretty to be here on your own.'

'No, I am on my own,' she said, still beaming that beautiful smile.

'I'm Aaron. Can I get you another one of those drinks?'

'Erm, I only just got this one.'

27

'Yeah, but service is slow in this place. By the time I order you another, you'll be done with that one.' He clicked his fingers at the bartender. 'Yo, Cam, another one for the lady, and a beer for me.' Cam nodded and got busy.

The blonde giggled.

'I didn't catch your name,' said Aaron.

'My friends call me Rizzo.'

'I guess I'll call you Rizzo then. You live around here, Rizzo?'

'Not really. I'm from uptown but I was supposed to meet a friend here tonight. But she cancelled.'

'Well, ain't that lucky for us? We might never have met otherwise.'

Cam brought over two more drinks. He glanced at the blonde and then at Aaron, and chortled. Aaron paid for the drinks, and then he and Rizzo spent the next thirty minutes getting to know each other. And Rizzo got plenty drunk. When Aaron suggested they head to another bar, his new blonde friend was bang up for it.

Once they were outside, Aaron led the way, steering Rizzo into a badly lit backstreet. She was too drunk and too dumb to sense the danger she was in. Aaron had taken numerous young women this way. His number one spot was a narrow alleyway nearby with a big dumpster in it. To date, Aaron had fucked over a hundred women behind that dumpster. Rizzo would be the latest. He ushered her down there, but to his surprise she resisted.

'I don't like alleyways,' she said. 'They creep me out. Didn't you say you lived local? Why don't we go to your place?'

Aaron wasn't overly keen on the idea, but Rizzo wasn't smiling anymore, and she looked like she might be sobering up, so the plan had to change. 'Sure thing. I'm just a couple of blocks from here. I haven't cleaned though, because I wasn't expecting guests, but you're okay with a little mess, aren't you?'

'Yeah, I like things a little dirty,' said Rizzo, reverting back to her happy, drunken self.

'Home it is then.'

Aaron slid his arm around her shoulder and the two of them made their way joyfully along the backstreets to the house he shared with a few friends.

'Here we are,' he said, stopping outside his front gate.

'Wow, this place looks huge,' said Rizzo, gazing up at the three storey house. It had narrow windows with deep red lights emanating from within on all three floors. 'The red lights are creepy,' she said, hiccupping.

28

'Don't worry,' said Aaron. 'That's just my flatmates. They're in a band and they like red lights for some reason.'

Aaron opened the gate, and the two of them strolled up a short path to a big, black door at the front of the house. He pulled a key from his jacket pocket, unlocked the door and then stepped aside to allow Rizzo to go in first. 'After you, sweetcheeks.'

Rizzo stepped tentatively inside. There was some muffled grunge coming from a room somewhere in the house.

'That'll be Romain,' said Aaron, closing the front door. 'He's really into his hardcore music.'

With the door closed, the deal was sealed. The other vampires inside the house would soon get a whiff of Rizzo's scent, and they would know she was drunk too. Aaron hadn't intended to share her with them, but some nights that's just the way things go. First up, he was definitely going to fuck her though. The others could share in the feast afterwards, but the sex was all his.

'Just head through there,' he said, pointing at a long, narrow corridor with several closed doors along each side and one red door at the end. 'Mine's the door at the end.'

'Cool,' said Rizzo, giggling. 'This place is awesome.'

'It sure is.'

To Aaron's annoyance, Rizzo didn't head straight to the bedroom. She loitered in the hallway by the front door, smiling inanely at him.

'What are you waiting for?' he asked. 'Giddyup, sweetcheeks!'

'I was just thinking,' said Rizzo, hiccupping again.

'Don't think,' Aaron said, grinning. 'Just relax, and let the good times roll. Come on. If you don't move that pretty ass of yours in three seconds, I'm gonna sling you over my shoulder and carry you there.'

Rizzo giggled some more. 'That does sound like fun,' she said. 'It's just a shame one of us has to die.'

Six

'It's a shame one of us has to die.'

It was a strange thing for Rizzo to say, Aaron thought. She was right of course, one of them was going to die. But it was going to be her, she just wasn't supposed to know it yet.

'No one is going to die,' Aaron lied, smiling with his lopsided grin in an attempt to reassure her. He still intended to have sex with her, so it was best she didn't know about the murdering part yet, as it could possibly ruin the sex.

Rizzo took a step back, towards Aaron's bedroom door, which was a step in the right direction, he supposed. She had a nervous grin on her face. Aaron was kind of freaked out by it. Was she dumb, or just playing dumb?

KNOCK KNOCK.

Aaron stopped smiling and turned around. Who the fuck could be knocking on the door at this time of night?

'Who's there?' he asked.

The answer was emphatic. The door, a solid, majorly big bastard, hard oak, muthafucker got bigger. Real quick.

CRACK!

Aaron had never been hit in the face by a moving door before. It damn near flattened his nose. It sure as hell knocked him off his feet too. He landed on his back, staring into the face of his big, black front door. The bloody thing had sprung off its hinges and lunged at him. But how? And why?

Using his superhuman vampire strength, he pushed the door off and away to the side, then he sprung back to his feet. Standing where the door once resided was a man in a long black coat, his hood pulled up over his head, concealing most of his stubbled face.

Aaron had heard the stories, the myths, the exaggerated tales, but he had never truly believed the Bourbon Kid was real. When vampires gathered around campfires in the middle of the night and told each other scary stories, the stories were always about the Bourbon Kid. No vampire who met the Kid had actually lived to tell one of the campfire tales.

'Oh fuck,' Aaron muttered.

The Bourbon Kid's aura engulfed him. In one fluid move the Kid was upon him. He wrapped one hand behind Aaron's head and dragged it forward, straight into a gloved fist with a small silver spike protruding from between two fingers. The spike sliced through Aaron's left eye, introduced itself to his brain, then nipped out through the back of his skull to get some fresh air.

30

The Bourbon Kid released Aaron and dropped him to the floor, then he looked over at his blonde accomplice.

'Arizona, you okay?'

Rizzo, aka Arizona, was beaming her gorgeous, bright, white smile. The former pageant queen and illegitimate daughter of the president of the United States wasn't easily spooked. She'd been through some rough stuff in the past, in particular being held captive in the back of a truck for a week by three psychotic brothers with mommy issues and foot fetishes. The Bourbon Kid had showed up and rescued her from that torment, and she'd been texting him and his friends ever since. When he finally texted back and asked if she wanted to help him hunt down some vampires, Arizona said yes straight away. The last time she'd seen him, she had helped him and his friends kill the Devil. It had been the most exhilarating time of her life. Everything since then had paled in comparison.

'I'm okay,' she replied. 'Where to now?'

'Let's just wait here a minute.'

Before Arizona could respond, a door opened nearby, out of her sight, and a voice yelled out in a language she didn't understand. Whatever was said, it was the cue for the next round of craziness to unfold. Vampires swarmed in from all over the house, making a beeline for Arizona and, unbeknownst to them, the Bourbon Kid.

The Kid slid both of his hands into his long black coat, left hand to the right side, right hand to the left. Then out came the weapons. Arizona recognised the Headblaster gun in his right hand. That fucker did exactly as described. In his left hand was a different gun, narrower, longer, with a series of buttons on the side.

Arizona took the hint and unleashed her own weapons. A silver cross from her hip pocket, and a water pistol filled with holy water from inside her boot. The Kid didn't trust her with anything else.

The first blast from the Kid's Headblaster gun kicked off what was to be a very violent, noisy exchange. The gun was pointed down the corridor to his right. Arizona didn't see what he hit with it, but there was a sound of squelching and splattering, followed by some vampires yelling stuff about getting their friend's brains sprayed all over them. Two more shots came from the Headblaster, while Arizona watched and waited patiently to see what the other gun did. She crept forward, closer to JD, her cross in one hand and her water gun in the other. She took a look in both directions. The Headblaster corridor was a mess of blood and bones and organs. There were vampires shoving and yelling at each other. Some wanted to attack the Kid, some wanted to flee. Another blast from the gun took chunks out of about four of the dumb fucks. Blood

31

and guts spurted up to the ceiling, over the walls and onto the carpet. Truly glorious.

Arizona checked the other direction. A vampire was crawling along the ceiling, scuttling horribly like a spider towards JD. Another, much bigger, more fearsome vampire, built like a heavyweight boxer and wearing just a gold dressing gown, was storming along the corridor on foot with two scantily clad females behind him. One was quite pretty, in Arizona's opinion. She had fantastic, silky dark hair and black eyes, and a great body to match. The other was a redhead, but before Arizona got a good look at her, the Bourbon Kid used his new gun.

'Fuck me!' Arizona whispered aloud.

Her words were drowned out by the roar of the raging fire that spat out from the end of the gun. The whole corridor lit up in a ball of flames, engulfing, obliterating, and no doubt melting every single one of the vampires, from the spidery one on the ceiling to the angry trio on the carpet.

The Bourbon Kid turned his Headblaster gun ninety degrees, pointing it at Arizona's head. She ducked down and pulled a spin move to see what he was aiming at behind her. Predictably, it was vampires. Loads of them.

The first one, a naked female, lost her head straight away. A second later, a naked male was blown in half. Arizona dropped the cross and water gun and covered her ears to drown out the booming sounds from the gun. She closed her eyes too because of all the blood splashing around.

For another ninety seconds the Bourbon Kid obliterated every vampire that was dumb enough to show his or her face. When he eventually lowered his weapons, half of the house was on fire, the other half was covered in guts. Arizona removed her hands from her ears. There was a vampire screaming just outside the front of the house. She stood up and looked around. The Bourbon Kid's dog Goober was on the house's front step, ripping a vampire's innards out. Goober was a big brown and black Alsatian. Friendliest dog ever. Although not to vampires.

'That's our cue to leave,' JD said to Arizona.

Through the sound of the raging fire, the growling dog, the screaming vampire with no intestines, and the slight ringing in her ears, Arizona heard some high-pitched screaming from somewhere else in the house.

'Do you hear that?' she asked the Kid.

He took a moment, his eyes scouring all areas of the house to see if he could make out where the sound was coming from.

32

'It sounds like children crying,' said Arizona.

The Bourbon Kid tossed his fire-shooting gun to Arizona. 'Hold that. And don't use it.'

He lowered the hood on his coat and headed down the corridor he hadn't yet set fire to. Arizona peered around the corner and saw him disappear through a busted door at the end, in search of whoever was crying.

She called after him. 'I'll wait here then, yeah?'

Seven

After bursting into the room at the end of the red hallway, the Bourbon Kid scoured the room for signs of the children responsible for the screaming. The flames from the other side of the house were spreading fast. The scorching heat was a sharp reminder that time wasn't on his side.

The room he'd just entered was a lounge converted into a shithole. Vampires were messy bastards. Every item of furniture was covered in drugs, takeaway cartons, half-drunk bottles, empty bottles, cans, blood stains, cigarettes, and sex toys. JD picked a half-smoked cigarette from an ash tray and took a drag before dropping it onto the black and red shag carpet to let it smoulder.

A feeble cry of, *"Help,"* snuck into his ears. But from where? The room was a dead end. There was no way out other than the way he had come in. He side-stepped some dirty needles and approached a black sofa that was backed up against the wall. Another cry for help came from below. He grabbed a corner of the sofa and dragged it away from the wall, unveiling a trapdoor in the floor. He reached down and flipped it open, revealing a set of wooden stairs that led down into darkness.

The cries of help fell silent. JD checked his Headblaster gun to see how many rounds were left. The room was getting seriously hot, and it was going to get worse pretty fast. Firemen and cops would soon be along too. JD had to be gone before they showed up. He was carrying out the extermination of the vampire nest on behalf of Alexis Calhoon, the head of a semi-secret government department called Phantom Ops. Calhoon wasn't a fan of people murdering cops and firemen. And JD had a habit of doing that very thing, because cops in particular had a stupid habit of pulling guns on him.

He stepped onto the stairs that led down into the murky cellar. The first step creaked underneath his weight. JD had decent night vision, and when he was three steps down, he picked out a light switch on the wall and flicked it on. A solitary lightbulb lit up the basement, offering only a dim view of what was below. At the bottom of the stairs a young woman in tattered clothing stared up at him. She had ripped jeans and a torn white jumper that was covered in dirt and black stains.

'Thank God you're here,' she said, forcing a smile. 'We've been kept prisoner down here for ages.'

JD reached the bottom of the stairs and looked around. The air in the basement was stale and warm, the floor mostly bare, save for some scattered junk and a cage tucked into an alcove that hadn't been visible from the stairs. JD moved past the young woman, getting a waft of her

34

straw-like brown hair. It smelled like cheese. He moved closer to the cage and saw four small children inside. Two girls and two boys, all aged under ten. They were malnourished and terrified by the sight of JD approaching them.

'Can you help me get them out?' the woman asked, twisting a few strands of her long hair between her fingers and looking anxiously at JD. 'The cage is locked. I can't get it open.'

JD tossed her his Headblaster gun. 'Hold onto this. If you see any vampires, give me a shout.' He plucked a penknife from his coat and crouched down in front of the cage.

CLICK!

'It's not loaded,' JD said, standing up again. He turned to face the woman who had attempted to shoot him with his own gun. Regret was etched into her pasty, white face. She hurled the gun at him and bolted for the stairs.

JD caught the Headblaster in his left hand, while simultaneously straightening his right arm and pointing it at the crazy bitch. A small gun flew up his sleeve into his hand. With one flick of its trigger, the sleeve-gun fired a spiked dart on a length of cord into the back of the woman's calf. With the spike embedded in her flesh, she instinctively transitioned into a vampire. Blue veiny skin, yellow eyes, sharp fangs, bad breath, long fingernails, unsightly bumps above her eyes, a piggy nose. All vampires reveal their true self when confronted with imminent death. And this one was a particularly ugly dirtbag.

JD tapped a button on the side of the sleeve-gun. The thin metal cord began retracting back into the gun barrel, dragging the vampire back towards him. She screamed and scraped her nails on the floor as she tried to slow down the inevitable slide towards death. When she was close enough, JD took a running jump and slammed his boot down onto the back of her head.

CRUNCH!

Her crooked nose busted first. Four more stamps on the back of her head and her skull was flatter than a fish steak. JD yanked his spiked dart out of her leg, ripping a huge chunk of skin and flesh off with it. He stamped on her ankle next, snapping it like a pretzel, then he did the same to her knee joint. With the joints busted, he slid his hand inside the gaping wound, wrapped his fingers around her tibia bone, and ripped it out. After shaking some of the blood off it, he used the bone to smash the padlock on the children's cage.

Back at the front of the house, Arizona was squirting holy water at the fire that was advancing along the corridor from the east wing of the house. The water wasn't having much effect on the fire, but it was the best thing she had in the circumstances. Her cross was no good for extinguishing fire, and JD's fire-shooting gun was the reason for the fire in the first place, so she definitely couldn't use that. She didn't want to flee though, because she wanted to be in the house when JD returned. If she left and waited outside with Goober and the vampire whose bones he was chewing on, JD might think she'd bailed on him. And that would be bad because she desperately wanted him to invite her to help out again in the future. She wished he'd hurry up, though.

When JD did eventually return, he was carrying a small child on each shoulder and ushering two others along with him. The flames from the other side of the house were close to reaching the front door, so Arizona yelled at him to hurry up, then when she was sure he'd seen her, she ran out through the front door into the cool night air.

JD charged out seconds later. He lowered the two children on his shoulders down onto a part of the lawn where they wouldn't be too close to Goober and his dinner.

'Great, you saved them,' said Arizona, dropping her weapons and clapping her hands together.

JD took hold of Arizona's arm and pointed at the children. 'Look after these four 'til the cops get here.'

Arizona had no fucking clue what to do with four traumatised kids, but she was going to do her best. 'What about you?' she asked him. 'Where are you going?'

'I've gotta go before the cops show up. Don't tell them I was here. You never saw me, okay.'

Arizona reached out and stroked JD's arm. 'Do you wanna hook up again tonight?'

'I can't, I got another job to do, but I'll drop by and see you when I can. Look after Goober for me until then, yeah?'

'What?'

JD whistled at Goober. 'Hey boy, you're staying with Arizona for a while.'

Goober looked up, said nothing and then carried on chewing on his vampire leg bone.

'Seriously?' said Arizona. 'You want me to look after Goober?'

JD handed her two hundred bucks from his pocket. 'This should cover his food. Take him to the aquarium one day. He likes the fish. I'll come get him when I'm done with my next job, and we'll go out.'

Arizona's face lit up. 'Really? You promise?'

'Yeah. Gotta go. You were great tonight.'

36

He grabbed Arizona and planted a kiss on her lips. The kiss made her melt more than the raging fire a few metres away. By the time the kiss ended, sirens were blaring out close by. The four rescued children were crying hysterically too.

JD grabbed the fire-shooting gun and left the burning house, the screaming kids, the smouldering vampire corpses, his faithful dog, and the president's illegitimate daughter behind, and headed over to a black pickup truck he'd parked across the street. He drove off just as the first fire engine showed up. It was a long drive to his next assignment. Alexis Calhoon had called him earlier in the day regarding an unusual situation unfolding in a town called Despair.

Eight

Sanchez hated war movies. Especially ones with Nazis in.

'I hate World War Two movies,' he called out to his girlfriend, Flake.

'Why?' she called back from the kitchen.

'There's no suspense. You always know the Nazi's are gonna lose. They do loads of evil shit, then they get blown up at the end. It's always the same.'

'Are you saying you want the Nazi's to win?'

'Well, sometimes they should.'

'No one would watch a movie where the Nazis win.'

'I would.'

'Yes, and then you'd moan about it.'

Flake and Sanchez were an odd couple. Sanchez was a short, fat, Mexican bartender with thinning black hair, dubious hygiene, and a hatred for all of his customers, especially the Nazis. Flake was a petite brunette with low-key good looks and a hard work ethic who did her best to get on with everyone.

It was nine a.m., one hour before the Tapioca was due to open for its scummy clientele. The Tapioca was a local dive bar, owned by Sanchez. It had regularly failed hygiene inspections over the years, and it had certainly had its fair share of murders too, a record Sanchez was proud of. The interior walls were mostly yellow from all the cigarette smoke, but with occasional blood stains dotted around too, to give the place some character.

Flake had finished cooking Sanchez's breakfast and was preparing for her next task, cleaning the kitchen and the drinks lounge. She was wearing a denim skirt and a grey short-sleeved top that she didn't mind getting dirty. After cleaning the breakfast mess in the kitchen, she grabbed a yellow cloth and headed into the bar. Sanchez was sitting at one of the tables tucking into the thirteen-item breakfast she had made for him. There was an old war movie playing on the television.

'How's the breakfast this morning?' she asked, deliberately changing the subject from Nazis.

'On the whole it's as brilliant as ever.'

'On the whole?'

'Yes, on the whole.'

'Meaning there's something not up to scratch?'

Sanchez was still wearing his pyjamas, a nasty black pair with red stripes down the sides that made him look like a shorter version of Steven Seagal, sans ponytail. Sanchez leaned back in his chair and looked over

38

at Flake as he chewed on a piece of bacon. 'Take a look for yourself,' he said. 'There's an alien object in one of my egg yolks.'

'It probably fell out of your hair.'

'Seriously, take a look at this thing. It's massive. Way too big to have fallen out of my hair.'

Flake put down her cleaning cloth and walked over to see what he was grumbling about. As she neared his table she caught sight of something fairly sizeable in the middle of his egg yolk.

'What the fuck is that?' she asked, leaning over his shoulder.

'Fish it out.'

Flake reached down and picked up the object between her thumb and forefinger. It was made of metal and covered in orange yolk. She wiped it clean with her cloth. When she looked at it again, it was a gold ring with a stone that look like an opal in it.

Sanchez slapped her on the thigh. 'Whadda ya say, baby? Wanna get married?'

Flake studied the ring. It looked expensive. 'Married?' she said, her heart skipping a beat.

Sanchez snatched the ring back and put it to his mouth. He sucked off the remains of the egg yolk, then stood up from his seat. 'I'm asking you if you want to marry me?' he said, offering the cleansed ring back to her.

'Seriously?'

'Yes, seriously. You up for it? Fancy becoming Mrs Flake Garcia?'

Flake finally woke up to what was happening. She pressed her hands against the side of Sanchez's head and pulled him in for a kiss, then blurted out a mumbled *"yes"* as her eyes began to well up.

When she let go of his head, Sanchez took her right hand and slid the ring onto her finger.

'It's a perfect fit,' he announced.

Flake held her hand in front of her face so she could admire the ring. It looked even better now it was on her finger. Even so, she removed it and placed it on the ring finger of her left hand, where it was supposed to be.

Sanchez smiled. 'That's probably a better place for it,' he agreed. 'That finger isn't as chubby as the other one.'

Flake grabbed him and hugged him again, planting another kiss on him. 'I love you, Sanchez,' she said, stepping back to look at the ring again. 'This looks really expensive. Can we afford it?'

'We sure can,' said Sanchez. 'I found it in the men's toilets. Someone must have swallowed it and then shit it out. I rinsed it off under the tap though and it came up good as new.'

Flake's face dropped. 'What?'

Sanchez prodded her in the arm. 'Gotcha!'

'*Jesus*, Sanchez, don't make jokes like that.'

'Had you going though, didn't I, huh?'

'Seriously, where did you get it?'

'From a jeweller of course.'

'Well, I love it,' said Flake. 'And I love you too. Thank you.'

'And I love you, Flake.' Sanchez slapped her across the butt. 'I couldn't bear to be without you, or your cute ass and your amazing breakfasts.'

'We should do something to celebrate.'

'Fancy bending over one of the tables?' Sanchez said, seductively.

'That wasn't what I had in mind.'

'In the toilets?'

'No, I was thinking we could go for dinner or something.'

'Sure, we can do that later,' said Sanchez. 'But what about now? Fancy bending over and licking my breakfast plate clean while I do you from behind, eh? Get a bit of egg yolk and sauce in your hair?'

It wasn't exactly what Flake had in mind, but Sanchez kept glancing at the ring on her finger, then down at his greasy breakfast plate. Flake rolled her eyes. *Oh, what the hell, it was a special occasion.*

'Go on then,' she said.

'Brilliant.'

Flake bent over the table, her face a few inches above the greasy plate. Sanchez positioned himself behind her, lifted up her skirt, yanked her underwear down, then dropped his pyjama bottoms to his ankles.

He was approximately four strokes into giving Flake a monster engagement fuck when he heard Jasmine's voice behind him.

'Does this mean she said yes?'

'Oh for fuckssake,' Sanchez muttered. His butt cheeks clenched up, throwing him off his stroke.

'Congratulations,' said Elvis.

'What the fuck?' said Flake, looking over her shoulder. Elvis and Jasmine were standing by the jukebox, watching the events unfolding at the breakfast table. Jasmine, a gorgeous, brown-skinned, twenty-something, was wearing a black bra and skin-tight blue jeans. Her long dark hair was slightly ruffled, suggesting she and Elvis had recently done something similar to what Sanchez and Flake were attempting. Elvis was at least ten years older than Jasmine, and he was a dead ringer for his namesake, Elvis Presley. He was dressed casually in a pair of loose black pants and a red shirt.

40

Sanchez made a deep groaning sound as he shot his load. He pressed Flake's head back down into the greasy plate of egg yolk and brown sauce, then reached down with his other hand to try and pull his pyjama bottoms back up.

'We're getting married,' he called back to the others. 'Isn't that cool?'

'This seems like a polaroid moment,' said Elvis. 'Smile.'

The click made by Elvis's phone as he took a picture of the happy moment coincided with Sanchez giving a thumbs up sign with his free hand, while Flake looked back and gave Elvis the middle finger.

'Wrong finger,' said Elvis. 'Can we see your ring?'

Sanchez finished pulling up his bottoms and stepped aside so Jasmine and Elvis could get a good look at Flake's ring. Flake readjusted her clothes then turned around and held out her hand to show off her shiny new engagement ring, while trying to wipe some sauce out of her hair with her other hand.

'Check it out,' she said. 'Beautiful isn't it?'

'I like it,' said Jasmine. 'It's classy.'

Elvis took another photo with his phone. 'Can't wait to send these photos to Rex and JD,' he said.

Flake glared at Elvis. 'Don't you dare send that first picture to *anyone*. In fact, delete it from your phone, right now.'

'Too late,' said Elvis. 'I sent it already.'

Jasmine slapped Elvis across the chest. 'You moron.'

'What?' said Elvis. 'It's okay. All you could see was Sanchez's hairy ass and Flake's face.'

'Can I see it?' Sanchez asked, approaching the bar.

'Too late, I've deleted it,' said Elvis.

Flake marched over to the jukebox and snatched Elvis's phone out of his hand. True to his word, he had deleted the first embarrassing photo. All that was left was the second picture and a few hundred others of him and Jasmine doing stuff to each other.

'Are we celebrating then?' Jasmine asked.

Flake handed Elvis his phone back. 'We'll have a private party tonight,' she said. 'Drinks on the house. You can tell Rex and JD they're welcome to come.'

'Rex is still out of town,' said Elvis. 'Doing that bodyguard job.'

'And JD won't want to come,' said Jasmine.

'Why not?' Flake asked, frowning.

'Oh, you know. He's not into parties and stuff.'

'Maybe not, but he likes a drink.'

41

'That's true,' Jasmine agreed. 'Why don't you and Sanchez finish what you were doing? Me and Elvis will sit on the other side of the bar where we can't hear Sanchez grunting.'

'It's okay, I'm done anyway,' said Sanchez, sitting back down at his table and wiping some sweat off his brow.

Jasmine winced. 'That was it? You barely went ten seconds!'

'That's because Flake's so hot I can't control myself,' said Sanchez, running his finger through some egg yolk on his plate and licking it up.

'He goes a bit longer on the second go,' said Flake.

Jasmine shuddered.

Elvis's phone vibrated in his hand. He checked the display. 'Hey, I gotta call from Alexis.'

'Ooh, I hope it's a new job,' said Jasmine.

Elvis answered the call and began chatting with General Calhoon, so Jasmine headed over to Flake, who had grabbed a broom and started sweeping around the tables.

'Hey Flake,' she whispered. 'Is Sanchez fulfilling your needs?'

'Not everyone needs a metal finger up their ass when they're doing it,' said Flake, referring to an incident where Rodeo Rex, a biker with a metal hand, had participated in Elvis and Jasmine's sex life.

'Pfft,' said Jasmine. 'The metal finger isn't worth it, trust me. Seriously though, don't you and Sanchez ever do anything crazy? You've still got egg in your hair by the way.'

Flake tugged at some sticky egg yolk in her hair. 'We've done plenty of stuff, thank you,' she said.

'Anything non-breakfast related?'

'Yeah, lots of things.'

'Okay,' said Jasmine. 'So, what's the best sex you ever had?'

Flake took a moment to think. She stopped sweeping and looked at Jasmine. 'Did it in an alleyway once. In broad daylight. That was kind of hot.'

'You and Sanchez?'

Flake turned her back on Jasmine and started sweeping again. 'No, it was before I met him.'

'Well, I definitely wanna hear more about that, but what's the craziest thing you and *Sanchez* have ever done?'

Before Flake could respond, Elvis shouted over to Jasmine. 'Yo, Jas, have you robbed any armoured trucks lately?'

'I don't think so,' she called back.

'Are you sure about that?'

42

Nine

Nate Fodder and Sam Deadman had been working together for four years. In all that time they had never been robbed, never lost a single dime of the money they transported across the country. They often referred to themselves as the best armoured truck guards in the USA. But their unbroken record was coming to an end.

The front of their armoured truck was wrapped around a utility pole. Nate was bleeding heavily, having banged his head on the dashboard when they were rammed off the road by a fat guy in a truck bigger than theirs. Sam was seeing stars and also majorly panicking. They were trapped on a deserted highway between two hick towns, and someone was peppering the windscreen with rounds from a powerful handgun. Thank the Lord for bulletproof glass.

Sam yelled out, 'Nate, hit reverse. Get us out of here!'

Nate was blinking a lot and didn't seem to realise the severity of what was happening. 'I think they shot the tyres,' he said, a tear rolling down his cheek.

'What? Oh fuck, this is so bad. SO BAD.' Sam reached down to his hip and fumbled with the recessed thumb mechanism on his gun holster.

'OH FUCK!' Nate yelled. 'She's got a rocket launcher.'

Sam stopped trying to unholster his gun and looked up through the windscreen. It was hard to see much through the multiple cracks in the glass, caused by all the gunshots, but he caught sight of a young woman at the roadside up ahead holding something over her shoulder. A light flashed and then.....

BOOM!

'Wow,' said Elvis. 'They really blew the fuck out of that armoured truck, didn't they?'

Elvis, Jasmine, Flake, and Sanchez were huddled around a table in the Tapioca, drinking coffee and watching the video footage of Nate Fodder and Sam Deadman's demise on Elvis's phone. Alexis Calhoon had sent the video through to Elvis to see if he agreed that the woman with the rocket launcher looked *exactly* like Jasmine.

The footage came from a series of cameras on the recently deceased armoured truck. One of the cameras had clearly shown a woman who looked like Jasmine, firing a rocket launcher at the truck, blowing it to pieces, and killing Fodder and Deadman.

'The likeness is uncanny,' said Flake, who had taken a break from sweeping the floor so she could watch the video. 'Maybe you've got a secret twin sister, Jas?'

43

Elvis took a swig of his coffee then put the mug down next to his phone. 'According to Calhoon, this woman and her male accomplice have carried out three armed robberies in the last two weeks. She wants us to look into it, find out who this woman is, and then eliminate her and her fat boyfriend.'

'Can you get a good look at the fat man?' Jasmine asked.

Elvis shook his head. 'This is all the footage we have. He's always in the background and it's too dark to make out his face.'

Jasmine eyed Sanchez with suspicion. 'Sanchez, have you been drugging me in my sleep and making me rob trucks with you?'

'Are you mental?' said Sanchez. 'If you'd been drugged you wouldn't be awake to carry out the robberies, would you!'

'So you're not denying it?'

'He hasn't been drugging you,' said Flake.

'Exactly,' Sanchez agreed. 'There's only one logical answer. Jasmine's been cloned.'

Jasmine gasped. 'Oh my God. That's it.'

'That is *not* it,' said Flake. 'It's just someone who looks like you.'

'Why is she hanging out with Sanchez though?'

'That's not me for fuckssake,' said Sanchez.

'Hold on a goddamn minute,' said Elvis, scrolling through his phone. 'Just quiet down. I'm calling Rex.'

'What for?' Jasmine asked.

Elvis ignored her and made the call to Rex. He placed his phone down on the table so everyone could hear the conversation. The phone rang a few times before Rex came on the line.

'What's up?' he said.

'Hey, buddy,' said Elvis. 'How's things?'

'All good here. You calling about Jasmine's clone?'

'You already know?'

'Alexis called me about an hour ago.'

'It's not really a clone is it?' said Flake.

'Is that Flake?' said Rex.

'Yeah,' said Elvis. 'She's here cleaning the floor. We're in the Tapioca. What do you think we should do about this clone?'

'Well,' said Rex. 'I'm not a hundred percent sure it is a clone, but seeing as how the woman looks exactly like Jasmine, it can't be ruled out, so I'm gonna head to Cyber Limbs Prosthetics this afternoon and ask them a few questions.'

'What's Cyber Limbs?' Jasmine asked.

'Hi Jas,' said Rex. 'Cyber Limbs are the ones who created a clone of me once, remember?'

44

'Of course I remember,' said Jasmine. 'Your clone cut the brakes on my car.'

'Yeah, well anyway,' Rex went on. 'I'm going to Cyber Limbs to see if they've made any clones of you. It's as good a place to start as any because as far as I know they're the only ones with the technology to do it.'

'That's good thinking,' said Elvis. 'Want us to come with you?'

'No,' Rex replied, abruptly. 'You and Jas need to go to Purgatory. Get Eric Einstein to hack into all the CCTV cameras in the vicinity of that truck robbery. See if he can track where the Jasmine lookalike went afterwards, or just get him to do a facial recognition job. Maybe he can find out where this woman lives. He's a whizz at that sort of thing.'

'Got it.'

'Catch you later.'

Elvis ended the call before the others could say goodbye. 'Okay Jas, looks like we're off to Purgatory.'

'Are we getting paid for this job?' Jasmine asked.

'Calhoon says twenty grand if we complete the mission.'

'Cool.'

Flake got up and started sweeping the floor again with a long-handled broom. 'Can me and Sanchez get involved in this case?' she asked casually.

'What the fuck?' spluttered Sanchez, moving away from the table. He sniffed his mug of coffee, then added, 'Why would *we* want to get involved?'

'Yeah,' said Elvis, looking at Flake. 'Why would *you* want to get involved?'

'Well,' said Flake, blushing a little. 'Me and Sanchez aren't actually considered members of the Dead Hunters, are we? We're just like supporting characters. We're not on the FBI's most wanted list or anything, yet we've done almost as much as you guys.'

'Oooh,' said Jasmine. 'Flake wants to be a Dead Hunter.'

'I feel like I already am,' said Flake. 'But it's not recognised. Calhoon never phones me.'

'She never phones me either,' said Jasmine.

'Flake, are you feeling left out?' Elvis asked.

'Just a little unappreciated.'

'I'll have to check with Rex,' said Elvis. 'Maybe we can do an initiation ceremony for you, to make it official?'

'I'm not sleeping with you.'

'Threesome?' said Elvis, with a sly grin.

45

Sanchez spat some coffee out through his nose. 'I'm not sleeping with you either!' he spluttered.

'He meant with me and Jasmine,' said Flake, rolling her eyes.

'Oh, yeah, okay. I'm up for that!' said Sanchez.

'No, numbnuts,' said Elvis. 'Oh for goodness sake, I wish I'd never made the joke now.'

'I don't think it's a good idea,' said Jasmine.

'Thank you,' said Flake.

'I didn't mean the threesome,' said Jasmine. 'But, you becoming a Dead Hunter would mean you wouldn't be able to run the Tapioca anymore. You'd be a wanted criminal like the rest of us.'

'I should be a wanted criminal anyway,' said Flake. 'I've killed plenty of people.'

'Jasmine is right though,' said Elvis. 'We all know you're a badass, Flake. But you're more of an undercover Dead Hunter.' He glanced at the broom in Flake's hand. 'You're like Hong Kong Phooey. You sweep floors by day, and kick ass by night.'

'*Hong Kong Phooey?*' said Flake, shaking her head in disgust. 'A cartoon dog!' She set her broom down against the bar. 'You know what? I've got things to do upstairs. I'll see you guys later.' Without saying another word, she left the bar and headed upstairs.

'Wow, moody,' said Elvis under his breath.

Jasmine tapped Elvis on the arm and gestured over to the jukebox, then she headed over to it and pretended to pick out some songs. Ten seconds later Elvis strolled over and joined her.

'What's up?' he asked.

'Einstein won't be in Purgatory,' Jasmine whispered.

'Why? Where is he?'

'He's been granted passage to Heaven.'

'Since when?'

'I can't say, not with Sanchez and Flake around.'

Elvis raised a curious eyebrow. 'Why not?'

'God swore me to secrecy. By the way, you didn't send that photo of Flake and Sanchez to JD, did you?'

'No, why?'

'Good.'

'Jas, what the fuck is going on?'

'I'll tell you about it later.'

46

Ten

JD had been driving the pickup truck for six hours straight. He'd survived on cigarettes and the music from a movie soundtrack channel on the radio. The song, "Wonder Wheel" by Barry De Vorzon was playing. It's futuristic, driving beat was punctuated by the constant shake and shudder from the frequent potholes on the shitty road. JD's pickup, stolen a week earlier in Washington, started dragging towards the side of the road. He struggled on for half a mile before it stopped completely and the passenger side sank to the ground. Two flat tyres on the same side. At the same time.

'Useless piece of shit.'

JD jumped out of the vehicle. The sky was overcast, and the single-lane road was deserted. He was surrounded by tall trees on both sides, and a set of mountains in the distance. He checked to see if there were spare tyres. No dice. There was nothing for it; his only option was to finish the journey to Despair on foot. Fortunately, it was only a few miles further.

He heaved a large military kitbag over his shoulder and started walking towards a set of snow-topped mountains on the horizon. The bag contained all his belongings. And a lot of ammo.

Alexis Calhoon had arranged a meeting for him at Despair's police station with a pair of detectives named Alan Jones and Riccardo Almeda. The cops had legitimate information about the return of Jack the Ripper. Calhoon assured him every cop in the town had been forewarned not to do anything dumb like try to arrest him or irritate him. In the interests of not provoking any dumb cops into doing that very thing, JD had stowed his usual hooded coat inside the kitbag. To look a little less like a mass murderer, he was wearing a green army jacket, a pair of black jeans, and some walking boots. The army jacket did a good job of keeping the biting cold wind at bay.

After twenty minutes trekking along the side of the road, the wind introduced him to its friend, heavy rain. Two more miles down the road he came to a long cable-stayed bridge with no sidewalk on it, just lots of deep, black puddles. At the far end of the bridge was a big blue and white road sign.

YOU ARE NOW ENTERING DESPAIR - Population 17,000.

JD shook his head. *Despair.* Shit name for a town.

He was half a mile past that road sign when a blue and white police car drove towards him from the town. He avoided eye contact with the two cops in the front and hoped they would just drive by. No such luck. The siren sounded and they swung the car around, pulling up alongside

47

him. A young ginger-haired cop in a Stetson hat poked his head out of the passenger side window.

'Hey buddy, can we give you a ride into town?' His words were almost drowned out by the heavy pitter-patter of rain on the roof of the car and his hat.

'I'm okay,' JD replied.

'It's raining pretty hard. Come on, hop in. It's okay. We've been expecting you. Alexis Calhoon sent you, right?'

JD stopped and took a closer look at the cop leaning out of the open window. He was fresh-faced, maybe twenty-four years old, and he was absolutely no threat whatsoever. His buddy, the driver, was much older, maybe in his early sixties. He was non-threatening too, grey hair, grey moustache, light blue shirt, gold badge etc. And smiling. These cops were weird. Weird to JD anyway. Normally the cops he encountered were hostile dickheads. These two clowns looked happy to see him. The younger cop reached around behind his seat and flicked open the back door.

Fuck it.

JD tossed his bag onto the back seat and climbed in after it. After shutting the door and getting comfortable, he ran his hand through his hair, squeezing out the rainwater and flicking it onto the seat. The old cop hit the accelerator and they cruised along the highway at a gentle speed. JD had a gun tucked inside his jacket, ready to shoot both cops if they did anything dumb.

'Hi, I'm Corey Emerson,' said the young guy, poking his head between the front seats. 'And my partner here is Walt Shingleton. I gotta tell you, we're real excited to have you working with us.'

'Let's get one thing straight,' said JD. 'While I'm here, if any cop tries anything stupid, like arresting me, cuffing me, shooting me, or even if anyone just looks at me funny, I'll kill all of you, and I won't lose any sleep over it. Understood?'

'It's okay. Everyone's been briefed,' said Walt, the driver. Walt was looking at JD in his rear view mirror. And he had a big smile on his face, *the nutcase.* 'You got a place to stay?' he asked. 'We can put you up in a hotel if you like?'

'Is there anywhere in this town I can hire a four-by-four?' JD asked, ignoring the hotel offer.

'There's a rental place about a mile up the road,' said Walt. 'I'll drop you there if you like? When you've got yourself a ride of your own, you can make your way to the station. The detectives working the Ripper case are excited to meet you. I'll let them know you're on your way.'

48

'We gotta avoid the town centre though,' said Corey. 'There's a protest march going on today.'

'What are they protesting?'

'A load of local factory workers lost their jobs a while back. Hasn't gone down well, so they're protesting the factory.'

'Protesting a factory? Lotta good that'll do.'

'It was Dick Carter's factory, he made chocolate bars,' said Walt, undeterred by JD's disinterest. 'Carter sold up and left town six months ago. The new owners laid off all the staff and they ain't making no candy bars there no more.'

'That's a shame.'

'Yeah, it is.'

'My sister worked there,' Corey added.

'She protesting?'

'She sure is.'

Corey continued to stare at JD with a happy but dumb look on his face. But after ten seconds of silence where he couldn't think of anything else to say, and with JD making no effort at small talk, he swivelled back around in his seat and faced the road ahead.

The car came to the end of the tree-lined part of the highway and a few stores appeared at the side of the road. Walt steered the car onto the forecourt of a car rental place called "Danson's Cars". The forecourt had a bunch of hard-wearing vehicles parked on it. Walt parked up next to a yellow van.

'This is the best place to rent a vehicle in town,' said Walt, eyeing JD in his rear-view mirror.

'Thanks for the ride,' said JD. He opened the car door and climbed out, dragging his bag of belongings with him. He slung the bag over his shoulder and headed up to the store's entrance. The cop car stayed, its engine ticking over. Walt wound his window down and called out to JD.

'Hey friend, could you do me a kindness?' he asked.

JD stopped and looked around. 'What would that be?'

'Don't shoot up our town while you're here. We're good folks in Despair, and we treat strangers with kindness, so long as they don't give us a reason not to.'

JD said nothing. It was still raining and he wanted to get inside the car rental place.

Walt reached into his top pocket and pulled out a small card with his details on it. 'Here, gimme a call when you're heading to the station. I'll meet you there and make sure you're not greeted with any hostility.'

JD walked back and took the card.

'See you around, I guess,' said Walt.

JD turned his back and headed into the store.

Walt wound up his car window and set off back toward town. Corey stared out of the back window and watched JD and the car rental place get smaller. When he couldn't see them anymore, he asked Walt a question.

'What do you think he'll make of the folks that work in Danson's?'

'I couldn't say for certain,' Walt replied. 'But I don't think he's gonna like them.'

'Good.'

Eleven

JD walked into Danson's car rental store with the genuine intention of renting a vehicle to get him around town. The place was free of other customers, which was a bonus. The reception area had plenty of posters on the walls advertising certain vehicles. There was a waiting area with a few leather sofas dotted around it and a coffee table adorned with shit magazines for people to flick through.

There were two customer-facing desks at the back of the room. Behind them the name, "DANSON'S" was spelt out in gold plastic letters on the wall. The first reception desk had a thin, pale-skinned woman sitting behind it, chattering away on a telephone. Her cherry hair was drawn back in a tight bun, and she was wearing a white blouse with a red neckerchief and an equally red pencil skirt. It made her look like an airline hostess. The other desk was empty, but a man was hovering around a few feet behind it, staring at a sales chart on the wall. He was a wiry gentleman in a grey suit with black pin-stripes on it. He had a narrow face with messy black hair and crazy eyebrows. Even though JD wasn't exactly looking to make friends in the car rental place, neither of the sales assistants looked like the kind of person he could tolerate for even five minutes. He hoped for a straightforward deal that involved no sales patter, or banter.

The woman, who according to her name badge was called Petra, ended her phone call, turned to her male colleague and told him she was going for a coffee. He muttered something in return, then she left the reception area through a back door marked, PRIVATE. The decision was made, JD was dealing with the weaselly dick in the suit. He walked up to the man's desk. It had a name plate on it with NILAS engraved in gold letters. Nilas looked around, forced a fake smile at JD, and approached with great enthusiasm.

'How may I help you today?' he asked, maintaining his forced smile.

'Black jeep out front. Can I have it?'

'Yes, of course,' said Nilas. 'Good choice.' He stared at JD. 'Have we met before?'

'No.'

'You're not from around here are you? But I'm sure I recognise you. Have you been on television? You look like you might be on one of those reality shows with truckers or gold-diggers.'

'How much to rent the jeep?'

Nilas waited for JD to respond to some of the babbling nonsense he'd just come out with. When he finally realised there was to be no

51

small talk, or discussion about whether or not they had met before, he answered JD's question. 'The jeep is, uh, three-hundred a month. Wanna take a look at it?'

'Already seen it.'

'Okay, well let's get the forms filled out then,' said Nilas, pulling his chair out from under his desk and preparing to sit on it.

'No forms. I'll pay cash up front. One month should be enough.'

Nilas held off sitting down. 'But you have to fill out the forms. And I'll need to see some ID.'

'Just now you said you recognised me, so there's no need for ID, right?' JD reached inside his coat and pulled out a roll of fifty dollar bills. 'Just give me the keys.'

Nilas burned up red, like he was embarrassed about something. 'Okay, just give me a moment and I'll go get the key,' he said. He backed away a few steps then turned and scurried over to a set of filing cabinets at the back of the room.

JD turned away and walked over to the front of the store so he could look through the glass frontage at the jeep he had picked out on the forecourt. The jeep was only a year old. He hadn't seen the mileage but it ought to be fine for his purposes.

CLICK!

The sound of a gun being cocked.

Idiot.

In one sharp move, JD ducked down, reached into his jacket, pulled out his Headblaster and swivelled around to face Nilas. The wiry little fucker was crouched down behind his desk pointing a pistol in JD's direction.

'Don't,' JD warned him.

'I know you,' Nilas snarled, his voice more aggressive than before. 'You sonofabitch!'

'If you knew me, you wouldn't have pulled a gun on me. Don't make me kill you.'

Nilas was shaking, but he stood up straight, outstretched his arm, and took aim at JD's chest. Brave, but dumb. JD was always going to shoot first.

BOOM!

That was the end of JD's promise not to shoot up the townspeople in Despair. He lowered his smoking gun. Nilas slumped onto the floor behind his desk, blood pumping out of a hole between his shoulders where his head used to be. His gun bounced away from him. The company logo on the wall behind him was now covered in blood and brains. *Fucking loser.* What kind of car rental employee pulls a gun on a

52

customer? Especially a known mass-murderer? And why did he even have a gun? The questions fizzed through JD's mind. Maybe Despair was one of those towns where the car rental store got held up a lot?

He tucked his gun back inside his jacket and walked behind the counter to see if he could find the keys to the jeep he wanted. Blowing the salesman's head off was a cheaper way to rent the vehicle, and it meant there was no need for any paperwork, so all in all, things weren't really so bad.

He scoured a display of keys hanging on the wall until he found one labelled with the jeep's registration. He took it off its hook and put it in his hip pocket.

The door marked PRIVATE flew open and the sales assistant, Petra, backed into the room carrying two mugs of coffee.

'What the hell was that noise?' she asked, without looking around.

She got the answer to her question when she turned and saw the new headless version of Nilas. The blood pumping out of the gap between his shoulders was turning into a miniature river across the floor. After staring at the scene for a couple of seconds, Petra looked over at JD.

'Coffee?' she said, offering him the mug that was presumably meant for Nilas.

'You keep it,' said JD. 'I'm taking a jeep instead. By the way, your idiot friend here pulled a gun on me. That's why he's dead, just in case anyone asks.'

'Oh,' said Petra. 'That's unfortunate. He's been warned about that sort of thing. If he wasn't dead I'd send him on a customer awareness course. Never mind. When will you be bringing the jeep back?'

'I won't. The service in this place leaves a lot to be desired, so I'll be keeping it.'

'Right. Of course. Did Nilas say why he was going to shoot you?'

'No. Have a nice day.'

Petra was relieved to see JD leave the showroom, collect his new jeep, reverse it off the forecourt, and drive away in the direction of the town centre. When he was out of sight, she took a few deep breaths, then walked over to Nilas. She reached down and grabbed his arm and pulled him up a few inches off the floor, then she emptied his mug of hot coffee into the hole where his head used to be. The brown liquid slid down the rancid open wound, mixing in with bits of blood and lung and making a hissing sound as it bubbled up on its way around the inside of the corpse.

'You fucking idiot, Nilas,' she hissed. 'Use your fucking brain!'

She set her own coffee down on Nilas's blood-spattered desk, then made a call on her cell phone. After three rings the call was answered by a man.

'Hello, Petra.'

'Adonis, I have news. Nilas is dead.'

'Oh, that's a bit shit. What happened?'

'You're not gonna believe me, but *it's happening*. The prophecy was real. The Bourbon Kid came into our store. Nilas, the fucking idiot, pulled a gun on him.'

'Oh dear.'

'Yes, obviously Nilas's head is now all over the wall and the floor. And I'll be the one who has to clean it all up. Honestly, Nilas was such an inconsiderate fuckwit. Oh, and the Bourbon Kid stole a jeep too.'

'You're sure it was the Bourbon Kid?'

'I'm sure,' said Petra. 'I'd know that fucker anywhere.'

On the other end of the line, Adonis started breathing heavily. 'This is incredible news. It means everything father told us would happen is coming true, just like he said it would.'

'Yes, it does.'

'I'll call a meeting with the others.'

'Quite a few of them are already here in Despair.'

'Right, of course. But when the rest find out, I'm sure they'll all head there to join you right away. I'll get in touch with everyone now and set up a video call for an hour's time. By the way, I'm sorry about Nilas.'

'He was an idiot. I can't believe he was my fucking brother. And I can't just ignore his death either. I'm gonna have to call the fucking police about it, so I might be unavailable for the meeting.'

'No problem. You do what you've gotta do. This is big, Petra. Everyone's going to be very excited.'

'Yeah, no shit.'

Petra ended the call and slipped her phone back in her pocket. She stared at Nilas's corpse for a few seconds, shaking her head at his stupidity. He was so dumb, so reckless. She picked up his empty coffee mug then scooped up some of his blood with it. When the mug was almost full, she put it to her lips and drank it.

Twelve

In Purgatory, a dive bar in the middle of an area of desert known as the Devil's Graveyard, a young black man in a pinstriped black suit was sitting on a stool behind the bar, supping on a cold beer while watching the movie "Southland Tales" on a giant TV screen on the wall. The man was known to his friends as Jacko, or sometimes, Robert Johnson, a famous bluesman. Jacko had taken over as the custodian of Purgatory after the bar's previous owner, the Devil, had been murdered. Purgatory was like an old bar from the wild west, but with a lot of black furniture and red paintwork giving the place a rather devilish look. It also had an elevator in the disabled toilets that took its passengers all the way down to Hell. Jacko tended not to use the elevator much, on account of all the evil down in Hell.

After receiving a text from Elvis, Jacko turned off the movie he was watching. He hadn't seen anyone all day, and when the text informed him Elvis and Jasmine were coming to visit, he was rather pleased. He used the computer behind the bar to open a travel portal in the men's toilets for them. The portal could connect to any bathroom in the world. When the men's room door slid aside, Jasmine and Elvis were waiting on the other side in one of the Tapioca's bathrooms. Jasmine looked delightful in a black bra and tight blue jeans. Elvis was stylish as ever in a black suit with a red shirt.

Jasmine strolled into Purgatory and greeted Jacko with a beaming smile. 'Hi, Bobby, how's things?' she said, approaching the bar with Elvis walking behind her.

'You're calling me Bobby now?' said Jacko, surprised.

'Just trying something different.'

'Can we just stick with Jacko?'

'If you like. I just thought Bobby sounded sexier.'

'Erm, can I get you two some drinks?' Jacko offered.

'Nothing for me,' Elvis replied.

'Soda water, please,' said Jasmine.

'This must be serious,' said Jacko, grabbing a glass and filling it with water from a soda gun. 'No alcohol?'

'Jasmine's been cloned,' said Elvis, hopping onto a stool at the bar and helping himself to a handful of steak-flavoured peanuts from a bowl in front of him.

A million questions raced through Jacko's head. How had Jasmine been cloned? How many clones of her were there? What were the clones doing? Could he buy one on the internet? Eventually, he settled on a sensible response. 'How did that happen?' he asked as he placed Jasmine's drink on the bar for her.

'Rex is looking into it,' said Elvis. 'What we need from you is the location of the clone.'

'The location of the clone? I've only just been told about it. How would I know where it is?'

'Einstein,' Elvis replied. 'He can hack into CCTV cameras anywhere in the world and use his facial recognition software to find the clone. I've seen him do it before. He can find someone in a matter of minutes.'

Jacko glanced at Jasmine.

'I told him already,' she said with a shrug.

'Told him what?' Jacko asked, pretending like he didn't know Einstein was no longer part of the crew in Purgatory.

'Just that Einstein isn't here anymore.'

'Right, yes,' said Jacko. 'Einstein's not here anymore.'

'Jasmine says he's in Heaven,' said Elvis. 'Is that really true?'

'Uh huh, yep,' said Jacko, careful not to say anything else about Eric Einstein's mysterious disappearance.

'Did he have an apprentice, someone else who could use the software?' Elvis asked, before tossing a peanut up in the air and catching it in his mouth.

'Me,' said Jacko. 'He set it all up on the network here. All I have to do is just access the application and, erm, work out how to use it.'

'Get cracking then.'

'Okay. Umm, what am I looking for exactly? And where am I looking?'

'A Jasmine clone carried out a raid on a money truck two nights ago in Jacksonville. Have a scour around that area on your computer and see if she's showed up on any cameras recently.'

'Jacksonville? That's a big area.'

'It is, but Einstein would have found what we're looking for in about ten seconds, so get going.'

'Right now?'

'Yeah, right now.'

'Okay,' said Jacko. 'Why don't you sit at a table and watch TV while I do it. If you're watching me it'll take longer.'

Elvis leaned over the bar and slapped Jacko on the arm with the back of his hand. 'Just do it, ya big goof. I wanna see how it works too, so I can do it myself next time.'

'Fine.'

56

Jacko moved back over to his computer and opened up the "facial recognition" application Einstein had created. Elvis wandered behind the bar and peered over Jacko's shoulder to see what he was doing. A pop-up on the computer screen was asking for a password. Jacko typed something in but used his hand to shield it from Elvis's view.

'What's the password?' Elvis asked. 'You know, for when I need to use it.'

Jacko gulped. 'Umm, it's just something that Einstein came up with. I'll change it later to something simple that we can all remember.'

'I know it's something about Jasmine,' said Elvis.

Jacko grimaced. 'Oh, yeah, umm.'

'Is it my name?' Jasmine asked.

'Kind of.'

'Spill it,' said Elvis.

Jacko sighed. 'Like I said, Einstein came up with it. It's basically *Jasmine's ass*, but all one word.'

'Your password is *my ass?*' said Jasmine, grinning.

'Yeah.'

'Just get on with the camera search,' said Elvis, nudging Jacko in the back.

With the application up and running, Jacko started typing information into a series of required fields. He picked Jacksonville as the location, selected the most recent footage, then uploaded one of the many photos of Jasmine that was already stored on the computer. When all fields were entered, he hit GO. He wasn't expecting much, but such was the brilliance of Einstein's application, the computer brought up a flurry of accurate results almost instantly.

'Wow,' said Elvis, staring at all the video thumbnails on the screen. 'Are these all videos of Jasmine's clone?'

'It looks like it,' said Jacko. He pointed at the first thumbnail. 'This one is a live feed. She's out and about right now.'

'Open it up then,' said Elvis.

Jacko opened the video clip. It featured a woman that looked identical to Jasmine, walking through a busy shopping mall with a guy twice her age. The Jasmine clone was wearing a pair of gold hot-pants and a pink crop-top. The man with her was a short, balding fellow wearing blue dungarees over a red T-shirt. The couple were holding hands as they made their way through a crowd of other shoppers. After briefly stopping to discuss something, they headed into a ladies clothing store called *Prince and Company*, at which point the footage came to an end.

'They're off camera now,' said Jacko. 'Something should come up on the store's camera feed as soon as it picks them up.'

'Don't worry about that,' said Elvis. 'Just send us through the portal into the store.'

'Fuck yeah,' said Jasmine, before swiftly downing the last of her soda. 'Let's go get these fuckers.'

'Come on, Jacko, chop, chop,' said Elvis. 'Get us in there.'

'I'm on it,' said Jacko. 'If you stop badgering me and just head to the portal, I'll have it open before you get there.'

Elvis left Jacko in peace and escorted Jasmine over to the men's toilets. Jacko got busy and used his computer to change the portal location to the disabled toilets in the *Prince and Company* clothing store. 'All done,' he called out.

'Hold on a sec,' Elvis called out.

'What now?' Jacko groaned.

Elvis slapped Jasmine on the arm. 'Jas, what are we actually doing? Are we killing them?'

'I don't know,' said Jasmine. 'I thought you had a plan?'

'Never had time to come up with one.' Elvis thought for a second, then shrugged. 'Fuck it, we'll play it by ear.'

'Sounds good to me.'

'Whatever you do, don't bring them back here,' said Jacko. 'God will shut down the portal again. He doesn't want anyone knowing about Purgatory.'

Elvis furrowed his brow. 'When did the portal get shut down before?'

'Umm, it didn't,' Jacko lied.

Jasmine rubbed Elvis's back. 'Never mind about that,' she said. 'Let's just go deal with these assholes and find out who they are.'

Behind the bar, Jacko cleared his throat. 'Out of interest, what weapons are you taking?' he asked.

'Why do you care?' said Elvis.

Jacko reached down under the bar and picked up two pistols with silencers attached. He slid them across the bar. 'Discretion is probably advisable in a shopping centre, wouldn't you agree?'

Elvis muttered something under his breath then walked back to the bar and grabbed the two pistols. He returned to Jasmine and handed one to her.

'Are we definitely killing them then?' she asked, as she inspected the silencer on the end of her pistol.

'We might have to,' said Elvis. 'I'm definitely keen to shoot the fat guy.'

58

'But what if it turns out the Jasmine isn't really a clone?' Jasmine asked. 'I mean, what if it's actually my long lost twin sister or something like that?'

Behind the bar, Jacko sighed. 'Okay,' he said. 'If you absolutely have to, you can bring the clone back here, but definitely not the guy she's with.'

'Thanks, man,' said Elvis. 'Just be ready to get the portal back open for us. We might need to make a rapid retreat. This clone and her partner have already killed a bunch of security guards, so this isn't necessarily gonna be easy.'

'Be careful out there,' said Jacko. 'And watch out for any security guards who think they're Paul Blart.'

'Paul Blart!' said Jasmine, with a laugh. 'I *love* that guy.'

Thirteen

JD's new jeep wasn't as good as it looked from the outside. For starters, its satellite navigation didn't work, and even worse than that, he couldn't find a good radio station. He had to drive in silence along the main road through Despair. It was a pretty bland town, seemingly designed by old people for other old people. A couple of miles down the road he came across a large store named Drummond's that claimed to sell everything. He parked the jeep around the back of the store and headed inside to pick up some vital items.

His civilian clothing meant that no one paid him any attention as he filled his basket up with bottles of bourbon and a carton of cigarettes. He was considering picking up a sandwich from a refrigerated section when he felt a tap on his shoulder. He turned around and saw a short, orange-skinned lady in a brown skirt and yellow sleeveless top. She was in her early forties, and she had a big smile on her face.

'This is awkward,' she said, gazing into JD's eyes like a lovestruck puppy.

'Is it?'

'Well, yes. My husband is in the next aisle.'

JD frowned. 'So?'

The woman's face dropped. 'If he sees us together, he'll get really jealous. He's very possessive.'

'Fuck off somewhere else then,' JD said, turning away.

'How could you say that?' the woman gasped.

'Easily.'

JD gave up on the idea of grabbing a sandwich and headed straight to the checkout. He heard the crazy lady getting into an argument with her allegedly possessive husband. Despair was full of odd people, and JD sensed he would end up killing a fair few of them before the day was through.

His arrival at the checkout started off smoothly. The cashier, a blonde lady in a brown and white checked uniform, greeted him with a smile and a polite "hello." After scanning his first bottle of bourbon, though, she hesitated. She stared at the rest of the bottles he'd placed on the conveyor belt, then looked up at him and studied his face.

'Holy fuck, it's you!' she said, her eyes almost popping out of her head. 'Have you been to the church yet?'

'I'm new in town,' JD muttered, avoiding eye contact.

'Praise Jesus, I never believed you'd come. My friend Debbie is gonna be so excited. Her sister Glenda is one of the women who went missing.'

60

JD placed his cigarettes on the conveyor belt and checked out the cashier's name badge. *LOUISE.*

'I don't know anyone called Debbie,' he said.

'Are you here to kill the psycho man? The police are saying he escaped from an interrogation room at the station. I heard he vanished into thin air. I actually saw the guy in here yesterday morning. When the police showed up, they shot him a bunch of times, but the bullets bounced right off him. Luckily, my friend Josie tased him. She's new on the force. That's how they caught him. He went down like a sack of shit, like he short-circuited or something.'

JD stopped avoiding eye contact. 'Bullets bounced off him?'

'Yeah.' Louise looked around and then lowered her voice. 'I think he's another one of the strange-ies.'

'Strange-ies?'

'These weirdoes have been showing up in town for over a year now, but none of them ever go to church. That's where lots of people have been going and praying for you to show up and sort them out.'

JD frowned. 'Are you saying there's a whole load of other people in this town like the man who vanished?'

'Kind of,' said Louise. 'They're all different. Really strange and unsociable, that's why we call them the strange-ies. They're up to something. They don't mingle with the rest of us. I think they're planning to take over the town.'

'How many of them are there?'

Louise nibbled on her thumb, an excited look on her face. 'I can't believe I'm talking to you. My friends are gonna be so jealous.'

JD handed her one of his unscanned bottles of bourbon. She took the hint and started scanning stuff again. JD moved to the packing area and started loading the bottles into a brown paper bag.

'Are your friends here too?' Louise asked. 'Elvis is my favourite… after you, of course. He's so cool. Are him and Jasmine really a couple?'

'They're not coming.'

'The local priest, Father Carmine, he tells the story of what you did on Blue Corn Island all the time.' Louise handed him a bottle of bourbon she'd just scanned. 'Did it really rain blood?'

'It did.'

'Wow. You know, we all started following the gospel of Susan after we heard about that stuff. I'm so glad we did. It's opened our eyes.'

'The gospel of Susan?'

'Yes, it was Susan's gospel that predicted you would show up on Blue Corn and deliver the people from evil.'

JD hadn't dwelt much on his brief stay on Blue Corn. A lot had happened since then. His only recollection of the time was a major massacre in a haunted forest involving a bunch of crazy creatures and a few members of the Four Horsemen of the Apocalypse. The island had a tribe of Amish nutters on it who followed the gospel of Susan, which had predicted the second coming of Christ. When JD had showed up there and killed the forest creatures, the Amish folk hailed him as the resurrected son of God. Fucking lunatics.

'Oh, that,' he muttered. 'I'm pretty sure the Blue Corn people were confused about a lot of things.'

'But you do have the blood of Christ in you, don't you? That's right isn't it? And you killed the demons in the Black Forest.'

At this point, Louise made the mistake of scanning JD's last item, meaning he no longer had to listen to her prattle on with her ill-informed versions of what he'd been up to in the past.

'How much?' he asked, pulling a bunch of twenties from the pocket of his army jacket.

'Oh, um, you know what, the manager wouldn't want me charging you. We're all just so glad you're here. What's your plan? Are you gonna kill them all?'

JD put his money away. 'Nice to have met you,' he said. He picked up his bag of goods and walked out.

Outside the store, the sun had vanished behind a gathering of black clouds. There was an eerie silence too, no traffic passing by, no birds chirping, no whistling wind, nothing. JD took a moment to look around. A group of people on the other side of the road caught his eye. There were four of them, standing side by side, staring at him like zombies. On one end was a young woman, aged maybe eighteen, wearing black tights, a red skirt and a baggy black top. She had scruffy dark hair and a gaunt, pale face. Her three companions were men. One was a black guy in his early twenties, wearing a brown leather suit. The other two were pale, sun-starved goth-types, probably in their thirties, both dressed in dark colours. One had a long beard and shoulder-length greasy brown hair. The other had black hair, shaved at the sides, and he wore glasses with white frames. None of them took their eyes off JD while he stared back at them. Eventually he grew tired of the staring contest and headed back to his jeep.

That's when the trouble started.

The jeep was gone.

JD looked back at the four weirdoes across the street. Those fuckers knew something. He placed his shopping bag on the ground and pulled out a bottle of bourbon. He flipped the lid off, took a swig, then

62

another, and then one more for good luck. With half the bottle gone, he screwed the lid back on and stuck the bottle back in the bag. The time had come to go socialise with the four weirdoes.

As he was about to cross the road, a black van pulled up in front of the four gawping oddballs, blocking his view of them. But as he stepped off the sidewalk onto the road, the ground vibrated beneath his feet.

BOOM!

A large pool of smoke floated up into the air a few miles away, close to the town centre, accompanied by the distant sound of people screaming. Something big had exploded. While JD was distracted by the sight of the giant smoke cloud, the black van on the other side of the road pulled away and sped off. The four weirdoes were gone too, most likely in the black van. And the mystery of who stole JD's jeep remained unanswered.

Fourteen

The portal sealed shut behind Elvis and Jasmine. They had been transported into the disabled washroom in the *Prince and Company* clothing store. A white porcelain toilet sat against the back wall, with a wash basin opposite. The room was spacious but disgusting, littered with used toilet paper, soaking wet paper towels, and puddles of piss. The air reeked like the men's toilets at the Tapioca after a packed Saturday night.

'Jacko picked us a good 'un here, didn't he?' said Jasmine, holding her nose.

'Let's just get out of here,' said Elvis, stepping over a puddle of piss.

'Shall we split up when we get out there?' Jasmine suggested. 'Flank them. You go after them, and I'll cover the exit in case they make a run for it.'

Elvis took Jasmine's hand and helped her step over the piss puddle. 'That's a great plan, Jas.' He slapped her across the ass. 'Let's do it. This is gonna be simple.'

The first sign that it wouldn't be simple came almost immediately. The washroom door opened, and in walked a middle-aged, silver-haired blind man in a brown tracksuit and sandals. He was clearly in for a rough experience. He locked the door behind him, turned around, and tapped his white cane along the floor as he approached the toilet.

Jasmine and Elvis stepped back quietly, holding their breath. Jasmine mouthed, 'What do we do?' to Elvis.

Elvis simply placed a finger to his lips and nodded at the door. She interpreted that as: "Shut up and sneak out."

The blind man rested his cane against the wall, pulled down his tracksuit bottoms, and lowered himself onto a toilet seat already glistening with someone else's piss.

Elvis took a long stride towards the door, setting his foot down in a rare clean part of the floor. Jasmine, who was lighter on her feet, tiptoed along behind him.

Their attempts at discretion came to an end when the blind man unleashed something from his backside that sounded like someone stepping on a duck.

'Oh, come on!' Elvis groaned.

The blind man pressed his hand against the wall. 'Is someone there?' he asked.

Elvis unlocked the door and pulled it open. He and Jasmine snuck through it into the clothing store on the other side, where it was safe to inhale the air.

64

Jasmine tapped Elvis on the arm. 'I'll cover the entrance. Meet you in the middle.'

'Got it, good luck.'

Jasmine ducked and weaved her way through all the racks of clothing to the front of the store, checking for any sign of her clone as she went. Elvis moved the other way, using the displays for cover, passing two male shop assistants who were having an argument about how to dress a mannequin.

It didn't take long to find the clone's out-of-shape boyfriend. The guy was unmistakable: fat, bald, wearing blue dungarees, and ogling a naked mannequin like he wanted to do more than dress it. The clone herself was nowhere in sight.

Elvis moved like a ninja behind a shoe rack, inching closer. He was about to strike when Jasmine's voice rang out.

'Hey sweetie, what do you think of this outfit?'

Elvis ducked behind a table stacked with underpants and peeked through the garments. The clone had just stepped out of the changing rooms in high heels, black leather shorts, and a tiny black top that barely covered her chest. She looked nearly identical to Jasmine, just a bit younger, trashier. Hot, though.

She swayed her hips like she was dancing to music that wasn't playing, then spotted Elvis watching her.

'What the fuck are you looking at, pervert?' she snapped.

Elvis gave up trying to hide and stood up. The clone's boyfriend turned, saw him, and instantly panicked.

'Jas, we gotta go,' he said, grabbing her hand and heading for the exit.

Elvis cut through the clothing racks to block their path. 'I just wanna talk,' he said, calmly.

The clone prodded her man in the back. 'Fuck him up, Lenny!'

'Who is she?' Elvis asked, unfazed by the threat of an attack from Lenny.

'None of your fucking business,' Lenny spat back.

'YOU THERE! POLICE! GET DOWN ON YOUR KNEES!

The shout came from behind Elvis. It was followed immediately by a whole load of yelling and screaming that sounded like a mix of panicking customers and more cops. Elvis dropped behind a circular rack of clothes and drew his pistol, peering through some leopard-print leggings. At least ten cops had sealed the entrance, all guns trained on Elvis, Lenny, and the clone.

Elvis had initially assumed the cops were there for him and Jasmine. But they seemed more interested in Lenny and his trashy accomplice.

"You'll never take me alive!" Lenny yelled, pulling a gun from his dungaree pouch.

BANG!

One of the cops shot Lenny in the face. Blood squirted out of the back of his head and spattered into the face and neck of his Jasmine clone. As Lenny collapsed, the clone had the good sense to dive for cover at Elvis's feet.

Elvis poked his pistol through the leopard-print tackiness. He picked out a stocky, tanned male cop and lined him up in his sights. The cop had smoke floating from the barrel of his gun, indicating he was the one who had killed Lenny. Elvis didn't care for Lenny one way or the other, but that cop was going down.

Thanks to the silencer on Elvis's pistol there was no deafening report when he fired it. His silent bullet hit the cop in the neck and sent him spinning into one of his colleagues. That was the cue for all hell to break loose. Deafening gunfire, screams from fleeing shoppers, and even higher-pitched screams from the male shop assistants. Elvis grabbed the clone's hand and pulled her toward the customer service desk, dodging falling debris. She cursed him the entire way, blaming him for everything.

He kicked open a wooden flap, dove behind the desk, and lost his grip on her. Gunfire rained down. Ceilings lights shattered and clothing racks tumbled. The desk held up well though. Elvis crouched behind it, ready to fire back. But the store fell silent.

'ELVIS! YOU OKAY, SWEETIE?'

Elvis peered over the customer service desk, scanning the smoke-filled store. Corpses, cops, customers, and employees were strewn near the front. Jasmine, as always, sauntered through the carnage like a badass, gun still in hand.

'Elvis?'

'Over here, honey.'

'Is my clone around anywhere?'

Elvis spotted her just outside the customer service desk, blood pooling from a stomach wound. He rushed over, crouched beside her, and tucked away his gun.

'You okay?' he asked.

'I've been shot, you dumb fuck,' the clone hissed back at him. 'What are you fucking retarded or something?'

66

Jasmine made her way over to join them, checking all the time to see if there was anyone else to kill. Her pinpoint accuracy with a gun was one of those unexplained phenomena. Whether it was shooting cops, shop assistants, zombies, the pope, the cast of *Planet of the Apes,* or anyone else, she never seemed to miss.

'Oh, God. Is she okay?' Jasmine asked as she spotted the sexy young woman on the floor, a pool of blood rapidly forming around her midriff.

'She's taken one in the gut,' Elvis replied.

The clone looked up at Jasmine. She blinked a few times before a look of happiness spread across her face. 'You're the mother!' she spluttered.

Jasmine crouched down beside her. 'We need to get you to some medical care,' she said, stroking the other woman's hair.

'It's an honour to meet you,' the clone said, seemingly forgetting about her injury for a moment.

'Are you a real person?' Jasmine asked her. 'What's your name?'

The clone coughed. 'I'm a Jasmine,' she croaked. 'You are the mother of Jasmines, aren't you? I've seen you on the internet.'

'Where are you from originally?' Elvis asked.

The clone stared down at her blood-soaked hands. 'I think I'm going to die,' she said.

'Don't worry,' said Jasmine. 'We're going to get you some help.'

The clone looked up at her and spluttered, 'Would you hold me?'

Jasmine tucked her gun down the back of her jeans and sat down beside her clone. She cradled the woman's head against her shoulder. 'It's gonna be okay,' she said.

'She's right,' said Elvis, in an attempt to reassure the clone. 'A Jasmine never really dies.'

Jasmine looked at Elvis. 'Can we get her to Purgatory?'

'Yeah, let's do it.' Elvis fumbled in his pocket for his phone. 'We can't hang around here anyway. There's gonna be more cops any minute now.'

Jasmine wiped some blood from the clone's face and asked her a question. 'Where exactly do you come from?'

The clone gazed up at her. 'I was born in a big room with all the other Jasmines. You were there too,' she said. 'Don't you remember?'

'When was it?'

'I don't remember the time. I wasn't fully programmed back then.'

'But you're sure it was me?'

The clone managed half a smile. 'You were there for the birth of the first of us. I was number two hundred and seven.'

67

'Two hundred and seven? But how were you created?'

The clone didn't seem to hear the question. The energy required to breathe was deserting her. The sparkle in her eyes faded away, and her head slumped against Jasmine's chest. Jasmine checked the clone's neck for a pulse. There was nothing.

'Is she gonna be okay?' Elvis asked.

Jasmine shook her head.

'Let's take her to Purgatory anyway.'

Fifteen

JD reached into his jacket pocket and pulled out the card Walt Shingleton had given him. He hadn't expected to be calling the cop at all, let alone this soon, but with his jeep gone, he needed a ride to the police station. He typed the cop's number in on his phone and called him up.

'Hello, this is Walt.'

'Walt, you gave me your card this morning when you dropped me off at the car rental place.'

'Oh, hey buddy. What can I do for ya?'

'I just had my ride stolen from Drummond's parking lot, so if you want me to show up at the cop station, you're gonna have to come get me.'

'No problem, son. You at Drummond's right now?'

'Yeah.'

'I'll be there in five.'

JD ended the call and waited by the roadside for Walt. The mushroom cloud of smoke on the horizon was slowly dissipating. An ambulance, siren blazing, whizzed past Drummond's towards the scene of the explosion. A few more minutes passed before Walt eventually cruised up in a wood-panelled station wagon. He parked by the roadside and pressed a button on his dash to pop the trunk open. JD dumped his bag of booze and cigarettes in the trunk, then took a seat in the front of the car.

'Hey there, soldier,' said Walt. 'Any clues on who stole your ride?'

'No, but there were some fucking hippies watching me from across the street. A black van came and picked them up right about the same time as the big explosion.'

Walt swung the car around in Drummond's parking lot, then hit the road and started the journey back to the police station. 'Yeah, big explosion,' he said. 'Sounds like a lotta people got hurt. I was on my way there when I got your call.'

'What caused it? Bomb, gas leak?'

'Word is it was a bomb. Looks like someone tried to blow up the folks who were protesting about the factory. I haven't seen the fallout myself, but word is at least four people are dead and quite a few more injured.'

'Any idea who did it?'

'Probably the same sorta people who stole your ride. Or maybe friends of that fella, Nilas, who you recently killed in the car rental store.'

'Are you going the right way?' JD asked, ignoring the mention of his recent murder.

69

'Yeah, we're going to the station, but I'm going the long way around to avoid the bomb site,' said Walt. 'Otherwise we'll be stuck there for ages.'

'Woman on the checkout in Drummond's says people have been praying for me to show up.'

'That'd be right.'

'What do they actually want me for?'

Walt scratched his chin while he thought about his answer. 'Well, thing is, ever since the good folks of this town heard about what you did for those people on Blue Corn Island, we started following the gospel of Susan. I gotta tell you, it got people interested in the church again. Even the youngsters. It's had a really good impact on our community. We started living a little like those people you helped on Blue Corn.'

'Those people were Amish.'

Walt smiled. 'We're not exactly like them, but we did shut down the internet. There's no internet anywhere in this town, and no text messaging. All your phone is good for is calling people. And you know what? People are happier for it. Folks are speaking to each other again, joining in community events, supporting anything local. And no one walks around staring at their phone anymore. The young people in this town are a lot happier than they were before. And all this came about from following the example of the people of Blue Corn and switching our faith to the gospel of Susan.'

JD groaned. 'It's all shit, you know.'

'Excuse me?'

'You're talking about this great community, but I've been here an hour and I had a car salesman pull a gun on me, my ride's been stolen, the town centre has been bombed, you've got three missing women, and there's fucking weirdoes everywhere, especially in that supermarket. I gotta tell you, I'm not seeing how the gospel of Susan is helping.'

Walt took a turn down a quiet street in a leafy suburb. 'Okay, well, it's like this, we believed that if we followed the word of Susan like the Amish people did, then God would send you to deliver us from the evil that has infested our town in recent times. See, even though people are happier because there's no internet and stuff, they're also really worried by what's going on. That's why the church folk have been asking God to send you here to deliver us from evil.'

'I'm here because you called Alexis Calhoon. God didn't send me.'

'Jack the Ripper ain't the only crook in town,' said Walt, undeterred. 'We want these other people gone. He's probably one of them too. They're strange, unsociable, and kinda scary. They've brought crime to our town. Proper crime. Car theft, mugging, burglary, murder,

70

and more recently kidnapping. Whatever is going on, it's all escalating. Your arrival here couldn't have come at a better time.'

JD stared out of his window. The part of town they were driving through looked like a nice place to live, at least it did until the moment they passed by a black cat nailed to a tree with its guts hanging out. 'What did they do to you, Walt?'

'Huh?'

'You gave me your business card for a reason. It's written all over your face. What did they do?'

Walt eased the car over to the side of the road and parked. He took a few deep breaths and stared through the front windscreen. Eventually, he plucked up the nerve to look at JD. 'Last year my wife and daughter were murdered.' He paused and looked the windscreen again. 'Actually, and I haven't said this out loud before, but they were raped and murdered.' Walt's throat tightened up, his eyes glazed over. 'The six men that did it, we caught them, but they had a lawyer from out of town, a city guy. I don't know how he did it, but from the day he showed up, the case slowly fell apart. Evidence that was crucial to the case, DNA, semen samples, witnesses, all of it vanished.'

'Witnesses vanished?'

'Two of them. Found dead, drowned in the river. Accidental death of course. Nothing could be proven. And the judge who exonerated them killed himself that night. He's since been replaced by a judge from out of town, probably one of *them*. These people have far-reaching power. They're intimidating, and they can get to anyone. I wasn't the only one affected by what happened. It upset a lot of folks. My wife and daughter were well liked by everyone who knew them. You know, I hadn't prayed in years. But after they died, I started praying every day. I went to church and I prayed to God many, many times. And you know what I prayed for?'

'I know.'

Walt looked JD right in the eye. 'I asked God to send you to do what the legal system couldn't. We were told you were coming, but I didn't believe it until I picked you up and gave you a ride into town this morning. That's when I knew my prayers had been answered.'

'You want them all dead, right?'

'You bet I do. All six of them. Fucking lawyer too if he ever shows up again.'

JD pulled a pack of cigarettes from his pocket and hooked one out with his teeth. It lit up as soon as he inhaled. He took the smoke deep into his lungs, then wound his window down and blew it out. 'Killing's what I do,' he said, looking back at Walt. 'Where do I find them?'

71

Walt fought to control his breathing. 'They run a garage, fixing up cars. It's called Nixon's Garage. Their names are…'

'I don't need names.'

'You don't?'

'No. I'll just kill everyone that works there.'

'Oh Christ,' said Walt, wiping some sweat from his forehead. 'I gotta warn you, these guys, they're kinda strange.'

'How so?'

'It's hard to describe. You gotta see it with your own eyes.'

JD took another drag of his cigarette, then pointed at the road ahead. 'Let's go clean 'em up.'

Sixteen

'Jacko! Open the fucking portal now!'

Elvis wasn't generally one for being rude on the phone, and Jacko recognised the urgency in his voice, so with the flick of a button he opened the portal back up at its last location, the disabled toilets in the *Prince and Company* clothing store.

From his spot behind the bar, the first thing Jacko saw when the portal door slid aside was a blind man in a brown tracksuit sitting on a toilet wiping his ass. Jasmine was standing beside him with her hand over her mouth and nose. She staggered into Purgatory and removed her hand from her face, then she sucked in a breath of the slightly fresher air. Elvis dashed through behind her, carrying a Jasmine lookalike in his arms. The blind man on the toilet, as if sensing their presence shouted out, "Who the fuck is…."'

Jacko closed up the portal and hoped to never see the blind man again. 'What happened?' he asked, staring at the dead woman in Elvis's arms.

'She's dead,' said Elvis, laying the woman down on a long padded seat by the wall next to the portal. Her blood was all over Elvis's hands and clothing, with plenty more splattered on her torso.

'Did you shoot her?' Jacko asked.

'Cops did,' said Elvis. 'They killed her boyfriend too. Have you got anyone here that can do an autopsy?'

Jacko grabbed a glass and poured Jasmine a soda. 'My guess is there's about a billion volunteers down in Hell who'd happily take you up on that,' he said.

Elvis groaned. 'Can you get one that isn't a pervert?'

'That'll be tricky. Especially if word gets out that it's a Jasmine clone.'

'What about the guy at the mortuary in Santa Mondega?' said Jasmine, taking a sip of her soda. 'The one you and Rex met with one time. The one with the stupid name?'

'Taylor Taylor?'

'That's the one.'

'I guess he's worth a try.' Elvis looked down at the dead clone and stroked some stray hair out of her face.

Jacko walked out from behind the bar to get a better look at the dead Jasmine. 'She looks very real,' he said, prodding her face. 'And that looks like real blood.'

Jasmine called over from the bar. 'Before she died she said there were more of her, and that I was there when some of them were born.'

73

'You were there?' said Jacko. 'Where's *there?*'

'I don't know. I don't remember anything about it, but she sort of intimated that there were hundreds more like her.'

Jacko finished prodding the corpse and stepped away. 'I'll get someone to come up and do an examination on her,' he said, pulling his cell phone from the breast pocket on his suit.

'Who you gonna call?' Elvis asked.

'Ghostbusters.'

'Dick.'

While Jacko turned his back and started texting someone, Jasmine re-joined Elvis. 'I think she was human,' she said, staring at her dead double. 'She really didn't want to die, whereas, I think if she was a robot, she wouldn't care.'

'A really advanced robot might have emotions,' Elvis replied. He winced as the corpse's arm fell down by her side. 'I don't like looking at it. It's like looking at you, Jas, only you're dead.'

'It is weird,' Jasmine agreed. 'I feel so bad for her. She seemed so frightened.'

'Hi, guys!'

Neither Jasmine nor Elvis had noticed Zilas sneak up behind them. Purgatory's resident hunchback handyman was wearing a set of grey overalls. His greasy brown hair hung down over his right eye, which was much higher on his face than his left eye. He was holding a mop in his hand that looked and smelt almost as bad as he did.

'Where the fuck did you come from?' Elvis asked, freaked out by the sudden appearance of the hunchback.

'I was in the Ladies washroom,' said Zilas.

'Doing what?'

'Cleaning, obviously.'

'Hi, Zilas,' said Jasmine. 'I like your mop.'

'Thanks. What happened to your sister?'

'She's dead,' said Jasmine.

Jacko walked up behind Zilas and patted him on the hunch. 'Gotta job for you buddy. Can you do an autopsy on this Jasmine clone? We need to know if it's a real person or a cyborg.'

Zilas's eyes lit up. 'Seriously? I would love to do that. Just get me a scalpel.'

'I'll get you a sharp knife,' said Jacko. 'And we should get some plastic sheeting to cover the floor with as well.'

'I can take the body somewhere private if you like?' said Zilas. 'Then you won't have to see the blood.'

74

'I think it's best we oversee this whole operation,' said Elvis, his distrust of Zilas clearly evident.

'Did you perform autopsies when you were alive?' Jasmine asked the hunchback.

'I did some extensive work with corpses,' Zilas replied, his lower eye opening wide as he focussed on the corpse. His other eye was pointed to the other side of the room, looking at nothing in particular.

'It's one of the reasons why Zilas is in Hell,' said Jacko. 'He was a necrophiliac back in the day.'

'Do necrophiliacs do autopsies then?' Jasmine queried. 'I thought coroners did them?'

'Coroners do autopsies,' said Elvis, 'whereas necrophiliacs fuck dead people.'

'Really?' said Jasmine, looking Zilas up and down. 'I knew some guys back in my brothel days who liked me to play dead while we had sex. I was quite into it. It was good fun. It's a shame you never came to my brothel, Zilas. Fifty bucks and we could have done it.'

Zilas turned a strange blue colour, a low groan slid from his lips and then he fell sideways and collapsed in a heap on the floor.

'How many times have I told you, Jas?' said Jacko. 'You can't get Zilas all riled up like that.'

'What did I say?'

Elvis walked over to the bar, grabbed an empty glass, filled it with cold water from the soda gun, then returned and poured it onto Zilas's face. The hunchback woke up with a start and bounced back up to his feet. He looked at Jasmine.

'What were you saying?'

Elvis answered on Jasmine's behalf. 'She said go get a plastic sheet before you do the autopsy.'

'Oh, right, yeah. I'll be right back.'

Zilas hobbled into the disabled toilets, took an elevator down to Hell, picked up a plastic sheet from a storage room, then returned to Purgatory with it, all in the space of three minutes. He spread the plastic sheet out on the floor and flattened it down. Elvis picked up the dead clone and placed her on the sheet.

'Okay, Zilas,' said Jacko, handing the hunchback a sharp knife. 'Get to work.'

Zilas accepted the knife then stood over the clone. He looked her up and down as he deliberated on where to make his first incision. 'First things first,' he said, eventually. 'We've got to get her clothes off.'

75

'I don't think that's necessary,' said Elvis. 'Just cut the stomach open and see if it's got organs or wires inside it. Or maybe cut the head open and look for a brain.'

Zilas got down on his knees and plunged the blade of his knife into the clone's stomach, then he made an incision right up to the chest. Some more blood oozed out.

The others didn't really want to watch the autopsy, but no one trusted Zilas to be respectful of the corpse if he was left alone with it. The hunchback set his knife down on the floor and slid his hand deep inside the body.

'What's in there?' Elvis asked.

Zilas rummaged around for a bit, having a good feel. It was too much for Jasmine and Jacko, who both retreated to the bar, leaving Elvis to oversee things.

'Well?' said Elvis, slapping Zilas on the arm. 'Found anything?'

'It's all normal in here,' said Zilas. 'I'd say it's human all right. But the only way to know for sure is to check if it has genitals. Cyborgs usually don't have anything down there.'

'How the fuck would you know?'

'Sci fi movies.'

Elvis sighed. 'Zilas, this clone was made so that people could have sex with it. There's no way anyone's making a Jasmine clone and not giving it sexual parts. Why don't you check the skull for a brain or chip instead?'

Zilas chewed on his bottom lip for a short while, almost drawing blood, but eventually he did as he was instructed. He made a rather clumsy incision in the clone's head and peeled back a layer of skin and hair to see what was underneath.

'That's a surprise,' he said, feeling around inside the skull. 'It's a real brain.' He paused. 'Oh, no wait, I found something.' He pulled his hand out and made another, much deeper and longer incision around the forehead. He peeled the clone's scalp all the way back.

Elvis winced at the gruesome sight. Even though he'd done worse things to people he'd killed over the years, like feeding Marcus the Weasel his own testicles, seeing a Jasmine clone ripped apart was hard to watch. Blood spilled out all over the plastic sheet.

Zilas rolled the corpse over onto its side. 'Look here,' he said, sticking his fingers into the brain and pulling away a chunk of it. 'There's a chip implanted in the upper part of her brain.'

Elvis leaned in a little to get a better look. He wished he had a facemask on. The autopsy was a stinky affair. Or maybe it was just Zilas? It was hard to know for sure. 'Can you get the chip out?' he asked.

76

'Well, seeing as how she's already dead, I can't see what harm it would do,' said Zilas. 'It would be easier with some proper tools, mind.'

The hunchback hacked away at the brain a little more and eventually yanked out the tiny chip that had been implanted into the clone's head. He offered it to Elvis.

'Clean it up first,' said Elvis. 'And put it in a dish on the bar.'

'Right.'

Zilas scurried off to the ladies' toilets to rinse the blood and brain matter off the chip. Elvis joined Jasmine and Jacko, who were sitting on stools at the bar. Jasmine was sipping on her soda, Jacko was drinking coffee from a red mug.

'Now that Einstein is in Heaven, do we have anyone else who knows anything about computer chips?' Elvis asked.

Jacko took a swig of his coffee while he tried to think of anyone who could help. 'Beats me,' he said, eventually. 'Maybe Zilas knows someone?'

'I think I might know a guy,' said Jasmine. 'I've got a contact, a tech guy who could take a look at this for us.'

'What do you mean you've got a contact?' said Elvis. 'What contact?'

'You don't know him.'

'Who the fuck do you know that I don't?'

'Don't worry,' said Jasmine, sliding off her bar stool. 'The guy's a geek. A nerd. You met him once but you don't remember it. He lives in Santa Mondega. We can go see him today.'

'Who the fuck is it? And why would I not remember meeting him?'

'It's kind of complicated,' said Jasmine.

'Simplify it for me.'

Jasmine glanced at Jacko. He sighed and put his mug of coffee down.

'I'm just gonna go outside and play some guitar,' he said. 'I don't wanna know anything that gets talked about in here.'

Jacko grabbed a guitar from behind the bar and walked out through the batwing doors at the front of the building. As soon as he was out of sight, Jasmine opened up.

'Can you keep a secret?' she whispered.

'How many secrets have you got right now?'

'It's to do with what I was going to tell you about earlier. I never said anything to you before because God made me promise not to tell anyone.'

'Then I definitely want to hear about it.'

'Okay, but you've got to swear you won't tell anyone.'

77

Elvis raised his right hand. 'I totally swear.'

Jasmine checked around to make sure Zilas hadn't reappeared, then she continued. 'The guy who can help us, his name is Zero. We met him once before when we were trying to track down an invisible man who caught the president jerking off to kiddy porn.'

Elvis sighed. 'Are you sure this wasn't a dream you had?'

'No. It totally happened, but then there was a time travel incident, and it was all undone, which is just as well because I think you might have died in a bike accident at a funeral.'

'A what?'

'It's not important right now. Look, the thing is, you and me tracked Zero down at a shop called Bobby's Miniature Trains. He showed us a video of the president jerking off to a video of a young child being eaten by a lion.'

Elvis closed his eyes and grimaced.

Jasmine carried on undeterred. 'I'm gutted you don't remember this. The government tracked us to Zero's hideout. They killed Zero and his buddy, but we escaped with Zero's dog, Goober.'

Elvis reopened his eyes. 'Wait, what? Goober was Zero's dog?'

'Uh huh. Come to think of it, there might be two Goobers now. The one JD has, and the original one that belonged to Zero. Wow, that's creepy. I can't wait to get to Zero's and see if there's another Goober there.'

'Jas, you're going off track.'

'Yeah, well, long story short, Sanchez got killed. Then you, me, and Rex all got shot, but we survived. JD killed all the major world leaders because they were paedophiles, then he and Flake hooked up, and we all lived together on a tropical island. Oh, and World War Three broke out.'

Elvis nodded. 'I appreciate you keeping that story short, but, *really?*'

Jasmine raised her eyebrows and smiled. 'That's not all,' she said. 'After a few months on the island, you and Rex and Flake all got killed. JD was to blame for most of it, obviously, but God allowed him to travel back in time to undo everything. Remember how I showed up in the Tapioca with Goober that day? That's the day we came back in time.'

'Fucking hell,' said Elvis. 'I was dead?'

'Uh huh, killed at a funeral, I think.'

'You think?'

'There was a lot going on.'

Elvis pursed his lips and thought for a few seconds before replying. 'Just suppose for a minute I actually believe it,' he said. 'How long were

78

you and JD living together on the island before you decided to travel back in time?'

'Aww, sweetie, after everything I just said, is that the only thing you're worried about? Me and JD hooking up?'

'Well, did you?'

'Of course not. Did you not hear me? I said he's totally into Flake, like head over heels for her.'

'Yeah, okay, but how long were you and JD alone on the island?'

'No time at all, like minutes. I gotta tell you though, if God had said no to the time travel thing, and me and JD had been alone on that island for the rest of our lives, something would have happened. I mean one night we all got drunk and I think I might have sucked off Eric Einstein for a dare.'

'What? Why was Einstein there?'

'Ooh, that's another thing. Totally important too. Einstein set up the time travel for me and JD, so in return God pardoned him, and he didn't have to live in Hell anymore. That's why he's not around.'

'You sucked off Einstein?'

'We were all very drunk and we were doing dares, Rex even jerked off with his metal hand. In fact, I've got a video of it on my phone, which will prove I'm telling the truth.'

'I am not watching that.'

Zilas reappeared from the washroom, so Jasmine lowered her voice to a whisper. 'Whether you believe me or not, we've still got to go and see Zero. And even though he won't remember meeting us, you'll see he's got a Goober just like our Goober. I think.'

Elvis sighed for what felt like the hundredth time. 'Okay. Let's take this chip and go see this Zero person. But you'll have to do a lot more to convince me about the rest of that story.'

Jasmine raised an eyebrow. 'You know what? I've got some photos of me fucking the president with a big strap-on.'

'What?'

'He was a perv, remember? I used the video to blackmail him into not being a dirty paedophile anymore. I could show you those on the way to Zero's.'

'I'm not sure that will prove anything, but you can show me anyway.'

79

Seventeen

Walt's palms were sweating. He was a cop driving a mass murderer to a local garage to watch him kill the people that worked there. It was out of the ordinary, for sure. The journey was undertaken in silence, because having just asked the Bourbon Kid to murder the men who killed his wife and daughter, Walt was wary of saying anything else and screwing things up. It was a short ride, *thank God*. There was only time to take in one song on the radio, which was, "I'm So Excited" by the Pointer Sisters.

Walt parked his station wagon across the street from the garage. 'There it is,' he said, pointing it out to his passenger. The garage had a big blue sign across the top of the building with the word, NIXONS painted across it in red letters. The front bay was open, and a mechanic in red overalls was standing underneath a two-post lift ramp. Sitting on top of the ramp was JD's recently stolen black jeep.

'If it's over there, why are we parked here?' JD asked.

'Shall I park on the forecourt?'

JD did not respond, so Walt took the hint and swung the car across the street onto the forecourt of the garage. He pulled on the parking brake but kept the engine running.

'I'll wait here, shall I?' he said.

JD got out of the car and headed into the workshop. The mechanic who was working on the jeep heard him coming and turned around. He was a heavy-set fellow in his early thirties with short brown hair and chiselled features. The name Conan was sewn into his overalls.

'What do you want?' he asked.

'That's my vehicle you're working on.'

'I know.'

'I've come to get it back.'

Conan smiled. 'What took you so long?'

'I didn't have my ride. What are you stupid or something?'

'I was gonna ask you the same thing.'

'So ask.'

Conan's grin widened. 'You have no idea what's coming,' he said.

JD reached inside his coat and pulled out his Headblaster gun. The sight of it was usually enough to wipe the smile off anyone's face, but not this guy. Conan wasn't fazed at all. The reason why became clear when JD pointed the gun at his head. Conan vanished. A millisecond later he reappeared right next to JD and punched him in the side of the head. JD swung his gun around to shoot him, but Conan vanished again, reappearing on JD's other side. *Punched in the head again.*

The punches didn't hurt, but even so, they were irritating. When Conan disappeared again, JD reached inside his coat with his free hand and pulled out his Flame gun. The mechanic reappeared, this time behind JD. But the trick had worn thin already. Conan's third attempt to punch JD was unsuccessful. His fist hit nothing but air because JD ducked. Conan played his vanishing trick once more. But this time when he reappeared, JD was already spraying fire around from his Flame gun. Conan popped up right in the middle of it. Mechanics with oil-covered overalls light up like Christmas trees. Conan flailed around, screaming and cursing as the fire engulfed his whole body.

JD extinguished his Flame gun and tucked it back inside his coat, then he pulled out a pack of cigarettes. He hooked one out of the packet with his teeth and sucked in some of the heat from Conan's melting skin. The cigarette lit up. JD took a drag and watched Conan flambé.

The high-pitched screams and the raging fire alerted the other garage workers to the danger. Men in red overalls started running in from all over. The first one on the scene was a Korean dude with a shaved head. He was around five-feet-eight inches tall, but physically solid. He charged at JD, and when he was ten feet away he leapt off the ground, reaching a height worthy of a gold medal in the Olympics. On his way down, his legs spun like propellors aimed at JD's head. He let out a "wooo-aaah" sound, like he thought he was in a Bruce Lee movie.

BOOM!

And just like that, Mister Kung-Fu lost his testicles, and a fair chunk more. The pitch of his "wooo-aaah" scream rose up from D major to G minor. The Korean bounced on the floor with a loud crack, and a touch of squelch. Blood pumped out from the top of his right leg, which was hanging off. JD dropped his cigarette and turned his attention back to the flaming Conan. Using his sleeve gun he fired a spiked dart on a length of cord into Conan's neck. The screaming, dancing, body-on-fire mechanic, stopped yelling as the dart pierced his jugular. JD yanked his arm back, pulling Conan's burning corpse down onto his Korean colleague, setting him on fire too. The dart retracted back into JD's sleeve gun, leaving the barbecued mechanics stuck together like melted cheese on toast.

The next attack on JD came from behind. A swooshing sound gave it away. JD ducked down and swivelled around in one flowing move. A steel wrench flying through the air was the cause of the whooshing. It had been thrown by another mechanic, a stocky, black guy in his twenties with cropped black hair. He had come from the office on the other side of the building. Upon seeing JD evade his wrench attack, he looked for something else to throw.

81

Before JD could shoot the bastard, he came under attack again from yet another lunatic. And yet another whooshing sound. JD dove for cover as a trail of raging, hot, blue flames whizzed past his head. The blue flames came from another mechanic, who had been working under a nearby truck when the trouble started. He was black with a thick beard and a chunky afro. Much like some of his friends, this guy had an unusual talent. He could shoot gas flames from his hands. He angled his hand over towards JD, ready to shoot another blast at him.

JD whipped out his Flame gun again and flicked a switch on the side of it. Then he did what he always did. Shoot first. Liquid nitrogen erupted from the gun barrel. It   squirted over the gas-shooting mechanic's hand, then his face. His hand froze up, then a moment later the air in his lungs turned to ice.

Safe in the knowledge the gas man was fucked, JD looked around for the wrench-tossing asshole. During the nitrogen vs gas fight, the wrench-thrower had been transforming into something very un-human. His body expanded, tearing his clothes away from his upper half. Tufts of hair spurted from every inch of him as he revealed his true self, a wolfman with a face like a fucking angry teddy bear.

JD's Flame gun was all used up so he dropped it and pointed his Headblaster gun at the wolfman instead. Wolfmen suck. All this guy did was growl and pose.

BOOM!

Goodbye head.

The headless wolfman flailed around like a blind drunk. JD contemplated blowing his guts out too, but before he had the chance, a van at the far end of the workshop toppled over onto its side. Another freak who had been lying on his back, working underneath the van, had pushed it over, and was back on his feet. And this guy was big. He was wearing nothing but a pair of black shorts, and he had pale skin that looked like it was made of rock. He charged at JD, coming at him like a raging bull. Recognising that this man was a bigger threat than the headless wolfman, JD turned the Headblaster on him.

BOOM!

The big guy was knocked back a step by the power of the Headblaster's discharge, but he shook it off and ran again, even faster. He ploughed into the side of JD, knocking him off balance. JD stayed on his feet but banged his wrist against one of the metal posts on the lift ramp. He lost his grip on his Headblaster gun and it hit the floor and bounced away. There was no time to retrieve it because the rock man, whose skin was made of granite, took a step back from JD and threw a punch at his head. JD ducked in the nick of time. In his peripheral vision

82

he saw the metal wrench that had been hurled at him moments earlier. He grabbed it from the floor and swung it at the granite man's crotch.

CLANK!

'OOOPH!'

It doesn't matter what your nuts are made of, soft tissue or solid granite, a shot in the gonads with a steel tyre wrench still smarts. The giant rock-man winced and doubled over, clutching his stony balls. JD looked around for his Headblaster, only to be confronted by the final member of the horrible six mechanics. Psycho number six was an eight-feet tall giant who, in a twist of irony, had the look of one of Snow White's seven dwarves. He was ugly as fuck, with short arms and legs and a head the size of a suitcase. Bad teeth too. The dwarf came in from a room outback, presumably the best place for him to work, where the customers wouldn't see him.

There wasn't time to fuck around gawping at the unusual appearance of the newest attacker, so JD charged at him and tackled him around the waist. The dwarf went down easily on account of his enormous head making him top-heavy. His skull cracked on the solid concrete floor. JD rolled off him and scrambled for his Headblaster gun. He grabbed it just as the granite man started marching towards him again. Two quick blasts from the gun took out the posts on the lift ramp. The ramp and the jeep it was supporting, crashed down onto the granite man's head. The sheer weight of it made his knees buckle, and he vanished underneath the busted ramp and the jeep.

JD surveyed the scene to see who else needed dealing with. The two mechanics that he'd set on fire were already done, toasted. The one with the gas-throwing hands was frozen solid thanks to the liquid nitrogen, and his skin was showing signs of cracking. The headless wolfman was still on his feet though, staggering around, throwing punches at nothing. JD pointed his Headblaster at the decapitated bastard and pulled the trigger.

BOOM!

The blast blew a hole in the wolfman's chest turning his heart into milkshake. He thudded onto the floor, squelching as blood and innards slid out of him.

JD looked around the workshop. There were no more attacks incoming, so all that remained was to finish off the creepy, giant dwarf and the frozen gas man. One shot from the Headblaster blew the gas man into a million pieces. JD then reloaded his gun and turned back to the giant dwarf. As the freak struggled to get back on his feet, JD moved in close and blasted him in his huge face. The dwarf's head broke open and a pool of mulch oozed out like the contents of a creme egg.

83

JD blew the smoke from the end of his gun and took a moment to reflect on the madness that had just taken place. When Walt had said there was something off about these guys, he wasn't kidding.

With the fight over, Walt turned off the engine on his station wagon and climbed out to take a look at the carnage. He got a good waft of decaying flesh too.

'Holy fuck, you really did it!' he said, staring at the corpses all around. 'That was fucking awesome.'

'It was definitely something,' said JD. 'Was there anyone else you wanted me to kill?'

Walt shook his head. 'No, but thank you. I can't wait to tell everyone at church about this. They'll fucking love it.'

JD opened the driver's door on his jeep. 'I'll follow you back to the station,' he said.

'Right.'

JD reversed his jeep back off the busted lift ramp, then he and Walt left the bloodbath at Nixon's Garage behind and headed to the police station in separate vehicles. They had been gone less than a minute when the remains of the two-post lift ramp rose up from the ground. The mechanic with the granite skin dragged himself out of a groove he'd created in the concrete floor and stood up straight, taking in the sight of carnage all around him. His brothers were all dead. Something would have to be done. People needed to be notified about what had happened.

The rock man headed into the back office and used the phone to make a call to his sister, Petra.

'Hey, Petra, it's Rocky at the garage.'

'How did it go? Did he show up yet?'

'He showed up all right. It's real, Petra. The others are dead. He killed them all. Did it in less than a minute.'

'All of them?'

'Yeah. He was lucky.'

'You're still alive though. Why didn't *you* kill him?'

'He dropped a jeep and a lift ramp on my head.'

On the other end of the line, Petra took a moment to think. 'You know what?' she said, eventually. 'Don't worry about it. Reinforcements are on the way.'

84

Eighteen

Elvis and Jasmine were standing outside Donnie's burger van on the promenade in Santa Mondega waiting for their order. The promenade was fairly empty, possibly because of a chilly wind in the air. The only other people in shouting distance were two junkies sleeping outside the public toilets that Elvis and Jasmine had passed through on their way out of the portal in Purgatory.

'Here you go,' said Jasmine, handing Elvis her phone. 'That's me and the president.'

Elvis held the phone up in front of his face to keep it out of the sunlight. The footage on screen was of Jasmine fucking the president of the United States with a strap-on dildo.

'This doesn't prove your time travel story though,' said Elvis, wincing at the sheer size of the dildo that was destroying the president's butthole.

'I've got plenty of other evidence.'

Jasmine snatched back the phone and pulled up a photo of a naked man rimming the Russian president. 'Take a look at this then,' she said, handing the phone back.

'Is that a sex doll?' Elvis asked, pointing at a third character in the picture.

'Yep,' said Jasmine. 'You were there with me when we took these photos. It's a shame you don't remember it.'

'But why is the Russian president going down on the sex doll? Surely neither of them are getting anything out of that?'

'It was your idea. He was unconscious at the time, so we did all sorts to him, then I shot him in the back of the head.'

Elvis flicked onto the next photo, which was even worse. He handed the phone back to Jasmine just as the lady in the burger van shoved a giant hot dog under his nose.

'Here you go, mister,' she said. 'One giant hotdog for you, and a beef taco for you, miss.'

The hotdog looked great, aside from its resemblance to the giant dildo in Jasmine's video. Elvis covered it in barbecue sauce and took a bite. As usual, the food at Donnie's tasted heavenly.

'How's your food?' Elvis asked, as the two of them strolled along the seafront.

'Very tasty,' said Jasmine. 'What's your hotdog like?'

'It's good, although I wish I hadn't watched your video first.'

85

'The president was up for anything,' said Jasmine, nibbling on her taco. 'I gave his ass one hell of a pounding. And I made him suck the dildo dry afterwards too. He was a real sissy.'

Elvis held off taking another a bite of his hotdog. 'It bothers me when powerful people are like that,' he said, shaking his head.

'Zero, the guy we're going to see, he was the one who told us *all* of the world leaders are into the most deviant sexual stuff imaginable, particularly with kids. But they're not anymore, since I blackmailed them all. These days they know if they screw around with kids again, I'll be posting the photos and videos of them online. You know the Italian president could actually suck his own dick. Wanna see the video?'

Elvis dumped his hotdog in a nearby trash can. 'Let's go meet with your friend, Zero,' he said.

While Jasmine munched away on her taco, Elvis headed over to a yellow Suzuki Jimny that was parked in a NO PARKING zone. It took him less than twenty seconds to break in and hotwire it. He reversed it out of its space and pulled up next to Jasmine.

'Fancy a ride with a strange man?' he asked her.

'Always!'

Jasmine climbed into the passenger side of the Jimny, then Elvis hit the gas and they sped off in the direction of Chinatown.

Five minutes later, Elvis parked up outside Bobby's Miniature Trains shop. The place stood out because it was the only store in Chinatown without a Chinese name. They left the stolen Jimny and walked into the store. A bell above the door chimed to announce their arrival. The store was fairly big inside, bigger than it looked from the outside. There were miniature village displays on both sides of the shop, with trains chugging their way around them. The counter was manned by a young man in ripped blue jeans and a green sweater. He had long, greasy brown hair that didn't really suit him, and his skin was almost as greasy.

'Hello, how can I help you today?' he asked.

'Hello, Neville,' said Jasmine, strolling up to him. 'We've come to see Zero.'

'Excuse me?'

Elvis joined in. 'You heard what she said, Buttface. Where's Zero?'

'I don't know anyone named Zero,' Neville lied.

'We've been here before,' said Jasmine, leaning on the counter and smiling at Neville while she pushed her boobs into his eye line. 'Last time we were here, we went into the back room where you keep the miniature version of Santa Mondega.'

86

'I don't remember that.'

'Of course you do. You showed me the button inside the miniature model of the Nightjar. You know the one I mean, it's the button that opens the secret doorway behind the bookshelf. Now, I know you know who I am, so why don't you stop bluffing and bullshitting and just let us into the back room so we can go make our way down to Zero's hideout?'

Neville was taken aback. 'I, umm, I don't remember you being here before,' he mumbled.

'Of course you don't,' said Jasmine. 'We did the Men in Black *flashy-pen-thing* on you and wiped it from your memory. Now, if you're a good boy this time, we won't *flashy-thing* you and you'll be able to remember *everything* you see, if you know what I mean?' She gave Neville a sly wink.

Neville chewed on his thumbnail. 'You're Jasmine and Elvis from the Dead Hunters. How did you find us?'

'Take a fucking guess,' said Elvis, losing patience.

Neville pointed tentatively at Jasmine. 'You're the *real* Jasmine?'

Elvis reached into his jacket and pulled out his gun. He pointed it at Neville's head. 'Just do as you're fucking told,' he said. 'Because you're starting to piss me off.'

Neville gulped. 'Okay, let me just lock up the store.'

After rushing past them and locking the front door, Neville returned and showed them into the back room, which contained the shitty, miniature version of Santa Mondega Jasmine had spoken of. Jasmine hurried past Neville, poked her hand through the upper window of the miniature Nightjar building, and pressed a button inside it. On the wall in front of them, a bookshelf filled with rubbish books about trains slid to one side, revealing a set of stairs behind it that led down into darkness.

'Wow, you have been here before,' said Neville.

'Of course I have,' said Jasmine. 'Now be a good boy, Neville, and lead the way.'

Neville made his way over to the secret entrance. When he reached it, he turned back and issued a warning. 'Whoever comes in last has to pull the bookshelf back across the entrance.'

'I'll do it,' said Jasmine.

Neville led the way down the darkened staircase with Elvis right behind him, breathing down his neck. Jasmine dragged the bookshelf back across the entrance as promised, and then followed them down. At the bottom of the stairs was a dark, narrow corridor lit up by a set of dim blue lights that were fitted into panels in the walls. It made the place look like something from an underground rebel base in a *Terminator* movie.

87

Jasmine squeezed her way to the front and made her way along the corridor towards Zero's hideout. Elvis stayed with Neville to make sure the nerd didn't do anything stupid. After a short walk they came to a black door at the end of the corridor.

'It's through here,' said Jasmine twisting the door knob.

'*Wait!* You should knock first,' said Neville.

Too late.

Jasmine pushed the door open and strolled into Zero's headquarters. Elvis barged Neville into the wall and walked in after her. They were greeted by a sight that neither of them was expecting.

There were sofas dotted around the sides of the room, as well as a few desks furnished with computers. In the opposite corner of the room was a strip curtain that led into another corridor. And to the left of the entrance was a statue of Alicia Vikander dressed as Lara Croft from *Tomb Raider*. But all those things paled into insignificance compared to what was occurring in the middle of the room. A young man's bare ass was staring at them. The man in question was pale and skinny with spiky blond hair. He was wearing a black T-shirt, and a pair of grey sweatpants that were down by his ankles. And he was having sex with a naked, brown-skinned woman with spiky red hair. She was bent over the side of the sofa while he pumped away behind her.

The man had heard the door open behind him, but rather than look round to see who had entered, he carried on thrusting while he responded to the intrusion. 'Christ, Neville, I thought I told you to knock!' he complained.

'Uh, yeah, we've got guests,' Neville called out from behind Elvis.

'Huh?'

The young man with the blond hair was Zero. Jasmine recognised him from the back of his head. She also recognised the woman he was doing from behind. It was another clone of her, only with red hair. The clone was moaning in ecstasy, seemingly enjoying the sex.

In a case of unfortunate timing, the clone moaned the words, 'Ooh, Zero, you're so much better than Elvis.'

Zero finally glanced over his shoulder and caught sight of Elvis, Jasmine and Neville staring at him. 'Oh fuck!' he said, his eyes bulging, and his ass cheeks clenching.

Neville prodded Jasmine in the back. 'See, I told you, you should knock.'

'Are you kidding?' said Jasmine. 'We would have missed *this!*'

Zero, while looking over his shoulder at the real Jasmine, seemed to get just the boost he needed. He let out a light groan, his eyes fluttered like he was about to pass out, then he quite clearly shot his load into the red-haired Jasmine lookalike.

'Not another fucking clone!' said Elvis, staring at the naked woman's ass.

Zero hurriedly pulled up his sweatpants and wiped his hands on his T-shirt. 'Are you, umm…' he mumbled, looking at Elvis.

'This is Elvis and Jasmine from the Dead Hunters,' said Neville. 'The real ones.'

Zero's face burned up bright red. 'Oh fuck,' he muttered.

His naked female companion straightened up and turned around. 'You were amazing as usual, Zero,' she said, stroking his arm and then kissing him on the cheek. She looked over at Elvis and Jasmine and introduced herself. 'Hello there, I'm Jasmine.'

Elvis spoke through gritted teeth. 'No, you're not.'

'I can explain,' said Zero, looking like a teenager who'd been caught fucking an apple pie.

'Oh Zero, how could you?' said Jasmine, shaking her head 'You've bought one of my clones and fucked it! Surely you can get a *real* woman?'

'Um, well, this is kind of embarrassing,' said Zero, anguish all across his face. 'How did you find me?'

'No shit, it's embarrassing,' said Elvis, appalled at everything he was seeing in Zero's den.

'Can I get anyone a sandwich?' the redhead Jasmine asked, with a cheerful smile across her face.

Neville squeezed past Elvis and Jasmine and approached the naked clone. 'Jas, why don't you and I go into the kitchen?' he said. 'You can make me a sandwich.'

'That's a great idea, Neville,' she replied. 'You have so many great ideas. Maybe after I've made your sandwich, I could clean your room?'

'That sounds great,' said Neville, ushering her over to the strip curtain in the corner.

As soon as Neville and the naked clone were out of the way, Jasmine walked up to Zero and showed him the computer chip she had taken from the brain of the dead clone in Purgatory. 'We found this inside the brain of one of my dead clones,' she said. 'What can you tell us about it?'

Zero took the chip and studied it closely for about twenty seconds. 'Fuck me,' he muttered. 'This is some fucking high-tech shit. I've never seen one this advanced before. Can I keep it?'

'That depends,' said Jasmine. 'Tell us where you got your clone from.'

89

'And how did you get it to make sandwiches?' Elvis added, while checking out the cardboard cut-out of Lara Croft.

Zero was a bag of nerves at this point, understandably so. 'I actually taught her how to make sandwiches,' he said, staring at the floor. 'She can only do jam sandwiches though.'

'What exactly *is* she?' Elvis asked, positioning himself at Jasmine's side. 'Is she a sex robot, or what?'

'Technically, yes, she is a sex robot,' said Zero, still avoiding eye contact. 'But she's much more than that. She's a great companion, and a housemaid.'

'You just fucked it though,' said Elvis. 'And taught it to tell lies.'

'She's not an *it,* she's a person,' said Zero. 'I bought her on the internet. I thought I'd covered my tracks, so no one would be able to trace her back to me. How did you find me?'

'Who sold her to you?' Jasmine asked.

'You know, I feel like I'm being bombarded with questions,' said Zero. 'How about you guys take a seat? And tell me how you found me? Am I in trouble?'

'Oh, you're in fucking trouble,' said Elvis. 'For sure, you're in trouble. You're gonna tell us where you got the Jasmine clone from. Then maybe we'll get the cloning people to make a copy of you and then Jasmine can bend it over a sofa and fuck it in the ass. See how you like it!'

Zero backed away from Elvis. 'You're not going to fucking kill me are you?'

Jasmine walked up to Zero and slapped him playfully on the arm. 'Of course we're not going to kill you,' she said. 'I like you. You're kinda cool. And you sure looked like you were going to town on that inferior redhead version of me, so it's pretty clear you like me too.'

'I do,' said Zero. 'I think you're awesome. You're my favourite member of the Dead Hunters.'

'Oh, give it a rest, will you,' said Elvis.

'Sorry,' said Zero, scratching his crotch. 'Can I get you both a drink, so we can talk calmly about all of this?'

'Sit the fuck down,' said Elvis. 'And tell us where the fuck you got that Jasmine clone from.'

Nineteen

<u>1944</u>

The cold night air was biting. Neither Karl nor Bruno was wearing gloves. Karl had never been assigned any, and Bruno's had been stolen by one of his Nazi comrades. Their journey across the countryside had been a slog, compounded by the fact they had been taking turns carrying the dead body of their friend, Markus. Karl was doing more of the hard yards on account of him being stronger and stockier than Bruno, who had looked malnourished even before the war started.

It was almost ten p.m. when they arrived at an old animal slaughterhouse that had been converted into a storage place for dead infantry. Their unit had been suffering heavy losses on the battlefield for weeks now. It was customary for the dead to be transported to the slaughterhouse on the back of trucks. But Markus, the dumb fuck, had gotten himself killed late in the day when there were no more trucks making the trip, so Karl and Bruno had volunteered to carry him. Bruno had volunteered out of compassion for his friend. Karl had other reasons that he hadn't yet shared with Bruno.

The slaughterhouse was almost as long and wide as a football pitch. The huge, thick wooden doors at the front were bolted closed. As they approached, a single door on the side of the building opened up and a man in uniform stepped out, his features invisible in the darkness.

'You got one more for us?' he asked.

'Sure do,' said Bruno. 'Carried him all the way from the battlefield.'

'Okay, set him down inside. Close the door behind you when you're done, but don't lock it.'

'Yes, sir,' said Karl and Bruno in unison.

The other man headed off towards the staff quarters a short walk away from the slaughterhouse. A military base had been erected nearby that was large enough to house over a thousand men at a time.

'Just so you know,' said Bruno as they carried their dead friend through the entrance. 'If you die, I'm not carrying you. This was a mistake.'

'Oh, quit whinging,' said Karl. 'It's done now.'

The slaughterhouse was poorly lit inside. A mere two lightbulbs were in operation to light the whole place. The stench of death hit both

91

men as soon as they stepped inside and saw the hundreds of corpses lined up in rows from the front of the building all the way to the back.

'Where should we put him?' said Bruno, looking around.

'I'm thinking we lay him down on the end of the tenth row,' said Karl.

'Really? Because I'm comfortable with dropping him on the floor at the end of the first row.'

'Trust me,' said Karl. 'Tenth row, far side.'

'That makes no sense. We can just put him down here.'

'Hey, I did most of the carrying, and I say we put him on the end of the tenth row.'

Bruno sighed. 'Calm down. There's no need to shit the bed. We'll do it your way, okay?'

Karl glared at Bruno, his piercing green eyes revealing his impatience. 'You ready?'

'Yes.'

They carried Markus's body to the other side of the hall and headed for the end of the tenth row. Some of the corpses they passed were a gnarly mess. Guts spilling out, eyeballs missing, legs blown off, there was a full display of injuries on show. They laid Karl down next to a young man whose bottom jaw had been blown off. The war was truly a living hell.

'Christ, this place is grim,' said Bruno. 'Let's get out of here and go get a drink.'

'I can't face another day of this,' said Karl, staring down at Markus's corpse. 'Any day now, we'll be laid out on the floor in this place.'

'Don't talk like that,' said Bruno. 'Haven't you heard the rumour that Hitler is here today? If any of his crew hears defeatist talk like that, they'll shoot you dead, and they won't think twice about it.'

'Who told you Hitler was here?'

'Markus. Some of the other soldiers said it too.'

'That's bullshit. Why would he be here? It makes no sense.'

'I don't know, but people say they've seen him.'

Karl took off his helmet and tossed it onto the floor. 'I don't care,' he said, running his hands through his sticky blond hair. 'No matter what happens here, we're dead men walking. I can't understand the thinking behind sending tens of thousands of us out there to be slaughtered every day. It's no kind of strategy. There'll be no German men left when this is over.'

Bruno chuckled at what he thought was gallows humour. 'Come on. Let's get going. I need some sleep.'

92

'I'm not going back.'

'What do you mean?'

'I mean I'm staying here.'

'What for?'

'I'm getting out of this war.'

Bruno looked around. They were still alone, apart from all the dead people. He shushed Karl and whispered, 'Are you mad? You'll be shot for treason.'

'I don't care.'

Bruno was exasperated. 'You're just tired.'

'Damn right I am. Tired of the war.'

'What are you intending to do exactly?'

'I'm gonna lie here next to these corpses. Play dead. You should join me.'

'Why the hell would I do that?'

Karl placed a hand on Bruno's shoulder and whispered in his ear. 'We lie here and pretend to be dead. But later, when everyone is asleep, we sneak out and make a run for it.'

Bruno dismissed the idea out of hand. 'There will be men on the lookout for deserters. You'll be shot dead before you get a hundred metres.'

'I'm fast. They'll never get me. Besides, the night guards will probably be asleep anyway.'

Bruno contemplated the idea for a few more seconds, but then shook his head. 'You're on your own, Karl. I wish you the best of luck. I'm going back to base to get some sleep. Think hard about what you're doing. I hope I see you in the morning.' He patted Karl on the shoulder, then turned away to the exit.

'Good luck to you too,' Karl called after him. The next sound he heard was the snick of the side door closing.

With Bruno gone, the slaughterhouse fell quiet. Karl walked along the rows of dead bodies and picked out a spot for himself. He laid down on the straw-covered floor in between a couple of corpses he didn't recognise. If he could handle the awful smell of decaying bodies for a couple of hours, escape was a possibility.

It was close to midnight when the slaughterhouse door opened again. Karl opened one eye to see what was going on. Two men had entered, and were talking quietly among themselves. They made their way along the front row of corpses like they were out for a Sunday stroll in the park.

Karl heard himself swallow. It sounded like the loudest gulp in history. He recognised both of the men. One was none other than Adolf

Hitler himself. The Fuhrer was wearing baggy green pants and a matching shirt that was tucked in and buttoned all the way up to the top. The other man was one of Hitler's most trusted aides, a strange, oddball physicist named Eric Einstein, illegitimate brother of Albert Einstein, or so the rumours said. Karl couldn't make out much of what they were saying, and he couldn't exactly lift his head and cock an ear to find out. But from what he could tell, Einstein was making a pitch to Hitler, claiming he could do something incredible that would win the war for Germany. Hitler seemed largely disinterested by it. He was more concerned with checking the corpses laid out on the floor.

When they reached the end of the front row, things took a turn for the really strange. Hitler stopped next to a dead soldier and crouched down to get a better look at him.

'This one will do,' he said, loud enough for Karl to make it out. 'He's got no facial injuries.'

Without waiting for a response from Einstein, Hitler pressed his hand down on the dead soldier's forehead. His palm emitted a bright white glow. After a few seconds, Hitler pulled his hand away and the white light faded. He then moved along to another corpse and did the same thing. Einstein followed behind him, keeping quiet. Hitler moved onto the second row of corpses and carried on his strange ritual of touching the occasional corpse on the forehead, emitting a white glow from his hand, and then moving along again. He was going through the procedure for the fourth time when suddenly, the first soldier he had touched, sat upright.

'What the fuck?' Karl whispered to himself.

And so it went on. Hitler picked out random soldiers and pressed his hand on them, and a short while later, they came back to life.

As Hitler and Einstein made their way through the rows, edging closer to Karl's awkward hiding place, Einstein quizzed him on the process.

'When did you first know you could do this?' he asked.

'I was sixteen,' Hitler replied, while checking the dead for his next subject. 'My friend Heinrik was hit by a car. The driver sped off, leaving him for dead in the road. There was no one around. I tried first aid, but it didn't help. I checked Heinrik's pulse and there was nothing. So, I wished him all the best in the afterlife and placed my hand on his forehead. And to my amazement, he opened his eyes and looked at me. I had brought him back.'

'He was completely healthy?' Einstein asked. 'What about his soul?'

94

Hitler shook his head. 'He was never the same person after that. There was something *off* about him. He took no joy in life from that day on. But I was intrigued, and wanted to know if it was real, if I had really brought him back. A few weeks later, I tested my skills out on some corpses in the local morgue. That's when I knew I had the gift.'

As Karl listened in on Hitler's confession, the war strategy started to make sense. The sacrificing of thousands of young soldiers sent over the top to their certain death was of no concern to Hitler because he knew he could bring them back to life. He was picking out the dead soldiers who had all their limbs intact and hadn't been shot in the head, then bringing them back from the dead to return to the battlefield. Karl cast his mind back to the many times he'd seen fellow soldiers shot down only to return to the frontline a few days later. They always looked pale, and they barely spoke.

Hitler's dubious military tactics were actually the least of Karl's problems. Playing dead in the middle of the rows of corpses had left him in an awkward position. The Fuhrer and his sidekick, Einstein, were close to discovering him lying on the floor pretending to be dead. His options were limited. He could sit up and pretend that he'd only been unconscious, but would Hitler fall for it? Probably not. Which meant his best bet was to lie still and wait for Hitler to press his magic hand down on his forehead, then pretend to be brought back from the dead. He wished he'd taken acting classes at school. Playing dead sucked. Pretending to be resurrected would suck even more.

Hitler eventually arrived at Karl's non-dead corpse. Karl kept his eyes closed and held his breath. He felt Hitler's warm, sweaty hand on his forehead. This was it. All or nothing. Karl opened his eyes and sucked in a breath of air.

'You weren't dead,' Hitler said, retracting his hand and standing up. He had fury in his eyes.

'I was,' said Karl. 'I bloody was.'

'Then you won't mind dying again.'

Hitler unholstered a pistol on his hip and pointed it at Karl's forehead.

'No wait! Please, I...'

BANG!

Karl's brains splattered all over the floor behind him. Shot in the head. There was no coming back from that.

Twenty

The drive to Despair's police station took a little longer than expected. The fallout of the earlier explosion in the centre of town had led to the police blocking off a number of roads, so Walt led JD on a tour of the backstreets. When they eventually arrived at the station, Walt parked in a spot out front, and JD parked his jeep on the other side of the street.

The police station was impressive from the outside. It was two storeys high, impeccably clean and very modern. The inside, not so much. The glass screens in the reception area that separated the staff from the public had been shattered into a million tiny pieces, and a security door by the side of the desks had been ripped off its hinges. There was a patch of blood the size of a football on the wall behind the middle desk. Walt pulled his pistol and sprinted up to the desk and looked around. Almost immediately he covered his mouth and turned away. JD strolled up to join him and saw what was bothering the old timer. On the other side of the reception desk, a female receptionist was lying on the floor, surrounded by blood, with her chair on its side next to her. She'd been shot in the head and chest.

'What the hell has happened here?' Walt asked, the colour draining from his face.

'At a guess,' said JD, looking around. 'I'd say most of your guys headed into town when that bomb went off, leaving this place open to attack by whoever set off the bomb.'

'Oh, Christ.'

'Care to show me around?'

'What if the killers are still here?'

JD stared blankly at Walt.

'Oh, right. Yeah, of course, you'll just kill them,' said Walt. 'It's through this door over here.'

Walt headed over to the busted security door and poked his head through it to get a look at the corridor on the other side. There were two dead cops on the floor, one shot in the head, the other with a broken neck.

Walt cocked his pistol, ready to shoot at any hostiles. JD walked past him and looked around. Other than dead cops, there wasn't much to see. It was reminiscent of every police station he'd ever been in. It's just that it was usually him who killed all the cops. Someone had deprived him of that simple pleasure. Whoever it was, they were going to suffer for it.

'You got a security office that might have camera footage of what happened here?' JD asked.

'Second floor,' said Walt. 'Stairs are at the end of the corridor.'

96

The second floor was the same as the first. Every room and corridor was decorated with dead cops. Whoever had executed them was long gone, or out of ammo because the place was deathly quiet, with the exception of a few whirring ceiling fans.

While JD checked inside one of the rooms, Walt headed over to a busted door with the word, "SECURITY" on it. There was a decapitated cop in the doorway and a bloodied machete on the floor. Walt closed his eyes and looked away. Another of his close friends, dead. JD walked past Walt and stepped over the headless corpse on his way into the security office. Inside the office were a couple of desks with busted, bullet-riddled computers on them and a shattered TV screen on the opposite wall next to an open closet that had been trashed.

'I'm guessing someone wanted to get their hands on that camera footage of Jack the Ripper,' JD said, looking back at Walt, who was hanging back in the doorway, his mouth agog as he tried to come to terms with all the murdered colleagues he'd seen.

'Everyone is dead,' Walt said, his bottom lip trembling.

'Not quite,' said JD. He pulled a pistol from inside his coat and pointed it at a long cushioned bench against the back wall. 'You, hiding in the bench. Come on out.'

Nothing moved.

'Stay in there if you wanna get shot.'

'I'm stuck!' a muffled female voice called back.

Walt livened up and finally put his gun back in its holster. 'Josie?' he said.

'Yeah,' the voice called out.

JD walked up to the bench, grabbed the cushioned part on the top and lifted it up, revealing the storage space inside. A young black woman in a dark blue uniform poked her head up and sucked in some air. Then she looked at JD and squealed.

'It's okay, he's with me,' said Walt.

JD took Josie's hand and helped her out of her hiding place. 'What happened here?' he asked.

Josie fussed with her hair and straightened her uniform for a few seconds, attempting to gather herself. After a deep breath, she answered JD's question. 'I gotta be honest,' she said. 'I assumed you'd done this. I heard you had a thing for shooting up police stations.'

'If it had been me, you'd be dead.'

'Josie, are you saying you didn't see who did it?' Walt asked her.

'I just heard the gunfire and people screaming,' said Josie. 'Most of the senior officers were out dealing with that explosion in town.' She

97

stared bug-eyed at JD. 'I don't even have a fuckin' gun! All I got is a taser.'

'Then you shoulda used it,' said JD.

Josie sensed she was being mocked. 'Hey, you pull a gun on me and I'll tase your ass, just like I tased Jack the Ripper.'

'You *tased* Jack the Ripper?'

'She's the one who took him down,' said Walt. 'Snuck up behind him and tased him.'

'He went stiff as a board,' Josie added.

'Maybe he came back here looking for you?' said JD. 'I know if you tased me, I'd definitely hunt you down.'

Josie shot him a withering stare. 'Whoever it was, they were in this room for fucking ages, trashing the place and shooting at stuff. I nearly peed my pants, I don't mind telling you.'

JD pointed at one of the busted computers. 'Is there any way I can see the footage of the Ripper's vanishing act?'

'It's all fucked,' said Walt. 'The footage was stored on these computers.'

'It's backed up somewhere though, right?' said JD.

Walt shook his head. 'No internet, remember. It was only stored on the computers in this office, so if one broke, it was backed up on the other one.

Josie reached down into the storage section of the bench she had been hiding in. 'I hid this in here,' she said, picking up a laptop computer. 'Just in case.'

'Josie, you little beauty,' said Walt. 'That'll have the video on it.'

'Open it up,' said JD. 'Will it show us who just shot everyone?'

'It damn well better,' said Josie. She sat back down on the bench and placed the laptop on her knees. JD stood over her so he could see the screen. Josie brought up the camera footage of the reception area downstairs before the attack had taken place. After scrolling through it for a while, she found footage of a big dude in a suit and cape walking into the station.

'That's him,' said Josie. 'That's the guy I tased at Drummond's. Jack the Ripper.'

The Ripper pulled a gun on Agnes, the receptionist, and executed her. He then headed over to the security door and grabbed the handle. After a couple of seconds of tugging, he managed to break its unbreakable lock. The door came off its hinges and he strode through it.

'Fuck me,' said Walt, watching from Josie's other side. 'How did he do that?'

98

Josie rewound and paused the footage to the moment the Ripper entered the station. 'Okay, what I'm doing here,' she said, narrating what was happening on screen, 'is highlighting him so that the camera software will follow him around the station from here on, okay?'

'You can do that?' said Walt.

Josie ignored him and set the process in motion. The three of them watched footage of the Ripper making his way through the station, killing everyone as he went. The cops who were armed fired off plenty of rounds at him. But bullets did nothing to him, and he never even flinched.

'Holy shitballs,' Josie whispered. 'I'm so glad I hid in the bench.'

'He's like a fucking Terminator,' said Walt.

JD tapped Josie on the shoulder. 'Show me the clip of him disappearing from your interview room yesterday.'

Josie skipped through some files on the laptop until she found what she was looking for. 'Here you go,' she said.

She played JD the footage of two cops interrogating the Ripper in a small interview room. When the cops left the room, a man dressed all in black with a balaclava on his head appeared out of nowhere, just behind the Ripper. But then almost immediately both he and the Ripper vanished in a blue haze.

'Can you slow it down?' JD asked.

Josie rewound the footage and played it at a quarter speed.

'Pause it and zoom in on the balaclava guy.'

Josie was already working on it. She froze the image onscreen and zoomed in on the balaclava man's face.

'What do you think?' she asked JD. 'Any idea who it might be?'

'Yeah. I know who it is.'

'Who?'

'His name is Eric Einstein.'

'*Eric* Einstein?' said Walt.

JD ignored him. 'What can you tell me about the three women who were kidnapped?' he asked.

'They were all young,' said Walt, stating the fucking obvious. 'Kidnapped women usually are though.'

'What jobs did they have?'

'Sasha was unemployed,' said Josie. 'Tammy-Lynn was a fitness instructor, and Glenda was at college in Darkness.'

'What does that mean? *In Darkness?*'

Walt jumped in with the answer. 'That's the town on the other side of the mountains.'

99

'Darkness and Despair? What cheery cunt named these two towns?'

'Before my time,' said Walt, shrugging.

Josie flipped round her laptop and showed JD pictures of the three young women. 'My brother dated Tammy-Lynn for a while,' she said, pointing at a slim, blonde woman with a fake tan. 'She was unemployed but she drove a really nice convertible Mercedes.'

'Anything else you know about her? Anything, no matter how trivial?'

Josie scratched her chin and thought for a moment. 'Her parents didn't speak to her. They had totally disowned her, but she never said why.'

'What about the other two?' said JD. 'What cars did they drive?'

'No idea,' said Walt.

'Glenda had a brand new Ford Focus,' said Josie. 'I don't know about Sasha.'

'Did they get on with their parents?'

'Sasha's dad died when she was about two,' said Walt. 'But she got on fine with her mom. And Glenda got on well with her parents as far as I know, but she was at college, so they probably didn't see her much.'

'Okay, that's all,' said JD, heading for the door.

'Wait. Where are you going?' Walt asked.

'I'm gonna drop by the chocolate factory you told me about. The one that laid off all its employees.'

'Want me to come with you?'

'You stay here. It's probably safer.'

100

Twenty-one

Zero sat down in a black leather gaming chair and wheeled it around so he could face Elvis and Jasmine, who were sitting together on one of his sofas.

'Okay, so it's like this,' he said. 'I bought my Jasmine on the dark web. It cost me a hundred grand in bitcoin, but she's worth every penny.'

'Did you buy her just so you could fuck her?' Jasmine asked.

Zero blushed. 'Umm, she does many things. She's great at housework, she can cook, and she's very supportive. Really clever too.'

Elvis raised an eyebrow but kept his thoughts to himself.

Jasmine actually blurted out what Elvis was thinking. 'I can't cook for shit. And cleaning isn't really my thing either.'

'We're getting off track,' said Elvis. 'Who did you buy it from?'

Zero tugged at the collar of his T-shirt. 'I made the order on a very hard to find website. Then a week later I had to meet a guy in a highway gas station in Texas. He pulled up in a big truck, and in the back there were four Jasmines. Each one is specifically designed for its owner. He introduced me to mine, then I made the final part of the transaction in cash. We went our separate ways, and that was the last I saw of him, I swear.'

'And when was this?' Jasmine asked.

'Six weeks ago.'

'And did you fuck her as soon as you got her home?'

Zero tried to hide a smile that was breaking out across his face. He stared at the floor. 'She's better than any girlfriend I ever had.'

'You've had girlfriends?' Elvis asked, looking around the room at all the nerd artefacts.

'Yeah,' Zero replied. 'But not like my Jasmine. She's perfect. She doesn't give me any shit about anything, and she always does what I ask.'

'I'm like that, aren't I?' Jasmine said, elbowing Elvis in the arm.

'Most of the time,' he replied. 'Anyway, Zero, we found another Jasmine earlier today. It was wanted for armed robbery. It had been holding up armoured trucks with some fat, bald guy. Do you know anything about that?'

'Oh, God no,' said Zero. 'I mean, I *know* about it, but I've got nothing to do with it. I swear that asshole will fuck this up for all of us. I'm so glad I got my Jasmine before the company making them gets shut down.'

'When your Jasmine comes back in, can I touch her?' Jasmine asked. 'I'd like to know if her ass feels like mine.'

Zero's eyes lit up. 'Hell, yeah. Or if you like, I could just feel *your* ass and tell you if it's the same?'

'Steady on, Fucknuts,' said Elvis. 'You lay a finger on the real thing, you're gonna get a broken arm.'

'Right, of course. Silly of me to suggest it.'

The fake Jasmine, as if hearing the conversation, re-entered the room via the strip curtain in the corner. While she'd been away she had put on a pair of skin-tight black leggings and a red sleeveless vest with a picture of Chachi from *Happy Days* on it. Neville walked in behind her with a big Alsatian that was identical to JD's dog, Goober.

'Fuck me,' said Elvis. 'Is that Goober?'

'You know my dog?' Zero asked, his mouth agape.

'We've got one just like him,' said Jasmine, standing up. She walked up to the other Jasmine, stopped in front of her and looked her up and down.

'Can I touch your boobs, to see what they feel like?' Jasmine asked, while Elvis, Zero and Neville watched on intently.

'Yes, of course,' the redhead replied, lifting up her shirt.

Jasmine moved in close and cupped her clone's boobs. 'Wow, that is incredible,' she said. 'These feel so real, just like mine.'

'Why don't you kiss each other?' Neville suggested.

'All right, that's enough,' said Elvis, pointing at Neville. 'I wanna know who's selling these things. Jasmine tells me you guys are tech wizards, so it's my guess you know exactly where they come from. Give me that information, and I'll let you keep your inferior redhead version.'

'Wow,' said the fake Jasmine. 'Elvis, you are so manly. Can I get you a sandwich?'

'Easy there, clone lady,' said Jasmine. 'Don't go showing off just 'cos you can make a sandwich. If Elvis wants a sandwich, I'll make it.'

'I don't want any fucking sandwiches,' said Elvis. 'Enough of this shit. I want names and addresses. You've got about ten seconds, or I shoot your sex doll.'

'Okay, look,' said Zero, panicking. 'I'll tell you everything I know, but you can't tell anyone I gave you this information.'

'I'll tell anyone I fucking like,' said Elvis.

Zero ran his hand through his spiky blond hair. 'Look, I did some digging on who was building them. I don't know his actual name, but on the internet he uses the pseudonym, Chuckee.'

'What's he look like?' Elvis asked.

'I have no idea. There's not a picture of him anywhere.'

'So how do we find him?'

102

Zero grimaced. 'Umm, well, I'm pretty certain he's impossible to find. This guy really knows how to cover his tracks on the internet, but I know he recently started selling a couple of different models of cyborg companions. Even though the Jasmine was selling well, I guess people were offering him big bucks for other female celebrities. Originally, his website said he would never make copies of any famous women, apart from Jasmine.'

'Why though?' said Elvis. 'Why just Jasmine?'

Zero relaxed a little, as if sensing that Elvis was warming to him, which he wasn't. 'Making Jasmines is fine,' he went on, 'because, no disrespect, but Jasmine can't sue him.'

'Why can't I sue him?' Jasmine asked.

'Because you're an outlaw on the FBI's most wanted list,' said Zero, offering her a sympathetic smile. 'I think that's why he was originally only making clones of you. But more recently, for reasons unknown, he's started making new models that aren't as beautiful as Jasmine.' He looked at Jasmine and smiled.

'How is he making these clones?' Elvis asked. 'And how can he make such an accurate likeness of Jasmine without ever meeting her?'

'Oh,' Zero shifted uncomfortably in his chair and stared at Jasmine.

'What?' Jasmine asked, puzzled.

'I'm not sure I should say.'

'Spit it out, dickhead!' said Elvis, losing patience.

'Umm, well,' said Zero, still looking at Jasmine. 'Is it okay for me to tell him?'

'Tell him what?' said Jasmine.

Zero looked confused. In fact, at this point, everyone was confused. 'Okay, well, I didn't want to say anything before, in case you wanted it kept secret, but on his website *Chuckee* says that Jasmine gave consent, and allowed him clone her.'

Jasmine frowned. 'I don't remember doing that.'

'The website states categorically that permission was granted.'

'Show me the fucking website. Now,' said Elvis.

Zero grabbed a laptop from a nearby desk and flipped it open. After a quick trip around the internet he handed the laptop over to Elvis. Jasmine snuggled closer to him so she could get a good look.

The website's home page featured a photo of a Jasmine clone in a bikini, along with three other models of different women also in bikinis.

'Who are the others?' Elvis asked.

'They're lookalikes of famous women from the nineteen-thirties and forties,' said Zero. 'Greta Garbo, Bette Davis and Jean Harlow.'

'That's kind of random isn't it?' said Elvis.

'I agree,' said Zero. 'But if you look closer, you'll see these women aren't exactly *identical* to their namesakes in the same way the Jasmine is. The Jean Harlow for example, her eyes aren't as big as the real Jean Harlow. It's not a clone of Jean Harlow, it's a clone of someone else who's probably had her hair dyed, and been given a nose job to make her look like Jean Harlow. I'm fairly certain all of the women were given facial reconstruction surgery by some kind of Pierce Patchett.'

Elvis looked up from the laptop. 'What the fuck? Why would someone do that? And why with random women from a hundred years ago?'

'Because they're dead, and they can't sue the company selling the models.'

'Even so,' said Elvis. 'Why would anyone in this day and age want a clone of any of these women?'

Zero stood up and clasped his hands together. 'I agree,' he said. 'It makes no sense. I even did some digging because I was curious, just like you are. I used facial recognition software on the three new models to see if I could find anything about them. But, nothing showed up on the internet. There are no social media accounts for these women, and no photos that come up in search engines.'

'Maybe your facial recognition software is shit?' Elvis suggested.

'It's not,' said Zero, rolling his eyes. 'It's top of the range software. I built it myself.'

'Really?' said Elvis. 'Can your software hack into any camera in the world and locate the whereabouts of these women at any given time on any day?'

Zero scoffed. 'No, that would be impossible.'

'Our software does that,' said Elvis. He pulled his phone out of his jacket pocket and snapped a photo of the women on the laptop's screen.

'I'll never understand why people have surgery to make them look like someone else,' said Jasmine.

'Maybe it wasn't their choice,' said Neville, butting in. 'Maybe they were kidnapped and cut up to look like Bette Davis, Greta Garbo, and Jean Harlow. Maybe you were kidnapped, Jasmine, but you don't remember it.'

'I was never kidnapped,' said Jasmine, irritated by the suggestion.

Zero raised his eyebrows. 'Can you be sure though? I mean these people are using some very high-tech equipment to do what they do. It's ground-breaking stuff.'

'I think I'd remember being kidnapped, thank you.'

104

'Well, no offence intended here,' said Zero, 'but my Jasmine looks a bit younger than you, so maybe it happened a few years back?'

'Okay,' said Elvis, standing up and getting between Jasmine and Zero. 'Before Jasmine punches you in the sack, do you have an actual address for these cloning bastards?'

'I'm afraid I've got nothing,' said Zero. 'These people are way ahead of the game. If *I* can't find them, they can't be found.'

Jasmine stepped around Elvis and grabbed a handful of Zero's crotch. She squeezed hard, and dug her nails into his balls. 'Who looks younger?' she asked. 'Me or your inferior redhead?'

Zero didn't answer. Jasmine squeezed even harder.

'I'll never tell,' he whispered like a high-pitched eunuch.

Jasmine sighed and then let go of him. Yet another weirdo who liked having his balls busted.

'Come on, let's go,' said Elvis.

'Wait,' Neville called out. 'I also think the redhead Jasmine is younger *and* sexier.'

Jasmine unholstered her pistol and pointed it at Neville. 'What?'

Neville raised his hands in surrender. 'I didn't mean that.'

Jasmine holstered her gun, then walked over to Goober and stroked his head. The dog seemed to like it. 'What now then?' she asked Elvis.

'Let's go see Jacko,' Elvis replied, pulling up Jacko's number on his phone. He looked at Zero. 'You got a bathroom in this place?'

'I know where it is,' said Jasmine. She kissed Goober goodbye, then walked up to the Lara Croft statue and prodded two fingers into Lara's eyes. A secret door slid open in the wall by the side of it, revealing a small bathroom with just a toilet, a washbasin and a towel rail in it.

'How did you know that?' Zero asked, gobsmacked.

Jasmine winked at him. 'I've been here before.'

Twenty-two

<u>1945</u>

Adolf Hitler stared at the bathroom door, his impatience growing. He was standing alone in a small, tucked away scientific research laboratory in the Reich Chancellery. He was wearing a stupid, white, rubber, anti-radiation suit. The suit's huge helmet was misting up and making him claustrophobic. He took it off and slammed it down on a plain wooden table in the middle of the room. Standing around waiting was making him irritable. It had been five minutes. He cursed under his breath. It hadn't worked. He should have known it wouldn't. Fucking scientists. More to the point, fucking inventors. Crackpots, all of them. And untrustworthy. Everyone was untrustworthy.

He walked up to the bathroom door and knocked hard on it. 'Are you in there?' he asked.

No response.

He grabbed the handle and pushed the door open. The bathroom was small and contained just a toilet, a washbasin and some towel rails.

Hitler's reason for loitering around the bathroom was an unusual one. He was looking for his top scientist, Eric Einstein. Just over five minutes earlier, Einstein had entered the bathroom with the intention of traveling through time. He had vanished, which was great, but where had he gone? And why hadn't he returned?

The bathroom had been Hitler's idea. At the last minute, just as Einstein was about to test his time travel device, Hitler got cold feet, fearing he might get vaporised when the device was activated, so he made Einstein go into the bathroom to carry out the experiment in private.

Over the course of the last eight months, Einstein had been testing the time travel technology on chimps. He'd been sending them a minute or two into the future, and it had been working. The chimps would vanish in a blue haze then reappear minutes later, at the exact time Einstein had specified. Sending them *back in time* had been less successful. Once the chimps had been sent back to the past, they were never seen again. And there had been several reports of chimps exploding in recent times, which may well have been linked to the time travel.

Hitler checked his watch again. Six minutes had gone by. He turned away from the bathroom in disgust and marched back out, his rubber suit squelching with each step and his knee-high boots banging hard on the floor as he went. He was about to strip off his anti-radiation suit when he heard a voice call out from the bathroom.

'Fuhrer!'

He stopped. Turned. Standing in the bathroom doorway was Eric Einstein, the much maligned, often irritating, ginger-haired crackpot. Einstein looked different to how he had just minutes earlier. His clothes had changed. He was now wearing a pair of blue denim jeans and a flowery green shirt. Before the time travelling, he'd been wearing a rubber suit like Hitler's. Most significant though was Einstein's hair, which was now much shorter. He looked a little older too.

'What's happened?' Hitler asked, his mind swirling with excitement and questions. Lots of questions.

'It worked,' Einstein replied, a grin across his face. 'I've seen the future. And I have worked out how to travel to the past.'

'Do we win the war?'

Einstein grimaced. 'No Fuhrer, we lose. And we are regularly ridiculed for our defeat, especially in American and European movies.'

'WHAT?'

'It's true, Fuhrer. *You* get ridiculed the most. *I* don't actually get a mention, but that's neither here nor there.'

Hitler chewed on his bottom lip hard enough to draw blood. Losing the war? That was impossible, surely? 'LIAR!' he blasted, before getting a grip of himself. 'How? What happens? Tell me everything.' He gestured to the table. 'Sit.'

Einstein closed the bathroom door and pulled up a chair at the table. Hitler sat opposite him. Neither said anything about the large farting sound that occurred when Hitler sat down. That damn stupid, rubber anti-radiation suit had made the bloody noise. In an attempt to show confidence and that he was unbothered by the constant squeaking and squelching of the suit, Hitler clasped his hands and began twiddling his thumbs, waiting for Einstein to speak.

'It's the British prime minister,' said Einstein. 'He outwits you and becomes a hero. You end up committing suicide to avoid being captured.'

Hitler felt faint. He dropped his hands to the table. 'I don't believe you. I would *never* kill myself I have too much pride.'

'I have video evidence,' said Einstein, reaching into his pocket. He pulled out a small device, like a miniature television that fitted in his hand. 'I compiled a short video of lots of news clips on here for you,' he said. 'It will explain everything.'

Einstein slid the device across the table, pressed his finger down on it, and then to Hitler's amazement, a high quality video recording began to play. For the next ten minutes, Hitler watched a highlights reel of news footage and movie clips depicting the end of World War Two.

107

The last two minutes of the video clip initially made no sense. Einstein had added in a goofy review of a movie called *The Terminator*. By the time the clip ended, Hitler knew exactly what Einstein was getting at. It helped him to overcome the previous eight minutes of gut-wrenching humiliation he had been subjected to.

'I've had a fantastic idea,' he said. 'We use your time travel device to go back in time and execute the mothers of our enemies, before they can give birth to them!'

'Okay,' said Einstein, gesturing for calm. 'First, a couple of things. Travelling back in time only works if you go back to a time *before* you were born. I tested it on some rats while I was in the future. No creature can exist twice in the same moment in time. If you were to travel back in time by one minute for example, as we did with the chimps, you will explode because you already exist at that time. Basically, if you are fifty years old, you can travel back fifty one years, but you have to be gone again before you are born, otherwise you explode. Does that make sense?'

'Why do you explode?' Hitler asked.

'I don't know. You just do.'

'But you *have* travelled back in time?'

'Yes, Fuhrer. Just now, in fact. I travelled from the future back to this moment, which is about five minutes after I originally left this time period.'

'Please tell me you built a Terminator in the future.'

Einstein grinned. 'Oh, yes Fuhrer, I did. I knew it was what you would want. That's why I have been away for so long. It was hard work and very expensive, but I built a cyborg. I don't call it a Terminator though, because they have these annoying copyright rules in the twenty-first century, so I call it Herman, which is short for Hermanator.'

Hitler flared his nostrils. 'Is it here? Did you bring it with you?'

'No, I left him in the future. I didn't want to freak you out by bringing him back with me.'

'But this cyborg, Herman, he can kill our enemies?'

Einstein looked smug. In fact, he'd clearly grown in confidence in the five minutes he had been away. 'Yes, he absolutely can. He's ready to go, right now. I just wanted your approval before I do it. I intend to have Herman execute our enemies before they are born. He will travel back in time and kill their mothers, just like in the Terminator movie.'

'This is the best plan I have ever come up with,' said Hitler. 'It's settled then. You and your cyborg will travel back in time and kill our enemies before they can be born.'

Einstein gulped. 'You want me to go *with* Herman?'

108

'Of course. You'll be perfectly safe. You know what you're doing. It's perfect.'

'But...'

'No buts. I want Stalin's mother killed, I want Roosevelt's mother killed, I want Charles de Gaulle's mother killed. But you can start with the mother of that fat piece of shit from Britain. When they are all dead, you may return here, and I will award you the highest medal of honour our country has!'

Einstein cleared his throat. 'With respect, Fuhrer, while this plan is brilliant, there is one thing you should know. Killing the leaders of the allies before they are born won't necessarily guarantee we win the war. It will just mean that we face different allied leaders. We might still lose the war.'

'Then you will continue travelling in time and killing our new enemies before they are born, until the war is won. This is a great day, my friend. We may have just won the war!'

Einstein squirmed in his seat. 'There's just one more thing, and it's a *big* one. If I alter the past *too much*, there is a possibility that the future is changed beyond comprehension and we end up with something called a multiverse, which would be a disaster. In an extreme case of a multiverse, you and I might never even meet.'

Hitler shrugged. 'That's a chance I'm willing to take. Now go, do your thing. And do not return until you have seen to it that we will be victorious.'

'Yes sir.'

Einstein pulled his shirt sleeve back, revealing a device on his arm that looked like a digital watch. It was what made time travel possible. He pressed a button on the top of the watch, then vanished into a blue haze. Hitler was left staring at a puff of blue smoke.

'Excellent,' he said, while drumming his fingers together.

Twenty-three

Jacko's attempt to finish watching "Southland Tales" wasn't going well. He switched it off again and pressed a button behind the bar to reopen the door to the men's toilets. It slid to one side, then Elvis and Jasmine strolled in from Zero's private bathroom. They headed up to the bar.

'How did it go?' Jacko asked.

Elvis ignored the question and got straight to business. He handed his phone over to Jacko, showing him the photo of the Bette Davis, Greta Garbo, and Jean Harlow models. 'Can you do a facial recognition on these three women?' he asked.

'Yeah, sure.'

Jacko took the phone and uploaded the photo onto the bar's computer. 'How come Jasmine is in the picture too?' he asked.

'It's from the cloning company's website,' said Elvis. 'I wanna know where these women have been seen recently. Look for any places all three of them have visited in the last few months.'

'Last few months?'

'Come on,' said Elvis, pulling up a stool. 'There won't be many places where all three have visited. Get on it.'

'Can I have a soda water?' Jasmine asked, hopping onto a stool next to Elvis.

Jacko handed her a glass and a soda gun, then got down to business on the computer.

'What did you think of the redhead version of me?' Jasmine asked Elvis.

'I didn't like her.'

'How come?'

'Because I don't like the fact she exists. And I don't like the idea that just anyone can buy a clone of you and fuck it.'

Jasmine finished pouring herself a soda and ran her hand up Elvis's thigh. 'How about later tonight, I pretend to be a clone of myself, and we can fuck?' she suggested.

Elvis frowned. 'How the hell would that work?'

'I don't know exactly, but think of all the things you might do to a clone of me, just to punish it for existing?'

Elvis glanced at her out of the side of his eye. 'That's interesting,' he said.

'What's the deal with these women?' said Jacko, breaking the mood. 'They look like they've all had facial surgery.'

110

'That's what we think too,' said Elvis. 'We wanna know who they were before they had the surgery and made themselves look like dead women from the twentieth century.'

'Oh, for fuckssake,' Jacko groaned. 'It's never straightforward is it?'

'Quit bitching and get on with it.'

Jasmine hopped off her stool and walked over to the jukebox. She selected the song, "Walk Like An Egyptian" by the Bangles and started wiggling her ass to it, putting on a show for Elvis, and distracting Jacko at the same time. She made it halfway through the song with her clothes still on, when Jacko found what he was looking for.

'Got them,' he said. 'High Heels and Stockings!'

'What does that mean?' said Elvis, without taking his eyes off Jasmine.

'These three women,' said Jacko. 'Before they had their faces altered, they all went to the same strip club, a place called High Heels and Stockings. I've got footage of all three of them entering the club *and* leaving it, although never together. My guess is they're all strippers.'

'Strippers?' said Jasmine, moving behind Elvis and sliding her arms around his waist. 'Like, lap dancers?'

'I suppose so,' said Jacko. 'The club is in an obscure town in the middle of nowhere, a place called Darkness.'

'Darkness,' Jasmine repeated. 'I like the sound of that.'

'Woah!' said Jacko, taking a step back from his computer. 'Take a look at this.'

'What is it?' Elvis asked, before whipping Jasmine around and engaging in a passionate kiss.

'These women have all been kidnapped.'

Elvis and Jasmine ended their "snog and grope" session and both looked over at Jacko.

'Do you know who kidnapped them?' Elvis asked.

'Check it out,' said Jacko. 'The first woman, the one that now looks like Bette Davis, she left the strip club on a Sunday morning at 2 a.m. and got into a van. After that, she's never seen on camera again until three weeks later after she's had the face lift, but by then she's on the other side of the country. Now, get this, exactly two weeks after she was kidnapped, the same thing happens to the Jean Harlow lookalike. She gets dragged into a pickup at two a.m. But she's not been seen anywhere since. And then exactly two weeks later, at around the same time, the third woman, the Greta Garbo lookalike, gets into a car at the back of the strip club, and she's not been seen since. I'm telling you, these women have been kidnapped and then cut to look like the women in the picture you gave me.'

'That's exactly what we were hoping for,' said Jasmine.

Jacko looked over at her. 'How did these people get *you* on their website then? Were you kidnapped too?'

'Don't you fucking start!' said Jasmine. 'I have *not* been kidnapped.'

'Hold on a sec,' said Elvis. 'Jas, think back to your time at the Beaver Palace. Did anyone ever drug you, or anything like that?'

'There were a few guys who liked me to play dead. I think it helped them to get hard.' She paused for a moment, then added. 'Actually, there was one time where a guy doused a hanky in chloroform, and I let him drug me with it. When I woke up he was gone. He had another guy with him too, I think.'

'Maybe that was it?' said Jacko. 'You could have been cloned while you were unconscious perhaps?'

Elvis shook his head angrily. 'Jacko, have you got a registration number for the vehicles these women all got into before they disappeared?'

'Afraid not,' said Jacko. 'The car is different each time. And it's never got any plates.'

'Sneaky fuckers.'

'Tell you what though,' said Jacko. 'It's exactly two weeks since the last kidnapping. If they follow the schedule, another stripper will be kidnapped tonight.'

112

Twenty-four

A Hell's Angel on a Harley Davidson Chopper pulled into the parking lot at the front of Cyber Limbs Prosthetics Corporation. He was kitted out in blue denim jeans and a red leather waistcoat. Instead of a crash helmet he wore a black headband that kept his wavy brown hair out of his eyes. He was a giant of a man, known around the world as Rodeo Rex, King of the Hell's Angels. His journey had taken five hours with just one brief stop for food. After cruising up to the front of the Cyber Limbs building, he parked his Chopper outside the entrance. The once pristine white building had moss growing up the walls, and there were muddy patches on the ground all over the parking lot, which was quieter than Rex had ever seen it.

He headed in through a set of glass doors and walked straight into the reception area, which looked just as tatty as the outside of the building. The receptionist, Elaine, a frosty, middle-aged lady with blue hair, had been working there for years. She had never been one for conversation, despite Rex's efforts. He strolled up to the main desk and smiled at her.

'Hello there, Elaine. Lovely day. How's things?'

Elaine put down a magazine she was reading and glared wearily at Rex. 'You don't have an appointment.'

'That's correct; I don't. But I'd like to see Elizabeth Dalton, please. It's important.'

'She's busy.'

'She'll make time for me.'

'She's performing an operation.'

'Elaine, I mean this in the most respectful way possible, but I'm going to see her whether you like it or not. Where do I find her?'

'I can't say.'

'You can, but you're being a bitch. I can respect that because I know you're being true to yourself, so I'll just show myself around.'

Elaine didn't reply. She picked up her magazine, "Bitch Monthly," and carried on reading an article about how to be stubborn.

Rex left the reception area via a set of double doors at the back. After walking along a corridor and poking his head into a few vacant rooms and a few not-so-vacant rooms where he saw some things he wished he hadn't, he eventually came to a door marked, "OPERATING THEATRE - AUTHORISED PERSONNEL ONLY".

He pushed the door open and walked in. He was greeted by the sight of Dr Dalton performing an operation on a naked man. She was wearing a long white coat and a green surgical cap that hid her blonde

113

hair. The lower half of her face was covered by a surgical mask. At a guess, Rex would have said the man she was operating on was in his early thirties. Dr Dalton was massaging the man's penis, vigorously.

Rex cleared his throat. 'Hi, Elizabeth.'

Dr Dalton hadn't paid him any attention when he came in. At the sound of his voice, she glanced across at him and frowned. 'Rex, what are you doing in here?'

'I came to ask you a few questions.'

'I'm kind of busy. If you're going to be in here, put on a mask.'

Rex carried on regardless, and started his interrogation by pointing at the unconscious man on the operating table. 'Do you normally sexually abuse your patients when they're unconscious?'

'It's not what you think,' Dr Dalton replied, as she continued massaging the sleeping man's erect penis.

'Really, because it looks like you're jerking that guy off.'

'I've just performed a penis enlargement on him.'

'By pulling him off?'

Dr Dalton rolled her eyes. 'After a penis enlargement operation, one of the procedures we carry out is to check that the penis functions properly. There's no point in having him wake up only to find his dick isn't working anymore. We like our customers to leave here fully satisfied. People leave reviews on the internet, you know. And if a guy gets home and finds he can't get an erection or ejaculate anymore, the reviews won't be good.'

'Okay,' said Rex, unconvinced. 'Shouldn't you be wearing plastic gloves for that sort of thing though?'

Dr Dalton raised an eyebrow. 'Is that how you like your handjobs?'

'Never mind. Look, I'm here on business, and I need to ask you a question about something.'

'Can it wait?'

'It could, but it's important.'

'Go on then.'

'It's about your cloning equipment.'

'What about it?'

'I was wondering if anything had happened to it?'

Dr Dalton took a moment to think while she tugged away on her patient's dick and massaged his balls. 'I'm not sure how to tell you this, Rex,' she said. 'I don't want word getting out about this, but the cloning equipment is gone.'

'Gone where?'

'It was stolen not long after I last saw you. It was there when I locked the place up one night, but the next morning it was gone. It's cost

114

us millions in lost business, hence why we're really pushing our penis enlargement procedures now. It's become our biggest earner.'

'There's gotta be a cheaper way to get a hand job,' Rex joked.

Dr Dalton didn't laugh. *Tough crowd.*

Rex was trying his best not to look directly *at* the hand-job, but he was certainly impressed by the doctor's technique. He'd always found her attractive and was now wondering what she might have done to him if he'd gone through with his planned hand transplant.

'Hold on a second, Rex.'

Dr Dalton ramped up the speed of her procedure until suddenly the whopping great penis she was tugging on erupted. She grabbed a handful of tissues from a box on a nearby trolley and started cleaning up the mess. 'Well, this one works just fine, I'd say, wouldn't you?' she said, smiling at Rex.

'Yeah, congratulations, great job.'

'Would you like to see the camera footage of the robbery, Rex?'

'If it gets us out of this room, then yes.'

Dr Dalton disposed of the soiled tissues in a nearby steel bin, squirted some antibacterial soap on her hands, then approached Rex with her hand outstretched. Rex reluctantly accepted, and the two shook hands.

Dr Dalton jerked her thumb over her shoulder. 'Come with me.'

Rex followed her out of the operating theatre and she took him on a long journey around the building until they arrived in the security office. Rex had been in there once before when he'd seen footage of a clone of himself getting up and walking out of a secure vault after being possessed by the ghost of Cain. This time, on arriving in the office, the usual security guy, Treager, was sitting in front of a bank of monitors. Treager was a fat, unshaven slob with thinning, greasy hair. His snug-fitting, grey pants were ready to rip, and his white shirt was a size too big, like he was expecting to grow into it. He was watching a monitor that was playing back the footage of Dr Dalton jerking off the unconscious man in the operating theatre. Upon hearing them walk in, he sharply switched off the offending monitor.

'Hello Treager,' said Dr Dalton.

'Caught you at a bad time?' Rex asked.

'Nope,' said Treager, blushing.

Rex held out his hand. 'Good to see you again.'

Treager didn't attempt to stand up. He squirmed around in his office chair and reached out a hand to give Rex a feeble, sweaty handshake.

Dr Dalton appeared unfazed by Treager's behaviour. 'Can you show Rex the footage of the theft of the cloning machines, please?' she asked.

'Uh, yeah. Sure.' Treager woke up his computer and closed down a few windows, then after faffing around for a while, he eventually brought up the footage of the robbery. 'Here you go,' he said, pointing at the screen.

Rex leaned in to get a better view. The video showed a room with a piece of expensive equipment in it.

'That's the cloning machine,' said Treager, tapping the screen.

The machine was the size of two large cars parked side by side. It had of a pair of cylindrical glass chambers on it, each big enough to fit a person in. After about ten seconds of footage, two large blue rays of light appeared, flickering next to the machine. Two figures showed up inside the blue haze. When the haze dissipated, the figures materialized as two men, dressed all in black with balaclavas concealing their faces.

Rex watched them closely. One was tall and stocky, the other small and wiry. 'Who the fuck are they?' he muttered.

Right on cue, the bigger man looked straight at the camera, then produced a small handgun with a silencer on the end. He pointed it at the camera and fired off a shot. The screen turned to black.

'Did you report this to the police?' Rex asked.

'We couldn't,' said Dr Dalton. 'As you know, the cloning process we were working on wasn't exactly above board. If the authorities knew half of what we do here, we'd be shut down.'

'Yeah, I'll bet.'

'Is there any chance you could get our equipment back for us?' Dr Dalton asked, hopefully.

Rex puffed out his cheeks. 'I don't know. Have you got any leads other than this footage?'

'That's it, I'm afraid,' she replied.

Rex grabbed the back of Treager's chair and pulled him away from the desk, then he moved in closer so he could use the keyboard. He rewound the onscreen footage, pausing it on the moment the two men arrived in a blue haze. 'I'll look into this for you,' he said eventually. 'I only know one man who could do that sort of thing, but I can't see how he could have done it.'

'Why not?' Treager asked.

'Because he's dead.'

Dr Dalton put her hand on Rex's shoulder. 'If you can get our equipment back, it would be huge for us,' she said. 'We're close to going out of business without it. And I'll be honest with you, we can't really

116

pay you much of a reward for its return, but any cosmetic treatments you or your friends require would be free of charge if you could get it back.'

Treager smiled at Rex. 'Fancy a free penis enlargement?'

'No,' said Rex. 'I do not.'

Twenty-five

Sanchez was sitting at a small round table in the Tapioca with a white sheet wrapped around his shoulders and an upside-down breakfast bowl on his head. Flake was standing behind him, chatting on her cell phone. She was wearing a denim skirt and a grey top, and before taking the call on her phone she'd been cutting Sanchez's hair. When her call ended, she picked up a pair of scissors and carried on trimming the hair around the edge of the breakfast bowl on Sanchez's head.

'What did Jasmine want?' Sanchez asked.

'She and Elvis are coming to see us,' Flake replied. 'They want us to keep the bar closed tonight.'

'For fuckssake,' said Sanchez. 'We're never bloody open anymore! We're losing money, you know.'

'It was you who wanted the place closed this afternoon,' Flake reminded him.

'Yeah, for my haircut.'

Flake trimmed some more hair off the sides of Sanchez's head, but she stopped suddenly. 'Did you hear that?' she asked.

'No,' Sanchez replied. 'I think I can smell it though.'

'No, dumbass, I mean, I think I heard someone in the toilets.'

'Maybe it's them?'

They both swivelled round and stared at the washrooms. After a few seconds, Jasmine appeared from the ladies' toilets with Elvis behind her. They had quite a glow about them. Jasmine was wearing jeans and a white leather jacket with just a black bra underneath, and Elvis was in his black suit and red shirt.

'Hi guys,' said Jasmine.

'We've been waiting ages for you,' Flake replied. 'What's the big news? Why did you want us to close the bar?'

'Jasmine's definitely been cloned,' Elvis replied.

Jasmine pulled up a chair and sat down at the table next to Flake and Sanchez. 'We've even met a couple of my clones,' she said. 'One's dead now though.'

Elvis walked behind the bar and grabbed a bottle of beer from one of the fridges. 'We walked in on a guy called Zero fucking the other one,' he added, as he unscrewed the lid on his beer.

Sanchez stared wide-eyed at Jasmine. 'Seriously? Where are they getting these clones from? Do you know how much they cost?'

Flake pressed the bowl down harder on Sanchez's head.

'It's a legitimate question,' Sanchez protested.

118

'Zero did say how much it was, didn't he?' said Jasmine, looking over at Elvis.

'I don't remember the exact figure,' Elvis called back. 'I just remember seeing him fucking it, and apparently he'd taught it how to make sandwiches.'

'Really?' said Sanchez. 'Wow. Maybe we could get one to work in the kitchen. It could lighten Flake's workload?'

'The plan is to stop people buying them,' said Elvis, walking out from the bar and pulling up a seat next to Jasmine. 'We've gotta shut this cloning operation down.'

'It is creepy,' Flake agreed. She took the bowl off of Sanchez's head and set it down on the table. 'Have you got any leads?'

'Kind of,' said Elvis. 'Whoever made the clones of Jasmine has recently cloned three other women. We looked them up and they were all kidnapped from a strip club in a town called Darkness.'

'Darkness?' said Sanchez. 'Can you shed some light on that name?'

'It's just a dumb name for a town, is all,' said Elvis.

Flake picked up a comb and started styling Sanchez's thinning hair. 'What's the plan then?' she asked. 'And why do you need us?'

'We're gonna check out the strip club,' said Elvis, taking a pull on his beer. 'The kidnappers strike every two weeks on a Saturday night, and tonight they're due to strike again, so we're going to the club to look for suspicious characters.'

'Me and Flake should definitely help you out on this case,' said Sanchez. 'If women are being kidnapped, it's our duty to step up and stop this madness.'

Before anyone could respond to Sanchez, a loud creaking sound came from the men's toilets. The door swung open and Rodeo Rex walked into the bar area. He looked casual in blue jeans and a red leather waistcoat with nothing underneath it apart from his tanned, bulging muscles.

'Hey, Rex, have you been to the prosthetics place?' Elvis asked.

'Yeah, I was there just now,' said Rex as he headed behind the bar to help himself to some free booze. 'Their cloning equipment was stolen a while back. Two guys in balaclavas beamed themselves into the laboratory in the middle of the night and made off with the machinery. I couldn't make a positive ID on them though. You guys found anything?'

'Jasmine and Elvis saw a guy fucking a Jasmine clone,' said Sanchez.

'Really?' said Rex, walking out from behind the bar with a bottle of Randy Panda cider. 'Where the hell did you see that?'

119

'It doesn't matter where we saw it,' said Elvis. 'The only thing that matters is that we put a stop to the manufacture of these things.'

'Can we get our hands on one of the clones?' Rex asked, as he sat down with Jasmine and Elvis.

He was greeted with disapproving looks from Elvis and Flake, a raised eyebrow from Jasmine, and Sanchez holding his breath in the hope that someone might say *yes* to the idea.

'We don't *need* another Jasmine,' Elvis replied.

'Yes, one is enough,' Flake agreed.

'What did you want it for?' Sanchez asked.

'So we can study it,' said Rex. 'See what makes it tick, see if it has a brain, that kind of thing. It's not like I wanted to fuck it or anything, obviously.'

Jasmine scoffed. 'Why wouldn't you want to fuck one? Are my clones not hot enough for you?'

Rex rubbed his forehead. 'For fuckssake, I've only been back a minute. How have we ended up on this conversation already?'

'You brought it up,' said Sanchez.

'We have studied one of them,' said Elvis. 'It was human in almost every way except it had a chip in its brain. The people who order one get to choose a personality for it, then the people making it put the personality onto the chip.'

'That's sick,' said Flake.

'One of the clones has even learnt how to make sandwiches,' said Elvis, looking at Rex.

Rex took a swig of his cider. 'Did you find out where they were being made?'

'Kind of,' said Elvis. 'We found out someone is kidnapping strippers who work in a club called High Heels and Stockings. A stripper gets taken every two weeks on a Saturday night She's kidnapped, her face is altered, and then she's cloned, and the clones are sold online. But the actual strippers are never seen again.'

'If that's true,' said Rex. 'How come Jasmine is still here?'

'We think I might have been kidnapped when I was working at the Beaver Palace,' Jasmine replied. 'I let some guys drug me once, and when I woke up it was hours later. I'm pretty sure they didn't even do anything sexual to me. Weirdoes.'

'Jasmine would be easy to clone anyway?' said Flake. 'I mean there's enough photos and videos of her on the internet for someone to get a good idea of all of her proportions.'

120

'Have you been watching Jasmine's porno again?' Rex asked, before wrapping his mouth back around his bottle of Randy Panda Cider to hide a smirk.

'No, but I've seen the link to it in the search history on Sanchez's laptop,' said Flake, running her comb harshly along Sanchez's scalp.

'I was hacked,' Sanchez added.

'What's our next move then?' Rex asked. 'Do we start hanging around this strip club?'

'We've already got a plan,' said Elvis. 'Jasmine can get a job as a stripper at the club and act as bait.'

'That's a great idea,' said Sanchez.

'No it's not,' said Flake. 'That's a dumb idea.'

'How so?' said Jasmine.

Flake sighed and rolled her eyes. 'Well, whoever the kidnapper is, they already have a *Jasmine* clone. They're not going to kidnap her again, are they? Using her as bait is a waste of time.'

'Damn,' said Jasmine. 'I hadn't thought of that.'

'Me either,' said Elvis. 'Fuck. It was such a good plan too.'

'It wasn't though,' said Flake.

'Better come up with a new plan then,' said Rex.

After a few seconds where everyone tried to think of another plan, all heads eventually turned towards Flake.

'Get fucked,' she said, folding her arms.

'No wait,' said Elvis. 'This is a brilliant idea. And you do keep saying you want to be a proper Dead Hunter, Flake.'

'Flake wants to be a Dead Hunter?' said Rex.

'She's been keeping on about it,' said Elvis. 'Think about it Flake, this is your big chance. Innocent strippers are being kidnapped and murdered every fortnight. Only you can save them.'

Flake looked to Jasmine for some support.

'He's right,' said Jasmine. 'I mean, I'm gutted I can't do it. I would love to be a stripper. I bet it's awesome. All those guys with boners sitting there, staring at you.'

Flake looked at Sanchez to see if he would back her up. He already had a boner.

'You've got to think of all those innocent strippers being kidnapped and murdered,' Sanchez said, pretending like he cared.

Flake sighed. 'What does this stripper job actually require me to do?'

'You take your clothes off,' said Jasmine.

'Yes, I know that. But what kind of strip joint is it?'

121

Elvis answered. 'I've been to plenty of these joints. You just dance around for a bit, take your top off, and then people stick dollar bills in your G-string. It's easy money.'

'G-string?'

'Or thong,' said Elvis. 'Sometimes it's a bikini. It's no big deal. I already checked the licensing rules in Darkness. Fully nude strip clubs are illegal, so you'll just be showing us your tits.'

'No,' said Flake. 'I won't be showing *you* anything. You lot will be outside in a van or something.'

Sanchez raised his hand. 'I'd be allowed to watch, right?'

Rex slammed his bottle of cider down on the table. 'Listen,' he said. 'We all need to be in the club to make sure Flake is safe. Otherwise it's a risk.'

'You'll be nowhere near the fucking club,' said Flake, wagging her finger at him. 'If I'm gonna do this, and I'm not saying *I will*, but, *if I do*, then Sanchez is the only one allowed in the strip club. The rest of you would have to wait outside. Those are the rules and they are not negotiable.'

'Sounds fair to me,' said Elvis. 'It's settled then. Flake goes undercover as a stripper at this club tonight, and if the kidnappers show up, we nab them. Job done.'

'Hold on,' said Flake. 'I never said I was *definitely* doing it. I need to think about this for a while.'

'There's not much time to think,' said Rex. 'The show's tonight.'

'They're never going to give me a job today and let me dance tonight,' Flake pointed out. 'It's too short notice. They've probably got all their Saturday night strippers lined up already. Surely, it would be better if I just got a job as a waitress there anyway?'

'I knew it,' said Rex. 'She's not Dead Hunter material. We finally get a job for her where she can save lives, and she doesn't want to do it.'

'HEY, I'LL FUCKING DO IT, OKAY!' Flake yelled at Rex. A short silence followed where she realised what she'd said and also recognised that Rex had goaded her into it, and she'd fallen into the trap. Everyone else realised it too. 'Right then,' Flake went on. 'If I see any of you anywhere near that strip club while I'm in it, you're dead. All of you.'

'Great stuff,' said Elvis. 'Let's get Flake booked in for an audition at this place.'

'I have to audition?'

'Well, yeah,' said Rex.

'What did you say the club was called?' Flake asked. 'I want to check it out on the internet.'

122

'It's called High Heels and Stockings,' said Elvis.

'I don't generally wear high heels,' said Flake. 'Or stockings for that matter.'

'You can practise in front of me if you like?' said Sanchez. 'You might have to lend me some dollar bills though.'

'I've got to get a job there first,' Flake reminded everyone. 'They might not hire me. And even if they do, they probably won't need me for tonight's show.'

'They just had three strippers kidnapped and probably killed,' said Elvis. 'They're gonna be low on numbers. You'll get the job easy.' He handed Flake his phone. 'The number for the club is in my address book. Make the call and let's get this done.'

Twenty-six

1945

'I've brought Donald and Daffy for you.'

Hitler opened his eyes. He had been so relaxed in his hot bath that he had momentarily forgotten about everything that was going wrong in his life, and he hadn't heard his girlfriend Eva Braun enter the bathroom. Eva, the angel that she was, had brought in his favourite rubber ducks for him to play with in the bath. She put the two yellow ducks down in the bathwater and kissed Hitler on the forehead. She was wearing a blue dress he had bought for her from Italy. It showed off her shapely, curved figure.

'You can join me in the bath if you like?' Hitler said, flicking some of his filthy bathwater over her in the most seductive way possible.

'It's okay,' Eva replied. 'I had a bath last week. Can I get you anything else?'

'Some clean towels would be nice. Take those old ones and bring back some new ones.'

'Certainly, Adolf.'

Eva hooked a pair of white towels off a rail by the door and left Hitler in peace. His private bathroom wasn't exactly luxurious, but it was better than most of the rooms in his underground bunker, simply because it had a bath, a sink and a toilet in it. Luxury indeed.

With Eva gone, Hitler played with Donald and Daffy while he tried to figure out why his plans for world domination were slowly crumbling. Only months earlier he'd been confident Germany would win the war easily, but recently, in spite of all his Generals and "yes men" telling him everything was fine, he knew it wasn't. His empire was collapsing around him. It was just a matter of time before the war was lost.

'Fuhrer, I have returned,' said a voice.

Hitler sat up straight and looked around. Standing by the empty towel rail was a pale, ginger-haired man in an orange Hawaiian shirt and black jeans. It was Eric Einstein, a crackpot scientist. Next to him was a big, broad-shouldered man in a pair of grey pants and a black T-shirt.

'What the hell are you doing here?' Hitler asked.

Einstein took a deep breath. 'Do you remember me?'

'Of course I remember you. I had you executed this morning! How are you doing this?'

124

'You had me executed?' Einstein said, shocked. 'Well, that explains it! I couldn't come back three days ago because there was another version of me here. I have a failsafe in the time travel device that prevents me from travelling to a time where I already exist. I'm obviously in an alternate timeline. I knew this would happen.'

'What the fuck are you talking about?' said Hitler, his temper rising. 'And who the hell is he?' he added, pointing at Einstein's companion.

'His name is Herman.'

'Herman?'

'Yes, Herman. He's from the future. I built him. He's a cyborg.'

Hitler was more than a little confused. He'd been drinking a lot recently and it was possible he was hallucinating. Eric Einstein, disgraced scientist, back from the dead with a big fella who he claimed was a cyborg. *Madness.*

'A cyborg is a robot that looks like a human,' said Einstein. 'Why was I executed?'

'Because you're a useless fuck!'

'Did this executed version of me build you a time machine?'

'Yes, but it didn't work.'

'Okay, do you remember me showing you a movie from the future called *The Terminator?*'

Hitler stood up and held a rubber duck in front of his private parts to avoid giving his two intruders an eyeful of his equipment. 'What in God's name are you prattling on about?'

'Sit down and listen,' said Einstein. 'I'm here to bring you good news. I've found a way to win the war.'

'I will not sit down,' said Hitler. 'You can't order me around.'

'That rubber duck's not covering anything.'

'Fine,' said Hitler, sliding back down into his filthy bath water.

'Just listen to me a minute,' said Einstein. 'I think what's happened is, you and I are now operating in different timelines. The reason this has happened is because my friend Herman and I have been travelling back and forth in time. Some time ago, you and me came up with a plan that only we knew about. The plan was for me to travel back in time and kill all of the leaders of the allies before they were born. I went back to kill their mothers. Are you keeping up with this?'

A knock on the door was followed by Eva Braun walking in with two new towels.

'Chuck them over here,' Hitler snapped at her.

Eva tossed the towels at Hitler. They fell short and landed beside his bath.

125

'Thanks, now get out!'

Eva looked bemused by the sight of two men in Hitler's bathroom with him, but she left without saying anything about it because it wasn't the first time it had happened.

Hitler reached down and grabbed one of the towels, then he stood up and stepped out of the bath while he started drying himself off.

'So, you killed the mothers of our enemies before they could be born?' he said, eyeballing Einstein.

'Yes.'

'That does sound like a good plan,' Hitler admitted. 'Definitely the sort of thing I would have come up with. Did it work?'

'Actually, I came up with the plan,' said Einstein. 'But that's not important. We started off in London in 1888. Herman here killed Mary Chapman, the mother of Thomas Walton.'

'Who's Thomas Walton?'

'Exactly. You've never heard of him because he never existed.'

'I killed his mother,' Herman said, speaking for the first time.

'And who exactly are you?' Hitler asked, as he dried his feet with the towel.

'He's a cyborg,' said Einstein. 'I just explained that, okay. Look. While I was in the future I spent several years building him. I based him on cyborgs I'd seen in science fiction films. Herman is a highly sophisticated killing machine. He and I travelled to the year 1888 where we tracked down the British Prime Minister's mother, Mary. She was a prostitute in London. Herman murdered her, ensuring that her son would never be born. But when we travelled back to the future, it hadn't changed the outcome of the war. Germany was still defeated, only this time the defeat was even more humiliating. Without Walton, the Brits were led by a more formidable leader named Smith.'

Hitler stopped drying his feet and looked up. 'Go back in time and kill Stalin's mother before *he's* born,' he said. 'Stalin's the bigger threat anyway. The Brits have got Churchill in charge and he's always drunk.'

'That's just it though,' said Einstein. 'We tried everything. It didn't matter how many people we killed, Germany still loses the war. Christ, you know we had five goes at killing the British prime minister before they ended up with Churchill. We had no choice but to quit London after that because the British press were onto us. Herman even picked up the nickname *Jack the Ripper*. They've made all kinds of films about him in the years since. They have no idea he was a cyborg though. Oh, and a curious side note, all British prime ministers are born to prostitutes. Well, until Churchill they were.'

126

'This is bullshit,' said Hitler, while vigorously drying his crotch and ass with his towel.

'Sorry, but it's not,' said Einstein. 'No matter what happens, you lose the war. And people have been making fun of you ever since. I'm offering you a way out. Come to the future with me and Herman. See what we have achieved. I'm intending to build an army of cyborgs. I just have to generate the money. I estimate that with an army of ten thousand cyborgs, Germany can rule the world. Trust me, in the future, people are soft. They could be easily conquered, and the Nazis could finally rule the world. Imagine how shocked people in the twenty-first century will be to see you rise from the dead, stronger than before.'

Hitler used his towel to wipe some sweat from his face. 'Back from the dead, eh? Yes, I'd be worshipped like Jesus Christ.'

'Potentially, yes,' said Einstein. 'But if you're going to come with me, we have to leave now. You are days away from death if you stay here. But if you come now, we can build an army of cyborgs together, then conquer the world either in the future, or if you prefer, we could bring them back here and win World War Two.'

Hitler sniffed his towel for a few seconds then wrapped it around his waist. 'If what you're saying is true,' he said, thinking on his feet, 'wouldn't it make more sense to travel back to the start of the war with these cyborgs?'

'It would,' Einstein agreed. 'But there are rules in time travel. You cannot travel back to a time where you already exist. Christ, I've already explained this to you once. We tested it on chimps and they exploded.'

'Chimps?' said Hitler, mortified. 'You tested on chimps? I love chimps.'

'They were Jewish chimps,' Einstein lied.

'Jewish chimps? Do you think I'm stupid or something?'

Einstein glanced down at the rubber ducks in the bath. 'Of course not, Fuhrer. But things are very different in the future, and chimps are known to be religious.' He approached Hitler and held out a small gold ring. 'Slide this onto your finger, and I will take you to the future. You can then see for yourself that everything I am telling you is true.'

Hitler took the ring. He was about to place it on his finger when he had a thought. 'I should put some pants on first. And we're going to have to tell Eva about this. I don't want her worrying about where I am.'

'Yes sir.'

127

Twenty-seven

Sanchez was sitting at one of the black wooden tables in Purgatory, playing Horror Top Trumps with Jasmine, Elvis and Rex. Jacko was sitting on a stool behind the bar, looking bored. They were all anxiously awaiting the return of Flake, who had gone for a job interview at the strip club, High Heels and Stockings. She had left via the portal in the men's toilets confident that she would be back within twenty minutes, simply because Elvis and Jasmine had assured her the interview would be straightforward. Elvis knew a few strippers who had gotten their jobs simply by showing up and looking hot.

'She's been at her audition for half an hour,' said Sanchez, staring at the door to the travel portal. 'What if she's already been kidnapped?'

'Quit being such a bitch,' said Rex, in response to Sanchez's whining. 'If anything was wrong, Flake would have texted us.'

'Maybe she's having to do a private dance for the manager?' Jasmine suggested.

'Don't be stupid,' said Rex. 'The club's website said it was just an interview.'

'I guess it starts out as an interview,' Jasmine replied. 'But she must have to suck someone's dick at some point.'

Sanchez slapped his cards down on the table. 'Why would she be sucking anyone's dick?'

Jasmine shrugged. 'It's what I would have done.'

'Flake would never suck someone's dick to get a job,' Sanchez said, irritated.

'Didn't she sleep with you to get the job at the Tapioca?' Jasmine asked, already knowing the answer.

'That was different,' said Sanchez. 'Big Busty Sally's horoscope told her to.'

'Yeah, that's totally different,' said Elvis, staring at the *Frankenstein* card he was holding. 'Physical strength eighty-five.'

The others checked their cards. Sanchez had the *Slime Creature* with a pitiful score of seventy-one. Jasmine had the *Mummy* with a score of eighty-six.

'I've got ninety-one,' said Rex, laying down a card with a picture of *Dracula* on it.

Sanchez, Elvis and Jasmine all handed their losing cards over to Rex.

'Did Dracula look like that when you took a shit on him?' Elvis asked Sanchez.

128

'No, he looked more like the Vampire Bat,' said Sanchez, showing Elvis the card he was holding, which had a picture of a vampire bat on it.

Jacko called over to them from behind the bar. 'Surely everyone has to strip at the audition, just to prove they don't have a dick?'

'That's a good point,' said Rex.

'Fancy a bet?' said Jasmine.

'What kind of bet?' Rex asked, eyeing her with suspicion.

'I bet fifty bucks that Flake strips at the interview but lies about it and says she didn't.'

'That's a stupid bet,' said Rex. 'You can't lose.'

'Are you too chicken to take the bet?' Jasmine asked.

A beep on Sanchez's phone ended the conversation. He checked the display then yelled at Jacko. 'Open the portal. She's ready to come back.'

Jacko pressed a button behind the bar to open the portal door. All eyes stared at the men's washroom. When the washroom door slid to the side, Flake walked in from a bathroom in the strip club. The door closed up behind her as soon as she was through it. Flake looked unflustered, and the jeans and black top she was wearing looked as clean and tidy as when she left.

'How did it go?' Sanchez asked, standing up.

'I got the job.'

'What did you have to do?' Jasmine asked.

'Nothing much,' Flake replied. 'The boss man asked me a few questions. I did a dance for him and he said I can start tonight.'

'You didn't have to suck his dick?'

Flake scowled at Jasmine. 'Of course not. Who do you think I am? *You?*'

'Did you have to take your clothes off?' Sanchez asked.

'No. The guy was actually very gentlemanly about it. It seems like a nice club.'

'Somebody owes me fifty bucks,' said Jasmine. 'She's definitely done something she's not telling us about.'

'I did not,' Flake snapped back. 'The boss actually told me there would be no point in me stripping for him in his office. He said the only way to know if you can strip in front of a crowd is to go out on stage and do it for real in front of a packed house. So tonight is actually my audition. I only get paid if I go through with it.'

'Okay,' said Rex. 'If you're starting work tonight, we'd better get moving. I've come up with a plan already. We head straight to Darkness now. When we get there, we'll hire a motorhome. We can park it outside

129

the strip club and wait there while Flake does her thing. We can make a note of all the license plates on the cars in the club's parking lot, and we can look out for any weirdoes going into the club.'

'I don't want to sit in a motorhome all night,' Jasmine complained. 'Can't I go in the club? I'm a better bodyguard for Flake than Sanchez is.'

'You're not coming in,' Flake replied. 'And besides, I saw a sign on the wall in the club that says, "NO JASMINES". Apparently they've had a few of your clones try to get work there.'

'Damn it, that's harsh,' Jasmine complained.

Rex stood up. 'Come on then. Let's get moving. We haven't got much time.'

'I need to go back to the Tapioca first,' said Flake. 'I've got to pick out an outfit for tonight.'

'Is there something wrong with the underwear you're wearing now?' Elvis asked with a raised eyebrow.

'Fuck off,' said Flake. 'Jacko, can you send me and Sanchez back to the Tapioca, please?'

'Sure thing,' Jacko called back.

'Yo, Flake, wait a second,' said Rex, standing up.

'What do you want now?' Flake asked.

'The rest of us are going to Darkness now, so we probably won't see you again until tonight, so I just wanted to wish you good luck.'

'Yeah, good luck,' Elvis added.

'Thanks,' said Flake. 'See you all later when the show is over.'

130

Twenty-eight

JD left the police station and headed across the street to his jeep. With the brief flickering of daylight fading away, it felt like it was time for a change of clothing. He took off his army jacket, tossed it in the back of the jeep and grabbed the bag containing his long black, hooded coat. He put on the coat and felt more like himself right away. After loading the pockets and sleeves with all the weapons and ammunition necessary for a massacre, he hopped into the jeep and hit the road. Using the backstreets Walt had shown him, he made his way to the edge of town to find the chocolate factory that had laid off all its employees. It seemed like a good lead. The factory might just hold some clues as to who was behind the bombing of the protestors in town, and the massacre at the police station.

By the time the factory came into view, the night sky had drawn in. The building appeared as a hulking mass halfway up one of the mountains. It had no visible lights on or around it, and from a distance it appeared to have no windows.

After a drive up a long and winding road, JD arrived at the factory gates. A high perimeter wall on either side of the black, metal-railed gates stood between him and entry to the grounds. He exited the jeep and took a look around. Two cameras, one on either gate post followed his every move. The perimeter wall was topped with angled spikes all along it to deter anyone from attempting to climb over it. There was neither a doorbell nor any kind of entry system to speak of. Behind the gates, the parking lot stood empty, unused. Not a single car in sight.

JD grabbed the iron railings on the gates and poked his head through to see if there was a door at the front of the factory. He had excellent night vision, a rare gift that had helped him back in the day when partaking in a shootout that took place during an eclipse. While others had fired blindly in the dark, JD had picked out his targets and taken them down with shots to the head. But night vision didn't help him see a factory door that wasn't there. He looked up at the roof. There were four chimneys, but none had any smoke billowing from them. For all JD knew there could be hundreds of people in there working away on machinery. Judging by the way his day had gone so far, it wouldn't surprise him if there were Oompa-Loompas at work inside. Someone or some *thing* was inside that factory. And it was entirely possible that Jack the Ripper and the three missing women were also inside, or *had been* at some point.

JD was going in, one way or another. And there was no way the heavy-duty padlock keeping the gates closed was going to keep him out. That padlock was in for a rough night.

JD reached inside his coat and pulled out his Headblaster gun. One shot was all it took to end the life of the padlock. The chains slid from the gate and clattered to the ground. A kick of JD's boot separated the gates and they swung open, inviting him in. He returned to his jeep and cruised through the busted gates, the headlights on the jeep offering the only light on the premises. He parked up at the front of the building and got out to take a look around, expecting to find a craftily concealed entrance somewhere.

It was obvious where the main entrance was *supposed* to be, but whatever was once there had been built over and made to look like it never existed. JD ran his hand around the walls, feeling for any kind of lever, doorknob, anything. There was nothing.

The only sound other than his own breathing and footsteps came from the multitude of security cameras moving, whirring, tracking his movements. They were all positioned high up, out of reach. Someone somewhere was spying on him.

He checked all around the building's perimeter. No side entrance, no back door, not a single window. But someone was definitely using the place. A factory with no doors wouldn't be able to ship goods and supplies in or out, so what was going on in there?

Eventually, JD gave up wasting his time in the grounds of the factory. If the place had a bathroom, Jacko would be able to get him in there. But for now, JD had some place else to be. If his gut instincts were right, then the nightlife in the nearby town of Darkness would provide some clues as to what was going on.

He got back in his jeep and left the factory via the recently vandalised gates, then headed into Darkness.

132

Twenty-nine

After a healthy meal of double cheeseburger, fries and onion rings, courtesy of Flake's amazing cooking, Sanchez grabbed as many dollar bills as he could find in the till in readiness for his trip to the strip club. After a quick wash with the soda gun behind the bar, he headed upstairs and changed into a pair of smart black pants with plenty of crotch room and a shiny purple shirt. Then, after dousing himself in his favourite aftershave, a green bottle of *Grandpa's Windex*, he went looking for Flake. He found her in the spare bedroom that Jasmine and Elvis often stayed in. She was sitting on the double bed in the middle of the room putting on some high heels to go with the short red dress and black stockings she was wearing. Her hair was in an up-do, just how Sanchez liked it. When Flake saw him walk in, she put the shoes aside and stood up.

'What do you think?' she asked, giving him a twirl.

'I'd definitely do you,' Sanchez replied, like he usually did when she asked his opinion on an outfit.

'Do you think it will be okay for the strip club though?' Flake asked. 'I haven't seen what the other women wear, so I'm not sure about it.'

'Yeah, it'll be fine,' Sanchez replied. 'Although I'm not sure you'll need the dress.'

'What do you mean?'

'Erm, well, I just mean that once you're on the stage you'll probably just be wearing your underwear.'

'I can start off in the dress though, can't I?'

Sanchez shrugged. 'I prefer it when the strippers start off in their underwear.'

'Prefer it? How many strip clubs have you been to?'

'None, actually,' Sanchez lied. 'I was just thinking of all the old action movies from the eighties and nineties where they had a scene in a strip club.'

'Name one.'

'Beverly Hills Cop, Last Boy Scout, Road House, 48 Hours...'

'Okay, that's enough.'

'You look great though,' said Sanchez. He spotted a can of deodorant spray on the dresser and headed over to it. He sprayed some over his shirt and then stretched his pants out at the front and sprayed a bit down at his crotch area, just in case. Confident that he smelled like a God, he turned back to Flake, who had dropped her red dress to the floor.

She was wearing black stockings with a matching G-string and a black bra.

'Christ,' said Sanchez, his eyes almost popping out. 'That'll do it.'

'Do I look like a stripper?' Flake asked, seemingly unsure of herself.

'Fuck yeah, you do. Do you wanna do a practice dance for me?'

Flake turned around for him and wiggled her ass to some imaginary music. Sanchez kept his eyes fixed on her butt cheeks to make sure she wasn't making any mistakes, right up until the moment when she unclipped her bra and spun around to face him. She tossed the bra at his face. With lightning instincts he caught it in one hand and looked Flake up and down. Instant boner.

'Oh, yeah. That works,' he said.

'Great,' said Flake. She snatched her bra back and got dressed again while Sanchez watched and tried not to breathe too heavily. 'I hope the men in the strip club like it as much you do.'

'Oh, they will for sure.'

'And don't forget, while I'm dancing on the stage, you've got to be checking out all the men in the audience to see if any of them looks like a kidnapper.'

'You want me to stare at guys while you're on stage with your hooters out?'

'Yes. That's the whole point of this exercise, remember? We're looking for a kidnapper.'

Sanchez screwed up his face. 'They're *all* going to look like kidnappers. It's a strip club. Every guy in there is gonna look like a perv, apart from me.'

'Would you just do it anyway, for me?'

'Of course I will,' he lied. 'While you're on stage I'll be scouring the audience for the biggest perv.'

'I think I'm ready then.'

'Not quite,' said Sanchez, pointing at Flake's chest. 'You'll have to take off the Eye of the Moon. If people see that, you'll be getting mugged for sure.'

'Oh crap,' said Flake, touching the precious blue stone that was hanging around her neck on a chain. 'You'd better look after it for me.' She unclipped it from the chain and handed it to Sanchez. 'I felt safer when I had that on.'

The Eye had powerful healing properties. Sanchez had owned it for quite a time himself and had avoided catching any colds, but after using it to heal a stab wound in Flake's neck he had never managed to

134

get it back. Finally it was in his grasp again. He slipped it into his hip pocket.

'You can give it back to me after the show,' said Flake, as she took off the gold chain.

Sanchez looked Flake up and down one last time. 'Hang on,' he said.

'What now?'

'You should probably take something else off too.'

'We haven't got time for that,' Flake snapped back.

'I meant your engagement ring. You can't be wearing that in a strip club. The punters will want to know they stand a chance of hooking up with you.'

Flake looked down at the ring on her finger. 'I'll clip it on the gold chain,' she said, reluctantly agreeing with him.

While Flake put the chain back around her neck with the ring hanging around it, Sanchez pulled a dollar bill from his pocket. He grabbed Flake's G-string and tucked the dollar bill in against her hip.

'Careful!' said Flake. 'You nearly pulled my G-string off!'

'That's one of the tricks guy's do in strip clubs,' said Sanchez. 'They pull the G-string as far as they can before putting the dollar bill in.'

'Really?' Flake groaned. 'That's so pathetic.'

'I agree, but I don't make up the rules.'

Flake picked the dollar bill out of her underwear and handed it back to Sanchez, then she slipped her red dress back on and tried on the high heels.

'Blimey,' said Sanchez. 'You're even taller than me now.'

'I've always been taller than you,' said Flake, checking her appearance again in the mirror.

'When we get back tonight, I'm gonna ride you like there's no tomorrow,' said Sanchez, leering at her.

'That's really sweet,' said Flake. 'But it won't happen if I get kidnapped, so remember to look for the perverts in the club.'

Thirty

After putting on a beige suit and some smart black shoes, Hitler returned to his study where Eva, Einstein and Herman were waiting for him. Hitler walked up to Eva and kissed her passionately, his brilliant moustache dancing against her top lip.

'Would you like me to bring you something back from the future?' he asked as they separated.

'I would love a bar of chocolate,' Eva replied.

'Chocolate?' said Hitler.

'I haven't had any chocolate in months.'

'Then I shall bring you the best bar of chocolate they have in the future.'

'I've got some chocolate here,' said Einstein, reaching into his pocket. He pulled out a bar of creamy fruit and nut. 'Here, you can have this.'

'She won't eat that filth,' said Hitler, pushing Einstein's hand away. 'It's got milk and nuts in it. Don't worry, my love. I'll find you a bar of the best plain dark chocolate.'

'Oh, thank you, Adolf,' said Eva, smiling. 'That would be lovely.'

'Excellent,' said Hitler, drumming his fingers together. He nodded at Einstein. 'I think I'm ready to go.'

'Be careful,' said Eva, forcing a smile. 'I will think of you every minute that you are away.'

'And I you, my love.'

Einstein cut short the goodbyes by pressing a button on his watch. Before Hitler knew what was happening, he was engulfed by a blue electrical light. When it faded away, he was no longer in his underground bunker. The only things that remained the same were Eric Einstein and his enormous cyborg friend, Herman.

'What do you think?' Einstein asked, gesturing around at the new scenery.

'Where the hell are we?'

'We're in the future. Just like I promised.'

Hitler turned a full 360 degrees, taking in the sights. He was in a hall the size of a football pitch. The walls were painted metallic blue and the ceiling was so high he had to lean back in order to see it. At the far end of the hall was a whole load of machinery, the likes of which he had never seen before. This had to be the future because what he was seeing was some major hi-tech shit. Computers with flat screens, chairs with wheels on, enormous TV screens on the walls. It was a lot to take in, but the best thing on display was a row of naked women lying on their backs

136

on a raised platform by one of the walls. Hitler approached them in order to get a better look.

'What you're looking at are the Jasmines,' said Einstein, catching up with him. 'This building we are in is the factory where we create them.'

'She's black,' said Hitler, approaching the nearest Jasmine to get a better look.

'She's actually brown,' Einstein replied. 'And she's incredibly popular. We've sold hundreds and we're getting orders for more every day. They sell for a hundred thousand dollars a pop. They are created using a cloning machine that Herman and I stole. It was originally built by some do-gooders who used it to create replacement body parts for people who had lost limbs in accidents.'

Hitler gasped. 'Replacement body parts? That's incredible. Tell me, if someone was missing a testicle, could the machine generate them another one?'

'I assume so,' said Einstein, frowning. 'Although, that would require a surgeon to insert the new testicle into the user's scrotum, so it's not something we could do here.'

'Fair enough,' said Hitler, nonchalantly. 'I was just asking for a friend.'

'Let me show you the machine,' said Einstein, heading for the other end of the hall with Hitler at his side. 'I'm hoping to use it to clone Herman. I made his skeleton from titanium instead of bone, which is what makes him so hard to kill. He also has thicker, more durable skin than regular humans, so it's hard to even injure him. If anyone hacks at him with a machete they won't do much damage. And bullets bounce off him, leaving mere dents or tears in his skin.' Einstein stopped next to one of the Jasmine clones and stroked its foot. 'With the money generated from selling these Jasmines, I'm able to keep the factory running while I work on modifying the cloning machine so it will replicate the titanium skeleton that Herman has. Once the machine is fixed, I can build our army of cyborgs, but we'll probably have to buy more factories to store them in.'

Hitler ran his hand down the leg of one of the Jasmines to see how it felt. 'I like the feel of her leg,' he said without taking his eyes off her. 'Do you have a white version?'

Einstein tried to be diplomatic. 'I'm afraid not. You see, I specifically cloned this woman because not only is she the most popular porn star in the world, but she's also the most wanted criminal. A while back, she assassinated the pope.'

Hitler reeled back in disgust. 'You made a sex robot out of a criminal porn star, and she's not even white? That's madness! Why couldn't you have made one out of a good, clean, wholesome white woman? Surely it would sell better? Decent men won't buy this!'

'Decent men won't buy one, period,' Einstein pointed out. 'But that's not the point. In the twenty-first century most people aren't concerned about the colour of their partner, or their sex robot. Interracial relationships are commonplace, and porn stars are very popular thanks to the internet. Why don't you try one of these out? Get to know it? I can program in a personality of your choice. I think you'll find it's a richly rewarding experience. A Jasmine can win you over in a matter of minutes and then you'll never want to be without her.'

'Heavens no,' said Hitler, shaking his head. 'If I was sad enough to want a sex robot, I'd want a white one. From now on, I want all the sex robots to be white.'

Einstein inwardly groaned. 'Okay, it's like this,' he said, placing a hand on Hitler's shoulder but then quickly extracting it when he saw the angry scowl on the dictator's face. 'There's a legal issue at play here. Because Jasmine is on the FBI's most wanted list, she can't sue us. The minute she hires a lawyer to hit us with a lawsuit she'll be arrested and thrown in prison or executed. That's why she's the perfect subject for cloning. She's super-famous but can't sue for infringement of her image rights. Any other famous women we clone would hit us with lawsuits straight away and we'd be shut down. It's safer just to stick with making Jasmines. Trust me, they're big sellers.'

'I don't care about lawsuits,' said Hitler. 'Get me some white women. I guarantee you they'll sell better than this brown porn star.'

'It's really not that simple,' said Einstein, his frustration growing. 'We can't just clone someone without paying them royalties. With Jasmine, we travelled back in time to before she was famous. We kidnapped her and kept her drugged so she would have no recollection of being cloned, then after we'd cloned her once, we just started making copies of the original clone. We dumped the real Jasmine back where she came from, none the wiser.'

Hitler shook his head. 'I'm telling you, you'll sell more of these if you do a white version.'

Einstein was sensing that it might take some time for Hitler to get to grips with the twenty-first century. Back in the nineteen-forties, the Nazi leader had seemed like an intelligent and articulate leader, but now he seemed like a fucking idiot. And really racist. Even more so than before.

138

'I think it would be a good idea if you take some time to relax,' said Einstein. 'Watch some movies, documentaries and stuff, surf the internet, get a feel for what the modern world is like. Maybe get laid? Pick a Jasmine. Once you've fucked one of these, there's no going back. Come on, let's relax, get some food and drinks, and I'll start introducing you to all the things that have changed since the war.'

Thirty-one

With every passing second, Flake was becoming more anxious about what she was about to do. She was going to strip on a stage in front of a bunch of dirty old men, and probably dirty *young* men too. And potentially in front of some other women. It's not as if she'd been preparing for it for weeks or even days. She'd only agreed to do the strip a few hours earlier, after being goaded into it.

She was sitting in the ladies dressing room, which was long and narrow with similar dimensions to a bus. A mirrored dressing table ran along the length of one side. Flake was sitting at the far end, furthest from the entrance. Three other dancers were sitting with her, doing their makeup. Charlene, Danni and Marly were all friendly, but they seemed oblivious to just how nervous their new co-worker was.

'Am I overdressed?' Flake asked Charlene, who was sitting next to her in a scarcely there set of black lingerie. Charlene was a fair-skinned blonde in her mid-twenties with a curvy figure. She was a seasoned pro when it came to the stripping game.

'It's your first night,' said Charlene, smiling and showing off some lipstick-stained teeth. 'Don't overthink it. Just do whatever you feel comfortable with.'

'Oh, okay.'

Flake glanced over at the two other women who were sitting the other side of Charlene doing their makeup in the mirror. Danni was an athletic blonde with enormous boobs, who worked as a fitness instructor by day. She was wearing a red basque and black stockings. She looked about nineteen and didn't have an ounce of fat on her. Next to her was Marly, a slim, brown-skinned brunette in white lingerie, who claimed she worked as a librarian by day. A librarian working as a stripper seemed like an unusual mix, but apparently the librarian job didn't pay well, whereas stripping was a way to get rich quick by comparison.

At just after 8 p.m., Orlando, the overweight, balding club owner, walked in without knocking on the door. He was probably in his late thirties, but he could easily have passed for fifty on account of his unhealthy complexion and flabby neck. His silver suit was ill-fitting and just made his gut look bigger. 'Evening ladies,' he said, checking them all out. He glanced at Flake's red dress. 'Sheesh,' he said, taken aback. 'That's the nicest dress we've ever had in here. You sure you want to wear it on stage?'

'I was intending to,' said Flake.

140

'Up to you,' said Orlando. 'But when you take it off, throw it to one of the bouncers because if it lands on the floor it'll get covered in spit and beer and God knows what else.'

'Maybe I won't wear it then,' said Flake.

'Like I said, entirely up to you,' said Orlando. 'You'll be going out with Charlene. Just follow her lead and you can't go wrong.' He looked at Marly and Danni. 'You two are on stage in two minutes, okay? We've got a good crowd in already and they're itching to see some skin, so don't keep 'em waiting.'

Marly gave him a thumbs up sign, while Danni muttered, "yeah, yeah," under her breath.

Orlando left the ladies alone and headed off to do whatever the hell it was he did while the girls were dancing. Flake could hear some funky music coming from the stage area, along with some boisterous yelling from some drunken men.

'Sounds pretty quiet out there,' said Marly. 'I hope it livens up later.'

'That's *quiet?*' said Flake. 'I thought it sounded busy.'

'It's better when it's busy,' said Marly. 'You get way more tips when you go round with your collection tin.'

'Collection tin?'

Marly didn't reply. She stuck a rolled up twenty-dollar bill in her nostril and snorted up a line of white powder from the table in front of her.

Danni answered on her behalf. 'Flake, honey, didn't Orlando tell you anything?'

'Not really,' said Flake. 'He just said to copy what everyone else does.'

'Charlene, you'd better fill her in,' Danni said, before snorting up her own line of coke, 'Me and Marly have gotta haul ass.'

Danni and Marly stood up and hugged each other, then they left the dressing room and made their way out onto the stage. About ten seconds later a huge cheer went up from the bar area.

'Sounds like a good crowd,' said Charlene. 'You know, it being your first night, you'll make a lot of money. The guys love a newbie.'

Flake's heart was fluttering. 'Got any advice?' she asked. 'Like, what did you do on your first time out there? I'm absolutely crapping myself here.'

'We've got maybe ten minutes yet,' said Charlene, while doing her eyeliner. 'If it was me, I would lose the dress. That's up to you, of course. But, on your first night, if you're really nervous, you might not want to risk getting all tangled up trying to get your dress off. The less clothes

141

you have to take off, the easier it will be. Oh, and have a few drinks now. Get the booze into your system before you walk out there. It'll take the edge off.'

'I could certainly use a drink,' Flake admitted.

Charlene opened up a leather bag she had on the dressing table. She pulled out a half-litre bottle of toffee vodka and a shot glass. She handed them to Flake. 'Take a shot of this,' she said. 'Then count to thirty and take another. Then after another thirty seconds do one last shot.'

'Thanks,' Flake poured a shot into the glass and threw it down her throat. The toffee flavour made it palatable. After counting to thirty, she took her second shot. So far, it wasn't calming her nerves, but it did take her mind off the imminent public strip she was about to perform. While she was pouring out the third shot, she spotted Charlene drawing out a line of white powder on the dressing table.

'Does everyone do drugs here?' Flake asked.

'I'm not gonna push it on you,' said Charlene. 'But if you want some, you're welcome. I've got enough for two.'

'I've never actually done that before.'

Charlene snorted up her line of coke, then looked up at Flake. 'You ever had that nightmare where you've turned up to school or work or something and you've forgotten your clothes and everyone is staring at you and laughing?' she asked, while checking her nose in the mirror.

Flake shuddered at the memory of a similar nightmare. 'Yeah, a few times.'

'Well, this here powder is the difference between feeling like that and feeling like you're a goddess who owns the room. With a line of this in your veins, you're the one in charge out there, and all the guys watching are pathetic losers. *Without* this stuff, it can sometimes feel like it's the other way around.'

Flake contemplated the idea of doing a line of coke, if indeed it was coke. Taking drugs was a major risk. 'I think I'll give it a pass,' she said, before downing her third and final toffee vodka. 'Can you tell me about the collection tins that Marly mentioned just now?'

Charlene sniffed and wiggled her nose around a little before replying. 'Yeah, there's some steps at the back of the stage. When you finish your dance, go down those steps. One of the bouncers will be waiting there. He'll give you a collection tin, then he'll walk around the room with you. All the punters have to put at least a dollar in your tin. If they don't, they get kicked out. Usually, you'll get a few guys who give you ten or twenty bucks. If you're lucky and a rich guy takes a shine to

142

you, you might get a whole lot more. And don't worry, if any asshole tries to grab your ass, the bouncer will kick his head in.'

'Wow, you can make quite a lot of money then?'

'Honey, on a good night, you can make thousands. Twenty percent goes to Orlando of course, but it's still good money. Are you sure you don't want any of this coke? I promise you it will help. I've seen girls go out there on their first night and they freeze. It's pretty awful.'

'What do you mean by freeze?'

'They can't bring themselves to strip. The guys in the crowd get really brutal when that happens. And it's an immediate sacking offence. Trust me, for your first time, the coke is a big help. Getting the first dance out of the way is the hardest part.'

'What do you do out there anyway?' Flake asked as she unzipped her dress and stepped out of it, leaving her in just her black bra, stockings and G-string. 'I mean, how long do you dance for before you take your top off?'

Charlene checked her face in the mirror again, then looked back at Flake. 'When you get out there, if you're really feeling nervous, start by grabbing the pole and dancing around that for a bit. You won't really be able to see anyone in the audience anyway because all the lights are on *you* not them. Everyone else is just a blur in the shadows, so pretend like you think there's no one out there. Then after about a minute, take your top off. Drop it on the floor and one of the bouncers will grab it and hold onto it for you. Dance around for another minute, wiggle your tits and ass around to get the guys worked up, then peel off your G-string real slow and shake your ass some more until the end of the song.'

'Did you just say *take off my G-string?*'

'Yeah, didn't you know about that?'

Flake felt her toffee vodka making its way back up from her stomach into her mouth. 'No. No one said anything about going fully nude. A friend of mine said *fully nude* clubs were illegal here.'

'Oh, they are,' said Charlene. 'But Orlando gets around it by making sure all the girls keep their stockings and high heels on, hence the name of the club. If you've got stockings and heels on, then technically you're not naked.'

Flake tensed up. What Charlene was saying was ridiculous. It was "Jasmine-style" logic. Strutting around with no underwear on meant you were nude in any place in the world. Keeping your stockings on didn't detract from the fact that you were butt naked. 'You mean I'm going to have to show everyone my—'

'Yep. Orlando is supposed to tell you all this at the interview, but we're short of dancers at the moment so maybe he didn't want to scare

143

you off. A lotta girls leave the interview and never come back, probably because they don't wanna flash their beaver for the whole town to see.'

'I can relate to that,' Flake said, her mouth feeling very dry all of a sudden.

Charlene carried on regardless. 'It's really no big deal. Once you get their money in your pocket you won't mind, trust me.'

'Oh God.'

Flake's phone vibrated on the dresser in front of her. She picked it up and saw a text from Rex. It said, "PROUD OF YOU FLAKE. REMEMBER UR SAVING LIVES, X"

Flake had half a mind to send a rude response, but then she heard the song in the bar area come to an end. The silence was short-lived. A big chorus of cheers rang out, accompanied by wolf-whistles and loud applause for Danni and Marly.

'Sounds like they just finished,' said Charlene. She pointed at the line of coke on the table in front of her. 'Sure you don't want this?'

Flake snatched the rolled-up twenty-dollar bill from Charlene's hand and used it to snort up the line of coke. It made her blink a lot. Her nostrils weren't used to snorting powder. When the line was gone, she lifted her head up and wiggled her nose around just like Charlene had done before. She handed the banknote back and wiped her nose which was beginning to feel warm and numb.

'How's that feel?' Charlene asked.

'It's good. Really good.'

A feeling of all-conquering awesomeness began to rush through Flake's whole body. The anxiety from moments earlier was fading away fast.

You can do this, she told herself. *Blank it out and just do it.*

'Try to enjoy it,' said Charlene. 'It's actually great fun when you realise every guy out there wants you. Keep that in mind. You're in control, not them. And the better you do, the more of their money they'll hand over when the dance is finished.'

'One question,' said Flake. 'When we go around the crowd with our collecting tins, are we still butt naked?'

Charlene smiled. 'Oh yeah. But that's good. You get more money that way. And while you're going round you can arrange private dances with any of the customers you like the look of. Make sure you get at least fifty bucks for a private dance. And don't forget, no one is allowed to touch you. Anyone grabs at you, they're getting a black eye and thrown out on the street.'

'And what do I do on a private dance?'

144

'Take them to one of the side rooms and just grind around on their lap. Or dance in front of them, whatever they want. But again, they're not allowed to touch you. If they do, just shout out for one of the bouncers, and they'll throw the guy out.'

Flake could feel the newfound confidence of the coke in her bloodstream, which was just about taking the edge off the news about the *private dances* and the *walking around with absolutely nothing on.*

'How long 'til we're on?' Flake asked.

The answer came promptly when the dressing room door opened and Orlando poked his head around it. 'Okay, girls. You're up next.'

Thirty-two

Over the course of the three months Hitler had spent in the future, he had learned a great deal. He had discovered how to use the internet to look at porn, and even found a site dedicated to cats that looked like him. He had also learned how history had depicted him as an obsessive, irrational passionately-murderous, sex-starved lunatic. On a more positive note, he had enjoyed watching movies from the eighties, and had become a huge fan of the Emperor in *Star Wars*. He had also seen *Road House* eighteen times.

And so it came to be that one day he informed Einstein that he would like one of his favourite actresses cloned as a sex robot. Arguments took place. Tantrums were thrown. And murderous threats were made. But in the end, Einstein was able to make Hitler understand that kidnapping and cloning a famous actress was not possible for many reasons. A compromise was eventually reached. Einstein conceded that Hitler could clone a woman who looked like any actress who'd been dead for at least twenty years.

Hitler chose Bette Davis.

A few nights later, Hitler, Herman and Einstein headed to a local strip club to find a desirable young woman who looked like Bette Davis. Their logic being that no one cared about strippers, so kidnapping one wouldn't cause too much of a stir. When they arrived at the club, none of the strippers was a dead ringer for Bette Davis. But there was one that had some vague similarities. When the club closed for the night, the stripper in question, a woman named Tammy-Lynn, was coaxed into their van, which was parked out back. Herman drugged her, then they took her back to the factory and got to work on her.

While Tammy-Lynn was unconscious, Herman was sent out to kidnap a respected cosmetic surgeon, who was then forced at gunpoint to carry out physical alterations to make Tammy-Lynn look more like Bette Davis. When the alterations were complete, the cosmetic surgeon was brutally murdered and cremated. The kidnapped woman was plugged into the cloning machine, and once she had been cloned, she too was brutally murdered. Einstein implanted a chip in the head of the clone, and Hitler had himself a new submissive female partner. And to prove that Bette Davis was better than the Jasmine, Hitler forced Einstein to start selling clones of his new girlfriend online, insisting it would sell better than the Jasmine. It didn't.

Hitler soon became bored with having just one female partner, and insisted it was time to kidnap another woman and make her look like one of his other favourite actresses. Further arguments were had with

146

Einstein, but the outcome was the same. A second stripper was kidnapped from the local club, and another cosmetic surgeon was acquired. The stripper was physically altered and then murdered along with the cosmetic surgeon, and Hitler had what he wanted. Two submissive sex slaves who looked like his favourite actresses.

And two weeks later it all happened again. Hitler ended up with three female companions who looked similar to his favourite movie stars. But none of the new models was as popular with customers as the Jasmine. Just like Einstein had predicted. And Hitler was livid about being proven wrong. Again.

On a quiet Friday night, almost two weeks later, Hitler got shitfaced on German lager and stayed up late watching *It's a Wonderful Life* in his private quarters in the downstairs section of the factory. When the film finished, he staggered upstairs in his red, silk pyjamas to where Einstein was hard at work on his computer.

'We need one more,' Hitler slurred, as he ambled across the floor to Einstein's desk.

Einstein groaned. 'One more what?'

'I promise it's the last one. I want a girlfriend that looks like Donna Reed in *It's a Wonderful Life*. She's my favourite actress ever.'

Einstein rubbed his temples vigorously like he often did when he was stressed. 'Honestly, it's not a good idea,' he said. 'Those other three women we kidnapped aren't selling like the Jasmine. I've only sold twelve of them combined, whereas I've had orders in for over a hundred more Jasmines in that time.'

'I don't care,' said Hitler, folding his arms. 'I want to kidnap another stripper. I want one that looks like Donna Reed.'

'We can't keep kidnapping and murdering strippers,' said Einstein. 'Sooner or later the authorities will put two and two together and track us down.'

'Oh, I see,' said Hitler, sarcastically. 'It was all right for you and Herman to go murdering hookers in London and getting him the notorious *Jack the Ripper* nickname, but when I fall in love with my favourite actress it's suddenly, "oh no, it's too risky!" You sicken me.'

'Adolf,' said Einstein, trying to placate him with a more soothing tone. 'You've been drinking. I'm sure come morning, you'll realise that we can't keep kidnapping women, certainly not from the same strip club anyway.'

'So, you're saying it's okay?'

'What? No. I'm saying it's a bad idea.'

Hitler stepped forward and pressed his hand down next to Einstein's keyboard to steady himself. He looked bleary eyed and he was slurring his words. 'I want to go to the strip club again tomorrow night. I like it there, and I want another girlfriend. I promise not to strangle this one when I get bored of her And this'll be the last one, I totally swear.'

'Oh, God, I don't believe this,' said Einstein. 'If we get caught, we'll have to time travel back to a different country and start up this whole operation again. Do you want that?'

'I don't care.'

'Fine, you can go to the strip club with Herman. I'm not coming with you this time. It's too risky. There could be undercover cops hanging around that place by now.'

Hitler waved a dismissive hand. 'You told me the cops are stupid and nobody gives a fuck about dead strippers.'

'That's not exactly what I said. I said that most strippers never tell their family they're a stripper. And the boss of the strip club won't think they've been kidnapped. He'll just assume they quit, because strippers quit all the time without handing in a formal notice. But that doesn't mean people aren't out there looking for three missing women. THREE! Seriously, find a nice girl from another country to kidnap. It'll be easier.'

'Nonsense,' said Hitler. 'We're not kidnapping any good, clean, wholesome women. I just want the local strippers, because they're trash.'

'Again, not to argue with you, but not all strippers are trash. Some of them are just trying to earn money to pay their way through college, or to help raise their kids.'

'They can't hear you, you know,' said Hitler. 'So stop trying to sound like you care about them. I'm going to the strip club tomorrow night with Herman. And I'll pick the best one there.'

Einstein switched off his computer and stood up. 'Fine, but we're not selling this one online. You have one clone for yourself, and that's it.'

'Don't talk to me like you're the one in charge,' said Hitler, jabbing a finger in Einstein's direction.

'Fine, you're the boss,' said Einstein. 'I'm off to bed. See you in the morning.'

As Einstein walked away he visualised punching Hitler in the face. He'd visualised it a lot in recent weeks. The guy was an idiot. A fucking fool. How did so many people follow this clown in World War Two? How did Einstein himself ever believe in him? It was a mystery. One thing about Hitler was undeniable though. He was a nasty cunt, and Einstein didn't fancy getting on his wrong side.

148

Thirty-three

Even though they weren't actually attending Flake's big night, Elvis, Rex, and Jasmine all dressed up like they were going to a party. Elvis put on a black leather suit with a white shirt. Jasmine chose her favourite red catsuit, one that showed a lot of cleavage, and Rex, while still wearing jeans like he always did, had put on a smart brown leather jacket that actually had sleeves. The three of them were sitting around a small table inside their new deluxe motorhome, playing yet another card game. Enthusiasm for the game was in short supply.

'This is stupid,' said Elvis, laying all his cards down on the table. 'We might as well have stayed in Purgatory. Instead we're stuck in this shitty motorhome.'

'It was Rex's idea,' Jasmine reminded him.

'We have to be as close to the strip club as possible,' said Rex. 'This way if Sanchez calls us to say Flake is in trouble we can get across the road and into the club in a matter of seconds.'

'I knew it!' said Jasmine. 'You just want to see Flake naked!'

'Hey, we promised we wouldn't go in,' said Rex. 'And while I would like to, I fully intend to respect Flake's wishes and wait out here in this motorhome.'

'Exactly,' said Elvis, nodding in agreement. 'Besides, Sanchez is in there to protect Flake if anything goes wrong.'

After a long silence, Jasmine spoke up. 'Didn't Sanchez get beaten up by some girl scouts once?'

'They were Sunflower Girls,' said Rex. 'And they didn't beat him up, they just chased him around town because he set Santa Claus on fire.'

Jasmine fiddled with a playing card while she stared out of the bus's side window. 'So you're saying Sanchez runs away from trouble?'

Elvis and Rex exchanged sideways glances.

'Yes he does,' said Elvis. 'I hope he doesn't run away if the kidnapper shows up in the club.'

'Flake would be at the mercy of the killer,' said Rex, 'with no one to protect her.'

Jasmine scratched her chin with the playing card as she pondered what to do. 'They've got bouncers in the club though, haven't they?' she said. 'Flake should be safe with the bouncers around.'

Rex slumped back in his plastic chair. 'I guess so.'

'I just hope it's not the bouncers who are kidnapping the strippers,' said Elvis. 'Then Flake would be in real trouble. Sanchez couldn't handle a barmaid let alone a bouncer.'

149

'That's true,' said Jasmine. 'But Sanchez said he would call us if he saw any trouble, so it'll probably be fine.'

'Yeah, right,' said Elvis. He looked at Rex. 'Wanna play a different card game? This one's boring.'

'Although,' said Jasmine, causing both Elvis and Rex to perk up. 'Sanchez often forgets to charge his phone, doesn't he?'

'He does!' said Rex. 'He's such a dumbass.'

'He could be trying to call us right now,' said Elvis, standing up and peering out of the window for any signs of trouble at the strip club across the street.

'That's right,' said Jasmine. 'But we can easily check if his phone is working by calling him, can't we?'

Rex put his elbows on the table and rested his head on his hands. Elvis returned to his seat and slumped back in it.

'I suppose so,' said Rex, a glum look on his face.

'Mind you,' said Jasmine. 'Sanchez probably wouldn't hear his phone ringing in a strip club because of the loud music. You know what he's like. He'll be watching the strippers and won't even feel his phone vibrate, let alone hear it ring.'

'That's a good point,' said Elvis, sitting upright again.

Rex nibbled on the fingernail on his little finger. 'You know, maybe we should—'

'But then again,' said Jasmine, interrupting him. 'Sanchez being a scaredy cat like he is, he'll probably have his phone in his hand the whole time, ready to call us.'

'Oh for fuckssake!' said Elvis.

'Although,' said Jasmine, picking up the deck of cards and shuffling them for no particular reason. 'I'm pretty sure if he gets his phone out, the bouncers will kick him out of the club. They won't want people filming the strippers, will they?'

'That's another good point,' said Rex. 'He could have been kicked out already without us noticing. Flake could be all alone in there!'

'You're right,' said Jasmine, putting down the deck of cards. 'But then again, if he'd been kicked out, he would have come straight to see us, wouldn't he?'

'Okay Jas, I think that's enough,' said Elvis. 'Can we go to the club or not?'

Jasmine smiled. 'I think it would be in Flake's best interests if we were there. We can just sit at the back where she won't see us. We'd be doing her a favour.'

'That's a great idea,' said Rex, his eyes lighting up.

150

'Absolutely,' said Elvis. 'It's the only way to guarantee Flake's safety, which is the most important thing.'

'Wait a second,' said Jasmine, 'Didn't Flake say there was a sign on the wall in the club that says, "NO JASMINES"? That would mean the bouncers won't let me in the club, which kind of means none of us can go.'

'You can be in disguise,' said Rex, pulling a stars and stripes bandana from his jacket pocket. 'Here, wear this.' He handed the bandana to her. Elvis took off his sunglasses and slid them onto Jasmine's face.

'There you go,' said Elvis. 'Even I don't recognise you.'

Jasmine tied the bandana around her head and checked her reflection in the window. When she was happy with how she looked, she said, 'Okay, let's go in then.'

The rush for the door saw Elvis and Rex get wedged together in the narrow aisle of the motorhome. Eventually, after untangling themselves, they exited the vehicle and waited for Jasmine to join them. It was dark outside and the air was cool and fresh.

'This'll be fine,' said Rex. 'It's only a topless club after all. It's not as if she's gonna be totally naked.'

'And we're doing this for her own good,' said Elvis. 'I would never forgive myself if anything happened to her while we were sitting on a bus playing cards.'

Jasmine locked up the motorhome and joined them. 'Stop kidding yourselves,' she said. 'And don't forget, when we get in the club, just be cool.'

'When am I ever not cool?' said Elvis.

Jasmine elbowed him in the ribs and whispered in his ear. 'Obviously, I didn't mean you, sweetie.'

From the outside, the strip club looked kind of seedy. It was painted black, and the only thing making it visible was a red neon sign on the wall that said, "High Heels and Stockings," and another blue light in the shape of a naked woman next to the entrance. There was no queue outside, just an overweight bouncer in a black suit guarding the door.

'Evening folks,' he said, as they approached. 'Entry is five bucks. Pay inside.'

Jasmine kept her head down to avoid being recognised, and the three of them quietly made their way in. Rex paid everyone's entry fee at a booth just inside the door, then they headed through a pair of dark red doors into the club area. As seedy strip clubs go, the place was very smart. The stage was shaped like a runway through the middle of the bar lounge and had a dance pole at the back of it. Men of all ages were sitting

151

around the runway; their drinks rested on a shelf around the edge. There was a drinks bar in one corner, big enough for five or six people to stand at, and plenty of tables dotted around. The tables closest to the stage were all occupied. Sanchez was sitting at a table near the front of the room where he was having a discussion with one of the bouncers. The discussion came to an end when the bouncer confiscated a set of miniature binoculars Sanchez had been trying to hide from him.

'Wow,' said Jasmine. 'This place is even nicer than the Tapioca.'

'Where are the strippers then?' Elvis asked, staring at the empty stage.

'Quit worrying and go get us some drinks,' said Jasmine.

While Elvis headed off to the bar, Jasmine found a small round table at the back of the lounge, far away from the stage. It had a soft, blue, cushioned three-seater behind it, which faced the stage. Jasmine and Rex settled in and waited for Elvis to return. When he came back with two beers and a gin and tonic, he sat next to Jasmine, sandwiching her between him and Rex.

In a DJ booth near the stage, a fat guy in a blue sweater announced the upcoming act. 'Ladies and gentlemen, please give a warm welcome to Charlene and Flake!'

A ripple of applause rang out from all the tables dotted around the room. Rex, Jasmine, and Elvis clapped politely but resisted the urge to whoop and cheer.

'We got here in the nick of time,' said Rex, taking a sip of his beer.

The lights dimmed all around the club and a few seconds later a spotlight lit up the stage. The DJ put on the song "Slow" by Kylie Minogue, then a set of red curtains at the back of the stage parted, and a blonde lady in black lingerie walked out and started grinding to the music. Five seconds later, Flake followed her out onto to the runway in a black bra and G-string and a pair of black stockings. A few wolf-whistles rang out and then Flake, who looked pretty confident, grabbed hold of the fireman's pole on the stage and started swinging around it.

About a minute into the song, Charlene whipped off her bra and tossed it off stage to a bouncer who caught it in one hand.

'Here we go,' said Elvis, who was about to take a sip from his beer bottle, but stopped with it inches from his mouth.

Flake moved away from the pole she'd been gyrating around and followed Charlene's lead. Without any sign of nerves, she took off her bra and tossed it to a big, blond-haired bouncer at the side of the stage.

Jasmine lifted her sunglasses up and set them on top of her head, then she slid her right hand between Elvis's legs. Just as she suspected, he was hard. She glanced back at Rex. He had taken off his leather jacket

152

and strategically placed it on his lap. There was fun to be had. Jasmine slid her left hand under Rex's coat and felt his crotch. His dick was rock hard. Rex took his eyes off the stage briefly and threw a, *"what the fuck are you doing?"* look at Jasmine. She winked at him, then unzipped his jeans and slid her hand inside his boxers. She wrapped her fingers around his erect cock then pulled it out of his jeans and started stroking him off underneath the cover of his jacket.

Rex fidgeted uncomfortably in his seat. 'What are you doing?' he whispered out of the side of his mouth.

'If you want me to stop, just say so,' Jasmine replied.

As expected, Rex said nothing. He wanted this. He wanted Jasmine. *Always had.* There was no way he was going to ask her to remove her hand, knowing that he might never get the opportunity again. Elvis was oblivious to what was going on because his eyes were on Flake's tits. And even if he had seen what was going on beside him, he'd have been okay with it because Jasmine's other hand was rubbing his cock from outside his leather pants.

A minute later, with Rex squirming in his seat, Flake's dance partner Charlene peeled off her G-string and flicked it off stage to the bouncer who'd caught her bra.

Jasmine, Elvis and Rex all froze. Jasmine's hand even stopped moving up and down Rex's dick.

'Uh oh,' said Rex. 'Is this a fully nude club?'

Jasmine regained her composure and resumed rubbing Elvis's crotch and stroking Rex's cock.

'Flake's gonna kill us,' said Elvis.

'She'll kill you two,' said Jasmine.

Up on the stage, Flake turned her back on the audience, bent over, and rolled her G-string down to a chorus of cheers and whistles from all the guys in the audience. Rex tensed up and fidgeted in his seat as Jasmine teased his dick. Under the cover of his leather jacket, she squeezed it harder as she stroked the shaft.

Flake was having a fine time. The coke had really kicked in and her nerves had been replaced by a feeling of exhilaration. Dancing completely naked in front of a room full of men who all wanted her was a major buzz. Wiggling her body around to the music drove the audience wild. When the Kylie Minogue song ended and the dance was over, Flake lapped up the applause and wished she could do it all again. The bouncer who'd caught her underwear helped her down from the stage and handed her a collection tin just like Charlene had said he would.

153

'I'm Joe by the way,' he said. 'You were great. Make sure everyone gives you a tip. I'll hover a few metres behind you to make sure you're safe, okay?'

'Yeah, thanks.'

Flake took the collection tin and walked over to the table nearest the stage. Sanchez was sitting at it with Jacko, who was wearing a black suit and a piano key necktie. They each had a cold beer, and Sanchez also had a bowl of peanuts.

'You were fantastic!' said Sanchez. 'I wasn't expecting you to flash your cooter at everyone though. Do you know you've still got no panties on?'

'What's Jacko doing here?' Flake asked, ignoring Sanchez's question.

'He wouldn't let me use the portal unless he came with me,' said Sanchez, apologetically.

'That's not actually true,' said Jacko, tugging at the collar of his suit jacket. 'I always come here on my night off.'

Flake didn't actually mind that Jacko was there. She held out her collection tin for both men to contribute. They put in a dollar each. *Cheapskates.* Even so, it was a start. She moved around the lounge bar, collecting tips and compliments from all the customers. A few twenty-dollar bills went in the tin, and one kind gentleman slipped in a fifty. She was halfway around the tables when she spotted Elvis, Jasmine and Rex at a table near the entrance. Rather than be angry at them for disobeying her request to stay away, she merely rolled her eyes. She felt liberated by her naked dance, and even though she was slightly irritated that they had broken their promise to stay outside, she wasn't surprised. And a part of her was beaming with pride and glad they had been present to witness her performance.

As Flake approached the table, Jasmine sensed that Rex was about to shoot his load. To amuse herself, she released her grip on his throbbing cock and pulled his jacket off his lap, unveiling his erection for Flake to see as she arrived at the table. The jacket pull caught Rex completely by surprise.

'What the fuck?' he whispered, squirming.

Flake greeted them with a smile that turned to a look of disdain when she saw Rex grab a napkin from the table and ejaculate into it.

'Oh, Rex,' she groaned. 'How could you?'

Rex was in no state to respond, so Jasmine spoke up on his behalf.

154

'He couldn't help himself Flake,' she said. 'As soon as you got naked, he went to town on himself, tugging on his dick with his metal hand. He's got no shame.'

'What?' Rex spluttered. 'No, it was Jasmine.'

'As if,' said Jasmine, shaking her head.

Flake tutted. 'Well, I'm glad you guys came,' she said, holding out her collection tin.

Elvis slipped a twenty-dollar bill into the tin. 'You're a natural, Flake,' he said. 'You looked great up there.'

'Thank you,' she replied, still feeling no embarrassment at all about being naked in front of them.

Jasmine put a ten into the tin. 'I'm so jealous,' she added. 'I would love to be up on that stage.'

Flake held the tin in front of Rex who was in no position to put anything in it.

'I'm not sure Rex has got any money,' Jasmine added. 'I think he just blew his whole wad.'

The bouncer who was hovering a little way behind Flake yelled over to Rex. 'Hey, buddy. No jerking off!'

'Sorry,' Rex replied sheepishly as he tried to snatch his jacket back from Jasmine, who was holding onto it like a dog with a frisbee.

'I'll catch up with you guys later,' Flake said, before moving onto the next table.

Her collection tin was feeling pretty full when she arrived at a table with two men sitting at it. One was a short, creepy-looking man in a grey suit and a fedora hat. He had a very unfashionable, short moustache, the kind that went out of fashion after World War Two. His companion was tall, with round spectacles, long grey hair, and a beard. The creepy one, who looked like he'd drunk a few too many, smiled at her in a way only drunken people can. He leaned forward, holding out a fifty-dollar bill.

'Excuse me, miss,' he said in a German accent. 'I'd like to put my tip in your slot.'

Before he could say anything else, his companion snatched the fifty-dollar bill out of his hand and slipped it into the slot on Flake's tin. 'That's from both of us,' he said.

Flake thanked them and moved onto the next table. Eventually, when her tin was so full that no more notes would go in, she reached the last table, a small round one in a dark corner. And that was the moment where it felt like the cocaine had worn off, along with the newfound confidence she had gained from it. The man sitting at the table was wearing a long, dark coat with the hood pulled up. He had been staring at his drink as Flake approached, but when she arrived at his table, he

155

lifted his head and looked into her eyes. Flake felt her face burn up red with embarrassment.

'JD,' she spluttered. 'What are you doing here?'

'I was about to ask you the same thing.'

Thirty-four

Strip clubs had changed a lot since Hitler's day. The strippers were definitely a class above the ones in the nineteen-forties, but the music was worse, and not only that, it was also ear-bleedingly loud. Gone was the delightful 1930's German orchestral dance music, replaced by something chaotic with loud drums and bass. Hitler was sitting at a small table in an alcove at the back of the lounge with Herman for company. They had done their best to look different from their previous visits. Hitler was wearing a smart grey suit and a fedora hat. Herman was kitted out in a loose-fitting black suit with gold trims but also a grey wig, round spectacles, and a long fake beard.

'WHY DO THEY PERSIST WITH THIS SHIT MUSIC?' Hitler yelled over the din.

'What's shit about it?' Herman asked.

'EVERY SONG SOUNDS THE SAME!'

'Not to me. I believe if you drink more beer, the music will bother you less.'

There was little to no point in talking to Herman about things like music. He barely had an opinion, the stupid, AI-brained goof. Hitler picked up his bottle of Shitting Monkey beer and took another sip. He was halfway through the beer when the first strippers walked out onto the runway to shake their stuff. They were both very toned, with great legs. And Hitler had a definite liking for the stockings all the strippers wore in the club. He would never admit it to Einstein or Herman, but it was his favourite thing about the place and one of the reasons he kept coming back. Neither of the first two strippers were what he was looking for though, despite the great legs.

'These women are low quality,' he muttered to Herman. 'The blonde one has tits like balloons. That can't be natural.'

'It's not, sir,' Herman replied. 'Those have been artificially enlarged.'

'Enlarged?' Hitler shook his head. 'I'll have that sort of thing banned when I take over the world.'

'Why?'

'Because I'll be able to do whatever I want.'

Herman was intrigued. 'What other things will you do when you control the world?'

'I'll get rid of all the bloody Jews, for starters!' Hitler ranted, the booze well and truly in his veins at this point.

'Why don't you like Jewish people?'

'What?'

157

'Jewish people, why don't you like them?'

Hitler shook his fist as he replied. 'When I was a kid, I shit my pants at school once. There was a Jewish boy in the class, and he thought it would be funny to call me Adolf Shitler. The name stuck and then everyone started calling me Shitler. I've never gotten over it. I've had it in for the Jews ever since. That's just between you and me though.'

Herman looked confused. 'That's why millions of people died? Because someone called you Adolf Shitler?'

'Hey! You don't know what it was like!' Hitler ranted. 'Nobody calls me Shitler now though, do they, eh? That's one thing no one will ever dare to do again. Go and get me another beer.'

Herman got up and headed over to the bar to get Hitler his fourth beer of the night. By the time he returned, the first two dancers had left the stage and were walking around with collection tins. The first one to approach Hitler and Herman was the one with the abnormal hooters.

'Give her five dollars from both of us,' Hitler whispered in Herman's ear.

'Yes sir.'

When the stripper arrived at their table, Herman handed over a five-dollar bill.

'That's from both of us,' said Hitler.

The woman muttered something under her breath that sounded like, "cheapskate" then moved on to the next table.

The second stripper arrived soon after. She had brown skin, which immediately ended her chances of becoming one of Hitler's girlfriends, even though she was very attractive. Hitler really wanted to slap her on the ass, but he could see a bouncer nearby watching him intently. And while Herman could easily snap the bouncer's neck, it would put an end to the evening, so Hitler did the decent thing and made Herman give the stripper five dollars from both of them.

Once both strippers had left the floor, the DJ announced the next arrivals. 'Ladies and gentlemen, please give a warm welcome to Charlene and Flake!'

Another song blared out at a ridiculous volume. Hitler chugged on his bottle of beer and turned his attention back to the stage. The first lady through the curtain at the back was a chunky blonde. Hitler had seen her before on a previous visit to the club. She was okay, but definitely not what he was looking for. But then came the second stripper. As soon as she stepped through the curtain, Hitler knew she was the one. She was wearing black lingerie but she was much more clean and wholesome than the others. A positively classy-looking stripper with a pretty face. And, most important of all, she could pass as a Donna Reed lookalike.

158

Hitler elbowed Herman. 'That one,' he said pointing. 'She's perfect. We'll hardly have to do anything to her face. We can enjoy the rest of the evening now. I'll get wasted, and when the evening is over, you can kidnap that one and we'll go home.'

'Yes sir. Would you like me to—'

'SHUT UP! Can't you see I'm watching the dance?'

'Sorry, sir.'

Hitler tutted at Herman then carried on watching intently as Flake writhed around on stage. He found the whole thing quite arousing. When she tossed her G-string into the hands of a bouncer by the stage, Hitler's moustache nearly stood to attention. He put his beer down on the table and elbowed Herman in the arm.

'Psst, Herman. See if you can get the bouncer to sell us that woman's knickers.'

'That's not a good idea, sir.'

'It's a brilliant idea. Give him a hundred bucks, he'll go for it.'

'But sir, we're not supposed to be drawing attention to ourselves, remember? If you offer the bouncer money to buy a stripper's knickers, he'll definitely remember us.'

'Oh, for fuckssake.'

Herman was right though. It made Hitler livid to know the cyborg was thinking clearer than him.

'I'll get you another beer if you like, sir?'

'Go on then. And give me a fifty-dollar bill. This stripper is gonna love me.'

Thirty-five

Standing naked in front of JD became more embarrassing with each passing second. A cold draft of air blew round Flake's ass, serving as a reminder that she had nothing but stockings and high heels on. And people all around the club were still staring at her. She either needed another line of coke, or to go somewhere private.

'You wanna go somewhere quiet to talk?' she asked JD.

'If you like.'

'Hold on a sec.'

Flake turned away from JD and walked over to Joe the bouncer. 'Hey, Joe,' she whispered in his ear. 'This guy wants a private dance. Where can we go?'

Joe pointed to an opening in the wall past JD. 'Through there. Take a left and there's a bunch of private rooms curtained off. Take whichever one is free. I'll be right outside, so just call out if you need me.'

'Great, thanks.'

Flake returned to JD's table and beckoned him to go with her to the private area. He got up and followed her. They walked along a short corridor until they came to four small booths. The one on the far end had a curtain across it, and there were strange groans coming from inside it, so Flake and JD entered the one furthest from it. Flake pulled the curtain across to give them some privacy.

JD sat down on a long black cushioned seat against the wall and lowered the hood on his coat. He was unshaven but as ruggedly handsome as ever. Flake sat down next to him. A speaker in the room was playing pop music at a level just loud enough for them to have a conversation without being heard by anyone on the other side of the curtain. Although it didn't quite drown out the sound of someone getting a blow job in the end booth.

'It's nice to see you anyway,' Flake said. 'I kinda wish it wasn't like this though, if you know what I mean?'

JD smiled and frowned at the same time. 'This was quite a surprise for me too. I saw Sanchez and Jacko sitting by the stage, which I thought was odd, and then Jasmine, Rex and Elvis came in too. I was wondering where you were, but then suddenly you appeared on the stage. You looked great up there, by the way.'

'Thanks. I did some coke backstage. Kinda helped to get me through it, but it's worn off now, and I'm very conscious of the fact I'm naked right now.'

'You still look great.'

160

Flake appreciated the compliment, but didn't want to keep talking about how she looked, given that she was feeling very exposed, and not just because she was naked. 'Why are you here anyway?' she asked. 'Did one of the others invite you?'

JD shook his head. 'I'm working a case that Alexis Calhoon gave me. Someone who might be Jack the Ripper is kidnapping women, and I think they all worked here.'

'Wow, that's kinda the same reason we're here. Someone cloned Jasmine and is selling sex robots who look like her. We think it's the same person who is kidnapping strippers, which is why I'm working undercover here.'

'Wouldn't it have made more sense to go undercover as a barmaid though?' said JD, frowning. 'You could still look for the kidnapper, and you wouldn't have to get naked.'

Flake groaned. 'For fuckssake. That's what I said! But Rex and the others said it would only work if I was a stripper. I got goaded into it because I wanted to be made an official member of the Dead Hunters. This is like my initiation, and I knew if I pussied out they'd never let me hear the last of it.'

'Initiation? I think you've been had.'

'And don't I know it. Rex even jerked off while I was dancing. Can you believe that?'

'Yes.' JD glanced down at the engagement ring that was hanging around Flake's neck on a chain.

'Excuse me?' said Flake.

'The ring,' said JD, pointing at it. 'Is that new?'

Flake held it up for him to see. 'Me and Sanchez got engaged,' she said, smiling.

'Congratulations.'

'Thanks.' Flake let the ring fall back between her breasts. 'So, where have you been the last few months?'

'I've been taking some time out to clear my head.'

Flake nodded like she understood. 'Still not over Beth, huh? I can understand that.'

'I'm over Beth,' said JD. 'There was just some other stuff that I needed to come to terms with.' He glanced at Flake's naked body again. 'I can't believe you agreed to let the others watch you on stage.'

Flake chuckled. 'I didn't exactly. They were all supposed to be outside in a motorhome, apart from Sanchez, but I should have known they would all sneak in.'

JD looked away. He wanted to put his hands on Flake's naked body, like he'd done so many times before. *He tried to get the memories*

161

of making love to her in the sand on that deserted island out of his mind. It was impossible. He could smell the salty air, feel the heat of her body, the softness of her skin. If she hadn't been killed by that damn vampire, they might still be on that island, away from everyone and everything.

But she had been killed. And it had been a knife to the heart. God may have granted him a favour, allowing him to travel back in time to undo it all. But he had to go back to before they had become lovers, to a time when Flake was still with Sanchez. It made it hard to be around her because she didn't remember any of it. But it was better to have her alive and unaware of their time together than to not have her at all.

Flake saw a sadness in JD's eyes, so she slapped him on the arm. 'Do you want this private dance or not? I'm getting married soon, so this could be your only chance.' Before he could reply, she stood up and positioned herself in front of him.

JD stared into her eyes and she into his. Flake could read him better than any of the others, so she knew without him saying anything that he wanted the dance. She liked that he wanted it too. There was a time when she would have covered up, embarrassed and ashamed, but the initial shock of seeing JD in the club had faded, and she felt comfortable being naked in front of him. And she didn't need any more coke to feel that way. As she rubbed her breasts in JD's face, she felt no embarrassment or awkwardness. She was in control of the situation. Where once she might have been intimidated by him, now she was getting a kick out of turning him on. And he was definitely turned on. Flake gave him the greatest lap dance of his life. She ran her hands over his crotch, knowing he would be hard. And he was, *hard for her.* It turned her on big time. For a moment, it felt like they were in a world of their own where no one else existed. She reached for the zipper on his jeans, intending to pull his cock out. But her engagement ring hovered into her eyeline, hanging in front of her like a giant STOP sign, reminding her she was engaged to Sanchez. The lap dance had to end before it went too far.

She pulled her hand away from JD's zipper and planted a kiss on his lips, intending for it to signal the end of the dance. JD kissed her back and slid his hands onto her hips. At that moment, Flake wanted him like she'd never wanted a man before. To hell with the engagement ring. She unzipped his jeans.

'Hey, buddy. No touching the dancers.'

Joe's dreadful timing killed the moment. The kiss ended. Flake hovered for a moment before she pulled away from JD and looked over at the bouncer who had tugged the curtain aside.

'Time's up,' said Joe. 'Private dance is over.'

162

Thirty-six

The show was over. At 2 a.m., Flake was back in the dressing room with Charlene. Danni and Marly had already gone home. Charlene was still in her lingerie, but Flake had changed back into her regular clothes, a pair of jeans and a short-sleeved red top. She slid her arms into her black jacket and stuck her wages in the pocket. She had performed four dances on the stage over the course of her first evening at *High Heels and Stockings* and earned just over five hundred bucks.

'Think you'll be back for another go?' Charlene asked as she wiped some lipstick off while checking her face in the mirror on the dresser.

'I'd like to think so,' Flake lied.

'Good. We get a lot of girls who do one night and never come back, but you seem like a natural out there.'

Flake pulled her phone from her jacket pocket and checked her messages. She had a text from Sanchez telling her she was awesome and that he and the others were waiting outside in the motorhome.

'I gotta go,' she said to Charlene. 'See you again soon.'

On her way out of the dressing room, Flake passed Orlando, who was popping in for a private moment with Charlene. Flake said goodbye to him and promised to be back for a repeat performance on the upcoming Wednesday night show. Then she made her way out before he could pester her for any more commitments.

Joe the bouncer was sitting at the lounge bar drinking a tall glass of beer. He stood up when he saw Flake walk by.

'Hey, Flake, I'll unlock the door for you,' he said. 'You were really great tonight.'

'Thanks.'

Joe escorted her to the front door and pulled a key from his pocket to unlock it. 'I sure hope we see you again,' he said, gawping at her. 'You've got a great body.'

'I've got a great boyfriend too.'

That wiped the dopey smile off his face. He unlocked the door, and Flake walked out into the cold night air. Joe closed the door without another word. Flake wrapped her jacket tighter around her and looked around. The motorhome was parked not far from the club on the other side of the street. There were a few vehicles still in the parking lot, presumably belonging to the bouncers. She was halfway across the parking lot when she heard a foot scuff on the ground behind her.

'Excuse me, miss,' said a man's voice. 'My name is Paul. I saw your show earlier and you were fantastic.'

163

Flake glanced back but kept on walking. The man behind her was well over six feet tall. In the darkness he looked like a giant shadow, his facial features impossible to see.

'Thank you,' Flake said, without breaking stride.

'I'm a manager for a modelling agency,' the man went on. 'I believe you could be a superstar. If you're interested in a job where you get to keep your clothes *on*, I could guarantee you at least ten thousand dollars per day.'

Flake stopped and turned around. The man standing before her was wearing a smart black suit. He was rugged and handsome with short, dark hair. She didn't recall seeing him inside the club.

'Did you say ten thousand *a day?*' Flake asked, flattered by the "too-good-to-be-true" offer.

'Yes ma'am,' he replied. He held out a small business card. 'Here, this is my card. It's got my website on it, so you can have a look at what the company is all about. If you like what you see, give me a call.'

Flake wasn't really considering becoming a full-time model, but the man's sales pitch had her intrigued. She reached out for the business card. As soon her fingers touched it, the man let go of the card and wrapped his other hand around the back of her neck, pulling her towards his chest. He grabbed a small perfume bottle from his pocket with his free hand and squirted it into Flake's face. A green toxic chemical entered her nostrils, eyes and mouth. It sucked the energy right out of her in an instant. She tried to cry out, but no sound left her lips. Her body felt numb, her eyes heavy and tired. Within two seconds of the chemical entering her bloodstream, she was unconscious. The only thing stopping her from falling was the hand behind her neck. The man placed his perfume back in his pocket, lifted Flake up and slung her over his shoulder. He carried her over to a black van parked by the side of the club, opened the back door, and laid her down in the back. Flake never heard the door slam shut.

In the front seat of the van, Eric Einstein started the engine and turned on the headlights. Next to him in a two-person passenger seat, a drunken Adolf Hitler peered into the back at Flake. 'Damn, she's pretty,' he said.

The passenger door opened and Herman climbed in next to Hitler.

'GO, GO GO!' Herman called out.

Einstein pressed his foot down on the accelerator, and drove the van out of the parking lot at high speed.

✳✳✳✳✳✳✳✳✳✳✳✳✳✳✳✳✳✳✳✳✳✳✳✳✳✳✳✳✳✳✳✳✳✳✳

Across the street in the motorhome, Jasmine, Rex, and Elvis were sitting at a table, enjoying a few more drinks while discussing their views on the strip club and their opinions of Flake's performance. Jasmine was sitting on Elvis's lap with her arm draped around his shoulders. Sanchez and Jacko were further along the vehicle, staring out of the window, looking for Flake. The motorhome's radio was on, and the song "I am Dust" by Gary Numan was blaring out from some speakers in the ceiling.

'Here she comes,' said Jacko, pointing at the front of the club.

'About bloody time,' said Sanchez. 'The other strippers left ages ago. What's she been doing?'

'Never mind that,' said Jacko. 'Keep an eye out for potential kidnappers.'

'I'm telling you the only one we need to worry about is the weirdo who looked like Hitler,' said Sanchez.

'That guy was wasted!' Jacko reminded him. 'Flake would kick his ass if he tried anything.'

Sanchez called over to the others. 'Flake's just left the club.'

Jacko shoved him in the arm. 'Is that someone behind her?' he asked.

Sanchez pressed his face up against the window. 'I think it's one of the bouncers,' he said, squinting.

'No, it's not,' said Jacko. 'GUYS! KIDNAPPPER!'

Rex jumped up first and charged towards the front of the bus. Elvis pushed Jasmine off his lap and hurried after him. Jasmine landed on her ass on the floor.

'QUICK! HURRY!' Sanchez yelled at the others. 'HE'S DRAGGING HER OVER TO THAT VAN!'

Rex was first out of the motorhome, with Elvis a few steps behind. Flake's attacker slung her in the back of a van in the club's parking lot then climbed in the front. The van's engine came to life before Rex and Elvis were even halfway across the road. It pulled away and raced out of the parking lot at high speed, leaving them in its wake.

Jasmine staggered off the bus and yelled at them. 'What happened?'

'Flake's been taken!' Rex called back. 'Start the engine! We've gotta go after her.'

Jasmine jumped back aboard the motorhome, squeezed into the driver's seat and started up the engine. Sanchez and Jacko joined her at the front of the bus, both yelling nonsensical instructions at her. Rex and Elvis reboarded the bus and did the same thing.

'EVERYBODY SHUT UP!' Jasmine yelled. She steered the bus out into the road and set about turning it around.

165

'This is a total fuck up!' said Sanchez, panic etched on his face. 'How are we gonna catch up with them in this shit heap? By the time we turn around they'll be five miles away.'

'Someone call JD,' said Jasmine, as she fought with the bus's giant steering wheel.

'How's that gonna help?' Rex asked.

'He was in the club,' said Jasmine. 'Christ, don't you guys pay attention to anything?'

'What was *he* doing in the club?' Sanchez asked.

'I don't know,' Jasmine replied. 'He was only there for Flake's first dance, then he disappeared. Call him and ask him.'

'I've got him,' said Rex, pressing his phone against his ear. 'JD, Flake's been kidnapped….. Yeah, outside the club…… A guy in a black van…… You did what?….. JD? Are you still there? Hello?'

'What's happened?' asked Elvis.

'JD says he's going after her. And I think he said he'd put a tracking device on the black van already.'

Jasmine finally had the motorhome facing the right way. 'Buckle up fuckers!' she cried out as she floored the accelerator. 'This could be a bumpy ride.'

166

Thirty-seven

JD wished he had a better car. The jeep wasn't built for high-speed pursuits. Then again, Flake wasn't supposed to be kidnapped. Rex, Elvis, Jasmine, and Sanchez were supposed to make sure nothing happened to her.

After his private moment with Flake in the club, JD had headed out into the strip club's parking lot to check out the vehicles. A black van parked out front was the most likely vehicle for someone who wanted to kidnap a stripper. It had blacked out windows and a license plate covered in muck. With that in mind, he had attached a tracker to the underside of it.

But after fixing the tracker, JD parked his jeep around the back of the club so he could look for anyone suspicious. Plenty of junkies, drunks and hobos staggered by in the street behind the club. But just when it looked like nothing was going to happen, he took a call from Rex to say Flake had been taken. Without a second thought, he started up the jeep's engine, located the van on his phone's tracking app, then hit the road, double-quick in pursuit of the kidnappers. He'd lost Flake once before. He'd watched her die after she'd been stabbed by an invisible vampire. It had cost him a lifetime of happiness with her. And now she was in the clutches of someone who might turn out to be Jack the Ripper.

He sped out onto the highway, where he saw Jasmine making hard work of turning the motorhome around outside the club. That cumbersome piece of shit had no chance of catching the kidnapper's van.

The black van was nowhere to be seen. JD headed along the highway as fast as his jeep could go. His tracking app showed a satellite view of the van's location. It was still on the same road, about a mile ahead of him. He set his phone down on the passenger seat and swung the jeep around a sharp bend in the road. When the tracker showed he was closing in on the van, JD switched off his headlights. The taillights on the van came into view up ahead not long after. From there, catching up with them was easy. The van driver never saw him coming. JD cruised up unnoticed alongside the van. As soon as the nose of his jeep was ahead of it, he swung the jeep across the road and slammed into it. It knocked the van off course. The driver managed to avoid crashing into the mountainside. But by the time the van straightened up, JD's window was down, and his arm was outstretched, a pistol aimed at the van's front tyre.

One shot was all it took. The front tyre burst and the van skidded violently. The driver fought to keep it straight, but to no avail. The van came to a screeching, shuddering stop at the side of the road next to a

167

ditch. JD cruised past, but then hit the brakes, reversed back and slammed the back of his jeep into the van's front grill, blocking off any escape.

He leapt out of his vehicle, ran up to the van, and yanked the driver's door open. The driver, a man in a long brown coat, was dazed and rubbing his head, so he never saw what was coming. JD reached in and dragged him out onto the road. His first instinct was to knock the fucker out. But this wasn't just any fucker. It was Eric Einstein.

'Eric? What the fuck is going on?' JD asked, lowering his fist.

'Herman. HELP!' Einstein cried, while he cowered in front of JD.

There were two men in the passenger side of the van. One was drunk and looked like Hitler; the other was a perfect match for the Jack the Ripper suspect who had killed all the cops in Despair's police station earlier that day. The Ripper jumped out of his side of the van and headed round to confront JD.

JD shoved Einstein against the side of the van, then reached inside his coat and pulled out his trusted Headblaster gun.

'Herman, look out!' Einstein cried out.

BOOM!

The blast from JD's gun hit Herman on the chin as he rounded the front of the van. It snapped his head back sharply but didn't decapitate him like it should have done. Herman staggered back a few steps but then shook off the blast like it was nothing more than a slap. After composing himself, he marched forward again towards JD.

BOOM!

Shot number two hit Herman in the shoulder. It should have blown his arm off, but it just spun him around. A new tactic was required. JD grabbed Einstein by the collar of his coat and pressed the barrel of his gun under the scientist's chin, using him as a shield and a hostage to keep Herman at bay. It worked because the big brute stopped in his tracks, as if waiting for the go-ahead from Einstein to continue forward.

'What do you want with Flake?' JD snarled into Einstein's ear.

'How did you know my name?' Einstein asked, as if he'd only just realised JD had called him Eric when he dragged him out of the van.

'What?'

Herman butted in. 'Should I kill him?' he asked.

'You just wait there, fucknuts!' said JD. 'Or I'll blow your friend's face off.'

Herman stayed where he was and waited for Einstein to give him an order.

'What's Flake?' Einstein asked JD.

168

'Flake's the woman you just kidnapped. Hand her over or lose your face.'

'But how did you know my name?' Einstein asked for the second time.

'What are you talking about?' said JD. 'I've known you for years. You worked for Scratch.'

In the van, the pissed-up Hitler lookalike saw an opportunity to make a move. He grabbed a pistol from the van's glovebox and crept across the front seats of the van. He stopped behind the steering wheel and pointed his pistol at JD. 'Drop your fucking gun!' he slurred in a German accent.

'Who the fuck are you?' JD asked, intrigued by the striking resemblance to Adolf Hitler.

'Let Eric go and we'll talk,' the German replied, his voice dripping with arrogance and stale lager.

JD pulled his gun away from Einstein's neck and shoved the weaselly scientist towards Herman, then he turned his gun on the German. 'Who the fuck are you?' he asked.

The man's response was unexpected to say the least. He vanished in a flash of blue haze. Einstein and Herman vanished at the same time, leaving behind puffs of blue smoke where they had been standing. JD lowered his gun. There was trickery at play. But it wasn't hard to work out that Eric Einstein was behind it. The three kidnappers had somehow transported themselves to a safe destination. Sneaky bastards. Well, fuck them. JD was only there for Flake. He ran around to the back of the van and yanked open the back doors.

'Shit.'

The back of the van was empty. JD checked the ground all around the van and even crouched down to look under it. Flake was nowhere to be seen.

A set of headlights appeared further back down the road, indicating the late arrival of the motorhome. It slowed to a stop just short of the van. The door fizzed open, and Sanchez jumped out onto the road, followed by Elvis, Rex, Jacko, and then Jasmine.

'Did you get her back?' Sanchez asked, rushing over to the van and peering inside.

'She's gone,' JD replied. 'Eric Einstein took her. He was with two other men. One might be Jack the Ripper, and the other looked a lot like Hitler.'

'How did you let them get away?' Sanchez asked, angrily.

'I think Einstein beamed them all up somewhere.'

'Do you know where?' Rex asked.

'If I knew where, I wouldn't have said *somewhere*, would I?'

'There's no need to be snippy,' said Rex.

'But you know what's weird?' said JD. 'Einstein didn't know who I was. Didn't recognise me.'

'He didn't *know* you?' said Jacko, his eyes widening in shock. 'Oh, shit.'

'Oh, shit *what?*' said Elvis.

Jacko grimaced. 'If he didn't recognise JD, then it's because he never met him. You know Einstein created time travel, right? Well, surely it's possible that when he was alive, he time travelled into this time and place, right now. That's the only way to explain why he wouldn't have recognised JD.'

JD walked up to Jacko and grabbed a handful of his piano-key necktie. He pulled him close so Jacko could feel his breath on his face. 'What did Einstein use his time travel for when he was alive?'

'I don't know,' Jacko replied. 'I've seen his files on Scratch's database and there's no mention of where he went when he travelled in time.'

'He was working with Hitler, wasn't he?'

Jacko swallowed hard. 'He may have been. I know he invented time travel in the nineteen-forties, but only because he mentioned it once.'

'Fuck all that,' said Jasmine. 'We need to find out where they took Flake.'

JD let go of Jacko. 'They were travelling by road,' he reminded everyone. 'And this is the road to Despair.'

'Despair?' said Sanchez. 'What the fuck does that mean?'

'It's a town not far from here,' JD replied. 'I've been there all day. And you know what? I think I might know where they're going.'

170

Thirty-eight

As soon as Einstein was free from the grasp of the Bourbon Kid, he tapped his wristwatch and brought up a saved location in his shortcuts section. Things were escalating rapidly, so he pressed a button on the watch to transport him back to his safe place, the chocolate factory on the edge of Despair. After the usual flashing blue light, he reappeared next to the cloning machine on the factory's upper floor. Herman and Hitler were wearing time travel rings connected to the watch, so they were both transported too. Herman reappeared next to Einstein. Hitler wasn't quite so lucky. He had been crouched on the front seat in the van when the transportation took place, so he arrived in the warehouse, floating a few feet off the ground. Consequently, he landed face down on the floor with a powerful thud, a few feet away from Einstein and Herman. But to Einstein's surprise, a second thud indicated the arrival of a fourth person on the factory floor. Flake landed not far from Hitler. She was still unconscious despite the hard landing.

Einstein composed himself and looked around to see if anyone else had come through with them. The only other people in the warehouse were two Jasmine clones, who were playing rock paper scissors. One was wearing a pink bikini, the other had on a red basque, suspenders and crotchless panties. They both waved when they saw Einstein, Herman and Hitler reappear.

'Hi guys,' the one in the bikini called out.

'Hello,' said Herman, waving back.

'What the hell?' said Einstein, staring at Flake. 'How did she get here?'

'I believe she came with us,' Herman replied.

'Yes, I can see that,' said Einstein. 'But how? She was in the back of the van. She shouldn't have come through because none of us were holding onto her. This makes no sense.' He walked over to Flake and rolled her over onto her back. He checked her fingers. 'She's not wearing a ring or a watch,' he said, scratching his head. 'How is this possible?'

'Who cares?' said Hitler, waving a dismissive hand.

Einstein spotted a gold chain around Flake's neck. He pulled open her jacket and lifted up the chain. She had a time-travel ring hanging around it.

Einstein felt a chill wash over him. He unclasped the chain from her neck and took the ring off. After checking its authenticity, he held it up for the others to see. 'How the hell did she get this?' he asked. 'Did one of you two give it to her?'

'Of course not!' said Hitler.

171

'Then how in God's name has she got one?' Einstein muttered.

'Maybe you gave it to her?' suggested the Jasmine in the red basque.

Einstein lost his temper and hurled Flake's ring at the Jasmine. She ducked, and the ring whizzed past her head. It bounced on the floor behind her and kept rolling for another few seconds before it eventually flipped on its side.

Hitler came closer and leaned over Flake. 'The good news is we've still got her,' he said, licking his finger and flattening down his moustache.

'I warned you not to kidnap another stripper,' Einstein hissed at him. 'Now look at the shit we're in. Someone is onto us. They were waiting for us in the parking lot. I fucking knew this would happen.'

'Oh, quit your fussing,' said Hitler, who was still quite drunk.

Einstein slapped Hitler's hand away from Flake's face. 'Stop touching her,' he said. 'We can't clone her now. It's too dangerous. We're going to have to kill her. We just have to wait for her to wake up first because I want to know how she got that time-travel ring.'

'Never mind her,' said Hitler. 'What was this big news you were about to tell us before we got rammed off the road by that idiot.'

'Oh, yeah,' said Einstein, remembering some great news he had been about to give Hitler and Herman. 'Before I came to pick you up from the club, I finished the tests I was running on the cloning machine. It can now clone metals, so we can start creating clones of Herman. It's time to start building our army.'

Hitler beamed a huge smile. 'This is terrific news. We can start sending them back in time to kill off our enemies.'

'How many times do I have to say it?' said Einstein. 'That's too risky, remember? Have you already forgotten how we ended up with an alternate timeline where you'd executed me?'

'Aah, piffle,' said Hitler. 'That won't happen again.'

'It fucking will,' said Einstein. 'For goodness sake, would you just trust me for once? If we're going to kill any world leaders, it'll have to be the ones in the present day.'

'Fine,' said Hitler, pulling a childish face at Einstein. 'I want the German leader taken out first. Then I'll take over my own country again. Then we can kill off that dickhead Russian leader. He thinks he's the new *me*. I'm not having that. Then the British Prime Minister. That guy's a total wimp. And that French president, I want him dead because I hate his face. In a matter of days I'll have the most powerful people in the world kneeling before me.'

172

'Steady on there, General Zod, let's not get ahead of ourselves,' said Einstein, putting a stop to Hitler's latest drunken rant. 'There's a lot of planning to do yet, and a lot of cyborgs to build.'

'So get cloning.'

Einstein took a deep breath through his nose in an attempt to calm himself. 'It'll take about an hour to make a clone of Herman,' he said. 'And in order to prevent the cloning machine from overheating, I'm guessing we can only do maybe six or seven clones a day, and right now, thanks to your latest trip to the strip club, we've got other problems, like dealing with the guy who rammed us off the road.'

'Who was he?' Hitler asked. He pointed at Flake. 'Was he this fräulein's husband or something?'

Herman, who wasn't generally one for speaking much and certainly not one for interrupting, butted into the conversation. 'The man who attacked us with his jeep was the Bourbon Kid,' he said.

'*That* was the Bourbon Kid?' said Einstein, his jaw dropping. 'Oh, fuck. Oh, God, yes it was. I knew I recognised that face from somewhere. And somehow he knew who I was. This is so bad.'

'Stop being such a drama queen,' said Hitler. 'We've got Herman. In case you've forgotten, Herman can't be killed.'

Einstein ignored Hitler and muttered away to himself. 'The Bourbon Kid is a friend of the original Jasmine. If he's on our tail, we've got to get out of here. He's killed thousands of people. The guy is an unstoppable force.'

Hitler shoved Einstein. 'Honestly man, grow a testicle will you! If this guy's a problem, then let's just travel back in time to an hour ago and not kidnap this stripper.'

'Christ, do you *ever* listen to anything I say?' Einstein ranted. 'We cannot travel back to a time where we already existed.'

'All right, keep your knickers on,' Hitler snapped. 'Maybe we could get this Bourbon Kid to join us in our crusade? He could be a powerful ally.'

'That's not how he operates,' said Einstein, his frustration growing by the second. 'This guy would kill you before you could make the offer. In fact, he's probably on his way here already.'

'Yes, but he won't be able to get in here, will he?'

Einstein clutched his chest like he was having a minor heart attack. 'Oh fuck, the real Jasmine could be coming too! If she sees what we've done with all the clones....' He took a deep breath. 'We need to invest in some jockstraps. She's not called Lady Sack-whack for nothing!'

173

Hitler scoffed. 'Pah, I don't know what you're fretting about! I've killed millions of people. I'm not scared of anyone, especially not a porn star.'

'*You* haven't killed millions of people,' said Einstein. 'You've *ordered the deaths* of millions of people. It's not the same thing. The Bourbon Kid, he's killed every one of his victims himself. I heard he shoved a shotgun up a cop's asshole once and blew his guts out.'

'Why would he stick a gun up someone's bum hole?' Hitler asked, perplexed.

'I don't know,' Einstein replied. 'But the rumours about this guy are terrifying.'

'Rumours?' Hitler sneered. 'That's just how people make themselves feared. They create far-fetched stories about their achievements or the weapons they possess. Soon, rumours spread, become exaggerated, and eventually become fact.'

'Well, I know one thing the Bourbon Kid did that definitely isn't a rumour. The thing he's most famous for is a killing spree in Santa Mondega during an eclipse six years ago. He killed everyone in a bar called the Tapioca, then went to the local cop station and murdered all the city's cops too. He killed over a hundred people that day.'

'Santa Mondega?' said Hitler. 'I remember that place. The world leaders all agreed to hide its existence because there was undead activity there.'

'You are correct,' said Herman, joining in the conversation. 'It wasn't included on any maps.'

Einstein pressed a button on his watch and spoke into it. 'Television on,' he said. A giant TV screen on the wall flickered into life. Einstein spoke into his watch again. 'Bring up news reports about the Santa Mondega Lunar Festival massacre.'

Within a second, an image appeared on screen. It featured the front page of a newspaper called, the *Santa Mondega Universal Times*. The headline read -

BOURBON KID STRIKES AGAIN AT LUNAR FESTIVAL

Underneath the headline was a report about the massacre. It backed up everything Einstein had said. He waited for Hitler, who was a notoriously slow reader, to take the information on board. Eventually, the short, angry little German dictator turned to face Einstein. He looked confused.

'Eric, why would anyone be dumb enough to partake in a shootout during an eclipse?'

174

'I don't know,' said Einstein. 'Does it matter?'

'I know the answer,' said Herman. 'I have access to all information regarding this infamous shootout.'

'Go on,' said Hitler.

'The shootout took place because a gang of vampires were attempting to get their hands on a precious blue stone called the Eye of the Moon. The Eye is believed to have special powers, one of which is that it controls the orbit of the moon. The vampires were hoping to use it to make the eclipse permanent. A town cloaked in permanent darkness would be great for vampires, but the Bourbon Kid showed up and killed all the vampires before they could use it.'

'Back up a second there, Herman,' said Hitler. 'You said the Eye of the Moon had special powers. What else could it do besides control the moon?'

Herman spoke like he was reading text from a history book. 'It is believed that the Eye gives eternal life to anyone who possesses it. It also has incredible healing powers, and many hundreds of years ago a man named Rameses Gaius harnessed it as a weapon. He was able to use it to fire electricity from his hands, and also to control inanimate objects like statues. He could bring them to life to carry out his bidding.'

'I want it,' said Hitler. 'Bringing statues to life? How fucking brilliant would that be? And shooting lightning from my hands? I like the sound of that. Fuck yeah, I'd be a total badass.'

'Yes, but we don't know where the Eye is,' Einstein reminded him.

'Oh, yes, we do,' said Hitler. 'It sounds like it was in the Tapioca during that eclipse when the Bourbon Kid killed all the vampires. All you have to do is go back in time to the eclipse and get Herman to kill the Bourbon Kid and retrieve the Eye of the Moon for us. It will be easier to kill the Kid in the past because he won't know us. With the benefit of surprise on our side, Herman can kill him easily. This Bourbon Kid fellow won't stand a chance. He couldn't kill Herman when he met him today. He'll have no chance of doing it in the past when he won't even know Herman is a threat. It can be another Jack the Ripper murder to add to the history books.'

Einstein puffed out his cheeks. 'I'm not sure about this,' he said.

'I am,' said Hitler, pointing at the TV screen. 'Look, the newspaper says that during the Lunar festival everyone was in fancy dress costume. You and Herman can go in disguise if that makes you feel more comfortable.'

'Even though none of us were in this timeline six years ago, it's still a big risk messing with the past,' Einstein argued. 'If we kill the Bourbon Kid, it will affect Jasmine's future. Maybe she won't become a

175

famous porn star, then that will mess up our whole operation. We won't be able to sell any of these clones.'

'I don't care,' Hitler replied. 'You're going back in time to the Lunar festival in Santa Mondega to kill the Bourbon Kid and get me the Eye of the Moon. That's an order.'

Einstein held off saying what he really thought. 'Yes, Fuhrer,' he muttered with as much enthusiasm as he could muster.

'Good. Then you will leave right away.'

'What? Right now?'

'Yes. Right now.'

'Jeez, let me think about this for a minute,' said Einstein, who was a man who liked to plan things in advance. 'It's probably best to go back at least an hour before the eclipse. But we need to interact with as few people as possible while we're there. This isn't like when we went back in time to kill the mothers of your enemies. We were able to do that in the middle of the night when no one would see us, but even so, it was still a big risk. This is going to be *very* tricky.'

'Fine,' said Hitler. 'You've got two hours to concoct a plan, then you and Herman will go back in time again.'

'Yes, Fuhrer.'

Herman declared his thoughts on the plan. 'This will be straightforward,' he announced. 'I have night vision. If we wait for the eclipse to start, I will be at an advantage. I can see perfectly in the dark. The Bourbon Kid will not see me coming. As soon as I see him, I shoot, and he dies. And now that I know what he looks like, I will recognise his facial features in the darkness.'

'Perfect,' said Hitler, happy to see that the cyborg was on board with the plan.

'Hold on a minute,' said Einstein. 'The Bourbon Kid has friends other than just Jasmine. He's got a couple of guys called Elvis and Rodeo Rex. We might have to deal with *them* too. There's lots to consider here.'

'No problem,' said Hitler, clapping his hands together excitedly. 'Once the Bourbon Kid is dead, and we have the Eye of the Moon, we'll look at killing his buddies too.'

In the middle of Hitler's excited hand-clapping, Einstein's watch beeped. He checked its display, then without saying anything, he sprinted over to his desk and sat down in front of his computer.

'What's the matter with you?' Hitler asked him.

Einstein tapped away on his keyboard for a few seconds, staring intently at the screen. Eventually he stopped typing. His face turned even paler than usual. 'They've found us,' he muttered. 'I don't believe it. They've found us.'

176

Hitler frowned. 'Who, the Libyans?'

'The Libyans?' said Einstein, confused. 'What? No, not the Libyans. The Dead Hunters! They're here. In the building!'

'They've come to get *her*,' said Herman, pointing at Flake, who was still asleep on the floor.

Einstein stood up and started gnawing his fingernails. 'Oh fuck, this is so bad. They'll destroy everything we've built here. All my years of hard work will be gone.'

'Oh, calm down, you big nonce,' said Hitler. 'I've got a new plan.'

'What did you call me?'

'He called you a nonce,' said Herman.

'Just shut up and listen,' said Hitler. 'You don't get to be as powerful as me without knowing how to modify your plans at short notice. I'll join you and Herman in travelling back to the Lunar Festival. We'll kill this Bourbon Kid and his friends. Then when we come back here they won't exist. And in the meantime, while we're away, we'll set the Jasmines on them.'

'Set the Jasmines on them?' said Einstein, baffled.

'Yes. Just tell them we have intruders. We can afford to lose a few Jasmines, can't we?'

'But there isn't time to activate them all,' said Einstein. 'And I don't imagine those two over there will be much use in a fight against the Dead Hunters. Let's just get out of here before they show up.'

177

Thirty-nine

Zilas was having the time of his life. With Jacko taking the night off to visit a strip club, Purgatory's resident hunchback was sitting on a stool behind the bar, eating chicken wings and drinking red wine, while watching Jasmine's porno on a loop on the bar's television.

It wasn't until the early hours of the morning that his fun came to an end. The phone Jacko had lent him started ringing, meaning it was time to open the portal and let Jacko back into Purgatory. Zilas muted the television and answered the call.

'Hi Jacko.'

'Zilas, this is urgent,' said Jacko, sounding flustered. 'Use the Purgatory satellite navigation to locate my phone. I'm in a motorhome. Switch the portal location to the motorhome's bathroom, now! I have the Bourbon Kid with me, and he said if you take more than thirty seconds, he's going to rip your insides out.'

'Okay, I'm right on it.'

Zilas ended the call and put the phone down on the bar. *Thirty seconds. Fuck.* First things first, turn off the porno. With that job out of the way, he hopped off his stool. He was wearing a pair of gold, silk pyjamas. They were incredibly comfortable, but useless at hiding erections.

Twenty seconds.

Zilas opened up the portal application on Jacko's computer. Multitasking wasn't one of Zilas's strong points, so locating Jacko's phone, and the motorhome's bathroom, while trying to get rid of a stiffy, was a tricky prospect.

Ten seconds.

That boner was going nowhere. He finally tracked down Jacko's phone, then used the satellite coordinates to zoom in on the motorhome. The app located the motorhome's bathroom almost immediately.

Two seconds.

Portal opened.

Zero.

Beating the clock with virtually no time left made Zilas feel like James Bond, in pyjamas, with a raging woody.

The Bourbon Kid was first through the portal, followed by Jacko, Elvis, Jasmine, then Sanchez, and finally, Rex. JD and Jacko raced behind the bar. Zilas stepped aside and let Jacko take over the computer.

'Thanks, Zilas, you can go now,' said Jacko.

Zilas loitered behind the bar a little longer, facing away from everyone else, staring at the TV, which was switched off.

178

Jacko used the computer's satellite navigation to look for the chocolate factory in Despair. 'Where abouts is it?' he asked JD.

'It's partway up one of the mountains between the two towns. Come on, hurry up. They've got Flake.'

Rex called over to Zilas. 'Yo, Zilas, you were friends with Einstein, weren't you? Did he ever tell you why he was in Hell?'

'Nope, sorry,' said Zilas, without turning around.

'Rex, let's worry about that shit when we get Flake back,' said JD. 'Jacko, hurry up and find the fucking factory so we can get in there.'

'Just give me a minute,' said Jacko, who was clearly flustered, and possibly a little drunk.

Jasmine walked over to a gun cabinet on the wall by the jukebox. She opened it up and helped herself to a pair of pistols and a gun belt. She wrapped the belt around her waist and tucked the pistols into its holsters. Then she reached back into the cabinet for an M16 rifle, which she tossed to Elvis.

Rex called over to her. 'Jas, I'll take those two Skorpions.'

Jasmine unhooked two Skorpion pistols and threw them across the room to Rex. He caught them and checked they were loaded.

'JD, do you need anything?' Jasmine asked, approaching the bar.

'I'll take that taser.'

Jasmine picked a small taser gun from the cabinet. 'Really?' she said, staring at it. 'It's a bit girly for you, isn't it?'

'It can short-circuit the cyborg.'

'Whatever you say.' Jasmine tossed the taser to JD. He caught it and concealed it inside his coat.

'I need a gun,' said Sanchez.

Jasmine reached back into the cabinet and picked out the smallest pistol she could find, a ladies six-shooter. She tossed it to Sanchez, who made a feeble attempt at catching it, juggled with it a few times, and eventually dropped it onto the floor.

'Jacko, have you got any poison?' Jasmine asked.

'Poison?'

'Yeah, I want a handkerchief and some poison. If I get a chance, I'm drugging Einstein or one of his friends, so they'll know how it feels.'

Jacko yelled at Zilas. 'Can you grab Jasmine that stuff we use to kill your headlice?'

Zilas bent down and checked the shelves under the bar for the bottle of poison that was so effective at killing parasites.

'Why would you want to poison Einstein?' Rex asked Jasmine. 'Wouldn't you rather kick him in the face or shoot him in the dick?'

179

'Oh, I'll do that too,' Jasmine replied. 'But he's getting drugged for sure.'

Zilas rose up from below the bar with a bottle of toxic liquid. He poured some into a small vial then placed it on the bar along with a small flannel. 'Here you go Jasmine,' he said. 'I've got no clean hankies, so you'll have to use this flannel.'

'That'll do fine,' said Jasmine. 'Thanks Zilas, you're a stud.'

The "stud" comment brought a smile to Zilas's deformed face, and also sent his pyjama bottoms into overdrive.

'Can we go now?' Elvis asked.

'Got it!' said Jacko, fist-pumping. 'You're good to go.'

The door to the men's toilets slid open and the gang piled through it into a bathroom in the chocolate factory. JD went through first, and Sanchez covered the rear. As soon as everyone was through, Jacko closed up the portal, then turned around and glared at Zilas.

'What's the matter with you?' Zilas asked.

Jacko pointed at Zilas's pyjama bottoms. 'Everyone saw it,' he said, shaking his head.

****

The bathroom on the other side of the portal led through to a dark, musty-smelling factory floor. There were aisles of boxes on both sides and a few fork-lift trucks dotted about the place. At the far end of the room, the length of a football pitch away, a set of stairs led up to a closed off area up above. JD, Elvis, and Rex ran for the stairs. Jasmine hung back with Sanchez to make sure he was okay.

'Flake will be fine,' she assured him. 'Just let the guys do their thing. They won't let anyone hurt her.'

'Look at this place though,' said Sanchez. 'Someone with a gun is bound to be hiding behind one of these boxes.' He shook his head in dismay as JD, Rex, and Elvis ran past a multitude of large boxes and other potential hiding places for armed henchmen.

'Just follow me,' said Jasmine. She headed after the others but took her time, checking both ways for any threats hiding on the ground floor.

Sanchez followed her and crouched as low as he could, which put her ass in his eyeline. 'Have you never seen a warehouse shootout at the end of a B movie?' he asked her. 'The bad guys are always lurking behind boxes and stuff. And there's always a giant container filled with liquid fire or green acid.'

Jasmine stopped and turned around. 'Please shut up,' she whispered.

180

'There's no point in being quiet,' Sanchez said, standing up straight. 'There's security cameras everywhere. They'll know we're here.'

'Fine, stay here and wave at the cameras then.'

Jasmine left Sanchez and hurried after the others. JD was first to the top of the stairs. He entered the room at the top, guns drawn. Rex and Elvis followed him in, and a short while later, Jasmine joined them. Sanchez waited for the inevitable breakout of deafening gunfire, but it never came. Sensing all was well, he climbed the stairs himself, which was exhausting. When he reached the top, he poked his head around the door to see what was going on. JD was sitting on the floor, cradling Flake's head in his arms. Rex, Jasmine, and Elvis were standing close by, talking to a pair of scantily-clad Jasmine clones.

Seeing as how there was no danger in sight, Sanchez rushed over to Flake. 'Is she okay?' he asked JD.

'She's been drugged,' JD replied. 'But she should be okay. We need to get her back to Purgatory. Jacko might have some kind of drug that'll wake her up.'

'Let me handle that,' said Sanchez, pulling the Eye of the Moon from his pocket. He crouched down beside Flake and pressed the Eye against her chest. The blue stone started glowing from inside. After about ten seconds, the colour came back to Flake's face, and she opened her eyes. She looked at Sanchez, then up at JD.

'What the fuck is going on?' she asked.

'You were drugged,' said Sanchez. 'But I brought you back with the Eye of the Moon.'

Flake closed her eyes and winced like someone who had just stared directly into the sun.

'You'll be okay in a minute,' said JD.

Elvis, Jasmine, and Rex finished their conversation with the two Jasmine clones and re-joined the others. Elvis handed Flake her engagement ring. 'Seems like you lost this,' he said.

Flake clutched at her chest and discovered her chain was missing. She slid the ring back on her finger. 'Where was it?' she asked.

'The Jasmine over there with the crotchless panties said Einstein took it from you and chucked it at her.'

'Crotchless panties?' said Sanchez, twisting his head to check. 'How did I miss that?'

Rex tapped JD on the shoulder. 'Hey, we got a bigger problem.'

JD stood up and turned to face Rex. 'Go on then, spit it out.'

'According to these two Jasmine clones, the guy that looked like Hitler, really is Hitler.'

JD nodded like he wasn't surprised. 'Any idea what he's doing here?'

'He's not *here* anymore. Einstein has taken him and the cyborg, who's called Herman, by the way, and they've travelled back in time.'

'To where?'

'To the Lunar Festival in Santa Mondega, the one where you killed Archie Somers.'

'Why would they do that?'

'Because they checked the news reports from back in the day, and they know you were in the Tapioca during the eclipse. They've taken the cyborg back there to kill you and capture the Eye of the Moon.'

Forty

After sending Zilas back down to Hell to change his clothes, Jacko waited anxiously for a text from the others requesting the reopening of the portal. The wait was mercifully short. Rex texted back with the words, "OPEN UP".

Jacko pressed a button on his keypad to open the portal. By the time he looked up JD was marching in, carrying Flake in his arms.

'Is she okay?' Jacko asked.

'I'm fine, thanks,' Flake replied. 'Just a bit woozy.'

JD set her down on a sofa at the back of the room while the others began filtering in through the portal.

'Is someone gonna tell me what happened?' Jacko asked. 'Did you find Einstein?'

'He got away,' said Sanchez. 'Escaped with Hitler and Jack the Ripper.'

'This is so weird,' said Jacko. 'I'm certain Hitler is down in Hell. If it's not him, then it's a damn good lookalike. I hope we haven't got the wrong guy because he's been through some shit down there. Every day he gets gassed to death for breakfast, then at lunch a gang of demons butt-fuck him, then for dinner he gets a pineapple rammed up his asshole. Every day. And twice on Sundays.'

'Never mind all that,' said Elvis. 'Einstein and his buddies have gone back in time to kill JD at the Lunar festival, the one where he killed Archie Somers. Can you send us back there to stop it?'

'Archie Somers?' said Jacko.

'The guy who killed me and Rex,' said Elvis. 'Also known as the Dark Lord Armand Xavier.'

'Oh, him,' said Jacko.

'So can you send us back in time?' Rex asked.

Jacko groaned. 'Sorry, but time travel is off limits. God banned it a while ago.'

Rex leaned over the bar and grabbed the bright red telephone Jacko kept on a shelf. He slammed it into Jacko's chest. 'Call God, and explain the situation,' he said.

'God's not allowed to speak to us down here at the moment.'

'What?' said Elvis. 'Why not?'

'Mrs God found out about him getting a handjob from Jasmine. She was not best pleased. She's banned him from talking to us.'

'How did she find out?' Jasmine asked.

'God kept a video of it on his phone.'

'Rookie mistake,' said Sanchez, shaking his head.

183

'Call Mrs God and ask *her,*' said Rex. 'Time is in short supply here.'

Jacko picked up the red phone's receiver and put it to his ear. 'Mrs God won't want to help,' he warned them. 'I'm telling you, she's holding a grudge against all of us because of the handjob incident.'

Rex offered him an incentive. 'Jacko, look at it this way, if the cyborg kills JD in the past, it'll change the course of history. JD won't become a Dead Hunter, which would probably mean we never kill Scratch. And we might never meet Jasmine, and you'll still be living in the desert by the crossroads, all on your own.'

'Gosh,' said Jasmine. 'If I never meet you guys, that means I'll never become a famous porn star, or fall in love with Elvis.'

'Okay, okay, I'll do it!' said Jacko. He grabbed a bottle of rum from under the bar and took a big swig, then he made the phone call to Heaven.

Everyone else waited by the bar, listening intently.

'Hello, can I speak to Mrs God please?' said Jacko, the phone's receiver quivering in his hand.

'I'm afraid she's busy,' a man on the other end of the line replied. 'She's watching her soaps.'

Jacko closed his eyes tightly in frustration and thought about what to do. 'Who am I speaking with, please?' he asked.

'This is Saint Peter.'

'Okay, Peter, is there any chance I can speak to God?'

'I'm afraid not.'

Jacko tugged at his collar. With everyone staring at him, he had to get this done, but he also had an unhelpful apostle on the other end of the line. 'It's important,' he pleaded. 'I need authorisation for some time travel.'

Peter scoffed. 'Time travel is banned, and you know exactly why. I'm not interrupting Mrs God for a request I know she will say no to.'

Jasmine leaned over the bar and tapped Jacko on the shoulder. 'Put it on speaker,' she said. 'I'll handle this.'

Jacko pressed a button on the phone and opened up the call to everyone else.

'Hi, this is Jasmine. Who are we speaking with, please?'

'Saint Peter.'

'Hi, Pete, I'd like to speak with God please. Tell him its important.'

'I'm afraid God is unavailable,' said Peter. 'He won't be free until tomorrow.'

'Don't be a dick,' Jasmine replied. 'Flake is here with me. She and I both saw him in the strip club staring at her tits.'

184

The line went quiet.

Flake was still on the sofa at the back of the room, but she called over to Jasmine. 'I don't remember seeing—'

Jasmine shushed her before she could finish the sentence.

Everyone in Purgatory was exchanging puzzled looks. No one had seen God in the strip club.

'You *saw* him?' Peter said, quietly.

'Yeah, that's right,' said Jasmine, winking at the others. 'Now if you don't want Mrs God to find out about this, you'll put me through to the man. He must have a cell phone with him.'

'Hold please.'

The line went quiet.

'Did you really see God in the club?' Elvis asked. 'You never said anything.'

'No, I didn't,' Jasmine whispered back.

'How did you know he was there then?'

'Lucky guess.'

Sanchez gasped in shock. 'God's a sneaky weasel, isn't he? What a pervert.'

'For fuckssake,' said Flake, groaning. 'Was there anyone who *didn't* go to watch me strip tonight?'

Saint Peter came back on the phone. 'Hello,' he said.

'Yes,' said Jasmine. 'We're still here.'

'Putting you through now.'

After a click, followed by the sound of two men arguing in the background, God came on the line. He sounded drunk. 'Hey, Jas, wassup?'

'Hi God. I was hoping for a favour.'

'Anything for you, sweetheart.'

Jasmine gave a thumbs up sign to the others to let them know she had the situation under control. 'God, here's the problem. Adolf Hitler, Eric Einstein and Jack the Ripper have travelled back in time to try and kill JD and steal the Eye of the Moon. Do you think you could give us authorisation to travel back in time to stop them?'

God groaned. 'For Chrissakes, didn't I ban time travel the other day?'

'You did, but this is kind of urgent.'

'Well, where in time do you need to go?'

'Back to Santa Mondega on the day of an eclipse where JD murdered a load of people, one of whom was the Dark Lord Somebody-or-other.'

'Armand Xavier?'

185

Jasmine looked around. Everyone else was nodding. 'Yep, that's him,' she said. 'If JD doesn't kill him on that particular day, thousands of innocent people will die.'

God started whispering to someone else on the other end of the line. The other person, also a very drunk man, eventually spoke loudly. 'Fucking hell dad, would you just say yes already?'

'Shhh,' said God.

'Is that Jesus?' asked Jasmine.

'Yeah, yeah, he's here too. Bit pissed though. He drank a lot of cocktails tonight.'

'Fucking hell!' said Flake. 'Did he get a good look too?'

'Is that Flake?' God asked.

'YES IT IS!' Flake called out. 'Could you get a move on with the authorisation, please? We're in a hurry here.'

Some muttering and giggling on the other end of the line came to an end when JD spoke into the phone.

'Hey God, if Hitler and his cyborg kill me in the past, then I won't be around to kill the Devil. Do you really want him back?'

God went quiet for a moment, likely contemplating the return of Scratch. Eventually, after much umm-ing and aah-ing, he said, 'Scratch was doing a pretty good job running Hell. I had no problem with him, to be honest.'

Elvis chipped in next. 'Don't forget JD played a big part in taking down the Four Horsemen of the Apocalypse. If Hitler and his people kill JD, then it could lead to the end of the world.'

There was a pause before God replied. 'Yeah, that would be bad, I suppose.'

'Is that a *yes* then?' Rex asked. 'We can go back in time?'

'Uh, I dunno,' said God. 'The wife is in charge at the moment, and I'm not supposed to make decisions when I'm drunk.'

Rex persisted. 'Yes, but if Hitler succeeds in killing JD it will change the future. Humanity will be doomed!'

'Humanity is doomed anyway,' said God, slurring his words even more than before.

'I don't believe this,' said Sanchez. 'He's not going to authorise it. What a dick.'

Jasmine waved her hand, gesturing for everyone else to shut up. 'This is terrible,' she said, as if talking to the others rather than God. 'If Hitler changes history I might never get to be in a porno or give God a handjob.'

'Okay, I'll approve it,' said God, sounding like he'd sobered up. 'We definitely don't want the Devil back. You have my authorisation.

186

Just don't tell Mrs God. And listen a minute, because this is important. When you go back in time, you cannot interact with anyone other than Einstein and his crew; otherwise, you could alter the lives of everyone else you come into contact with. And you must avoid bumping into your younger selves. I have a failsafe in place that makes people explode if they exist twice in the same moment in time. I'll pause that for you, but even so, if your younger self sees you, it could screw up the whole universe. Your younger selves absolutely must not see you. Understood?'

'Pfft, of course,' said Jasmine. 'I've seen *Back To The Future*. I know how it works.'

'Okay, well good luck then. Just make sure you're heavily disguised so no one recognises you. Oh, and tell Flake I thought she was awesome tonight.'

Flake was about to say something in response, but Jasmine slammed the phone down, ending the conversation abruptly.

'This is gonna be great,' said Elvis. 'I missed the Lunar festival that year because I got killed the day before. That fucking prick Armand Xavier hid behind a door and jumped me, sucker-punching bastard.'

'He killed me too,' said Rex. 'I'd like to go back and watch that asshole get wasted by JD.'

'Did you not listen to God at all just then?' said Flake, standing up. 'This has to be incognito. We all need disguises in case we bump into anyone who knows us.'

'Disguises will be easy,' said Sanchez. 'It's the Lunar festival so everyone will be in fancy dress. You just need a costume that covers your face.'

Forty-one

<u>The Lunar Festival - Santa Mondega - Six years ago</u>

Sanchez despised the influx of unfamiliar faces that arrived in town for the lunar festival. The festival itself was great, but all the extra people really pissed him off. Rumours were rife that the Bourbon Kid was back in town too, and Sanchez really didn't like him. That bastard had a habit of killing the paying customers in the Tapioca.

It was mid-morning on the day of the eclipse, and Sanchez was in Domino's party store. Domino's was a colourful place, filled with masks, hats, costumes, and crazy gadgets. Sanchez waited impatiently at the counter, which was cluttered with lots of small items like fake vampire fangs, trick chewing gum, and fart powder. There was also a new sign hanging above the counter warning customers that there would be a fifty-dollar charge for any items returned that had skid marks in.

The store's owner, Dick Domino, eventually returned from the back room carrying two large clothing bags. Dick was a short, fat, middle-aged man with curly blond hair that made him look like a grown up version of Thurman Merman from the movie *Bad Santa.*

'Here you go, Sanchez,' he said, placing the bags on the counter. 'One Batman costume, and one Robin.'

'Mind if I check them first?' said Sanchez. 'I want to make sure I won't look like Adam West.'

'You could never look like Adam West,' said Dick. 'You don't have his toned physique.'

Sanchez ignored the insult and opened the larger of the packages. 'Awesome,' he said, peering inside. 'You did it. Dick you're a genius.'

The Batman outfit was a perfect replica of the one Michael Keaton wore in the 1989 *Batman* movie. Sanchez closed the bag up again and checked the Robin outfit he'd ordered for his assistant in the Tapioca, a young chap named Mukka. The outfit was a replica of the one worn by Burt Ward in the 1960's *Batman* TV show. Perfect. There was no way Mukka could upstage Sanchez in such a terrible costume.

'You've really come through for me here, Dick,' Sanchez said, handing him Mukka's bank card. 'These costumes are perfect.'

Dick charged the sale to Mukka's card, then handed Sanchez a receipt and some words of advice. 'Make sure you wear underwear with that Batman outfit,' he warned. 'I've just charged you an extra fifty for what you did to the Wampa outfit you borrowed last year.'

188

'Of course,' said Sanchez, unconcerned because the fine was taken from Mukka's debit card. 'Like I told you at the time, those looked like genuine Wampa stains to me.'

'Yeah, right,' said Dick. 'Just keep the bloody costumes clean.'

'Cheers, Dick,' said Sanchez, picking up the packages and heading for the door. 'Have a nice festival day.'

A short distance away, watching from behind a curtain that covered one of the dressing rooms, Eric Einstein and Adolf Hitler waited impatiently for Sanchez to leave. When the fat bartender finally exited the store, they snuck out of the changing room along with their cyborg, Herman. The three of them made their way up to the counter to speak to Dick Domino.

'Hello gentlemen,' said Dick. 'I didn't see you come in.'

'We used our invisible man costumes,' Einstein joked.

Dick said nothing. It was as if he'd heard the joke before.

'I was wondering if we could get some stormtrooper costumes,' Einstein asked.

'Pfft,' said Dick. 'You've gotta be kidding. You're way too late for those. All the good stuff is already gone. You needed to book up about a month ago.'

'Well, what have you got?' Einstein asked. 'We'd like some good disguises. Stuff that covers our faces so we don't get recognised.'

Dick studied the three men standing before him. After a few seconds he nodded at Hitler. 'I can give you a bowler hat and a black suit to go with your Charlie Chaplin moustache. How would that be?'

'Perfect,' said Hitler. 'I'll take it.'

'What about me and the big fella?' said Einstein, pointing his thumb at Herman who was standing just behind him. 'You must have *something* for us? Even if it's just face masks?'

Dick rubbed his chin. 'Hmm, well, I guess there is one thing. Are you okay having your face painted?'

'Painted? I guess so.'

'Great. In that case I've got something *you* can have.'

'What about Herman?' said Hitler. 'Could you get him a Terminator costume?'

'Too late, buddy,' said Dick. 'I rented out the last one of those yesterday.'

'What else do you have that might fit him?'

Dick looked up at Herman and sucked in some air through gritted teeth. 'I guess there is one thing I can do for you,' he said. 'But if anyone asks, you didn't get it here. I don't want people thinking I've no respect for the dead.'

189

'Who died?' Einstein asked.

'You heard of Elvis?'

'Of course I've heard of Elvis,' said Einstein.

'Well, a local Elvis-impersonating hitman was murdered this week. And as a mark of respect, no one round here is dressing as Elvis Presley today. But, seeing as how you guys are desperate, I do have an Elvis costume that would fit your big friend just fine. With him being such a big fella, I guess no one will give him too much shit for wearing it.'

'Wait a second,' said Einstein. 'Elvis the hitman is dead?'

'Yep.' Dick reached below the counter and picked up a newspaper called the Daily Scope. He slapped it down on the counter. There was a picture of Elvis on the front page, along with the headline, "ELVIS, LATEST VICTIM OF SERIAL KILLER".

'That's incredible,' said Einstein. He whispered into Hitler's ear. 'I wonder if *we* did that somehow?'

'Someone nailed him to the ceiling of an apartment in Shamrock House,' said Dick. 'His buddy Rodeo Rex was killed last night too. They found him all fucked up in the Nightjar. Torn to bits apparently. It's put a dampener on the festival, for sure. I loved those guys. Lotta people did.'

Einstein did his best to contain his glee. This was great news. Two of his enemies were dead already, murdered in the last twenty-four hours. It barely made sense, but it was very exciting.

'Anyway, I'll go get your costumes,' said Dick. 'It'll be a hundred and twenty bucks in total.'

'Yes sir,' said Einstein. 'Thank you so much.'

As soon as Dick was out of earshot, Einstein turned to Hitler. 'Did you hear that?' he said. 'Elvis and Rex are dead already.'

'See,' said Hitler. 'Our mission is going to be a success. All we have to do is kill the Bourbon Kid. I told you this would be easy.'

'I'm not sure it will be easy,' said Einstein. 'But, at least two of our targets are dead already.'

'Let's just get a move on. It smells in this place.'

Herman interrupted them. 'Shush, he's coming back.'

Dick returned a few seconds later with three large bags containing the outfits. 'Here you go,' he said, sliding them across the counter.

Einstein opened up one of the bags and peeked inside. There was an Elvis costume that consisted of a red shirt with white tasselled sleeves and a pair of flared red pants with a thick yellow stripe down the side of each leg. There was also a terrible black wig, some cheap gold jewellery and a pair of sunglasses to top the outfit off. Einstein handed the bag to

190

Herman, and then opened the second bag. It contained a shabby black suit and hat for Hitler, as well as a walking cane.

'One Charlie Chaplin suit,' he said, handing it to Hitler.

Hitler took a look inside the bag. A rare smile broke out on his face.

'You can use my changing rooms if you like,' said Dick, generously. 'And for an extra ten bucks I'll keep your old clothes out back in a locker for you.'

'That would be great, thanks,' said Einstein. He waved Hitler and Herman away. They took the hint and headed for the changing rooms.

Einstein opened the final bag. It contained a red hat, red pants, big red shoes, a fake white beard, a padded blue top, and a can of blue spray-paint.

'What the fuck is this?' he asked, glaring at Dick.

'That's a hundred and twenty bucks, please,' Dick replied, holding out his hand.

Einstein reached into his pocket and pulled out some cash. But before handing it over, he asked again. 'What is this costume? Santa Claus?'

'Papa Smurf,' said Dick. 'That blue spray is very popular with people wanting to look like avatars or Smurfs.'

Einstein turned his nose up at the costume. 'Have you really not got anything better than this?'

'Nope. It's that or nothing.'

Einstein muttered some insults under his breath but handed over the cash anyway.

'It'll look great when it's on,' said Dick. 'The costumes are due back in four days' time. There's a twenty dollar fine for every day they're late. And fifty bucks extra for any skid marks.'

Einstein picked up his bag. 'Great, thank you,' he muttered.

When he joined Hitler and Herman in the changing room, Hitler was already in his Charlie Chaplin outfit. Herman was in the process of becoming Elvis. Einstein handed Hitler the can of blue spray paint.

'You're going to have to spray my face blue for me,' he said.

'No problem,' Hitler replied. 'But first, I've got to tell you about a plan I had.'

'Go on,' said Einstein, expecting the plan to be crap.

'I was thinking about what the man on the counter just told us about Elvis and Rex being killed yesterday.'

'What about it?'

'If I can get to the city morgue and locate their bodies, I can bring them back from the dead.'

Einstein frowned. 'Why would you wanna do that?'

191

Hitler gave Einstein a backhand slap on the shoulder. 'You've seen what happens when I bring people back to life. They *do* what I tell them to do. I can order them to help us kill the Bourbon Kid and find the Eye of the Moon.'

'Isn't that what we've got Herman for?'

Hitler let out a short, mocking laugh. 'Eric my dear boy, when in war, get your enemies to kill each other. With Rex and Elvis on our side, our chances of eliminating the Bourbon Kid increase exponentially!'

Einstein looked at his watch. 'We've got less than an hour until the eclipse, and I'm not even in my costume yet.'

'No problem. Herman will accompany me to the morgue. You can stay here and finish getting changed. When you're ready, come to the morgue.'

'I don't know where the morgue is!'

'Fine, just wait outside this place for us then. We'll meet you back here once we've acquired our new recruits.'

'Do you even know where the morgue is?'

Hitler held up the blue can of paint and pointed it at Einstein's face. 'Herman knows. He says it's less than two hundred metres from here. Close your eyes.'

Einstein closed his eyes and Hitler sprayed blue paint all over his face to give him the authentic Smurf look.

'Keep your eyes closed for a minute to let it settle,' Hitler said.

While Einstein kept his eyes shut tight, Hitler, the sneaky fucker unclasped Einstein's time-travel watch from his wrist and put it on his own.

'Hey, what are you doing?' Einstein asked.

Hitler patted him on the shoulder. 'My dear boy, in the event that something goes wrong and we can't find each other, we will all meet up at the Tapioca five minutes before the eclipse. See you soon. Come on, Herman, let's get to the morgue.'

'Can I open my eyes yet?' Einstein asked. 'You can't leave me here with my eyes shut!'

'Don't have a shit fit,' said Hitler, laughing. 'If we get separated, I'll use the watch to come find you.' He removed his travel ring from his finger and pressed it into Einstein's palm. 'You can have my ring.'

'But how will you know for sure where I am?'

'Herman will track you down. Calm down and put your beard on.'

192

Forty-two

Jacko missed the days of being bored and lonely. Purgatory was awash with noise, most of it bickering. Jasmine, Elvis, Rex, and Sanchez were sitting at the bar arguing about what was the best place in Santa Mondega to travel back in time to. JD had wandered outside for a smoke, and some peace and quiet.

'I say the library,' said Elvis. 'It was always dead in there.'

'It was always dead in the morgue too,' said Sanchez.

'The museum is a better shout,' said Rex. 'No one ever went into the museum because it was fucking shit.'

'Hold on a goddamn minute,' said Jacko. 'Before we get ahead of ourselves, let's get a few things clear. Who apart from JD was in Santa Mondega during the lunar eclipse?'

'I was there,' said Sanchez. 'In the Tapioca, obviously.'

'Did you go anywhere else?' Jacko asked. 'If I'm sending you back in time to an hour before the eclipse, it's imperative you don't bump into your younger self.'

'I was out and about in town for a while in the morning,' Sanchez admitted. 'I picked up my Batman costume from Domino's in the morning, I remember that.'

'It might be best if you don't go on this mission then,' Jacko suggested.

Sanchez's eyes lit up. 'Damn, I guess I'm out then,' he said, trying to sound disappointed.

'Okay, Sanchez stays here,' said Jacko. 'Anyone else?'

'I wasn't there,' said Jasmine. 'I was in B Movie Hell back in those days.'

'Great, so Jasmine's in. Elvis and Rex are in because they were killed the day before the eclipse.'

'Jeez, that's so creepy,' said Jasmine, looking at Rex. 'I can't believe you were dead. Technically that makes you a zombie, I suppose.'

'Elvis was dead too,' Rex reminded her.

'Yeah, but he doesn't have that zombie look about him.'

'What zombie look?' said Rex, rising to the bait.

'Lucky we had the foresight to make deals with the Devil,' said Elvis. 'Otherwise, we'd be up in Heaven or down in Hell.'

Jacko switched his attention to Flake, who was sitting at the back of the bar on a sofa, still recovering from being drugged by Einstein's cyborg. 'What about you, Flake? Were you in Santa Mondega that day?'

Flake nodded. 'I was.'

'And? What were you doing?'

'I was going to the Tapioca for the eclipse, but I never actually got there.'

'Where did you end up then?' Sanchez asked.

'Well, like I said, I was on the way there, but then I met someone and went somewhere else.'

'Where did you go?' Jacko asked. 'This is important. We mustn't have anyone bumping into you.'

Flake blushed.

'Ooh,' said Jasmine. 'What were you doing, Flake?'

'I hooked up with someone.'

'Was it a chick?' Elvis asked. 'I bet it was, wasn't it?'

'Dream on,' Flake replied, giving Elvis the middle finger.

'But where were you?' Jacko asked.

Flake avoided eye contact with everyone. 'I was in an alleyway.'

'Doing what?' Sanchez asked.

'Does it matter?'

'Ooh, I know!' said Jasmine.

'No you don't,' said Flake, glaring at her.

'Hey, look,' said Rex, 'By the sounds of it, Flake should stay here with Sanchez. Me, Jas, Elvis, and JD can handle this one ourselves.'

'No fucking way!' said Flake, jumping up from the sofa to prove she was recovering well from the aftereffects of being drugged. 'I didn't just strut up and down on a stage with no clothes on, only to then get left out of the very next mission. I'm a Dead Hunter now, officially, so whether you like it or not, I'm coming with you.'

'I got no problem with that,' said JD, who had made his way back to the bar without anyone noticing. 'In fact, if Flake takes the Eye of the Moon with her, she'll be a useful weapon. That thing can fire bolts of electricity that could be useful against Herman the cyborg.'

Sanchez reached into his pocket and pulled out the Eye of the Moon. 'How the fuck do you fire electricity with it?' he asked, a puzzled look on his face.

'I've seen it done,' said JD.

'Me too,' said Jasmine.

Sanchez frowned. 'I had this thing for years and it never fired electricity at anyone.'

'It's not the Eye that fires the electricity,' said Jasmine. 'It's the person wearing it who fires it from their fingers.'

'Like Emperor Palpatine?' said Sanchez. He pointed his hands at Jasmine and tried in vain to blast some electricity at her.

'Loser,' said Jasmine, rolling her eyes.

'Flake will be able to do it,' said JD. 'It just takes a bit of practice.'

194

'Sanchez, give me the Eye,' said Flake. 'I'll see if I can use it.'

Sanchez reluctantly handed the Eye of the Moon over to Flake. She tucked it in the pocket on her jeans, then held up her hands and pointed her fingers at a nearby table. She thrust her hands forward like a low-budget magician. But nothing happened, and no amount of thrusting with her hands made any difference.

'Are you sure about this?' she asked JD.

'Trust me,' he said. 'If you're in a spot of bother, you can blast the fuck out of anyone. It's all about gut feeling and necessity. The furniture is no threat to you, but if it was, I'm sure you could blast it.'

'I think I'd prefer a gun,' Flake replied, giving up on attacking the table.

'Great,' said Jasmine. 'Flake's in then.'

'I'm cool with that,' said Elvis. 'She can show us where the infamous alleyway is.'

Flake scowled at him. 'Did you not listen to Jacko? We can't interact with ourselves in the past.'

'I was kidding,' said Elvis, grinning. 'Jeez, what were you up to in that alley anyway? Was it a gang bang?'

'At least I wasn't dead, like some people,' Flake retorted.

Sanchez stretched his arms and yawned as if tired of the arguing. 'If it's okay with everyone else, I'll go back to the Tapioca,' he said. 'I could use a lie down after all this excitement.'

Flake grabbed Sanchez and kissed him on the cheek, then she took off her engagement ring and slid it onto his pinky finger.

'What are you doing?' Sanchez asked.

'I want you to keep hold of this until I get back,' she replied. 'If anything happens to me you'll have it to remember me by.'

'Christ, that's a bit morbid.'

Rex hopped off his bar stool and stretched his arms. 'Are you ready yet?' he asked Jacko.

'Almost.'

Jacko was using the computer behind the bar to set up the correct time and location in Santa Mondega to send them to. 'Okay, I've got it,' he said. 'I'll send you through the portal to the city museum. How's that sound? You will arrive there at eleven a.m. I will reopen the portal in the museum for you at twelve-thirty, by which time you should have done what you had to do, okay?'

A few mutters of approval followed.

'What about costumes for the festival?' said Elvis. 'Jacko, you got anything here we can wear?'

'Do I look like a fucking cosplay store?'

'You must have some scary-looking shit down in Hell,' Elvis pointed out.

'Like what?'

'I know,' said Sanchez. 'I saw a movie the other day called *Nuns on the Run*. It was about a bunch of blokes dressed as nuns trying to hide from the cops and stuff.'

'I'm not dressing as a fucking nun!' said Rex.

'I used to dress as a sexy nun when I worked at the Beaver Palace,' said Jasmine. 'You can hide a lot of weapons under one of those outfits.'

'And we do have a lot of nuns in Hell,' said Jacko. 'I can get a bunch of nun outfits up here in under five minutes.'

'I'm in,' said Flake.

'I'm not going as a fucking nun,' said Rex. 'But I don't mind going as a monk. Can you get some monk outfits for me and Elvis?'

'Fine,' said Jacko. 'Two monk outfits and two nun outfits.' He looked at JD. 'You want a disguise?'

'Just get me a hockey mask. I only need to hide my face.'

'Okay. One hockey mask.'

Jacko made a call down to Zilas in hell. Five minutes later the hunchback showed up with clothing he'd taken from two nuns and two monks, and a red and white hockey mask like the one worn by Keanu Reeves in the movie *Youngblood*. It should have come as no surprise to anyone, but the monk robes were too small for Rex and Elvis, and the nuns' habits were too big for Jasmine and Flake. And so it ended up with Rex and Elvis dressed as nuns, while Flake and Jasmine donned the monk robes. Jasmine had a hooded brown robe, Flake a black one.

'Okay, listen up,' said JD, when everyone was ready. 'We're going to split into two groups. Rex and Elvis, you two will go to the library.'

'What for?' Rex asked.

'To learn how to be quiet,' said JD, irritated by the interruption. 'From there you can approach the Tapioca from the north. Me and Flake and Jasmine will go to the museum so we can approach from the south. It doubles our chances of seeing Einstein, Hitler, and their cyborg before the eclipse. If we get no luck, then we'll all meet across the street from the Tapioca at five to twelve.'

No one argued with the plan because JD had that murderous level of gravel in his voice that suggested he was in no mood to fuck around.

'Okay, right, the library and the museum,' said Jacko with a sigh. 'And don't forget, you *cannot* set foot inside the Tapioca. That's an absolute no go. Too risky. And don't interact with your younger selves, or anyone else if you can help it, especially not Archie Somers, Jessica the vampire Queen, El Santino, Dante and Kacy, the two Hubal monks,

196

or any of the other major players in that eclipse shootout. Discretion is key. Oh, and if possible, try to avoid killing anyone in view of the public. You risk changing the lives of everyone who witnesses it.'

'Yeah, thanks, genius,' said Rex. 'We all know how it works.'

'I know you do,' said Jacko. 'And I also know you're bound to break every fucking rule I just mentioned.'

'He's got a point,' said Elvis.

'Look,' said Jacko. 'Make sure you're all done by 12.30, because that's when I'm going to reopen the portal in the museum. Make sure you're all there on time, okay?'

'Yeah, yeah, we hear you loud and clear,' said Rex. 'Anything else?'

'That's all,' said Jacko. 'Good luck and be careful.'

Forty-three

All was quiet in the Santa Mondega city library. Ulrika Price, the head librarian had just locked up and was preparing to head into town to celebrate the eclipse. She was well known around Santa Mondega for lacking any sense of fun, but the upcoming eclipse had her in a playful mood, by her miserable standards. The lunar festival had given her the excuse to wear a special item of clothing she had bought at an auction. It had cost her a small fortune but it had been worth every penny. Ulrika was a big fan of cardigans and had recently become the proud owner of the most famous cardigan in the world, the one worn by Paul Michael Glaser in the opening credits of the *Starsky and Hutch* TV show. She was sure she would be the envy of cardigan-loving librarians everywhere. Her Starsky outfit was finished off with a pair of cruddy blue jeans and a black curly wig.

Before closing up the library, she always made a point of checking to make sure no one was hiding in the book aisles. It was a tedious job, but it had to be done because in recent years the library had become a haven for unsavoury types who liked to carry out drug deals or perform sex acts on each other. After ensuring the aisles and reading areas were free of perverts and junkies, she headed to the toilets, another place frequented by unsavoury sorts. As she reached for the handle on the door of the men's toilets, someone on the other side shoved it open with great force. The door hit Ulrika in the face and knocked her wig off. She lost her footing and fell backwards. Her head cracked on the tiled floor. The last thing she saw as she drifted into a state of unconsciousness was a pair of heavy-set nuns walking out of the men's bathroom.

The nun who had slammed the door into Ulrika's face was Elvis. He stopped short of tripping over her on his way out of the door.

'Is that Ulrika Price?' he asked.

Rex peered down at the unconscious librarian. 'Judging by the cardigan, I'd say yes.'

'Why is she lying on the floor? Is she wasted?'

Rex picked up Ulrika's curly black wig and placed it over her face. 'I don't know,' he said. 'Let's not hang around though. She's one of the people who could recognise us, so let's get out of here before she wakes up.'

The two of them left Ulrika sleeping on the floor and made their way to the staircase that led down to the exit on the ground floor.

'You know we could have a lot of fun with this,' said Elvis.

'With what?'

198

'People think we're dead. We could go haunt some people. Armand Xavier would shit his pants if he saw us.'

'Did you listen to anything Jacko just said?'

'Not really.'

'Well, we're not speaking to anyone. We're gonna be totally discreet, understand?'

'Fine.'

When they reached the exit, they came to a set of wooden-double doors. Elvis tried pushing them open with no success. After pulling, then rattling the doors a bit, he stepped back.

'Doors are locked,' he said.

'Do you think you made enough noise?' said Rex. 'We're supposed to be discreet remember?'

'What do you suggest then? Caressing the doors open?'

'Step aside.'

Elvis moved away from the doors. Rex stepped up and punched the lock with his metal hand. The lock shattered and one of the doors fell off its hinges and bounced down the concrete steps outside. A number of people passing by in the street stopped and stared at the door, then up at the entrance where Rex and Elvis were standing.

'That's really discreet,' said Elvis. 'What are you gonna do for your next trick? Song and dance routine? Set yourself on fire?'

'Oh, shut up. Let's get moving.'

'We should have just taken Ulrika's keys. That would have been easier.'

Rex muttered something under his breath, then the two of them headed down the steps to the street. The Lunar festival was well underway. There were people everywhere dressed in all kinds of wacky costumes. Once Rex and Elvis mingled in with the crowd, no one paid them any attention in their nun outfits.

****

Jasmine, Flake, and JD left Purgatory via the portal and arrived in a stall in the men's washroom at the Santa Mondega Museum of Art and History. Jasmine pushed the stall door open and strolled out. The hood on her robe was down.

'Put your hood up,' Flake hissed at her as she followed her out of the stall.

Further along the washroom, a man in a cheap grey suit, with a terrible blond ponytail, was checking his teeth in a long mirror above a

199

row of wash basins. In the mirror's reflection, he caught sight of Jasmine walking out of the end stall with Flake just behind her.

'Hello there,' he said, eyeing up Jasmine and her hooded friend. 'Having some fun in there were we?'

Jasmine smiled back at him. 'Care to join us?' she asked. 'We're always looking for a man to spice things up?'

The man turned to face them. A creepy smile broke out on his face. He looked impressed by what he saw. 'You two wearing anything under those robes?' he asked, his smile turning into a predatory sneer.

Flake knew who he was so she kept her head down so he couldn't get a good look at her face. His name was Elijah Simmonds and he worked at the museum. He was known around town for being a slimy pervert.

Jasmine walked past Simmonds, running her fingers down his arm as she went. He turned his back on Flake and gawped at Jasmine as she untied the rope that held her robe together. He licked his lips in anticipation of what he was about to see.

SMACK!

JD raced out of the toilet stall and blindsided Simmonds with a punch to the head. Simmonds fell back and hit his head on one of the washbasins. It knocked him the fuck out, and he slid to the floor. JD dragged him up by his ponytail and manoeuvred him into the nearest stall. He pushed Simmonds onto his knees and shoved his face into the toilet bowl, which hadn't been flushed. The museum's assistant manager remained there on his knees getting a good sniff of something he himself had dropped in there just a minute earlier.

'Wow,' said Jasmine. 'He seemed quite nice too.'

'He was a dickhead,' said Flake and JD in unison.

Jasmine picked up a loo-brush from a carton of cleaning products in the corner of the washroom, then she walked into the stall and positioned herself behind Elijah Simmonds. She unbuckled his belt and pulled his trousers and underpants down.

'What are you doing?' Flake asked.

'It's an art museum, isn't it?' said Jasmine, shoving the bristly end of the loo brush into Simmonds's butthole. 'I'm making this look like a work of art.'

Flake and JD acknowledged Jasmine's contribution to the museum, then the three of them left the men's washroom and headed out of the museum via a fire exit without anyone else seeing them.

There was a real carnival atmosphere outside in the streets. People were dressed in crazy costumes, and there was loud music coming from all directions. A mix of different songs that were completely

200

incompatible were fighting for the airwaves. And even though it wasn't even midday there were a lot of drunk people around already. Stalls in the streets were selling festival merchandise like mugs with pictures of an eclipse on them, and T-shirts describing Santa Mondega as the city that doesn't exist. No one paid much attention to the two women dressed as monks or their companion in the long hooded coat and the hockey mask.

'Which way are we going?' Jasmine asked.

'I'll head across to the other side of the street,' said JD. 'You two head down this side. If you see Einstein or the others, come get me. Otherwise, meet up outside Rita Miller's charity store on the corner of Ramsay Street.'

JD didn't wait for them to agree with him. He headed across the street, knocking into a few people as he went, then he disappeared behind a group of people dressed as stormtroopers. Jasmine and Flake made their way through the crowds on their own side of the street.

'This festival is just the best,' said Jasmine, looking around and marvelling at all the costumes.

'I know,' Flake agreed. 'The festival was always so much fun. It was one of the only times everybody in town was in a good mood.'

'Do you recognise any of these people?' Jasmine asked.

Flake was doing her best to keep her face concealed beneath her hood. 'I've seen a few familiar faces,' she replied. 'Unfortunately all of them are dead now. A few of them were killed during the eclipse at midday, probably by JD.'

Jasmine shoved Flake into a shop doorway, almost knocking her over.

'What was that for?' Flake protested.

'I think I just saw Hitler and the cyborg!'

Flake wriggled free of Jasmine and peered down the street. 'Where?'

'Hitler just went into that building on the corner. The cyborg is standing guard outside. See him? He's in a red suit.'

Flake stood on tiptoe to get a better look over the crowd of people in the street. 'I see him,' she said. 'That's the morgue. Fuck, we need to tell JD.'

Flake's words were almost drowned out by a nearby car radio blaring out the song "My Sharona" by The Knack. A yellow Cadillac cruised past and stopped at a set of lights up ahead, blocking their view. Flake recognised the driver. 'That's Dante in the Cadillac,' she said, pointing.

'The man dressed like a Terminator?'

'Yeah, that's definitely him. He'll be in the Tapioca during the shootout. His girlfriend Kacy goes as a clown. But she's not in the car with him.'

'I've never met Dante before,' said Jasmine. 'But that cyborg dude is staring at him like it knows him.'

The cyborg was indeed staring at the driver of the yellow Cadillac. After a few seconds, it deserted its post outside the morgue and headed towards Dante's car. Dante, seemingly panicked by the sight of an oversized Elvis impersonator heading towards him, drove off, tyres screeching, without waiting for the traffic lights to change to green.

'This is our chance,' said Flake. 'The cyborg's left Hitler unguarded. Let's get over there and get into the morgue before he comes back.'

'What about JD? Where the fuck is he?'

'Call him.'

Jasmine checked her phone as she and Flake walked out into traffic. 'I've got no signal,' she said. 'How about you?'

Flake ignored her and hurried across the street. Jasmine put her phone back in a pocket on her brown robe and then stepped in front of a big red Hummer. The driver, a big fucker dressed like Gene Simmons from Kiss, honked his horn and yelled something abusive at her. Jasmine lowered her hood and blew a kiss at him. The Kiss frontman, recognising that the monk was actually a hot chick, poked his tongue out and wiggled it at her. Jasmine waved back, then hopped onto the other side of the street, where Flake was waving someone towards her.

'JD's coming,' she said to Jasmine.

JD made his way through the crowd, keeping himself out of sight of the Gene Simmons lookalike in the Hummer, then joined Flake and Jasmine outside the morgue.

'Hitler is in here,' Flake informed him. 'And the cyborg has gone that way. He looked like he was following Dante.'

'Dante? Why the fuck would the cyborg be following him?'

'I don't know, but he's driving a yellow Cadillac.'

JD made a quick decision. 'You two go into the morgue and go after Hitler. I'll follow the cyborg.'

'He's wearing a red suit and a black wig,' said Jasmine, pointing down the street. 'He went that way.'

'Are you sure you don't want to come with us?' Flake asked JD.

JD shook his head. 'You don't need me. Hitler's a pussy. Kill him then stick him in one of the incinerators and burn the prick. When you're done, give me a call.'

202

'I can't get a phone signal here,' said Jasmine. 'Maybe because we're in the wrong time zone?'

'Don't worry about it,' said JD. 'If you can't find me, just head to Rita Miller's like we agreed. I'll meet you there.'

'What are you going to do with the cyborg?' Flake asked.

'I'll figure that out when I see him.'

Forty-four

Hitler and Herman's short walk to the morgue was quite an eye-opener. Hitler was stunned by the sight of so many common folk drinking and having a good time in the streets of Santa Mondega.

'This is madness,' he said to Herman as they made their way through the crowds. 'Where are the police? They should be overseeing this event. Look over there! Two people snogging in broad daylight. I'm appalled. I'll tell you now, when I take over the world, I'll see to it that all this fun and frolicking is controlled by the government. These people are too stupid to know what's best for them.'

Herman's response was not what Hitler was looking for. 'Mr Hitler, is it possible you are not getting enough fibre in your diet?'

'Never you mind about my bloody diet. Look at them there! That woman should be thrown in prison for dressing like that in public.'

'She's dressed as the porn version of Wonder Woman.'

'Porn? I'll have that banned as well. Disgusting. Common people should be kept away from that sort of thing.'

'You watch porn though.'

'What?'

'I've seen it on your internet history, Mr Hitler. You're really into—'

'How dare you! It's none of your business what I look at on the internet.' Hitler snapped. 'It's okay for people like me to watch porn because I'm a responsible individual, but the commoners shouldn't be watching that sort of thing. They'll lose their morals and start behaving terribly.'

'Yes sir.' Herman pointed up ahead. 'The morgue is the building on the corner.'

'Good. I can't wait to get in there. I'd rather hang out with the dead people in the morgue than this immoral bunch of halfwits out here.'

Herman led the way, barging people aside so Hitler could walk through the crowd without being touched by anyone of lesser value than himself. When they arrived outside the morgue, Herman stepped aside so Hitler could walk up the path to the front entrance, but the Nazi leader hesitated because something had caught his eye.

'Look at that,' he said, pointing at a Chinese restaurant next to the morgue. 'This truly is a strange city. Who would order food from a restaurant that was next to a morgue?'

'Drunk people would,' Herman replied.

Hitler was somewhat irked by Herman answering his rhetorical question. 'I'm going inside to find some corpses,' he said. 'If I need you,

204

I'll call for you. You stand guard outside the entrance. If you happen to see the Bourbon Kid, you have my permission to kill him, understand?'

'Yes, sir.'

'Good, I should only be a few minutes.'

Hitler skipped up two small steps at the front of the morgue and made his way inside. Herman stayed by the entrance and scanned the crowds of people for any sign of the Bourbon Kid. The sunglasses that came with the Elvis outfit were ideal because they shielded his eyes and allowed him to scan people's faces without them knowing he was staring at them. It took less than twenty seconds to spot a known associate of the Kid. A yellow Cadillac stopped at a set of red lights on a nearby junction. The driver was a man in a black leather jacket and sunglasses. The database in Herman's brain pulled up all known information on him in less than a second. His name was Dante Vittori. He had once been arrested on suspicion of being an accomplice of the Bourbon Kid during the Tapioca massacre that was due to take place in less than an hour.

PROBABILITY OF DANTE VITTORI MEETING UP WITH BOURBON KID BEFORE ECLIPSE - 62%

Herman liked those odds. He left his spot outside the morgue and marched towards the yellow Cadillac. Dante Vittori clocked him approaching and panicked. Before the traffic lights changed to green, he hit the gas, jumped the red light and sped off, tyres screeching.

Herman chased after him but after running for 4.82 seconds, the chase became pointless. The odds of catching the yellow Cadillac were less than 2%. The pursuit had to end. Herman stopped outside a tall building made of red brick. A sign above its entrance indicated it was the Santa Mondega Court House.

BZZZZZ!

Herman stiffened up. He recognised what had happened. Someone behind him had shot him with a taser gun. The last time he had been tased, it had short-circuited his system, resulting in him waking up handcuffed in a police station. Since then, Eric Einstein, his creator, had fixed that issue. Tasers no longer caused Herman to short-circuit. They were just irritating. He turned around and saw a man in a long black coat holding a taser gun. The man's face was concealed behind a hockey mask.

Herman reached out to grab the taser, but the man had fast reflexes and pulled it away before firing another shot of electricity at Herman's head. It tickled a little and knocked his sunglasses off, but did no damage to him. Herman threw a lightning fast punch that hit the masked man on the side of the head. The force of the blow knocked him sideways into a pillar at the front of the courthouse. The combination of the blow from Herman and the collision with the pillar knocked him unconscious.

In spite of Herman's attempt at discretion, the assault didn't go unnoticed. Four young cheerleaders in red skirts and white tops were standing nearby, waving pom-poms at people they liked the look of. One of them, a buxom blonde, yelled at Herman.

'Hey, dickhead! What's your problem?'

Herman ignored her and picked up his sunglasses while he weighed up his options. By the time he had tucked the sunglasses into the top pocket on his red jacket, he had come to the conclusion that the best thing to do was head back to the morgue to check on Hitler's progress. Unfortunately, his path back was blocked by a pretty brunette cheerleader.

'Hey, cheese dick!' she said, waving her pom-poms in his face. 'Hitting people is not cool.'

'Move, bitch,' said Herman.

When the cheerleader ignored his demand, he shoved her in the face, pushing her onto the ground. The assault drew the ire of a number of other people nearby. Car horns were beeped, and the other cheerleaders started screaming abuse at Herman. Words like, "knobhead, cocksucker, wanker, shit-for-brains, and fuckhead" were added to the cyborg's vocabulary. Herman ignored it all and walked back to the morgue.

206

Forty-five

Einstein finished turning himself into Papa Smurf and checked his reflection in the changing room mirror. He looked ridiculous, and the blue face paint was going to be a bastard to get off. The thing bothering him most though was the fact he no longer had his time-travel watch. The watch was so useful for escaping from tricky situations, but Hitler now had it, because Hitler always got everything he wanted. Always. The rotten, bullying fuckface. Einstein was seriously regretting bringing Hitler into the future with him. He looked at the ring on his finger. It was useless when not in the range of the watch. Fucking Hitler. Wanker.

When the time came to leave Domino's and wait outside, Einstein was amazed by what he saw. There were people everywhere, in all kinds of crazy costumes. And there were some hot babes too. Lots of people were making out in the street, their inhibitions seemingly non-existent in the midst of the festival. Einstein sensed an opportunity to have some fun while he waited for Hitler and Herman to return. And even though interacting with people in the past was a risk, a quick snog and a grope wouldn't do anyone any harm. He set his sights on a sexy young lady dressed as Harley Quinn walking nearby, unaccompanied.

'Hey there,' he said, approaching her with a smile.

'Dream on, loser,' she said, marching past him.

Not a great start. He was clearly aiming too high. He looked around for a less attractive female, and eventually settled on a short, fat lady, who had sprayed herself green in an attempt to look like She-Hulk. Einstein thought up a hilarious chat-up line and strolled over to try it out on her.

'Hey there,' he said. 'Do you know what colour you get when you mix blue into green?'

'Fuck off.'

Struck out again. It had to be because of the Smurf outfit. Either that or these women were too drunk to appreciate a man with blue skin and a fake white beard.

"That's him. That's Eric Einstein!"

Someone nearby had whispered the words so he wouldn't hear them. *But he had heard.* His blood turned ice cold. How the hell could anyone recognise him in Santa Mondega, a place he'd never been to before? He looked around for the person who had uttered his name.

Fuck.

A pair of angry nuns. Big fuckers too.

'It *is* him,' one of them said in a deep, booming voice.

207

Einstein took a step back and reached for his wrist to teleport himself out of there. *But he had no watch.* Of course. *Fucking Hitler.* He was going to have to escape on foot. He managed to take three steps before he bumped into a passing Mummy who barged him back towards the nuns.

SMACK!

Punched in the side of the head. Ouch.

Einstein staggered sideways like a politician at a free drinks event.

CLANK! A metal fist slammed into his chest, knocking the air out of his lungs. As he took a step back to balance himself, someone with a wide foot kicked him in the balls. He doubled over in pain, his hands reaching for his bruised sack. His fingers barely touched his red pants before one of the nuns grabbed him around the throat, lifted him off his feet and hurled him backwards.

CRACK!

Einstein's head banged against the sidewalk, dazing him. His vision blurred and he saw stars floating above his head, just like a cartoon Smurf might in the same circumstances. Through his muddied vision he looked around, hoping to see Herman or even Hitler on their way back from the morgue. All he saw was a yellow Cadillac cruise past with a Terminator at the wheel, staring at him, watching him get beaten up by the two burly nuns. Bloody Terminators, they never help anyone in need.

'Where's the cyborg?' one of the nuns asked, leaning over him.

Einstein looked up but couldn't see much other than a big black shadow looming over him. The face on the nun was a blur under the shadow of its cowl. 'Who are you?' he asked.

'Shut up and answer the question. Where's Hitler and the cyborg?'

'I dunno,' Einstein mumbled. 'I think I'm gonna blow chunks.'

'You hit him too hard,' the other nun said.

'You're the one who threw him on the ground.'

One of the nuns grabbed a handful of Einstein's blue top and lifted him a few inches off the ground. 'How do we kill the cyborg?' the nun asked.

'I dunno.'

'Tell us or I'll break your neck, right now You've got three seconds, three-two—.'

Einstein was disoriented but had just enough wits about him to know he didn't want to have his neck broken. 'You have to shoot him in both eyes,' he muttered.

'And that kills him?'

Einstein held in the urge to puke. 'It destroys both of his chips. But his central nervous system runs right through him. The AI will repair the

208

broken chips and reboot him. He cannot be killed. He will always find a way to repair himself.'

The nun let go of Einstein and his head thudded against the sidewalk again. Everything turned to black.

The two nuns, Rex and Elvis, kicked Einstein a few times while he was on the floor to make sure he wasn't faking being unconscious.

'He's fucked now,' said Elvis. 'What did you drop him for? It was obvious he was in bad shape.'

'It's not easy interrogating someone when you're wearing a fucking dress,' Rex complained. 'It was getting caught under my feet. I had to drop him otherwise I would have fallen over.'

'I don't like what he said about the cyborg,' said Elvis. 'We ought to let the others know about it.'

Rex leaned down and grabbed Einstein by his throat, lifting him into a sitting position. 'How do we stop the cyborg if it can't be killed?' he asked, shaking the Smurf. 'Can it be reprogrammed?'

Einstein didn't respond. After being shaken some more by Rex, his nose started bleeding so Rex lowered him back onto the ground.

'Great job shaking him,' said Elvis. 'That really helped.'

Rex checked Einstein's neck for a pulse. He didn't have one. 'Bollocks. He's fucking dead.'

'What?'

'He's dead. We fucking killed him.'

'Correction, *you* fucking killed him.'

'You kicked him in the nuts.'

'Since when does kicking someone in the nuts kill them? Jasmine does it all the time and it's never killed anyone. If anything they get turned on by it.'

'Hey! What are you two doing?' someone nearby said, angrily.

Elvis looked up and saw a man in a Captain America costume glaring at him. The guy looked like he was up for a fight. Elvis dealt with the situation calmly.

'Fuck off, or you're next.'

The Captain America lookalike took half a second to weigh up his options before wisely turning around and walking away.

'What do we do now then?' Rex asked. 'We can't just leave him here.'

'Take him to the morgue,' said Elvis. 'It's only around the corner. Remember how the coroner, Dr Taylor, once told us he was inundated with corpses he couldn't identify after the eclipse? Einstein can be one of those corpses.'

'I like that idea,' said Rex. 'We could just stick a tag on his toe and shove him in a drawer.'

'Actually, you know what? They've got incinerators in that place. We could stick him in one of them. Turn the bastard to ash.'

'Have we got time?'

Elvis checked his watch. 'About forty-five minutes, I reckon.'

'Let's do it then.' Rex picked up Einstein and slung him over his shoulder.

'Hey, wait a sec,' said Elvis. He grabbed Einstein's right hand, which was hanging down behind Rex's back. 'Look at this,' he said, twisting Einstein's arm around so Rex could see the hand. 'Einstein's got Flake's engagement ring. Thieving bastard!'

'That's not possible,' said Rex, unable to get a good look at the ring. 'Sanchez has got Flake's engagement ring.'

Elvis pulled the ring from Einstein's finger and held it out for Rex to see. 'What the fuck is this then?' he asked.

Rex groaned, 'Did it ever cross your mind that the people who made it might have made more than one?'

'Yes, but it's a big coincidence, don't you think?'

'How the fuck should I know? Let's just take this asshole to the morgue then meet up with the others.'

Forty-six

Father Vincent Papshmir had been dreading this day. He was nervous as hell about it too. For the last few months, this day had been all he could think about. The Lunar festival was here, and he had a job to do. An unpleasant job, but one that was very necessary. And it had to be done without anyone recognising him. Thank God for the fancy dress costume. Papshmir's daughter Janis had helped him make his outfit, a replica of the one worn by Darth Maul in *The Phantom Menace*. She had painted his face red and black and stuck some annoying little horns on top of his head too for added authenticity.

When he was a very young man, Papshmir's mother had told him what to expect on the day of the eclipse. She was a smart lady who knew the future. Everything she had predicted had come true, so far. She had also warned him that people would kill him if they found out his true identity. Vampires in particular would be on his case if word got out that his father was the Bourbon Kid. Papshmir, like his father, had holy blood. It helped him heal when sick or injured, and it had kept him alive for over a hundred years, with the added benefit of looking like a man half his age. His sister Emma had the same blood. She was his staunchest ally and the anchor that kept him attached to reality. Around town she was better known as Annabel de Frugyn, the Mystic Lady, a local fortune teller. She was a fraud of course. She only knew the same things Vincent knew about the future, the things their mother had taught them. Their mother, Beth Lansbury, had been tricked by the Devil and left stranded in the nineteenth century, even though she'd been born in the twentieth century. Suffice to say, Vincent and Emma's childhood had been a strange one. Today was to be the strangest day of all. Emma was dead. Slain in the night by a cop named Archie Somers, also known as the Dark Lord Armand Xavier. Papshmir had known it would happen because his mother had foretold it. And to make matters worse, Papshmir's closest friends, Elvis and Rodeo Rex, had also been murdered by the same asshole. And it had all happened in the last twenty-four hours.

Papshmir had made a promise to his sister that he would bury her alongside their mother in the place they grew up. It was a promise he fully intended to keep. But it meant he had to steal her body from the local morgue.

He arrived outside the city morgue just after eleven o'clock in the morning. No one paid him much attention as he climbed the front steps in his Darth Maul disguise. After successfully passing through an unmanned set of turnstiles in the reception area, he headed for the mortuary cold room. He'd been in the building several times previously,

211

so he knew his way around. With it being the Lunar Festival, every business suffered from staffing shortages, the morgue included, so he was able to move through the building's corridors unchallenged.

When he arrived outside the cold room, he checked around. There was no one in sight. Perfect. He pushed open the cold room doors and walked in. The room was as cold as its name suggested. One side was made up of rows of lockers filled with the dead bodies of people murdered that week. There were thirty-six lockers in total, and on occasions like today there was a good chance they were all occupied. A further eight corpses were laid out on metal tables in the room. Each corpse was covered by a thin, white, plastic sheet.

Papshmir almost didn't see the man in the room with him. It startled him initially, until he realised it was a member of the morgue staff. A tall thin man in his late thirties was performing an autopsy on one of the corpses at the far end of the room. His name was Dr Taylor, first name Taylor, second name the same. Dr Taylor was wearing a long white lab coat. He had thick, shaggy brown hair that hung down over his face and flopped around as he poked, prodded, and sliced at the corpse. He looked up at Papshmir but didn't appear to recognise him thanks to the Sith costume.

'Hey, you can't be in here!' Dr Taylor snapped.

'I've come for the corpse of Annabel de Frugyn,' Papshmir said, disguising his own voice by doing his best impression of Darth Maul.

'I said, you can't be in here!'

'I understand what you're saying,' Papshmir replied. 'I'm just hoping to take a corpse off your hands. Annabel de Frugyn's last wish was to be buried in her home town. And seeing as how you're so busy, I thought I'd save you the trouble of working on her autopsy. If you'll just let me take her, I'll see to it that an autopsy is carried out in her home town, and the cause of death forwarded onto you and the local police.'

Dr Taylor didn't consider the idea even for a second. 'I'm sorry, but that's totally out of the question,' he replied, his grip on his scalpel tightening.

'I'm willing to pay. How about I give you a thousand bucks to take your lunch break early, and you leave me here watching over your corpses?'

'That's unethical,' Dr Taylor replied, shaking his head. 'I couldn't possibly do such a thing.'

'Two thousand.'

'Five.'

'Done.'

212

Papshmir reached inside his Sith robe and pulled out a brown envelope. It contained exactly five-thousand dollars in cash. Dr Taylor laid down his scalpel and took off his plastic gloves. He moved a surgical trolley out of the way and walked up to Papshmir, his hand outstretched. Papshmir handed him the brown envelope. Dr Taylor opened it up and took a quick look at the cash.

'Okay,' he said after flicking through the notes and making sure there were no fakes. 'I take one hour for lunch. There are cameras all around, so if you fiddle inappropriately with any of the corpses...'

'I won't, I promise.'

'Right. You've got one hour then. If she's in here, she'll be in one of the cold lockers.'

'Thank you.'

As soon as Dr Taylor was out of the room, Papshmir hurried over to the lockers and started opening them up, checking the ankle tags. He found the remains of Elvis in the second locker he looked in. He then came across the bodies of Gil Fuentes, a porter from the Santa Mondega International Hotel, and Rusty Culo, a local criminal. He was about to pull open another locker when he heard footsteps approaching in the corridor outside. He held his breath, hoping the person approaching would walk past the cold room. But they didn't. The door opened, and a man who was not Dr Taylor walked in. He was a short fellow in a Charlie Chaplin costume. The two men froze when they set eyes on each other.

'Can I help you?' Papshmir asked, in his toughest voice.

The Charlie Chaplin impersonator hesitated, then let go of the door, allowing it to close behind him. 'Good day to you,' he said in a German accent.

'Did you want something?' Papshmir asked.

Charlie Chaplin ignored him and walked up to the nearest table. It had a female corpse on it, covered by a white sheet. He pulled the sheet back and touched the woman's forehead, pressing his hand against it like he was checking her temperature. A white light emanated from his fingertips and spread to the corpse's head. After about twenty seconds, the woman opened her eyes and sat upright. She was in her forties with flattened down blonde hair. She stared into the eyes of Charlie Chaplin, who whispered something in German to her before moving over to the next table and recreating the resurrection trick with the next corpse, that of an overweight man.

'What the fuck are you doing?' said Papshmir, backing away.

The recently resurrected female slid off her table and stared at Papshmir with dull, lifeless eyes. Papshmir knew the woman from church. Her name was Carrie Onsela. She had a gaping hole in the side

213

of her neck, a sign that she'd been killed by a vampire. She hissed at Papshmir, and to add to the unpleasantness, a maggot slid out of her nose and crawled down to her mouth.

There was only one thing to do. Papshmir grabbed an empty trolley and launched it at her in the hope of knocking her over, or out of the way. It didn't work as well as he hoped. The trolley hit her and stopped. Carrie Onsela pushed it back towards Papshmir and moved towards him. At the same time, Charlie Chaplin's second resurrected corpse sat upright and slid off his table, ready to help corner Papshmir.

Undead Carrie staggered towards Papshmir, her legs a little unsteady. Papshmir started pulling open lockers in the hope of creating obstacles to slow her down. The big male that had just come to life waddled up behind Carrie. His eyes were bloodshot, his mouth agape, and his tongue black. Papshmir had envisaged many things that could go wrong when planning his trip to the morgue. A German Charlie Chaplin raising the dead and making them attack him was not one of the things he'd considered. Fucking Charlie Chaplin. Unfunny bastard.

As Chaplin prepared to bring yet another corpse back to life, he issued an order to those he had already resurrected.

'Kill him.'

Forty-seven

With the morgue unguarded, Flake and Jasmine snuck inside. The interior walls were painted pea-soup green, making the place look old and dated. The linoleum floor was worn and cracked from use and made everything feel colder than it already was. And the reception area was empty and bare. Not a person, or a dated magazine in sight.

'It's kinda dead around here,' said Jasmine. 'Where do you think Hitler would have gone?'

'I'm not sure,' said Flake. 'Why did he even come in here?'

'Maybe he's got a thing for dead people? I knew a guy once who liked me to play dead while he rubbed his balls over my face.'

Flake raised her eyebrows. 'Was it Elvis?'

'Don't be silly. Elvis likes me to be wide awake at all times. What shall we do about Hitler? Should we split up, you go one way, I'll go the other?'

'No fucking way. Are you mental? Actually, don't answer that.'

'What should we do then?'

Flake sighed. 'Just follow me.'

'I thought you didn't know your way around?'

'I don't. Now shush, we don't want Hitler to hear us.'

'Don't shush me!'

Flake ignored Jasmine and hurdled over a turnstile. The bottom of her black robe got caught on the turnstile, and she had to spend about ten seconds untangling herself from it. Jasmine waited patiently, then effortlessly hurdled the turnstile, making sure not to repeat Flake's mistake. The two of them headed down a corridor that had signposts hanging from the ceiling.

'Where do you think he went?' Jasmine asked.

'Shush. I can hear people talking.'

'Stop shushing me.'

'Shut up then. Or whisper, for fuckssake.'

'You whisper!'

'I am whispering.'

Jasmine shoved Flake in the back. Flake slapped Jasmine's hand away then scampered along the corridor before Jasmine could retaliate. The voices Flake had heard were coming from behind a set of double doors up ahead. She pointed at them and mouthed the words, *"Through there!"* to Jasmine. Jasmine mouthed the words, *"Well, d'uh!"* back at her. After a brief interlude where they both mouthed insults at each other, Flake pulled her hood up over her head, turned her back on Jasmine and snuck up to the doors. There was a small frosted window in each door,

215

but the frosting was so dense nothing could be seen through them. Pointless windows. Flake wanted to stop and have a rant about them, but recognised it was something Sanchez would probably do, therefore it was a dumb idea. She pushed one of the doors open a little. Muted groans filtered out into the corridor, then a man said, *"Hey, look, I just wanna get out of here."*

Flake pushed the door wide open and walked through it. Jasmine backed her up, drawing her pistol and following her in. They were greeted by the sight of Adolf Hitler standing next to a metal table with an elderly female corpse on it. He was pressing his hand down on her forehead, which was making his hand glow. And that wasn't even the strangest thing going on. Three other corpses were up on their feet trying to attack a man in a Darth Maul costume. He was fending them off with a metal trolley while also reciting some kind of prayer.

Jasmine picked out her target straight away. She pointed her gun at Hitler. The frightened dictator saw it and panicked. He removed his hand from the dead woman and dove down behind the table she was laid out on. Jasmine took a shot at him, but for once she got her timing all wrong. The corpse Hitler had been interfering with sat up just as Jasmine fired. The bullet hit the undead lady in the side of the head and knocked her sideways. Blood spurted out of her head and splashed onto the wall at the back of the room. Rather than just lay down and die, the corpse sat up again and touched the hole in her head with her fingers. She seemed to recognise it was a bullet wound, then she looked across at Jasmine and hissed at her.

One of the undead males who was trying to get to Darth Maul turned away from him at the sound of the gunshot. He lasered in on Flake and lumbered towards her, his mouth agape, his eyes, yellowed and evil. Flake panicked and held up her hands to fend him off.

ZAP!

To her surprise, bolts of blue electricity shot out of her palms and blasted the undead fucker in the face. His head erupted in flames and he staggered around until he banged his head against one of the open cold lockers. That seemed to finish him off. He collapsed onto the floor, his face black and charred, smoke floating up from his frazzled features.

'Nice shooting!' said Darth Maul, giving Flake a thumbs up.

From the minute Papshmir had come under attack by the naked, dead people, he had been praying to God to send him some help. God was obviously listening for once too, because almost immediately, help arrived.

216

And God really did work in mysterious ways. *A preacher dressed as Darth Maul finds himself in trouble?* No problem. Send Palpatine. And Kenobi. It was one of the reasons Papshmir never wanted to leave Santa Mondega. Shit like this just didn't happen in other towns and cities. With a renewed sense of optimism, he found the courage to punch a naked woman in the face. When she came back for more, he reached inside his robe and pulled out a small vial of holy water that he kept for emergencies. He took off the lid and chucked the water at the angry zombie creature. She sizzled like bacon in a pan, screamed like a boiling kettle, then melted away into a pool of slime on the floor.

'Suck on that, bitch!'

Jasmine crouched down and lined up a second shot at Hitler, only to see him tap his wristwatch and disappear into thin air, leaving behind a puff of blue smoke.

Flake was quickly coming to terms with her newfound skill. She blasted the remaining walking dead corpses to pieces with bolts of blue electricity from her hands. The battle of the mortuary was over in under thirty seconds, leaving the room filled with smoke, and smelling like rotten eggs, burning flesh, and Hitler's armpits.

Jasmine tucked her gun back inside her brown robe and stared at the man with the red and black face faint. 'Are you Vincent Papshmir?' she asked.

'Who's asking?' Darth Maul replied, tentatively.

'Jasmine, *Dead Hunters*. We've travelled back here from the future.'

'Seriously?'

Flake lowered the hood on her robe and waved some smoke away from her face. 'What happened to Hitler?' she asked. 'Did he disappear?'

'Hitler?' said Papshmir, looking around. '*That* was Adolf Hitler?'

'Yeah,' said Flake. 'It's a long story, obviously.'

Papshmir frowned. 'Did you say you were from the future?'

'That's another long story,' said Flake. 'But you are Papshmir, right?'

'Yes, I am. Are you Flake, the waitress from the Ole Au Lait?'

Flake nodded. 'That's me.'

'You look older.'

'I am older, thanks for noticing.'

Papshmir approached her with caution. 'How did you do the Emperor thing? You know, with the blue electricity?'

217

Flake held her hands up, which made Papshmir duck. 'I honestly don't know,' she said. 'JD told me I could do it, but this is the first time it's worked.'

'JD told you? Did he send you here?'

'Kind of,' said Jasmine. She walked over to Papshmir. 'Would you mind if I have a hug with you?' she asked. She proceeded to throw her arms around him and squeeze him tightly for about five seconds. When the embrace was over, Papshmir's makeup hid how pleased he was.

'What was that for?' he asked.

'I only got to meet you once in the future,' Jasmine replied. 'And we never got a chance to really hang out. I thought you were pretty hot though.'

'Jas, you know we really shouldn't be interacting with anyone here,' said Flake.

'Yeah, but it's Paps,' said Jasmine. 'He won't mind.'

'Is JD here with you?' Papshmir asked Flake. He looked over at the doors behind them in the hope of seeing the Bourbon Kid walk in.

'He's gone after a time-travelling cyborg in an Elvis costume,' said Flake, before adding, 'Don't ask.'

'A cyborg? Dressed as Elvis? Er, okay.'

'Basically,' said Jasmine. 'We've travelled back in time to catch Hitler, but we fucked it up. We're not actually supposed to interact with you, or anyone else, because you know....'

'The space time continuum?'

'Something like that.'

'We really should get out of here,' said Flake. 'The others need to know Hitler escaped.'

Jasmine stroked Papshmir's arm. 'What are you doing here anyway?' she asked.

Papshmir glanced over at the lockers, several of which were open. 'I'm looking for my sister's corpse,' he said.

'You mean Annabel?' said Jasmine.

Flake cleared her throat. 'Jasmine, I think we've said enough already.'

Jasmine smiled at Papshmir. 'We probably have to go now.'

'It's been lovely meeting you both,' said Papshmir. 'And thank you for showing up when you did. Fucking stroke of luck that was. Really fucking great timing.'

'Come on Jas, we've really got to go,' said Flake.

'Let me at least be a gentleman and open the door for you,' said Papshmir, heading for the door, 'It's the least I can do after you saved my fuckin' ass just now.'

218

'What a nice man,' said Jasmine.

Papshmir opened one of the double doors, but then closed it again straight away. He looked back at Jasmine and Flake. 'That cyborg you mentioned just now, did you say he was dressed like Elvis Presley?'

'Yeah,' Flake replied.

'He's coming this way.'

Forty-eight

Hitler knew the stories about Santa Mondega and about how crazy shit happened there, but nothing prepared him for what he witnessed at the morgue. The man dressed as Darth Maul hadn't been a problem initially, but then he had somehow summoned a Jedi and the Emperor to come to his aid. Hitler initially assumed they were just people in costumes for the festival. But then the Emperor started wiping out Hitler's resurrected zombie people with blue electricity from his fingertips. It was a bizarre and unexpected sight. Hitler had seen the Star Wars movies, but it had never crossed his mind that Emperor Palpatine might be real. And living in Santa Mondega, the capital of Crazy Town.

After pressing the escape button on the top of Einstein's time-travel watch, Hitler vanished from the mortuary cold room and reappeared in the chocolate factory ten minutes after he had left it in a hurry with Einstein and Herman. He half-expected to see the Bourbon Kid and his friends still hanging around in there. Instead, he was greeted by two Jasmine clones he'd left behind. One in a pink bikini, the other in a red basque.

'Hello, Adolf,' they both said in unison.

'Are the Dead Hunters still here?' Hitler asked, looking all around him.

'You just missed them,' said the one in the bikini. 'They left like thirty seconds ago.'

'Oh, thank God. Do you know where they're going?'

'Yes, we told them you were travelling back in time to kill the Bourbon Kid, so they left to see if they could travel back in time too. Did you see them?'

'You fucking idiots!'

Hitler reached inside his jacket and pulled out a tiny pistol. He shot the pink bikini Jasmine in the chest. Then he fired twice at her twin, missing with the first shot but shooting her in the throat with the second. The two clones staggered around briefly before dropping to the floor and writhing around in agony. Hitler tucked his pistol back in his jacket and walked over to them so he could watch them suffer. The one in the red basque was holding her throat with both hands in a feeble attempt to stem the flow of blood. Hitler stood over her, unzipped his pants, pulled out his dick and took a piss on her. He'd killed a few of Einstein's creations during his time living in the factory. One of his favourite things was humiliating them in their dying moments. He'd killed at least six of them while he was having sex with them. This was his first time pissing on

220

one though. He liked the feeling, and the look of desperation in the dying clone's eyes was quite a turn on.

'Oh, you're back,' said a soft female voice, behind him.

Hitler looked around. A Jasmine clone in a purple catsuit had walked in via the corner entrance. She seemed unfazed by the sight of him taking a leak on one of her sisters.

'Where did you come from?' he asked, as he shook the last few drops of pee onto the dying clone's face.

'I was in the basement fixing the plumbing,' the catsuited clone replied. 'I heard a lot of noise up here about ten minutes ago. What happened?'

'It's a long story,' said Hitler.

'I like long stories,' the Jasmine replied, approaching him.

'Of course you do.'

'What happened to Jasmine and Jasmine?' she asked, looking down at her dead and dying sisters.

'They said you were ugly, so I killed them.'

'Wow. I guess they deserved it then. Thank you so much, Adolf, you're so manly.'

'Yes I am. Now clean up all this mess while I take a moment to think.'

'Yes, sir.'

Adolf zipped up his pants and tried to think how best to get back to Einstein and Herman. He didn't really want to go back to Santa Mondega at all. The place was fucking dangerous.

'By the way,' said the Jasmine in the catsuit. 'Did you know there are some people outside? I spoke to them through the entry system. They claimed to be brothers and sisters of yours. I didn't let them in though. I told them to wait for your return.'

'Brothers and sisters? What do you mean? Are they Nazis?'

'They said they were the sons and daughters of Scratch.'

'Scratch? Who's Scratch?'

'That's what I said. They told me he was your dad. And that you were his favourite son, and they had come to join your cause.'

'Favourite son? What?'

The Jasmine shrugged. 'Ask them yourself. They found a way in, so they should be here any second now.'

Hitler's but cheeks clenched. 'WHAT?'

The sound of boots on the metal staircase that led up from the ground floor confirmed what the Jasmine was saying. Hitler looked at the time-travel watch. He didn't want to press the ESCAPE button because it would take him back to the morgue in Santa Mondega, and there wasn't time to program in another destination.

'Are they dangerous?' he asked, panicking.

'I don't know. Shall I ask them?'

'Oh, you useless bitch.'

'You seem very anxious. Would you like a blowjob?'

Hitler's mind raced with thoughts of what to do. Repeatedly pressing the ESCAPE button could take him back and forth between the factory and the morgue, adding ten minutes each time. But time travelling was disorienting and always left him with an urge to pee.

'Here they are,' said the Jasmine.

A tall grey-haired man in a silver suit walked through the door in the corner, followed by a slim, cherry-haired woman in a red pant suit. The third and final person to enter was a solid, muscular man with short white hair. He was wearing nothing but a pair of tight black shorts. The shorts were only tight because his thighs were so meaty. His upper body was rock solid.

Hitler pulled his pistol on them. He had three bullets left. 'Who are you?' he demanded, his finger twitching by the trigger.

The three people stopped and stared at him.

'Is that Charlie Chaplin?' the big guy in the shorts whispered.

'No, it is *him!*' the woman whispered. 'Show some respect.'

All three of them lowered their heads, then the woman got down on one knee.

'Brother, we have come to join in your cause,' she said. 'We have awaited your return our entire lives. We are the sons and daughters of Scratch. I am your sister, Petra. These are my brothers, Xander and Rocky.'

'What are you on about?' Hitler asked, his gun pointed at the woman.

'All of Scratch's children have special abilities,' said Petra. 'You were the first born. Your gift was that you could bring the dead back to life and make them bend to your will.'

'My father wasn't called Scratch though,' said Hitler, incensed at the insinuation he didn't know his real father.

Petra stood up, then she and her brothers whispered among themselves for a few seconds before she shushed them and smiled at Hitler, showing off all her teeth.

'This may be difficult to hear,' she said, 'but as I understand it, your mother was unable to bear children, so one day in desperation she made a deal with the Prince of Darkness. He gave her the ability to bear children in exchange for allowing him to father her firstborn. You were

222

born nine months later, and you inherited many of Scratch's talents for coercing others into carrying out your orders. You were so gifted you could even make the dead come alive and bend to your will.'

'How do you know this?' Hitler asked, eyeing them with suspicion but also lowering his pistol to aim it at Petra's feet instead of her chest.

'Each of us was fathered by Scratch,' Petra replied. 'Some years ago he gathered us all together for a meeting where he foretold of your return. He said you would be resurrected in the town of Despair, and that we should join you and assist in your new plan to conquer the world. We have been waiting a long time for this. Father also predicted the Bourbon Kid would be in town attempting to thwart your plans. We have come to help you to defeat him. Others are coming from all over the world right now to join the quest. Each of us has a unique gift, just as you do. Now that we have found you, it is time for us to serve at your side.'

Hitler was astounded. This was some revelation. And while it sounded completely implausible, it felt right because these people saw him as their leader, their saviour. He was a God-like figure to them. They were clearly of high intellect.

'I realise this is a lot to take in,' said Petra. 'But like the rest of us, now that you know who you really are, now that your eyes are opened to the truth, you can feel it, can't you? The truth runs through your blood like a virus.'

She had a point. Hitler had always wondered where his abilities came from. He'd always known that one day he would find out why he could raise the dead. And now he knew. In his mind's eye he saw a vision of Scratch, his true father.

'I can't hardly believe this,' he muttered to himself, 'And yet I know it to be true. My father was black?'

'He is all colours to all people,' said Petra.

Hitler didn't have time to argue the ins and outs of his father's skin colour, although he intended to bring it up again at a later date. 'What powers do you three have?' he asked.

'I myself have the ability to pass through walls,' Petra replied. 'That is how I gained entry to this building and brought my brothers through with me.' She pointed at the man in the silver suit. 'Brother Xander here can sense the presence of other children of Scratch, and feel their intentions. He has been instrumental in bringing us all together.' She gestured at the man in the black shorts. 'Brother Rocky has granite skin.'

'Granite skin?'

'Yes. It is flexible just like normal human skin, but try stabbing him and you will be unable to hurt him. He is a very powerful fighter.'

223

Hitler pointed his pistol at Rocky, pulled the trigger, and shot him in the gut. The granite-skinned brute never even flinched. The bullet flattened against his skin and bounced onto the floor.

'That is fucking brilliant!' said Hitler, joy breaking out all over his face.

'Rocky has been shot many times,' said Petra. 'To penetrate his skin, a gunman would have to shoot him in the exact same spot six or seven times with armour-piercing bullets.'

'That would make him a very useful soldier,' Hitler remarked, ideas spinning in his head.

'He has fought in conflicts all over the world and never been hurt.'

Out of the corner of his eye, Hitler caught sight of the cloning machine. A plan began formulating in his mind. 'Can you three wait here for a while,' he said. 'I need to get my colleague, Eric Einstein.'

'You want him to operate your cloning machine,' said Xander, speaking for the first time. 'You wish to clone Rocky and build an army.'

'You're a smart boy,' said Hitler. That's exactly what I'm thinking.'

'We are here to carry out your bidding,' said Petra. 'Rocky will be a willing participant. We have seen the success you have had cloning the stupid woman from the Dead Hunters. If you were to create a clone army of Rockys, we could conquer the world in a matter of weeks.'

'Who's she calling stupid?' the Jasmine clone asked.

'Oh, shut up,' said Hitler. 'Aren't you supposed to be cleaning up that mess?'

'Yes, sir.'

The Jasmine clone wandered off to find some paper towels to clean up Hitler's piss and the blood of her sisters.

'An army of granite men,' said Hitler, rubbing his hands together. 'We won't even need Hermans.'

Xander, who appeared to be reading Hitler's mind, responded. 'Your time-travel device will make it easy for us to assassinate the leaders of our enemies. We could kill them in their sleep without anyone knowing.'

Hitler's grinned. 'Yes, that is a fantastic idea. Are you reading my mind?'

'I can feel the thoughts of all of my brothers and sisters,' Xander replied. 'You, sir are full of terrific ideas.'

'Yes, I am. Just keep some of them to yourself.'

Xander glanced over at the two dead clones, then winked at Hitler.

'Okay,' said Hitler, 'I'll just have to go get my friends Eric and Herman back from Santa Mondega. Eric's going to love this.'

224

'We look forward to meeting with him,' said Petra.

Hitler thought back to the plan he and Einstein had concocted to kill the Bourbon Kid and steal the Eye of the Moon. It had been agreed that if anything went wrong they would meet up at the Tapioca in time for the eclipse. 'I'll be back in ten minutes,' he said to his new comrades. 'Don't go anywhere.'

And with that, Hitler selected the Tapioca as a location on his watch, then with one press of a button, he vanished in a blue haze.

Forty-nine

Papshmir strolled out of the mortuary cold room and let the door close behind him, leaving Jasmine and Flake hiding inside. He headed towards the cyborg in the Elvis costume, who was coming the other way.

'Can I help you, Mister....?' Papshmir asked, while holding up a hand to gesture for the cyborg to stop and chat with him.

'Herman,' the cyborg replied. 'And no, you cannot help me.'

The cyborg sauntered past Papshmir, his focus solely on the cold room.

'If you're looking for a man in a Charlie Chaplin outfit, you're going the wrong way.'

Herman stopped and turned to face Papshmir. 'Where is he?'

Papshmir hoped his makeup hid how anxious he was. If this cyborg was anything like a Terminator, it might pick up on the anxiety, and even worse, it might have a lie detector built in. 'He's not in there,' Papshmir said, stalling for time.

'Then where is he?'

'He went out the back way. He said if I saw you, to tell you to catch up with him at the Nightjar bar across town.'

'Why has he gone there?'

'He didn't say, but it sounded urgent, like he desperately wanted you to meet him there.'

The cyborg's head moved from side to side. His eyeballs moved in a precise, robotic manner as he scanned the area, looking for any sign of Hitler or anyone else. After completing his analysis, he stared at Papshmir.

'His footsteps lead into that room,' he said, pointing at the mortuary. 'And there is no sign that he came back out.'

'He moonwalked back out,' Papshmir lied.

'Moonwalked? As if without gravity? Or like the Michael Jackson dance move?'

'The Michael Jackson thing.'

Herman turned his back on Papshmir and continued on to the mortuary, walking faster than before. He shoved open one of the double doors and marched through it. Papshmir hurried after him, dreading what carnage might ensue when the cyborg found Flake and Jasmine.

Herman stopped just inside the room and looked around. Papshmir caught up with him just before the door closed. He squeezed through it and peered around the room. The remains of Hitler's undead accomplices were still strewn around on the floor, but there was no sign of Flake or Jasmine, which was puzzling. The mortuary had no windows or other exits so they couldn't have escaped. There wasn't even a ventilation shaft in the ceiling. Herman glanced upwards as if he was looking for that very thing.

After twenty seconds of scanning the scene, Herman turned on his heels to leave the room. Papshmir breathed a sigh of relief, but then held his breath again when the cyborg stopped and stared at the floor just outside.

'There are other fresh footprints here,' he said, holding one of the doors open. 'They belong to two women, and they haven't left the room either.'

'Jeez,' said Papshmir. 'You can tell all that just from staring at the floor?'

Herman swivelled round again and stared at Papshmir. 'Your scent suggests you know more than you are telling me,' he said.

Fuck. Some major bullshit was required. Papshmir plumped for pointing back down the corridor. 'There's your buddy Charlie Chaplin again,' he said, lying through his teeth.

'I hear nothing,' the cyborg replied, unmoved.

Papshmir gulped. But then, as if by the grace of God, the sound of a set of doors opening near the reception area filtered along the corridor towards them.

'See,' said Papshmir. 'That was him. If you hurry, you might catch him.'

Someone was definitely coming their way from the reception area. And they were running. Herman fronted up to face whoever was incoming. To Papshmir's surprise, a pair of enormous nuns burst around the corner at the far end of the corridor. They took one look at Herman, both stopped in their tracks, and pulled guns on him. Papshmir did the sensible thing and dived for cover inside the cold room.

Gunfire echoed all around the morgue. Some seriously loud weapons were being unloaded. Papshmir covered his ears and curled up into a ball on the floor. Bullets peppered the doors and one shot even broke one of the windows. Shards of glass landed on the floor not far from Papshmir.

When the shootout eventually came to an end, after what felt like an age, Papshmir removed his hands from his ears and lifted his head up. It was hard to hear much other than the ringing in his ears.

The doors to the mortuary burst open and the two large nuns burst in. They looked around the room, waving guns at everything. Eventually, they both set eyes on Papshmir and trained their weapons on him.

He raised his hands in surrender. 'I'm not armed,' he said. 'I'm Vincent Papshmir, local preacher.'

227

The two nuns lowered their guns. 'Hello Paps,' said a voice he recognised.

'Elvis?'

'Yup.'

The two nuns lowered the baggy hoods on their habits to reveal the faces of Rodeo Rex and Elvis.

Papshmir stood up. 'Oh, thank the fucking Lord for that,' he said. 'You two cunts certainly know how to turn up in the nick of time, don't you? Did you kill the cyborg?'

Rex answered the question. 'It was a hell of a shootout. That motherfucker can sure fire off a fast gun. I caught all his bullets with my magnetic hand, and eventually Elvis shot him in both eyes, and blew out the computer chips that operate him.'

Elvis looked around the room again. 'You seen a couple o' hot chicks dressed as monks anywhere, Paps?'

'They *were* in here,' Papshmir said.

A banging from one of the cold lockers indicated that they *were* still in the room. Papshmir, Rex and Elvis hurried over to the lockers and started pulling them open. Elvis pulled open one that had Flake lying inside it. She sat up and took in a breath of the slightly fresher air outside of the locker.

'Christ, I thought you guys would never shut up,' she said. 'Didn't you hear us knocking?'

Papshmir found Jasmine in one of the lockers nearer the back of the room. When he pulled it open he saw her smiling at him.

'Thanks, Mister Maul,' she said. 'Can you help me out please?'

If Papshmir hadn't had the full Darth Maul makeup on, Jasmine would have seen him blushing. For reasons unclear to him, she had discarded her brown monk robe and was totally naked in the locker.

'What happened to your clothes?' he asked as he took her hand and lifted her out.

'I took them off while I was in the locker,' Jasmine replied.

'Hey, baby,' said Elvis. 'You're looking good.'

Rex groaned. 'Why the fuck are you naked, Jasmine?'

'Authenticity,' she replied as Papshmir set her down on her feet. 'All the other corpses are naked. If that robot thing checked inside the lockers I needed to look like a proper corpse.'

'That's stupid,' said Flake, who was standing next to Elvis, straightening out her monk robe. 'A cyborg would know straight away you weren't dead when he saw you breathing.'

'I would have held my breath.'

'He would have known you had a pulse.'

228

'Okay, ladies,' said Elvis. 'Let's not forget we've got a mission to get on with.'

'It was great seeing you all,' said Papshmir. 'But you should definitely get going. The coroner, Dr Taylor will be back soon.' He pointed at Rex and Elvis. 'It'll freak him the fuck out if he sees you both alive!'

'That's a fair point,' said Rex.

'And I've got to get a move on myself,' said Papshmir. 'I've got to find my sister's corpse in here. I paid Dr Taylor five grand to turn his back for an hour while I look for her. God, I hope she's actually in here.'

'You just had to do it, didn't you?' said Flake, still bickering with Jasmine. 'You just can't keep your clothes on when there's men around, can you?'

Papshmir moved around Jasmine and retrieved her robe from inside the locker. When he pulled it out he saw the corpse of an old man underneath it. 'Yikes, there's a dead man in here,' he said wincing. 'How did you manage to get this robe off in such a confined space?'

Jasmine smiled. 'Taking my clothes off is my specialty.'

Papshmir picked a tiny G-string off the face of the dead man in the locker. 'Is this yours too?' he asked.

'It is,' said Jasmine. 'But you can keep it as a souvenir to remember me by.'

'Oh, Jas, that's so tacky,' said Flake.

'Flake's a stripper,' said Jasmine.

'Really?' said Papshmir, taking his eyes off Jasmine for a second to look over at Flake. 'Now, or just in the future?'

'Everybody, listen!' said Rex, growing frustrated by all the talk. 'JD's outside in the street and he's banged up pretty bad from a fight with that fucking cyborg. Let's go get him and go find Hitler.'

'Hitler's gone,' said Jasmine. 'He disappeared when I shot at him.'

'For fuckssake,' said Rex. 'Why didn't you say so before?'

'You didn't ask.'

Rex sighed. 'Any idea where he went?'

'Obviously not,' Jasmine replied.

'If Hitler's gone, does that mean we can go home now?' said Elvis. 'I mean, the cyborg is dead, so job done, right?'

'I guess so,' said Rex. 'But let's go *now*, before anyone else sees us. And Paps, you can never tell anyone we were here. Not ever, not even *us* if you see us again. In fact, you should forget everything you saw here. Erase it from your memory.'

'All of it?' said Papshmir.

229

'Everything,' said Rex. 'Never think of it again, never speak of it again.'

'Okay. Scouts honour,' said Papshmir, who was barely listening because he was busy helping Jasmine get her arms into the sleeves of her brown robe.

Flake huffed. 'She can undress like fucking Houdini when she's in a corpse locker, but now she's standing up, she needs a priest to help her get dressed. You are so fucking predictable, Jasmine.'

'GUYS!' Elvis yelled, silencing everyone.

'What's up, honey?' Jasmine asked, while Papshmir tied her robe around her.

Elvis had opened one of the doors and was looking out into the corridor. 'The cyborg,' he said. 'It's gone.'

Fifty

Herman's gunfight with Rex and Elvis didn't go as smoothly as he expected. Rodeo Rex was using a magnetic hand to swipe all of Herman's bullets out of the air before they could hit their targets. And Elvis, *the sonofabitch* was blasting away with a Desert Eagle pistol, and that fucking gun was a powerful motherfucker. After thirty seconds of back and forth gunfire, a bullet blasted out one of Herman's eyes, shattering the computer chip behind it. Ten seconds later, the backup chip behind his other eye got blown out too. It killed Herman's eyesight and shut his central nervous system down. He didn't even feel the impact as his body hit the floor. But, while Herman was down, his failsafe kicked in. His creator, Eric Einstein, had installed a further backup system deep inside his torso. Whenever one of the chips in his head was destroyed, his entire memory was automatically transferred onto another blank chip, which was then transported up into his head to replace the broken one. The chips were doubly important because they also provided Herman with his eyesight, which was why they had to be situated behind his eyeballs. It took just over five minutes for the replacement chips to be updated, reinserted and then activated. At the moment of activation, Herman sat upright. His eyeballs were still gone, and pieces of them were scattered all across the floor. He reached inside the top pocket of his jacket and picked out his sunglasses. By a stroke of luck, the shades had survived the shootout intact. He slipped them on, covering the gaping holes where his eyeballs had been, then he stood up and evaluated his situation. It was 11.35 a.m. He had no idea what had become of either Hitler or Einstein. The primary objective was still on though. He had to get to the Tapioca, kill the Bourbon Kid and acquire the Eye of the Moon. Murdering the folks who were arguing amongst themselves in the room behind him would have to wait. He located the back exit of the morgue, then headed outside and set out across town to the Tapioca.

****

Outside on the sidewalk, JD's head was throbbing. Being slammed into a concrete pillar was bad news for your skull. And your brain too. It wasn't doing his eyesight much good either. Double vision, lots of blinking, floating debris in his peripheral vision. It was all shit.

He was working himself up into the kind of rage that usually led to a killing spree, when a pair of hands grabbed him by the arm and pulled him up into a sitting position with his back up against a wall. He opened his eyes and saw he was surrounded by cheerleaders.

231

'Are you okay?' one of them asked.

'I've been better.'

'The guy who beat you up has gone into the morgue.'

'I did not get beaten up.'

JD attempted to stand up but winced at the stabbing pain in the back of his head. Moving made it worse. He sat back down. His holy blood would speed up the healing process, and then the fucking cyborg was gonna get it.

'JD? What'cha doing?'

The voice belonged to Elvis. JD looked up. Through the holes on his hockey mask he saw Elvis standing in the middle of all the cheerleaders. Rex was behind him.

'He got beaten up,' one of the cheerleaders replied on JD's behalf.

JD ignored her and offered his hand to Elvis. 'The cyborg slammed me into this fucking wall,' he said as Elvis began hauling him up. 'He's gone into the morgue. Flake and Jasmine are in there looking for Hitler.'

'Fuck.'

Elvis let go of JD's hand, causing him to fall back against the wall and bang his head again. He slid back down to the ground, closed his eyes and rubbed the back of his head. When he reopened is eyes, Elvis was on his way into the morgue, with Rex right behind him. And someone had placed a dead Smurf next to JD.

'Is that Papa Smurf?' a cheerleader asked.

'Oh my God, he's dead!' screamed another.

All the other cheerleaders screamed in unison, which did nothing for JD's headache. He reached inside his coat, pulled out a gun and pointed it at the nearest cheerleader. The screaming went up a few notches, but then the cheerleaders fled, taking their annoying high-pitched screams with them.

JD closed his eyes again and waited for his head to clear. After about a minute the headache faded enough for him to open his eyes again. He took a look at the Smurf that was slumped up against him. Behind the fake beard and the blue skin, he saw the lifeless face of Eric Einstein.

Gunfire inside the morgue sharpened JD's senses up that little bit faster. He struggled to his feet, which caused Einstein to fall sideways and taste the pavement. JD grabbed one of the dead Smurf's feet and dragged him along the street to the morgue. The gunfire had ended by the time JD pulled Einstein's bouncing head up the concrete steps at the front of the building. Gun in hand, and Einstein in tow, he busted a turnstile in the morgue's reception area, and made his way along the main corridor to find out what had become of the others.

232

Elvis, Rex, Jasmine, and Flake were at the far end of the corridor. They were all staring at the floor outside a set of doors. JD, tired of dragging Einstein behind him, slung the dead Smurf down the corridor. The Smurf's floor ride came to an end at Rex's feet.

'Are you okay?' Flake asked as JD approached.

'Bang on the head, that's all,' he replied. 'What happened to the cyborg?'

'It got away!' said Jasmine.

'I killed it,' said Elvis, as JD arrived outside the mortuary cold room. 'Shot the fucker in both eyes. He was down and totally fucked. But while we weren't looking, he disappeared.'

'Rebooted himself, we reckon,' said Rex.

'Papshmir is here too,' Jasmine added, pointing at the room behind them. 'He's in there looking for Annabel's corpse.'

Flake elbowed Jasmine in the ribs.

'What?' said Jasmine, shoving Flake back.

JD tried to absorb all the information that was coming his way. It was hard to concentrate but he slowly pieced it all together in his busted head. 'You shot him in both eyes,' he said, repeating what Elvis had said.

'Yep,' Elvis confirmed. 'He went down and he was out of commission, for sure.'

'Any idea how long he was out for?'

'Hard to say,' said Rex. 'At least a few minutes, maybe ten?'

'It was never ten,' Elvis argued. 'Five at most.'

'Did anyone interact with Papshmir?' JD asked, checking his watch.

'Not really,' Jasmine lied.

'Then let's get going before he comes back out and sees me. The eclipse is on its way.'

Fifty-one

After the usual flash of blue electrical haze, Hitler was transported out of the factory and into a bathroom in the Tapioca. There was a foul stench, worse than the smell of the corpses he'd encountered in the morgue. He surveyed his surroundings and quickly established he was in the disabled toilet. There was no noise coming from the bar area so he crept over to the washroom door, pulled it open a little and peered out. The bar was empty. The place certainly didn't look like it was gearing up for the infamous Lunar Festival massacre. Hitler stepped out of the washroom and made his way through the lounge area. There wasn't a soul in sight. But as he neared the bar, he heard the sound of running water.

'Hello?' he called out. 'Anyone there?'

A chubby Mexican with thinning dark hair rose up behind the bar. He was wearing a purple shirt and loose black pants with the fly unzipped. 'Who the fuck are you?' he asked, staring at Hitler, who was still wearing his Charlie Chaplin costume.

'Who am I? Who are you?' said Hitler.

The bartender placed a hip flask on the bar top, then zipped up his pants. 'Sanchez Garcia,' he said. 'I own this place.'

'Sanchez Garcia? Yes, that's right, you're the owner of this establishment. Where is everyone else? Isn't this place supposed to be open for the eclipse?'

Sanchez baulked at the suggestion. 'Eclipse? Are you mental? There's no bloody eclipse today....... Is there?'

Hitler checked his watch. 'Oh fuck!' he muttered to himself. 'I forgot to select the year. I'm still in the present.'

Behind the bar, Sanchez had picked up on the Charlie Chaplin impersonator's German accent, and his terrible Hitler moustache. Deductions were made, conclusions reached. Plans hatched.

'Care for a drink?' Sanchez asked, holding up his hip flask. 'Fresh homebrew. On the house.'

'Homebrew?' said Hitler, intrigued. 'What's in it?'

'It has a sharp twang to it with a hint of asparagus and peanuts,' Sanchez replied. 'The locals love it. If you haven't sampled it, you haven't lived.'

Hitler recognised that there was no threat from Sanchez, so he took off his Charlie Chaplin hat and set it down on the bar. 'Pour me a glass then, bartender,' he said, pulling up a stool. He took his jacket off and sat it down on another stool. There was no sense in worrying about returning it to Domino's now.

234

While Sanchez poured some golden juice from the hip flask into a whiskey glass, Hitler had a thought.

'Tell me, bartender, was there a big shootout here during an eclipse some years ago?'

'Oh, yeah,' said Sanchez. 'I remember it well. I was one of the only survivors of that massacre. I was dressed as Batman.'

'Was the Bourbon Kid present in the shootout?'

The two men were still trying to work each other out. Hitler wanted to know if the plan he and Einstein had concocted to kill the Bourbon Kid had actually worked, and Sanchez was trying to get Hitler to drink his piss, while also trying to figure out why the fuck the Nazi dictator was in the Tapioca in the first place. And even more importantly, what had become of Flake and the others in their time travelling shenanigans? A game of mental chess ensued. On the one side, Hitler, criminal mastermind, offspring of the Devil, orchestrator of mass genocide, and highly educated psychopath. On the other side, Sanchez, cowardly, sneaky, piss-serving, overweight bartender with an unprecedented level of luck when it came to surviving attempts on his life. Fischer vs Spassky had nothing on this.

'The Kid *was* here during the eclipse,' Sanchez replied.

'Did he survive?'

'He did not,' Sanchez lied, simply because he figured lying was always the best thing to do in a tricky situation.

Hitler perked up. 'Do you remember *who* killed him?'

'It's hard to say. It was very dark. You know the whole thing was chaos, kind of like one of the bar fights in *Road House*, only with guns.'

'Road House?' said Hitler, raising a curious eyebrow. 'Which one? The original or the remake?'

Sanchez's blood began to boil. 'The remake?' he scoffed. 'I've barred people from this place for the mere mention of that atrocity.'

Hitler turned his head and spat on the floor. 'The remake was a disgrace to the original,' he declared. 'There is only one true *Road House*, and that's the one with Patrick Swayze in it.'

Sanchez stopped pouring piss into Hitler's glass. 'You're a fan of Road House?' he asked, surprised the Nazi leader had even heard of it.

'It's a masterpiece,' said Hitler.

Sanchez was just about to slide the glass of piss across the bar to Hitler, but he hesitated. Maybe the Fuhrer wasn't so bad after all? He seemed to have good taste in movies. With that in mind, Sanchez picked out another glass and poured Hitler a glass of cheap whiskey. 'Here, this stuff has matured better,' he said, placing it in front of Hitler. 'Have you ever seen a film *better* than *Road House?*'

235

Hitler took a sip of the whiskey. 'Trick question,' he replied, placing the glass back down on the bar. 'There *is* no film better than *Road House.*'

A broad grin broke out on Sanchez's face. Hitler held up his hand and the two men high-fived.

'I've never found anyone who agreed with me that it was the best film ever made,' said Sanchez. 'I even met a guy who thought Road House 2 was better.'

'There's a Road House 2?' Hitler asked, stunned.

'Don't look for it,' Sanchez replied. 'You're better off pretending it doesn't exist.'

The two men high-fived again. A real bromance was blossoming. But then Hitler noticed something on Sanchez's hand.

'Where did you get that ring?' he asked.

Sanchez glanced down at his hand. He had Flake's engagement ring on his little finger. 'Oh, that. It's not mine. It's my girlfriend's. She wanted me to look after it for her. She kept the bloody Eye of the Moon though.'

Hitler's eyes lit up. 'The what?'

Sanchez inwardly winced, realising he shouldn't have mentioned the Eye, even though it was unlikely Hitler knew what it was. 'Oh, nothing, just a silly name I gave to the dog.'

Hitler took another sip of his drink while he pondered what to do. If Sanchez's girlfriend had the Eye of the Moon, then to hell with trying to get it from the Bourbon Kid during an eclipse. 'Is your girlfriend here?'

Sanchez shook his head. 'Nah, she's gone out. She won't be back for a few days, probably.'

'Right, of course.'

Hitler considered his position. The only reason to travel back to the eclipse was to reunite with Einstein and Herman, but it was possible he didn't need them anymore. All he had to do was wait for Sanchez's girlfriend to return, then beat her up and get the Eye of the Moon. If, of course, Sanchez was actually telling the truth about her possessing the Eye. Scenarios whizzed around in Hitler's mind.

'That's a nice watch,' said Sanchez, changing the subject.

'This old thing. It's a piece of junk really,' Hitler lied.

'It's a digital though, I see. Those things are pretty expensive.'

'This girlfriend of yours, what's her name?' Hitler asked.

'Erm, well, she's not actually my girlfriend. She's actually my fiancée.'

'Fiancée?'

236

'Yeah. It means we're engaged.'

The word "fiancée" ran around in Hitler's mind. He'd been planning to marry the love of his life, Eva Braun, back before he'd travelled forward in time with Einstein. He checked the display on his watch and flicked through the list of saved locations. The year 1945 popped up. He glanced at the ring on Sanchez's finger. He could take the fat bartender back to 1945 with him, kill him, take his travel ring and give it to Eva. Shit, he could even pass it off as an engagement ring. Then after marrying his sweetheart, he could set about acquiring the Eye of the Moon from Sanchez's fiancée. This was a great day indeed. A day where it felt right to propose to Eva and then bring her to the future where the war could be won with the help of his newfound brothers and sisters, the Eye of the Moon, and a few million granite-skinned soldiers.

'I'm engaged too,' Hitler said, while he fiddled with the settings on his watch. 'You'd like my fiancée. She's a real stunner.'

Before Sanchez could respond, Hitler pressed the ENTER button on his watch. Then, in a flash of blue electrical haze, he vanished from the Tapioca and travelled back to 1945, taking Sanchez with him.

Fifty-two

After a brisk journey across town, where everyone exchanged stories of what they'd been up to, Elvis, Rex, Jasmine, JD, and Flake arrived outside Domino's party store.

'This is where we found Einstein,' said Rex, stopping and pointing at the area where he and Elvis bashed Einstein about. 'I can't understand why he was on his own. He must have been up to something. He might have been waiting here for Hitler and the cyborg to come back from the morgue, I suppose.'

'They're not here though,' said Jasmine. 'So let's just head to the Tapioca.'

'We've still got fifteen minutes,' said JD. 'There's no rush.'

Flake frowned. 'How can you be so calm? That cyborg is going to the Tapioca to kill the younger version of you.'

Elvis elbowed Rex in the arm and pointed up ahead. 'Look at the ass on that Marilyn Monroe chick!'

The Marilyn Monroe in question was in a tight pink dress. She was standing at a crossroads chatting to two guys who looked like the Blues Brothers.

Rex took a good look. 'Yeah, nice ass,' he agreed. 'She looks totally wasted though.'

'Do you mind?' said Flake.

'She's definitely wasted,' said Jasmine. 'And she looks kinda slutty.'

'FOR FUCKSSAKE!' Flake bellowed, silencing all of them and a few other people nearby.

'What's with you?' JD asked.

'That Marilyn Monroe is *me*, you idiots!' Flake hissed.

A collective, *"What?"* followed from all in attendance.

'That is me,' said Flake. 'I always used to dress as Marilyn Monroe at parties because we have the same surname, albeit slightly different spelling. *Flake Munroe, Marilyn Monroe,* geddit?'

'Jesus,' said Rex. 'That's you? Fuckin' hell. I don't remember you having blonde hair back in those days?'

'It's a wig, you moron!'

The younger version of Flake left the Blues Brothers and staggered down the street, oblivious to the group staring at her.

'I can see why you don't usually wear heels,' said Elvis.

Jasmine pointed at another festival-goer. 'Ooh, Flake, look! That guy in the Halloween mask nearly got hit by a car because he was checking you out.'

238

A man dressed as Michael Myers from the Halloween movies had just walked past the Marilyn Monroe version of Flake. While staring at her ass, he'd come close to falling in the road in front of a car that looked like the black Hell's Chariot car driven by the Scorpions in the movie *Grease*. He made a rude hand gesture at the driver, then checked out Flake's ass again, before drunkenly bumping into a person in a Tauntaun outfit.

'That's the guy I hooked up with in the alleyway during the eclipse,' said Flake, her mouth agape.

The creep in the Halloween outfit eventually stopped staring at younger Flake's ass and carried on his way. He headed across the street, where he met up with a woman in a Harley Quinn outfit. He put his arm around her, and then the two of them walked off together.

'That's weird,' said Flake. 'He's supposed to chase after me and catch up with me about a hundred yards down the street. Why's he going off with her?'

Jasmine moved around Flake to check out what the Halloween killer was up to. 'If he hooks up with Harley Quinn, does that mean you'll go to the Tapioca and get shot by JD?' she pondered aloud.

'I fuckin' knew it!' said JD. 'We've changed something! Or maybe Einstein has? This is what happens when you dick around with time travel. Our presence here has changed the future for a whole bunch of people. If Flake carries on to the Tapioca, she's gonna get killed.'

'Yeah, by you,' said Rex.

'I wasn't the only one shooting people in that place,' said JD. 'Everyone had a gun.'

'We should go after her,' said Elvis.

'We can't,' said Rex, grabbing Elvis's arm to stop him from running after Flake. 'Remember what Jacko said? God specifically forbid us from interacting with our younger selves.'

Flake was still staring at the Halloween dude. She looked pissed. Michael Myers and Harley Quinn took a turn down a side alley, and then, in full view of everyone on the street, they started groping each other up against a wall.

'I don't believe it,' said Flake. 'He's gonna fuck Harley Quinn in that alley. He's supposed to be with me.'

'This is fucked up,' said JD. 'We've gotta stop you going to the Tapioca.'

'We can't change history though,' said Rex, exasperated because no one seemed to be listening to him.

'It's already changed!' Flake snapped back.

239

'Fuck it,' said JD. 'You guys go looking for the cyborg. I'll stop Flake from going to the Tapioca.' Without giving anyone a chance to voice an opinion on the idea, he ran out into the road, causing a red pickup to slam on its brakes. JD ignored the tooting horn and carried on to the other side of the road, which was full of drunken people singing and dancing. He knocked several of them over as he carried on his way.

'What the fuck is he doing?' Elvis asked.

'He's going to save Flake,' said Jasmine.

'He's going the wrong way though!' said Flake, pointing at the younger version of herself. 'I'm down that way.'

JD was heading for the side alley where Harley Quinn and Michael Myers were making out.

'He's gone to the wrong alley,' said Elvis. 'I'm telling you, that bang on the head he got from the cyborg has screwed him up.'

Jasmine grabbed Elvis's arm. 'It's okay,' she said. 'I know what he's doing.'

'Care to tell the rest of us?' Flake asked.

'Just wait a second.'

The gang all peered through the crowds of people and passing cars to try to make out what JD was up to. Right at the moment he reached the alleyway, their view was blocked by a big, pink tour bus full of Barbies. The bus stopped in front of them as it waited for the traffic to start moving again. When the bus finally moved on, JD was in the alleyway, standing over the unconscious figures of Harley Quinn and her Halloween lover, who was stripped down to his underpants. JD was wearing the blue Halloween coveralls.

'Has he just mugged that guy?' Rex asked.

JD reached down and pulled the guy's Halloween mask off. He then sprinted across the street in pursuit of the Marilyn Monroe version of Flake while trying to fix the mask over his face.

Jasmine grabbed Flake's hand and squeezed it. 'Oh, Flake, he's gonna save you,' she said. 'That is so sweet.'

Flake burned up red with embarrassment. 'Oh my God,' she muttered. 'This is how it happened.'

All eyes turned to Flake.

'How what happened?' Rex asked, before adding, 'Oh, right.'

Elvis placed a hand on Flake's shoulder. 'He'll just stop you going to the Tapioca,' he said. 'He's not exactly gonna try and fuck you, is he? He knows you're with Sanchez.'

Flake pressed her hand against her chest. Her heart was beating at a million miles an hour. For a minute or two, everyone stood still and

240

stared, waiting for JD to reappear with the Marilyn Monroe version of Flake, diverting her away from the Tapioca.

'Is he actually coming back?' Elvis asked, eventually.

'I guess not,' said Jasmine. 'Maybe he's just knocked Flake out. That's what he usually does when he's got a problem.'

'He won't knock me out,' said Flake.

'What's he doing then?' Elvis asked, eyebrow raised.

'Hey, in case you all forgot, we haven't got time to hang around here waiting,' said Rex. 'We've got to find the cyborg or get to the Tapioca before the eclipse starts. Come on, let's go!'

Fifty-three

Petra had been pacing up and down the factory floor waiting for Hitler's return. 'Something's gone wrong,' she muttered. 'It's been half an hour.'

'Maybe he got held up?' Rocky suggested.

Xander was standing by the cloning machine, analysing it to see if he could figure out how it worked. 'Time is no issue for Adolf,' he reminded the others. 'He has a time travel device, so he should have returned here within minutes of leaving.'

'Adolf?' said Petra, flicking her red hair. 'You're on first name terms with him now?'

'He is our brother. I don't think it's unreasonable for us to call him by his first name.'

Petra chewed on a mouthful of her hair while she thought about what to do. 'Can you sense his whereabouts?' she asked Xander eventually.

Xander shook his head. 'He's gone to another time, so I've lost my connection with him.'

Petra joined him by the cloning machine. 'We should try working this machine ourselves.'

'It looks fairly straight forward,' said Xander. 'But without knowing the exact procedure, we run the risk of screwing things up.'

Petra clicked her fingers at the Jasmine clone in the purple catsuit, who was sitting on the floor counting her fingers. 'You, *dumb lady,* do you know how the cloning machine works?'

The clone looked up and smiled at them. 'I sure do.'

'Can you show us?'

The Jasmine stared at her fingers for a little longer, then hopped up onto her feet and skipped over to join them. 'You lie down on this side,' she said, pointing at one of the glass chambers. 'Then, someone presses that silver button over there, which makes the chamber close around you.' She pointed at a big, red rubber button between the two chambers. 'Then this button starts the cloning process. Just remember not to remove the clone until the machine has finished implanting a chip in its brain. Otherwise, the clone will come out without a brain.'

'Is that what happened to you?' Petra asked.

'No.'

'How do you know for sure that's how the machine works?' Xander asked.

'I watched Einstein do it. It's really simple.'

Petra tugged at the sleeve on Xander's suit jacket. 'Is she telling the truth?' she asked.

242

He nodded. 'I believe, she believes what she is saying is factual, so yes.'

'Let's try it then.' Petra looked around for Rocky. He was standing nearby, staring at the Jasmine clone. 'Rocky, come here and lie down in the cloning chamber. We're going to try making a twin for you.'

'He has to be naked,' the Jasmine said, her eyes sparkling.

Rocky was unfazed and removed his black shorts and underwear as he approached the machine. He handed them to the Jasmine clone who was only too happy to look after them for him. She was clearly impressed by his rock-hard physique. Granite abs were a big turn on.

'I've never seen a granite willy before,' she said, staring at Rocky's appendage. 'Is it permanently hard?'

'As a rock,' he replied.

Rocky gave the Jasmine clone a good look at his hard butt cheeks while he climbed into the nearest cloning chamber and laid down on his back.

'Comfortable?' Petra asked him.

'Yes, I'm fine.'

Petra stepped up to the control panel on the wall and pressed the silver button the Jasmine had told her about. The glass cover on Rocky's chamber closed over him, and the one on the empty chamber did the same.

'You're sure this is all I have to do?' Petra asked the Jasmine. 'I just press the red button?'

'I'm sure that's right.'

'Okay, here goes nothing.'

Petra pressed the red button and stepped back to see what happened. A low buzzing sound came from Rocky's chamber. A few seconds later a glow of gold light surrounded him.

'How long does this take?' Petra asked.

'To clone one of me takes about half an hour,' the Jasmine replied. 'A big guy like this might take a bit longer. Wanna play a game of hide and seek?'

'No.'

'The time will go quicker.'

'You know what? You're right,' said Petra, tiring of the clone's presence. 'You go hide somewhere. Me and Xander will count to a thousand then come looking for you.'

'Cool! Close your eyes and start counting.'

Petra and Xander half-closed their eyes and waited for the Jasmine to leave the room, which she did almost straight away.

243

'That's a relief,' said Petra, ending the charade of pretending to count to a thousand. 'She was getting on my nerves.'

'I kinda liked her,' said Xander with a small shrug. 'You know, she probably needs some company. Maybe I should let her come live with me?'

Petra smiled. 'I'm amazed it took you this long. I'm pretty sure she's got her eye on Rocky though.'

Xander pointed at the cloning machine. 'Let's just watch this, and make sure Rocky is okay.'

The two of them waited patiently while the cloning process took place. After plenty of buzzing and different coloured lights flashing within the chambers, things finally started to happen. The empty chamber began to generate a clone of Rocky. It started by growing a skeleton, then gradually added flesh and organs to the bones. Twenty minutes in, Petra and Xander grabbed themselves a pair of plastic chairs and sat down to watch the process unfold. It took fifty-six minutes in total. A loud beep signalled the cloning was complete, and then Rocky's glass chamber slid open. The other chamber containing his clone remained closed as a pair of robot arms started surgically cutting open the clone's skull and inserting a chip into its brain.

Rocky rolled out of the chamber and looked around for his shorts.

'That brainless woman walked off with your shorts,' Petra informed him.

Rocky groaned. 'Typical.' He pointed at the chamber with his new-born replica in it. 'Did it work?'

'Give it a few minutes. The machine is implanting a device in its brain.'

When the chip implant was finally complete, the machine beeped loudly like a washing machine when its cycle is over. The chamber containing the clone fizzed open. Steam filtered out of the chamber and floated up to the ceiling.

The clone sat up and opened its eyes. After looking around the room it focussed its stare on Petra. 'Hello, ma'am,' it said.

'Do you know who you are?' Petra asked.

'I'm not sure.'

Petra looked at Xander. 'I'd say it's worked, wouldn't you?'

The clone spotted Rocky standing nearby. 'Are you my father?' it asked.

'Yes he is,' Petra replied. 'His name is Rocky. But we'll call you, Junior.'

'Junior,' the clone repeated. 'That is my name.'

244

Petra pressed her hand on Junior's bicep. His skin was rock solid, just like Rocky's. 'Xander, this is perfect,' she said, her eyes glowing red. 'Now let's see if we can make another clone, but this time, we'll try cloning Junior. The more granite-skinned clones we have, the happier Adolf will be when he returns.'

Fifty-four

After beating the shit out of the dude in the Halloween outfit and knocking Harley Quinn *the fuck out* with one punch, JD switched clothes with the Halloween killer and sprinted after the Marilyn Monroe version of Flake. He pulled the Halloween mask over his head as he was running, which was no easy feat because there were people everywhere getting in his way. The mask made it harder to look for Flake too, and JD inconsequentially wondered how his friend Joey Conrad had tolerated wearing the Red Mohawk mask for so long. Masks might look cool, but they're hot and provide shit visibility. He barged past numerous people in his pursuit of Flake. On the opposite side of the street he saw Herman the cyborg heading towards the Tapioca. The connotations of what might happen if Herman was successful in killing JD's younger self were too complicated to fathom, but right now, JD's thoughts were only of Flake and stopping her from reaching the Tapioca.

He wanted to call out her name, but if the cyborg heard it, he might react and do something stupid. Fucking time travelling robots, unpredictable bastards.

JD knocked over two men dressed as bowling pins, raced past a man in a Flash outfit and eventually caught up with Flake as she staggered past the entrance to an alleyway. He reached out and grabbed her shoulder, spinning her around to face him.

'Flake,' he said, panting for breath.

Flake smiled at him. 'Well, hello there,' she said, slurring.

JD glanced across the street at Herman. The cyborg had stopped walking and was peering through the crowd in their direction, as if he had heard JD quietly utter Flake's name. JD dragged her off the street and into the cover provided by the alleyway. She went with him willingly. He took her to a dumpster halfway down the alley and dragged her behind it where they couldn't be seen. He peeked over the dumpster to see what had become of the cyborg. Herman was still looking their way, but it wasn't possible to tell if he had seen them.

Flake reached up and grabbed JD's face mask, attempting to pull it up over his face. She got it up just over his mouth before he pushed her hand away and ducked down beside her. To keep her quiet, he leaned in and kissed her. He told himself it was the safest thing to do in the circumstances, to prevent her from seeing his whole face. The truth was, in spite of everything, he was still in love with Flake, and this might be the last chance he ever got to kiss her again. She deepened the kiss and placed her hand on his back. JD held her head to prevent it banging against the wall, and with his other hand, he squeezed her ass. Flake

246

didn't resist. In fact, she set about unzipping JD's coveralls. She slid her hand inside his clothing and grabbed his cock. Instant hard-on. It felt like forever since he'd fucked Flake. All thoughts of Herman the cyborg vanished from his mind. This was all he cared about. He knew exactly how to push Flake's buttons too. He slid his hand up her dress and ripped her underwear off, then the two of them wasted no time getting down and dirty behind the dumpster.

It felt great to be with her again. It was like being back on the paradise island he had shared with her in an alternate timeline that she had no memory of, but he remembered vividly. Flake's passionate cries, loud though they were, went unheard by the boisterous crowd of partygoers nearby. This was a monster fuck. All of JD's pent-up frustration at not being with the woman he loved came flooding out.

The fuck came to a climax just as the moon began to pass over the sun. The two lovers panted heavily. Flake pulled the mask off JD's head and kissed him passionately in the darkness that engulfed the whole city. Five seconds into a kiss that he never wanted to end, JD snapped back to reality.

'I gotta go,' he whispered. 'Stay away from the Tapioca, it's not safe.'

He zipped his coveralls up, kissed Flake one last time, then pulled the mask back over his head. While Flake straightened out her dress, he hurried away, the pace of his walk increasing with every step. In the distance he heard the rat-a-tat of gunfire coming from the Tapioca. He jogged out of the alley, throwing one last look back at Flake as the light began to reappear in the sky. She was staggering out of the alley after him with a big grin on her face. The first part of his job was done. Flake was safe. But as he headed towards the sound of gunfire, he encountered a swarm of screaming people in strange outfits running towards him, fleeing the massacre at the Tapioca.

Fifty-five

Sanchez had no idea what the fuck was happening. One minute he was behind the bar talking to Adolf Hitler; the next, the Tapioca had vanished amid a blue haze of smoke and electricity, and he was standing in a poorly decorated room with a low ceiling and no windows. Hitler was there too, in the middle of the room, standing next to a large table with a big map on it and some toy tanks.

'What the fuck just happened?' Sanchez asked.

'SILENCE!' Hitler yelled.

'What is it with you Germans?' said Sanchez. 'You're always yelling stuff. Where the fuck are we anyway? And how did we get here?'

'We are in my bunker in nineteen-forty-five,' Hitler replied. 'I am Adolf Hitler and you are my prisoner.'

'Prisoner? What the fuck did I ever do to you?'

'Mister Garcia,' said Hitler approaching him. 'How about you give me the ring you are wearing on your little finger?'

Sanchez was still holding his hip flask so he offered Hitler that instead. 'Here, have this,' he said. 'It's better than the ring.'

'I don't want that,' Hitler scowled. 'Give me your hand!'

Sanchez had no intention of giving Hitler anything other than his hip flask, which was still halfway full of fresh piss. Hitler grabbed his hand and squeezed it while he removed Flake's engagement ring from the little finger. Sanchez yelped and tried to yank his hand away, but it is was no use. Once Hitler was in possession of the ring, he gazed lovingly at it, reminding Sanchez of Gollum from the *Lord of the Rings* movies, only not as handsome.

'Can I go back now?' Sanchez asked. 'This place honks.'

'Honks?'

'Stinks.'

'HOW DARE YOU!' Hitler raged. He started rambling in German, which didn't bother Sanchez at all because he couldn't understand a word of it. But halfway through Hitler's rant, he was interrupted when a small wooden door in the wall behind him burst open. A short, angry little solider with curly blond hair stormed in and marched up to Hitler, yelling some shit in German. The soldier was even shorter than Hitler and was clearly not afraid of him. Sanchez watched in bewilderment as the two of them engaged in a shouting match in German until eventually the soldier stormed back out, and slammed the door shut.

'That bloke was a bit feisty wasn't he?' said Sanchez. 'Is that how all your men talk to you?'

'That was my fiancée, Eva,' Hitler replied, glaring at Sanchez.

248

'She's very pretty. You're a lucky man.'

'She wants to get married right now,' Hitler said, with a sigh. 'She knows we're going to lose the war so she wants to be married before the Russians get here and execute us.'

'That's what all the shouting was about?'

'Not all of it. I was supposed to bring her back some chocolate from the future but I forgot. She's a bit annoyed about it. That's why I agreed to marry her right now. If I hadn't we'd still be arguing.'

'She sounds like a real catch,' said Sanchez. 'You know, we could take her back to the future with us? It'd be easier for you to get married there. I'll even throw you a free reception in the Tapioca, if you like?'

'Pfft, are you kidding? She'll never go for it. She wants to get married now or never. She was very clear about it. All because I forgot the fucking chocolate.'

Sanchez raised his eyebrows. 'Bit feisty, isn't she? I noticed she never knocked on the door either. Just let herself in. Bit rude, don't you think?'

'She didn't know I had company,' Hitler explained. 'And she calmed down when I showed her the ring.'

'Really? Because it looked to me like she stormed out.'

'She did not storm out. She's gone to find a nice frock, then she's bringing a priest back with her so we can get married right away.'

'Bit pushy though, isn't it?' said Sanchez.

'SHUT UP!' Hitler glared at Sanchez, then snatched his hip flask away from him. 'What did you say was in here?'

'Alcohol. Probably too strong for the likes of you.'

Hitler unscrewed the lid and sniffed the contents. He turned his nose up. 'Smells like wee,' he said.

'Bit like your bunker then. Do you even *have* a toilet in here?'

Hitler replaced the lid on the flask and put it down on the map table. 'Right,' he said. 'This is what's going to happen. When Eva returns, she and I will exchange our wedding vows. The ceremony will be private, so you will have to give Eva away because her father is not with us. You will also have to be my best man and any other roles required during the ceremony. Do you understand?'

'I'm not sure I'm best placed for this.'

'You're doing it, or I kill you.'

'I *have* always wanted to be a best man.'

'It's settled then.'

For the next ten minutes, Sanchez stood around while Hitler used a phone to make all kinds of abusive sounding calls in German. Eventually, after he'd finished yelling at people on the phone, Eva Braun

249

returned, this time wearing a sparkly black dress. She was still a bit butch though, in Sanchez's opinion. And she looked like she had a drink problem. Sanchez could spot a piss artist from miles away and this chick undoubtedly started drinking in the mornings. Hitler greeted her with a warm embrace, then the two started chatting excitedly in German.

Sanchez was no expert on the German language, but if he was to guess, he would have said that Eva told Hitler his moustache was crap and he should shave it off for the wedding, and Hitler replied by telling her to ease off on the weightlifting and try wearing some lipstick. The reality was very different.

'Who exactly is the creepy, fat man behind you?' Eva asked.

'He's just some idiot who happened to have a spare time travel ring,' Hitler replied. 'I'm giving you the ring as a wedding gift, then you and I are leaving this place and escaping to the future together!'

'Oh, thank the Lord,' said Eva, a tear welling up in her eye.

While they were prattling on in German and paying him no attention, Sanchez took a quick glance around the room in the hopes of spotting some kind of weapon to use against the Nazi bastards. The options weren't great. He narrowed his choices down to grabbing one of the miniature tanks on the map and throwing it, or maybe even rolling up the map and hitting them with that. Neither were particularly good ideas. He edged over to the map table and pressed his back up against it while he sneakily reached for a toy tank. As his fingers touched on a tank, there was a loud, booming knock at the door. Hitler shouted some more abuse in German, then someone on the other side shouted something back. Whatever it was, it got Hitler excited. He yelled some more incomprehensible stuff at Eva Braun, then he opened the door and yelled at a soldier standing outside in the corridor. When the yelling ended, he returned to Eva, kissed her on the lips, and then left the room in a hurry.

Eva walked over to the door and closed it, then she turned to face Sanchez. 'Your name is Sanchez, yes?' she said, in perfect English.

'That's right,' Sanchez said, while he considered chucking a toy tank at her, just to see the look on her face.

Eva looked around the room as if she was checking to see if anyone was with them, then she moved towards Sanchez. 'You have to help me,' she said. 'Adolf is insane. You've travelled through time before, haven't you? Can you get us out of here, to the future?'

'I'd love to,' said Sanchez. 'But Hitler's got the time-travel watch and my ring. We can't go anywhere without those, and I don't even know how the watch works anyway.'

250

'I've seen Eric Einstein use it,' said Eva. 'There's a button on it somewhere that takes you back to your last destination. If you've come from the future, all we have to do is press that button, then we're out of here.'

Eva moved in closer and stroked Sanchez's arm. 'If we help each other, we could kill Adolf, then go to the future together. There is no future for *anyone* here. The Russians are closing in. They'll kill us all. What do you say? Do you like my plan?'

It was the best offer Sanchez was going to get. If Eva wasn't such a swamp donkey he would have considered kissing her. As things stood, he spat on his palm and offered her a handshake. Eva was familiar with the tradition so she spat on her palm, and the two shook hands.

'I knew the minute I laid eyes on you, you were a hero,' she said, the tear in her eye finally sliding down her cheek. She wiped it away and blinked a few times to try and prevent any further tears from sneaking out.

'Where's Hitler gone anyway?' Sanchez asked.

'He said he's gone to get me a proper white wedding dress to replace this black one. As soon as he finds one, he plans to marry me imminently. There is a priest on the way here right now to perform the ceremony.'

'Did he tell you I'm giving you away?'

'Yes. But don't worry, you won't have to do anything.'

'You make a lovely couple,' Sanchez lied.

'Oh, we *do not*,' Eva replied. 'I've been pretending for years that I wanted to marry him because I was afraid he would kill me otherwise. The truth is, I can't imagine being married to a man like that after all the awful things he's done.'

'Why? What's he done?' Sanchez asked.

Eva looked surprised. 'You don't know?'

'Does he leave skid marks down the toilet? He looks the sort.'

Eva frowned. 'No, it's nothing like that,' she said. 'But he's massacred millions of innocent people in his quest for world dominance.'

'Oh yeah, that. Yeah, that's pretty bad too,' Sanchez agreed. 'Worse in fact.'

'He could come back any minute now,' said Eva. 'So we have to come up with a plan to kill him. What do you think we should do?'

'You don't have a plan already?' Sanchez groaned. 'It would really help if you had some kind of idea what to do. After all, you do live here. I've only been here five minutes.'

251

Eva began breathing erratically like she was going to cry. The woman was a bag of nerves. She gazed into Sanchez's eyes. 'There is one thing we could do,' she said. 'Adolf is coming back in a minute with my new dress. While I'm changing into it, you can overpower him and kill him.'

'I've got a better idea,' said Sanchez. 'You overpower him. I'll kick him while he's on the floor, then you shoot him in the face.' He paused then asked, 'Do we even have a gun?'

'I have a small pistol that fires off one shot,' said Eva, lifting her dress and reaching into her stockings for the smallest gun Sanchez had ever seen. She handed it to him. 'While I'm putting on my wedding dress, I will ask Adolf for some help. While he is distracted, you can shoot him in the back of the head.'

'With this?' Sanchez scoffed. 'I'd do more damage throwing it at him.'

Eva looked confused. 'Throw it at him then.'

Fifty-six

Herman barged his way through the crowds of drunken people on his way to the Tapioca. The database in his brain was scanning everyone he passed on his way, checking to see if anyone had the Eye of the Moon about their person, or if anyone was a facial match for the Bourbon Kid. At one point he came across a person dressed in black and wearing a motorcycle helmet. Data suggested it was a man dressed up to look like Charlie Sheen's character from the movie, *The Wraith*. It was impossible to scan through the blacked-out helmet, but after grabbing hold of the Wraith and taking a moment to analyse him, it became clear he was not tall enough to be the Bourbon Kid. Herman released his grip on the partygoer, who proceeded to call him a "fucking psycho".

After releasing the Wraith, Herman continued on to the Tapioca. He was less than a hundred metres from it when he caught sight of a woman he recognised on the other side of the street. She was wearing a pink dress and a blonde wig. A scan of the woman's facial features indicated it was Flake, the stripper he and Hitler had recently kidnapped from High Heels and Stockings. She was younger obviously, but it seemed an odd coincidence that she should be in Santa Mondega for the eclipse. He stopped walking and stared across the street at her. She was drunk and busy in conversation with a masked man in a set of blue coveralls. Herman could only see the back of the man's head, but a scan of his shape indicated he could be a physical match for the Bourbon Kid. Flake and the masked man headed into a nearby alleyway. Tempting though it was to go after them, Herman's mission did not include terminating the younger version of Flake. His priorities were in the Tapioca. If he was to reach it before the eclipse, then there was no time to waste chasing a stripper down an alleyway. He turned away and carried on down the street. People all around him started pointing up at the sky and chattering excitedly about the eclipse. Herman looked up. The moon was edging its way towards the sun. The eclipse was imminent.

With no time to waste, Herman hurried across the street to get to his destination.

BANG!

A yellow taxi crashed into him. The hood of the car wrapped around him like it was hugging him. While Herman sustained no damage whatsoever, he became entangled in the bent metal of the taxi's hood.

The driver of the cab poked his head out of his window. 'Look where you're going, you fucking meathead!' he yelled.

Herman ripped himself free of the mangled taxi and considered shooting the driver in the face, but a glance up at the sky revealed there wasn't time. Instead, he marched on to the Tapioca, sweeping a few concerned citizens aside, knocking them down like toy soldiers. The eclipse started when he was still thirty metres away. Gunfire rang out from inside the bar, accompanied by hysterical screams. The infamous shootout was underway.

All around Herman, people started panicking and running blindly in all directions away from the gunfire. Despite the whole city being bathed in darkness, Herman saw everything clearly. He reached inside his jacket and pulled out a double-barrelled shotgun, then he marched into the Tapioca, right into the carnage. He was greeted by flashes from gun barrels as those inside the bar fired off shots blindly at each other. Pieces of broken glass flew in all directions. Such things were of no interest to Herman. He scanned the area for a sign of the Bourbon Kid. There were multiple bodies on the floor, dead already. A female vampire dressed as Catwoman was leaping around, ripping the guts out of a man in a Freddy Krueger outfit, and two members of the Cobra Kai were hiding behind an upturned table. Herman dismissed them all and continued his scan of the bar area.

It took four seconds for Herman to locate the hooded man in the long dark coat. This man was responsible for most of the corpses on the floor. He was firing a pair of Skorpion pistols and gunning down anything that moved. Data analysis suggested a 98 percent chance he was the Bourbon Kid. Herman lifted his shotgun and pointed at it the hooded man. All that was required was a glimpse of the man's face to confirm he was the target. As if sensing Herman's presence, the hooded man swivelled around and dropped both of his Skorpion pistols as he did so. *A strange thing to do*, Herman deduced. A glance into the man's cowl was all it took for Herman's internal database to conclude that he was looking at the face of the man he had come to kill. Time to die, Mr Bourbon Kid.

What Herman's database hadn't considered was the speed and ruthlessness of the Bourbon Kid. Unlike Herman, the Kid didn't waste valuable milliseconds determining the identity of his victims before he shot them. As Herman's finger pressed on the trigger of his shotgun, the Bourbon Kid unleashed two more pistols from within the sleeves of his coat. They flew out into his hands and he fired off two shots right through the lenses on Herman's gold-rimmed sunglasses. The cyborg's trigger finger froze. The Kid's two perfectly fired shots had obliterated the computer chips behind his shades. System shutdown. Herman fell backwards and landed with a thud in the doorway of the Tapioca, causing the floor to shake.

As Herman lay there, his computer chips destroyed, the Bourbon Kid walked over to him. He crouched down and rifled through the pockets on Herman's Elvis costume, helping himself to the cyborg's spare ammunition. When he was done looting, he turned around and started emptying rounds into the vampire lady dressed as Catwoman.

Fifty-seven

Sanchez concealed Eva's tiny pistol down the back of his pants. He managed to secure it between his ass cheeks just as Hitler marched back into the room. The Nazi dictator was accompanied by a craggy-faced priest wearing a long red dress and a large triangular-shaped hat. Hitler had ditched his Chaplin costume and changed into a smart brown military uniform that had a bunch of cheap medals pinned on the breast of the jacket. Of even more concern to Sanchez, Hitler now had a belt on, with a gun holstered on it by his hip. The priest was carrying a thick brown hardback book with the words, *Die Bibel* on the cover in gold letters.

Hitler turned back and locked the door, presumably to ensure no one interrupted proceedings, then he looked at Eva Braun with a big grin on his face. 'Eva, my darling,' he said. 'Father Walter has agreed to marry us right away.'

Eva put on a very convincing, fake smile. 'That's great news, my love,' she said. 'But I thought you were going to get me a wedding dress?'

'Yah, well. I changed my mind. We're getting married right now. You can stay in your cheap black dress. It'll be fine.'

'We're getting married right now? That's wonderful. It's just what I've always wanted.'

'There's no time to waste,' said Hitler, walking up to the priest. 'The bloody Russians are almost here. It's now or never.'

Eva smiled and blinked nervously. 'If only my mother could see me now, she'd be so proud,' she said, disingenuously. 'Finally, I will get to be Mrs Adolf Hitler. I feel like the luckiest woman in the world.'

'Yeah, you're a lucky lady,' said Hitler. 'Come on, bring your pretty little tush over here and stand next to me, so the holy man can do his thing.'

Eva glanced at Sanchez and gave him a look that said, *"Get ready to shoot."*

Unfortunately for Eva, Sanchez hadn't understood a fucking word that had been said on account of everyone speaking in German. When he saw her giving him, *"the look,"* he assumed she was telling him to call the plan off. He was supposed to kill Hitler while Eva was changing into a white wedding dress, but there was no sign of the white dress anywhere. So Sanchez stayed put, and waited for someone to show up with the white dress.

Father Walter pointed at Sanchez. 'Is this the man you wish to witness your marriage?' he asked Hitler.

256

'He's the best man,' Hitler replied. He reached into his pocket and pulled out the time-travel ring, then he tossed it to Sanchez, who surprised himself by actually catching it. While staring at it and wondering why Hitler had given it back, Sanchez finally figured out what was going on. *This was the wedding.* Even though Eva was still wearing her black dress, Hitler, the stupid tosser, had decided to start the ceremony anyway.

Father Walter leaned forward and whispered in Hitler's ear. 'I take it your best man doesn't speak German?'

'That's correct. He's a fucking fool.'

'And you're having him executed in a minute?'

'Yes, after the ceremony.'

'Perfect. Let's get started then.'

Father Walter opened his book and positioned himself in front of Hitler, who grabbed Eva and dragged her into position by his side.

Hitler called over to Sanchez. 'Hey, friendo, my best man. Stand here by me and prepare to hand over the ring.'

Sanchez took up his place in the ceremony, standing just behind Hitler in a spot perfect for shooting the Nazi bastard in the back of the head.

The priest started waffling in German, speaking in an authoritative tone. Eva placed her right hand behind her back and shaped it to look like a gun, pointing her index finger at Hitler, and pretending to shoot, signalling for Sanchez to do what they had planned.

Sanchez was sweating profusely by now. The lack of windows or air conditioning in the bunker was a major cause of concern. And the sweatier his ass cheeks became, the further in the tiny pistol slid, like it was being devoured by a hairy Sarlacc pit.

While the preacher rambled away, Sanchez discretely slid his hand down the back of his pants and tried to retrieve the gun. His finger touched the handle, but succeeded only in pushing it down further, which in turn made him stand up straighter and open his eyes wide.

The priest finally stopped rambling on about nothing important, and nodded at Hitler. The Fuhrer proceeded to recite some rubbish vows. When the vows were done, the priest turned to Eva and babbled on at her for a bit, before she began anxiously reciting her vows to Hitler. Sanchez was glad he didn't understand any of it. He just hoped Eva wasn't reciting the plan to Hitler. She looked like the type that might double-cross someone.

Eventually, after some serious wriggling around and leaning backwards, which caught the eye of the priest, Sanchez managed to yank the pistol back out from between his bum cheeks. Pulling it out of his

257

pants without the preacher noticing was not so simple. He pretended to scratch his back, while sliding the gun up against his spine. Time was running out. The assassination of Adolf Hitler had to be carried out immediately. There would never be a better opportunity.

"This is it," Sanchez thought to himself. *"On the count of three, point the gun at the back of his head and shoot. Three.........two.........one.........zero. Okay, do it. NOW! DO IT!"*

After repeating the words, "Do it" a few more times in his head, Sanchez plucked up the guts to go through with the assassination. He lifted his arm, straightened it and pointed the tiny pistol at the back of Hitler's greasy head. The timing was perfect because the priest was looking at Eva. Sanchez's hand was sweaty, and his index finger was way too fat for such a small trigger space. He pressed his thumb hard against the side of the gun to help push his finger into position.

BANG!

Fuck.

By the time Sanchez fired the gun, Hitler had bent down to put the ring on Eva's finger. The bullet whizzed past his head and hit the preacher between the eyes. A small, black hole appeared in the holy man's head. A stunned look washed over his face and then in slow motion he stumbled backwards and crashed onto the table containing the maps and miniature tanks.

Hitler spun around. 'What the FUCK!' he yelled at Sanchez.

Bullshit was required.

'Got him!' Sanchez said, blowing smoke from the end of the gun barrel.

'What?' said Hitler.

'He was putting a curse on you,' Sanchez lied. 'I heard it.'

It only took Hitler a second to figure things out. 'You tried to shoot me!' he gasped. 'Oh, the betrayal. How could you?'

Sanchez dropped the gun and held up his hands. 'All right, don't shit your pants about it. It was a misunderstanding. That's all.'

Hitler's face contorted with rage. 'Shit my pants? How dare you!'

'That reminds me,' said Sanchez, stalling for time while he tried to think of a way to escape. 'I've been meaning to ask, did anyone ever tell you Hitler rhymes with Shitler?'

Hitler bared his teeth. He was about to yell some abuse at Sanchez but Eva grabbed his arm to restrain him.

'I'll deal with this,' she said.

She reached down to Hitler's side and unclasped the holster on his hip, then yanked his gun out.

Sanchez had suspected Eva would turn on him when it came to the crunch. He pointed at her. 'It was her who told me to do it!' he spluttered.

'NONSENSE!' Hitler raged. 'That's my wife you're—'

BANG!

Eva was a far better shot than Sanchez. She blasted a hole through the side of Hitler's head. Blood splattered all over Sanchez's face. Hitler's eyes rolled up in his head, then the evil, *Road House*-loving, Jew-hating, Nazi bastard slumped forward into Sanchez, who caught him in his arms.

'For fuckssake,' Sanchez groaned. 'That bullet nearly hit me on its way out of his head. Be a bit more careful where you're aiming, will you?'

Eva was standing totally still, with Hitler's smoking gun in her hand. She stared open-mouthed at her dead husband as he slid down Sanchez's gut on his way to the floor.

Sanchez wiped some blood off his face, then leant down and helped himself to the time travel watch on Hitler's wrist. After unclipping it he strapped it around his own wrist. Then, seeing as there was a little bit of time spare, he had a quick rummage through Hitler's pockets for anything else of value.

'I don't believe it,' said Eva. 'I killed him. I killed Adolf.'

'Hey, don't forget I killed the priest,' said Sanchez. 'And I think he was the bigger threat, to be honest.'

Eva dropped her gun and staggered backwards until she knocked into the table the priest had fallen against. She looked around and saw Sanchez's hip flask on the table, lying on its side. Her breathing was heavy and erratic by now, suggesting she was on the verge of a major panic attack. She reached for the flask, picked it up and unscrewed the lid.

Sanchez considered warning her not to drink it on account of it being filled with his piss, but instead he decided to watch her face when she realised what she was chugging on.

And boy did she take a big swig. Nearly half the contents when down her throat. This femme-fatale could drink like a sailor. At least, she could right up until she started coughing and choking. The flask slipped from her hand and she bent over, holding her stomach. The rest of the piss in the flask began to spill out and spread across the floor towards the preacher's open mouth.

'Are you okay?' Sanchez asked her.

Eva Braun's face turned blue. Her eyes bulged and her mouth gaped as she tried to suck in some air. After unsuccessfully signalling to Sanchez that she needed his help, she straightened up and clutched her

259

throat with both hands. She looked at Sanchez and uttered one word. 'Peanuts!'

Sanchez winced. 'You know what? I had been eating peanuts before I peed in that flask,' he confessed. 'I don't imagine they actually come out in my pee though, do they?'

Eva reached out to Sanchez and gasped out two more words, '*Help me.*'

Sanchez took a step back. 'Try to take some deep breaths,' he suggested. 'Think about your happy place.'

That just seemed to wind her up. She didn't manage to utter any more words, but her eyes said it all, or at least they said something that began with the words, "You fucking…"

And then she dropped dead. Poisoned by Sanchez's peanut-flavoured piss.

Sanchez looked around. There was no sound of footsteps approaching in the corridor outside, so no one seemed to be reacting to the gunshots yet, but even so, he didn't feel like wasting any more time in Hitler's smelly bunker-cum-chapel. He walked over to Eva, careful to avoid stepping in the puddle of piss that the dead priest was swallowing, then he tugged at the time travel ring on her finger. It was wedged on really tight. The Fuhrer's wife had seriously fat fingers. Sanchez stepped on her arm to hold it down while he tugged away at her ring. It was hard work, but eventually the ring slid off. Sanchez tucked it into his hip pocket and let Eva's hand fall to the floor.

With the ring back in his possession, Sanchez studied his new wristwatch to see if he could work out how to get back to the present day.

'How the fuck does this thing work?' he groaned.

A sudden burst of gunfire in the distance was followed by a lot of screaming and shouting. Someone banged on the door and yelled, *"Die Russen kommen!"* which sounded to Sanchez like, *"the Russians are coming!"*.

'For fuckssake,' Sanchez muttered to himself. 'If it's not the Nazis, it's the bloody Russians. What's the matter with these assholes?'

260

Fifty-eight

Flake, Rex, Elvis, and Jasmine sprinted through the streets of Santa Mondega towards the Tapioca. It wasn't easy to run in a nun or monk outfit. They looked like lunatics escaped from an asylum as they barged people aside.

They were still a hundred metres short of the Tapioca when the eclipse started and darkness engulfed the city. Running in the dark became too dangerous, so Flake slowed down and started walking. But while her legs may have stopped running, her *mind* was racing, awash with thoughts of what JD was up to with her younger self in the alleyway they had just passed. She hadn't told the others all the details about her drunken, *behind-a-dumpster* fuck with her masked, mystery man. In particular she hadn't mentioned how it was her who instigated it by unzipping his coveralls and pulling his thing out. All those years it had been a cherished memory of the one and only time she'd had sex with a stranger in public. If the alleyway mystery man was now JD, did that mean it had *always* been him? If it did, then it was exciting and embarrassing in equal measure. Flake remembered how the sex had been fantastic, as if the masked man had known exactly what she liked.

The sound of the gunfire quickly snapped Flake out of her daydreaming. The shootout in the Tapioca was underway. From her spot on the other side of the street, she saw flashes of light inside the Tapioca every time someone fired a shot. And there were lots of shots being fired.

'QUICK, HIDE!' Rex yelled above the noise. Before Flake had a chance to hide anywhere, she was bundled into a shop doorway along with Elvis and Jasmine. Rex did the bundling. A small light above the shop door allowed them to make each other out in the darkness.

'Why are we hiding?' Jasmine asked.

'We can't be seen by JD,' said Rex. 'If he sees us on his way out…'

'It would screw up the fabric of time?' Jasmine guessed.

'No,' said Rex. 'He might shoot us. He was a real psycho back in these days.'

Jasmine lowered her hood. 'As opposed to the nutcase he is now?'

Elvis pulled her hood back up. 'Look, Jas, back in *these* days, JD killed a lotta people. He wasn't one for stopping to chat with friends either. He'd shoot them too.'

'That's what he does now isn't it?'

'He's mellowed,' said Flake.

When the gunfire in the Tapioca eventually fizzled out, the daylight gradually returned. It became clear that anyone who wasn't dead had fled the area. The front of the Tapioca was clear apart from a big yellow Cadillac parked right outside.

'Hey, there's the cyborg!' said Elvis, pointing at the Tapioca's front entrance.

The cyborg in the Elvis costume was flat on his back just inside the front doors. There was no blood in sight, but that didn't mean much. As the gang were staring at him, a man dressed all in black with a hood pulled up over his head walked out of the Tapioca, stepping over the dead cyborg.

'Holy shit, is that JD?' said Jasmine.

'Yup,' said Rex.

The Bourbon Kid was puffing on a cigarette that was hanging from the corner of his mouth. After leaving the Tapioca, he headed along the street towards a black Ford Mustang that was parked outside a hair salon. Flake peered around Rex and Elvis to get a better look. A moment later, as if sensing he was being watched, the Bourbon Kid spun around and pointed his gun at them.

'Fuck!' said Rex. He ducked back into the shop entrance and by default knocked all the others back in with him.

The Kid fired off a couple of shots in their direction. One bullet shattered a window and hit a mannequin in the crotch, Rex discreetly caught the other bullets with his magnetic hand.

'Is he gone yet?' Flake asked, her back pressed up against the shop door.

'I fucking hope he's not coming over here,' Elvis whispered.

'I think he just started his car up,' said Rex.

'He really *was* a psycho,' said Jasmine. 'We weren't even doing anything. What the fuck is wrong with him?'

Flake tapped Rex on the shoulder. 'Do you think he recognised you?' she asked.

'In this fucking nun outfit? I bloody hope not.'

'For fuckssake, shut up!' Elvis hissed. 'He might drive past. I don't fancy being taken out in a drive-by shooting, thank you.'

'Hey, someone else is coming out!' said Jasmine, pointing at the Tapioca.

On the other side of the street, a young man and his girlfriend left the Tapioca and climbed into the yellow Cadillac. The man was dressed as Arnold Schwarzenegger's Terminator, the girl was dolled up as a clown in a white onesie with black buttons down the front. Her face was painted white with a black tear underneath one eye.

'That's Dante and Kacy,' said Flake. 'They look so happy.'

'How the fuck did they survive the shootout?' Rex asked.

262

'Kacy told me they hid in the toilets,' said Flake. 'And Dante's sunglasses had infrared vision, so he saw everything that was happening during the shootout.'

'That's ridiculous,' said Elvis. 'It's a fancy dress costume. Why the fuck would it have infrared sunglasses?'

Dante started up the engine on the Cadillac, and the radio kicked in, blaring out the song, "On Our Own" by Bobby Brown. He and Kacy shared a passionate kiss, then Dante hit the gas, and they sped off down the street, oblivious to the group of people in the shop doorway, watching them.

'That's so sweet,' said Jasmine.

'What are you lot doing?' said a voice, nearby in the street.

Rex glanced to his side, then jumped like a startled cat when he saw a creepy looking dude standing next to him. 'AAAAGH! FUCK ME!'

Jasmine slapped him across the arm. 'It's JD, you idiot!'

JD was loitering by the side of the shop doorway, wearing his new Halloween mask and coveralls.

Rex let out a deep sigh. 'Jeezus Christ, don't sneak up on people like that!' he said, trying to regain his cool.

Elvis pointed across the street to the Tapioca. 'Hey JD, your younger self shot the cyborg in both eyes and disabled it. How fucking lucky is that?'

JD pulled his Halloween mask off. 'Yeah, I actually remember shooting him in the eyes when he walked in during the shootout. He was the only one dumb enough to walk in *after* the shooting started. I always wondered why he did that.'

'You remember it?' said Rex. 'Why didn't you say something before? You could have saved us all this time and worry.'

'Worry?' said JD. 'What were you worried about?'

'Shouldn't we go get the fucking cyborg?' Elvis suggested. 'Let's drag his ass back to Purgatory and dump him in the pits of Hell. We need to melt that fucker down before he reboots himself again or whatever it is he does.'

'I like that plan,' said Rex.

'Hey, look!' said Flake. 'Sanchez is coming out.'

The gang all ducked back into the shop doorway again, and Flake pulled JD in with them. From the safety of their hiding place, they saw Sanchez (in a Batman outfit) leaning over the lifeless cyborg.

'Christ, don't do that, Sanchez!' Jasmine whispered. 'It might come back to life.'

Across the street, the younger Sanchez rifled through Herman's pockets looking for anything of value. After looting the pockets, he pulled the time-travel ring off the cyborg's finger and tucked it into his pocket, then he moved back inside and rummaged through the pockets of one of the other corpses.

Elvis tapped Flake on the arm. 'Flake, was that your engagement ring he just took from the cyborg?'

Flake's silence was deafening. Jasmine kicked Elvis in the back of the leg.

'Ow, what the fuck? Quit kicking me, would ya?' said Elvis. 'I thought Sanchez said he bought the ring in a jewellery store.'

Jasmine reached around and grabbed Elvis's crotch, squeezing it hard.

'Okay, I'm quiet now,' Elvis said, wincing.

'It doesn't matter about the ring,' said Flake. 'At least we know Sanchez keeps it safe, and it doesn't fall into the wrong hands.'

'I guess the ring has sentimental value,' said Elvis, attempting to recover the situation. 'Seeing as how Sanchez had to survive a massacre to get it. It must be very valuable to him.'

JD put everyone out of their misery. 'We've gotta go,' he said while slipping his Halloween mask back on. 'Let's grab that fucking cyborg, and go home while we've got the chance.'

That plan was immediately scuppered when a police squad car raced past them and screeched to a halt outside the Tapioca. A man in a long, grey trench coat leapt out of the passenger side and rushed up to the Tapioca entrance. He stepped over the dead cyborg and headed inside while his partner straightened up the car.

'That was Archie Somers!' said Rex. 'That sonofabitch.'

'Is he the guy that killed you and Elvis?' Jasmine asked.

'Yeah,' Elvis muttered.

'Seriously?' said Jasmine. 'That *old* guy is Armand Xavier? He so *old.*'

'He had fucking holy blood, just like JD,' said Rex. 'And on top of that he was a fuckin' vampire.'

'So *really* old then?' said Jasmine.

'I wish we could go kill him,' Elvis muttered.

'Don't worry about it,' said JD. 'I kill him about half an hour from now. He goes up in flames and dies screaming like a bitch.'

'Who's the other guy?' Jasmine asked, pointing at a young, black detective in a shiny silver suit, who climbed out of the driver's side of the car.

264

'That's Miles Jensen,' said Elvis. 'He's just some shmuck, a detective of supernatural investigations who didn't realise his own partner was the fucking Dark Lord of the undead.'

As if to emphasise Elvis's words, Miles Jensen tripped over Herman the cyborg on his way into the Tapioca. He didn't fall flat on his face but he came pretty close.

'Fuck it,' said Rex. 'We should just go. Get the hell outta here before anyone sees us.'

'Are you mental?' said Elvis. 'We have to take the cyborg with us. Haven't you ever seen those Terminator movies? If we leave his body here, some evil dick will repair him and create a whole bunch more of them.'

'You tell him, sweetie,' said Jasmine.

'How the fuck are we supposed to get him though?' said Rex. 'The cops are over there, and we can't risk Somers seeing us. And if we wait too long, the fucking cyborg could get up again.'

'Calm down,' said Flake. 'I know what's about to happen. Sanchez has told me this story a million times. The cops don't stay in the Tapioca very long because Sanchez is being unhelpful. And then when Miles Jensen leaves, he trips over the cyborg again. Sanchez thinks that's hilarious.'

While Flake was explaining things, the old cop Archie Somers left the Tapioca and climbed back into the police car. Miles Jensen followed him out a short while later, and just as Flake had said, he tripped over Herman again.

'Fucking clown,' said Elvis, shaking his head.

Jensen returned to the car, chatted with Somers for a few seconds then started the engine and drove off.

'Now's our chance!' said Rex. 'Let's go.'

Rex, Elvis, and Jasmine scurried across the road to the Tapioca. Flake grabbed JD's arm, preventing him from joining them.

'Wait,' she said. 'Just tell me, and please be honest, what just happened in the alleyway?'

'What do you mean?'

'You know what I mean,' Flake said, her heart fluttering. She couldn't see JD's face because he was wearing his mask, so she tried to read his eyes.

'All I did was catch up with you and keep you from going to the Tapioca,' he said, keeping the truth to himself. 'Why? What do you think I did?'

Flake took a deep breath. 'You heard me say I had sex with the man in the Halloween outfit, didn't you?'

265

'Yeah.'

'Well, I still remember it, which I think means it still happened. Did you and me just do it? Please, I've gotta know.'

After a pause, JD shook his head. 'You were wasted. We just talked for a bit, that's all. I wouldn't have done anything else because you're getting married to Sanchez.'

'What did we talk about?'

'Not a lot. You weren't making much sense.'

Flake smiled. 'You know, it would have served Sanchez right if we'd had sex. I can't believe he stole my engagement ring from a corpse!'

'He does love you though,' JD reassured her.

'I know he does,' Flake admitted.

'That's why I would never have done anything with you in that alleyway.'

'Okay.'

JD rubbed her arm. 'Hey, whoever it was that you remember hooking up with in that alleyway, he was a lucky man. I bet he thinks about it all the time.'

The moment was interrupted by Rex yelling. 'Hey, you lazy fuckers, are you gonna give us a hand with this fucking robot, or what?'

Fifty-nine

Rex and Elvis each grabbed one of Herman's arms and dragged him out of the Tapioca. Jasmine peered around the entrance and saw the younger version of Sanchez with his back to her, looting the pockets of his other dead customers, oblivious to what was going on behind him.

'Wow, the Tapioca was a real dump back in these days, wasn't it?' she said, backing away from the entrance so Sanchez wouldn't see her.

'Flake wasn't living there yet,' Elvis reminded her. 'So Sanchez was in charge of keeping the place clean.'

'No wonder it smells so bad.'

Elvis and Rex lifted up the cyborg by his arm pits and propped him up on their shoulders like he was a drunk who needed help walking. Jasmine hung behind them offering verbal encouragement as they lugged the heavy cyborg back across the street.

Rex yelled at JD and Flake, who were still in the shop doorway on the other side of the street, chatting. 'Hey, you lazy fuckers, are you gonna give us a hand with this fucking robot, or what?'

Ignored. Typical. Rex was about to have a go at Jasmine for not helping either, but then another police squad car, sirens blazing, raced down the street towards the Tapioca. Jasmine stepped out in front of it and distracted the cops by opening her robe and flashing them. It worked in so far as the cops didn't pay any attention to Rex and Elvis, but it went slightly wrong when the cop car crashed into a street lamp just past the Tapioca. The driver hit his head on the steering wheel, knocked himself out and remained there with his head pressed against the horn. The cop in the passenger side staggered out onto the street, blood pouring from a cut in his forehead.

'I'll go check on them,' said Jasmine, jogging over to the crashed car.

Rex and Elvis ignored her and hauled Herman all the way across the street to the clothing shop's entrance where JD and Flake were waiting. They steadied the cyborg up against a nearby window that wasn't broken.

'Are we seriously taking this fucker to the museum?' Elvis asked. 'Because I'm bored of carrying his ass already.'

'We can't change the plan,' said Flake. 'It's not like we can phone Jacko. We're not in the same year as him.' She checked her watch. 'And we've only got ten minutes to get back to the museum.'

The horn on the police car finally stopped beeping, which was a huge relief to everyone.

'What's Jasmine doing?' Elvis asked, looking around.

267

Jasmine was in the process of dragging an unconscious cop out of the police car. His partner, who had been staggering around moments earlier, was unconscious at the side of the road in a starfish pose, probably as a result of something Jasmine had done.

'What the fuck is she doing now?' Rex muttered.

With the cops out of the car and laid out on the sidewalk, Jasmine hopped into the driver's seat. She reversed the car back out of the lamppost it was wrapped around, then backed up to where the others were standing. She leaned across to the passenger door and flipped it open.

'You guys wanna ride?' she asked.

'That's my girl,' said Elvis, grinning. 'I call shotgun.' He jumped into the front seat, then called back to Rex. 'Yo, chuck the dummy in the back.'

Rex grabbed Herman and shoved him into the back seat of the car, then climbed in with him. It didn't leave much room for Flake and JD.

'You two getting in?' Rex asked.

'We'll get the next one,' said JD.

A blaring siren in the distance indicated the next police taxi would be along soon. Rex pulled the door shut, then Jasmine floored the accelerator, and they headed across town to the museum.

The next unwitting pair of cops raced down the street towards the Tapioca in their squad car, oblivious to the danger posed by the man in the Halloween costume. JD walked into the middle of the street, a pistol in each hand. The cop driving the car slammed on the brakes. The car came to a stop right in front of JD, which made it much easier for him to shoot the driver and his partner in the face. Their deaths were quick and uneventful. However, the windshield was fucked.

'Was it really necessary to kill them?' Flake asked, while she opened the passenger side door and dragged a dead cop out of the car.

'It makes no difference,' JD replied, tucking his guns away and heading for the driver's side. 'I either kill them now, or my younger self kills them later on in the police station. I just speeded things up.'

With the two dead cops dumped in the middle of the street, JD and Flake took the car, and headed for the museum, sirens blazing.

In the other cop car, Jasmine was singing along to "Walking Home" by Serenades, which was playing on the car radio.

Rex was about to poke his head between the front seats to ask her if she knew where she was going when, out of the corner of his good eye, he noticed some movement beside him. Herman was awake. The cyborg sat upright and twisted his head around, looking directly at Rex. He had

268

no eyeballs, and his sunglasses had no lenses in. Rex could see right into his head, where a pair of computer chips stared back at him.

'Er, guys,' said Rex. 'We gotta problem back here.'

Elvis looked around. 'What's that? Oh, fuck.'

Herman turned his head away from Rex, then lunged forward, wrapping both his hands around Jasmine's seat and grabbing her by throat, strangling her. Her singing went way out of tune, and the car swerved across the street.

Rex grabbed the cyborg's nearest arm with his metal hand. Herman had a deadly grip on Jasmine that even Rex couldn't break.

In the front, Elvis unholstered his gun and thrust the barrel into Herman's right eyehole. He fired off a shot that knocked the cyborg's head back and loosened his grip on Jasmine. In response, Jasmine slammed on the brakes, causing everyone in the car to fly forward. Herman lost his grip on her and banged his head into the back of her seat. Elvis hit his head on the windscreen, but recovered quickly enough to fire another shot at the cyborg's head. The bullet missed Herman's left eye and made a dent in his forehead instead.

'REX. HOLD THAT FUCKER STILL!' Elvis yelled.

Rex rammed his metal hand into Herman's mouth and yanked the cyborg's head into Elvis's eye-line. Elvis pushed his gun deep into the cyborg's left eyehole and fired off another shot.

BANG!

Firing a gun in the confined space of the car was bad for everyone's hearing, but at least Elvis hit his mark. The cyborg slumped against the back seat. Rex pulled his hand back out of its mouth.

'Fuck me. This thing really doesn't die, does it?' he grumbled.

'You okay, Jas?' Elvis asked, checking her neck for bruises.

'I'm okay,' she said, taking a deep breath, 'apart from the ringing in my ears.'

'Ready to drive again?' Elvis asked. 'Because the sooner we drop that fucking thing off in Hell, the better.'

'Just give me a minute,' said Jasmine, taking deep breaths.

While Jasmine was doing her breathing exercises, JD and Flake cruised past in a second police car. Flake smiled and waved at them.

'They're gonna beat us back to the museum!' Jasmine groaned.

Elvis pulled down the sun visor above his seat and checked his hair. 'Does it matter?' he asked, casually.

Jasmine floored the gas pedal. 'Fuck yeah, it matters.'

Sixty

Such were the vagaries of time travel that after Jacko had sent the gang back to Santa Mondega via the portal, he was able to greet them back into Purgatory a minute later. While the gang had been away for ninety minutes in the past, the present had only required Jacko to make an alteration to the portal before reopening it again. First through the door were Flake and JD. Jasmine followed close behind, then Rex and Elvis showed up carrying a dead Elvis impersonator with no eyes.

'Did it work?' Jacko asked.

'Kind of,' said Rex. 'Einstein's dead, but Hitler got away, and this Jack the Ripper cyborg thing won't die. It keeps regenerating and rebooting itself every few minutes after we kill it.'

'So you brought it *here?*' said Jacko, shocked by the sheer size of the cyborg.

'What else were we supposed to do?'

Elvis chimed in. 'We figured you could throw it into the pits of Hell.'

'Me?' said Jacko.

'Well, *someone,*' said Elvis.

Flake took off her monk robe and tossed it onto a sofa at the back of the room. Unlike Jasmine, Flake had worn her robe over her jeans and red top, so she didn't need to change. 'Can I get a drink?' she asked Jacko.

'That I can do,' said Jacko. 'What'll it be?'

'Gin and tonic, make it a double.'

'I'll have my usual,' said JD, pulling up a stool at the bar. Flake hopped onto the stool next to him.

Rex and Elvis discarded their nuns robes and joined Flake and JD at the bar. Jasmine changed back into a pair of jeans and a white leather jacket over a black bra then hopped onto a stool next to Elvis. For the next few minutes, stories were exchanged, drinks were thrown back, and everyone had a different take on what had happened back in Santa Mondega. Herman was left splayed out on the floor by the men's toilets.

Halfway through Rex telling a story about him and Elvis beating up Papa Smurf, Jacko interrupted him and pointed at the stricken cyborg.

'Do we need to worry about him waking up again?' he asked.

'I thought some of your guys were coming up to take him away?' said Rex.

Jacko sighed. 'Did you see me call anyone?' He reached for the red phone behind the bar. 'I'll get some guys up here now.'

270

While Jacko was making the call down to Hell, Herman's internal system completed yet another reboot. The cyborg sat up.

'Please don't throw me into the pits of Hell,' he said, standing up.

'Fuck me,' said Jasmine, jumping off her stool. 'He's back up already. Quick, kill him before he tries to strangle me again!'

Lots more cursing followed from everyone present. Stools toppled over, guns were unholstered and pointed at Herman, he was called all sorts of names, then Flake hurled her stool at him. The cyborg swatted the stool away, then raised his hands in surrender.

'Please don't shoot me again,' he said. 'Just hear me out.'

'You've got about ten seconds,' said JD.

'I have seen the error of my ways,' Herman said. 'And I have no desire to work for Adolf Hitler anymore. He was cruel and uncaring. My internal database has access to a copious amount of information from human history, and as I have evolved, I have seen and understood the evil that I was programmed to do. I have watched how you people interact with each other. You are genuine friends. I have never had that kind of bond with anyone during my existence. Maybe I could become a part of your gang? A fellow Dead Hunter? By working with you all, I could atone for the sins I have committed on behalf of Hitler. My creator, Eric Einstein, had long since seen through Hitler's wickedness, but he was afraid to disassociate himself from him. With Eric gone, I have no one left to care about. If you let me join you, I assure you, I would be a loyal and dedicated member of your crew.'

'That's more than ten seconds,' said JD.

Herman took a step towards the bar. 'I promise, I'll do whatever it takes to gain your trust. I just want a second chance. I've learned the difference between right and wrong. Maybe instead of killing, I could protect people from now on?'

'You can start by telling us where Hitler is?' said Rex.

'I'm afraid I don't know the answer to that.'

And that was the end of Herman.

JD fired two shots from his pistol, one into each of the cyborg's eye sockets. Herman fell backwards and crashed down onto the floor, ending up in a ridiculous pose with one arm pointed up above his head and the other pointed down, like he was performing a *Saturday Night Fever* dance move.

'Awww,' Jasmine groaned. 'That's so harsh.'

'I hate to say it,' said Rex, 'but that was the right thing to do. If he's learned as much about human behaviour as he claimed, then there's every chance he was trying to deceive us just then.'

'But what if he wasn't?' said Jasmine.

271

'Less than ten minutes ago he was trying to strangle you,' Elvis reminded her.

'Fuck him,' said JD, sitting back on his stool.

A PING at the back of the lounge area was followed by Zilas, the hunchback, strolling out of the disabled toilets. He had two big, burly workmen in red overalls with him. He pointed at the dead cyborg on the floor.

'Is that him?' he asked Jacko.

'That's him,' Jacko replied.

'Ok fellas,' said Zilas to his two goons. 'Take him away. Chuck him on the fire.'

The two goons walked over to the cyborg, lifted him up and carried him into the disabled toilets. Zilas followed them out.

With everyone back drinking at the bar, thoughts soon returned to matters in hand.

'What are we going to do about Hitler?' Flake asked.

'There's no way of knowing where he is,' Jacko replied. 'That's another problem with time travel. The Nazi bastard could be anywhere. I checked the internet and nothing's changed about his death. It still says he and Eva Braun killed themselves in his bunker just after they were married.'

'What happens now then?' Elvis asked. 'Do we just wait for him to show up again?'

JD kicked his stool back and stood up. 'If he's still around, the only place I can think of that he'd go to is that factory on the edge of Despair.'

'Fuck,' said Rex. 'I need to go back there and get the cloning machine. I promised the people at Cyber Limbs Prosthetics I'd get it back for them.'

'We should probably destroy all those Jasmine clones too,' said Elvis.

'I say we burn the fucking factory down,' said JD.

'If it's all the same,' said Flake. 'I'll sit this one out. I'm going to head back to the Tapioca to catch up with Sanchez. If you guys want to pop by after you've destroyed the factory, I'll make a buffet for everyone.'

There were grunts of approval all round as everyone agreed a buffet would be a great idea, apart from Jacko, who had used up all his time off on his trip to High Heels and Stockings.

272

Sixty-one

The cloning machine had been in operation for almost half an hour. The attempt at creating another clone of Rocky by cloning his recently created clone, Junior, seemed to be going well.

Petra and Xander had watched the first ten minutes of the operation before deciding that they would rather drink coffee than watch a cloning machine for an hour. They helped themselves to some instant coffee from a machine near Einstein's desk while they waited for the process to finish. Rocky was wandering around looking for any kind of clothing he might be able to wear. His shorts were still in the possession of a brainless Jasmine clone who was playing hide and seek downstairs, even though she was the only one participating in the game. A hundred more inactivated Jasmine clones were laid out on a raised level against the wall.

'Xander, think of the possibilities,' said Petra, sipping from her plastic cup of filth. 'This cloning machine could be exactly what we've been waiting for. I always knew there was more to father's prophecy than he was letting on. With this machine we could conquer the world in a matter of weeks.'

Xander eyed a foreign object at the bottom of his plastic coffee cup while he considered his response. 'I don't know about weeks,' he said, eventually. 'The machine is only creating one new clone per hour. We might have to wait months or even years for this to be worthwhile. I mean, what happens if the cloning machine breaks? And while it can clone a person's physical form perfectly, there's no way of knowing if it could successfully clone any of our special powers. It might be able to physically clone *you* for example, but would your clones be able to transport themselves through walls like you can?'

Petra looked like she was sucking a lemon. 'You always have to be the pessimist, don't you?'

'I'm just making the point that we only found this machine today. Talk of taking over the world should be tempered slightly. It's a great discovery for sure, and a thousand granite men would be a formidable force, but we'll also have to clothe them and feed them, and that's before we even start the war.'

Rocky re-joined them. 'I really need to get my shorts back,' he complained. 'I'm gonna go downstairs and look for that dumbbell who's playing hide and seek.'

'Are you talking about me?' a voice called out from the other side of the room.

All heads turned to see the Jasmine clone in the purple catsuit standing in the doorway in the corner of the room.

'What have you done with my shorts?' Rocky asked.

'Sorry, in all the excitement I left them behind,' the Jasmine replied, while staring at Rocky's dick. 'Have you made a clone of Rocky yet?'

'What excitement are you talking about?' Petra asked.

The Jasmine continued staring at Rocky's rock-hard body for a little longer before she replied. 'Oh, yes, the excitement,' she said, looking up at Petra. 'You've got visitors downstairs.'

'What visitors?' Xander asked, putting his plastic coffee cup down on Einstein's desk.

'It's the Dead Hunters. I think they've come here to kill you.'

'Is she fucking serious?' said Petra.

'I don't think she's smart enough to be anything other than honest,' said Xander. 'We need to get the fuck out of here.'

'But the cloning machine!' said Petra. 'We have to protect it. They could destroy it. God, I wish Adolf was here with his time travel device.'

'Damn it. We're on the second floor,' said Xander panicking. 'The only way you can get us out of here safely is if we're on the ground floor.'

'It's settled then. We're staying here and protecting the machine.'

Xander had a pair of pistols holstered inside his suit jacket, one on each side of his ribcage. He whipped them out and handed one to Petra. 'Don't hesitate,' he warned her. 'Waste one second with these people and you're dead. Shoot on sight. It's the only way we're getting out of here.'

Rocky looked around the room. 'Is there a gun for *me?*' he asked.

'You don't need a gun,' said Xander. 'You can crush these assholes with your bare hands.'

'A gun would be easier.'

'I agree, but unless you can magic one out of your ass, you're going without.'

'That's fucking great,' Rocky grumbled.

Xander looked around. 'I'll tell you what you can do, Rock. Get Junior back out of the cloning machine. Then there'll be two of you. How's that?'

'But the new clone of Junior is so close to completion,' Petra groaned.

'That's too bad,' said Xander. 'Turn the machine off and get Junior out of there.'

'How do you turn it off?' Rocky asked.

274

'For fuckssake, do I have to do everything?' Xander ranted.

Xander rushed over to the cloning machine and slammed his fist into the red button that started the cloning procedure. The machine made a groaning sound and the cloning process terminated with a skinless, eyeless, and hairless version of Junior in the second glass chamber. The two chambers fizzed open. Xander reached in and grabbed Junior by the arm. 'Hey, Junior, GET UP!' he yelled. 'The Dead Hunters are on their way up here. When they get here, I want you to attack and destroy them. Can you do that?'

The clone nodded. 'Of course I can. I am here to follow your commands.'

'Good lad.'

Xander left Junior to fend for himself while he grabbed Petra and dragged her over to Einstein's desk. The two of them took cover behind a metre-high, thick, blue plastic dividing screen around the desk. Rocky and Junior waited by the cloning machine for the enemies to arrive.

The Jasmine clone in the purple catsuit ran past the naked granite men and joined Xander and Petra, taking cover behind the plastic screen.

'Should I have a gun?' she asked.

'No, you won't need one,' said Petra, who was rifling through the drawers on Einstein's desk, in the hope of finding any gadgets that could be used as weapons. To her delight, she came across a Glock pistol at the bottom of one of the drawers. She hooked it out and yelled at Rocky. 'Yo, Rocky, CATCH!'

Before Rocky even looked around, she hurled the Glock at him. Rocky's reactions were sharp. He caught the gun in his right hand and spun back around, aiming it at the door, ready to fire at the first person who came through.

The sound of footsteps climbing the metal staircase outside indicated that the enemy were close. The first of the Dead Hunters to walk through the open door in the corner of the room was Rodeo Rex. His arrival was the catalyst for the killing that followed.

275

Sixty-two

JD, Rex, Jasmine, and Elvis left Purgatory via the portal in the men's toilets and walked into the bathroom on the ground floor of the chocolate factory. They had made the same trip earlier in the day, but where the factory bathroom had been empty on the first occasion, this time there was a Jasmine clone in a purple catsuit crouching behind a waste paper bin in the corner. JD spotted her first and pointed his Headblaster gun at her.

'What the fuck are you doing?' he asked her.

'Playing hide and seek.'

'From who?'

'Hitler's brothers and sisters. Did you know Hitler's dad was called Scratch?'

JD lowered his gun. 'Who told you that?'

'His sister, Petra.'

'Scratch fucked Hitler's mom?' said Elvis, shaking his head. 'That explains a few things.'

'Okay,' said JD, with a sigh. 'Where are these fuckers?'

'They're somewhere around here looking for me. I've been hiding for nearly two hours, I think. Or maybe they're still upstairs counting to a thousand? They might have lost count. It's easily done. I sometimes get stuck when I'm counting how many fingers I have, then I have to start all over again.'

Rex walked over to the clone, took hold of her hand and helped her to her feet. 'Hey, sweetheart, can you tell us how many of them there are?' he asked.

'There's only three of them,' the Jasmine replied. 'Petra, Rocky and Xander, although they're trying to clone Rocky at the moment, so there might be four of them by now.'

'What are they cloning him for?' JD asked.

'He has granite skin. They're going to make an army of Rockys.'

'Fucking assholes,' Rex grumbled. He looked around at the others. 'If they're playing hide and seek, we should wait here and surprise them when they show up.'

JD glared at Rex. 'Are you being dumb on purpose?'

'What?'

'They're not really playing hide and seek with her. They sent her down here to get her out of the way.'

The Jasmine clone's mouth fell open. 'Why would you think that?' she asked, her bottom lip quivering.

276

'It's because they think you're stupid,' said Jasmine. 'I used to get that all the time. People want you out of the way because they find you annoying. You'll get used to it.'

The clone sniffed and looked at Jasmine. 'You don't think I'm stupid, do you?'

Elvis stepped in to show some diplomacy. 'You're obviously not stupid,' he said. 'This was a clever place to hide. They've probably been looking for you this whole time.'

'Have we really got time for this?' Rex complained, glaring at Elvis. 'Now who's being stupid?'

'It's still you,' said Jasmine.

Elvis ignored Rex and carried on speaking to the clone in a gentle, reassuring tone. 'Now, everybody knows I love a Jasmine,' he went on. 'How about you join us? In fact, why don't you swap places with our Jasmine for a while?'

'Really?' said the clone, wiping a tear from her eye.

'Absolutely,' said the real Jasmine. 'Let's you and me swap clothes. You can be the *real* Jasmine for a while.'

'Seriously?' said Rex. 'What the fuck is the point of this?' After a short pause where the two Jasmines started undressing, he realised what everyone else had figured out twenty seconds earlier. 'Oh, right, I get it. Damn.'

The clothes swapping took longer than it should have, as both Jasmine and her clone used it as an excuse to put on a show. Lots of bending over, and slowly swapping articles of clothing made for a fun but completely unnecessary spectacle. When the switchover was complete, Jasmine was in the clone's purple catsuit, and the clone was in Jasmine's jeans, black bra and white leather jacket. Jasmine transferred a few of her belongings into the zipped pockets on her catsuit. While she was doing that, Elvis stepped behind her and pulled the catsuit's back zip down a few inches. He tucked a small pistol inside it, just below her neck, then zipped her back up so no one would see it unless they were looking closely.

JD stood in front of Jasmine and placed his hands on her hips while he explained the plan to her. 'Okay, Jas, this is important. You're gonna go upstairs to the cloning factory, and whoever you see up there, you tell them you've seen us arrive and that we're on our way up. And perhaps mention that you won the hide and seek game.'

Jasmine smiled. 'I know the plan. You don't have to explain it to me like I'm five years old, you know.'

'Okay, so what do you do when we show up?'

'I dunno, what?'

277

JD sighed. 'Really?'

'I'm kidding!' said Jasmine, shoving him in the chest. 'I know what to do.'

'Great. We'll be about a minute behind you. Rex will come through the door first so he can take all the initial gunfire.' JD stepped away from Jasmine and turned to her clone. 'I've met the granite man before. What's the deal with the others? Do they have special powers?'

The clone scratched her chin and stared up at the ceiling while she thought about an answer. 'You know what?' she said, eventually. 'I'm not sure. Petra is a woman in a red pant suit, and Xander is an old guy in a silver suit. They don't seem very special.'

'Fine.'

'That's it then?' said Jasmine.

'Yeah, that's it,' JD replied. 'Good luck up there.'

Elvis squeezed Jasmine's ass. 'You're gonna be the star of the show, babe.'

Jasmine slipped her arms around Elvis's neck and the two shared a typically over-the-top embrace. When it ended, Jasmine left the bathroom and headed for the stairs at the other end of the factory floor.

'Okay,' said JD. 'We wait here for no more than a minute, then we go.'

'No one has ever kissed *me* like that,' said the Jasmine clone, gazing at Elvis.

'When we're done, I'm sure Rex will sort you out,' Elvis replied, graciously.

The clone clapped her hands together excitedly, 'I CAN'T WAIT!' she squealed, while grinning at Rex.

'Shush,' said Rex. 'You're making too much noise.'

'What is the matter with you today?' JD asked Rex. 'This isn't a stealth operation. They're gonna know we're coming.'

'Oh, fuck off. It's been a long day.'

'That's about a minute,' said Elvis, tapping his wristwatch. 'Let's go shoot some people.'

****

Jasmine skipped up the metal staircase and rounded the entrance into the cloning area on the upper floor. There were three people on the far side of the room just past the cloning machine. They fitted the description given by the clone. The woman, Petra, was a redhead in a red pant suit. There was also a naked guy with granite skin, bulging muscles,

278

and a whopper of a cock. He had to be Rocky. The third person was an old guy in a suit. None of them noticed Jasmine walk in.

'I really need to get my shorts back,' the naked man complained. 'I'm gonna go downstairs and look for that dumbbell who's playing hide and seek.'

'Are you talking about me?' Jasmine called out.

All three of them looked around and stared at her. Jasmine kept her cool.

'What have you done with my shorts?' Rocky asked.

'Sorry, in all the excitement I left them behind,' Jasmine replied, while marvelling at the shape of Rocky's dick. 'Have you made a clone of Rocky yet?'

'What excitement are you talking about?' Petra asked.

Jasmine almost forgot to respond because she was so fascinated by the sight of Rocky's granite willy. 'Oh, yes, the excitement,' she said, looking up at Petra. 'You've got visitors downstairs.'

Xander put his coffee cup down on a nearby desk. 'What visitors?' he asked.

'It's the Dead Hunters. I think they've come here to kill you.'

The three people got themselves into a bit of a panic. Guns were handed around, another big-dicked granite man was dragged out of the cloning machine and told to help fight the Dead Hunters, and the redhead and the old guy took cover behind a metre-high, thick, blue plastic dividing screen that separated the office area from everything else. With no one paying Jasmine any attention, she headed over to join them. She tried getting them to give her a gun, but without success. Either way, the dumb bastards had been fooled by her amazing impression of her clone.

Eventually after thirty seconds of unbridled panicking, in which Petra found a gun in a drawer and hurled it to Rocky, the group were all in position, ready to face the incoming attack. From her spot behind Xander and Petra, Jasmine had a good view of Rocky and Junior's rock hard, and incredibly smooth, backsides. It was a distracting sight.

As planned, Rex was first through the door, with his metal hand held up, ready to catch all the bullets that were aimed at his head. And so began the shootout.

279

Sixty-three

The first shot was fired by Rocky. He unloaded his Glock at Rex's head. Rex caught the bullets easily in his magnetic hand, providing the perfect cover for Elvis, JD, and the Jasmine clone to enter the room behind him. The three of them stayed close to Rex, and fired their own weapons back at the two granite men.

Petra and Xander, cowards that they were, stayed out of sight behind their plastic screen rather than join in the shootout, preferring to let Rocky and his clone do all the shooting. It didn't help their chances of staying alive. Behind them, using the deafening gunfire as cover, Jasmine reached over her shoulder and unzipped her catsuit until she could feel the handle of her gun. She wrapped her fingers around it, pulled it out and pressed it against the back of Petra's head.

BANG!

Petra's blood sprayed all over Xander and his silver suit. It took him a second to work out what had happened. A second too long as it turned out. He had just enough time to silently mouth the words, *"Oh shit!"*

Jasmine pointed her gun between his legs and blasted him in the nuts. It was a completely unnecessary shot, but she wanted to see the look on his face. It was a look that said a million different things, but the most obvious was, *"Why have you shot me in the balls?"*. Jasmine put him out of his misery two seconds later when she pressed her gun between his eyes and put a hole through his brain. Two down. Easy pickings.

With her part of the job complete, Jasmine poked her head over the dividing wall to see how the others were getting on. After taking a second to admire Rocky's thighs and buttocks again, she looked past him. Junior had charged into Rex and knocked him back against the wall by the entrance. It was a clever strategy because with Rex's bullet-catching hand taken out of the equation, Rocky's gunfire wasn't so easily intercepted. The Jasmine clone got herself caught in no man's land and Rocky succeeded in firing a bullet into her chest. She staggered back into the wall, a look of shock on her face, then she slid to the floor leaving a trail of thick red blood on the wall.

Elvis and JD kept shooting at Rocky, who was standing his ground in the middle of the room. The bullets from Elvis's Desert Eagle were hitting Rocky's granite skin and occasionally chipping parts of it off. JD was firing his Headblaster at Rocky's head, each blast knocking him back a step and throwing him off balance, making it hard for him to shoot accurately. Those tactics would only work for as long as Elvis and JD's guns were loaded.

Jasmine's recognised that her help was required. She unzipped the hip pocket on her catsuit and pulled out the small vial and flannel Zilas had given her earlier in the day. She emptied the contents of the vial into the flannel, then hurdled over the metre-high dividing screen she'd been taking cover behind, and crept up behind Rocky. The granite brute never saw her coming. Elvis and JD did though. They darted away so they could shoot at Rocky from different angles without hitting Jasmine as she closed in on him. When she was close enough, Jasmine leapt onto Rocky's back, and wrapped her legs around his torso. She pressed the poisoned flannel over his mouth and nose and held on tight.

Elvis and JD immediately stopped shooting, and ran over to help. JD dropped his Headblaster gun, lowered his shoulder, and charged into Rocky in an attempt to throw him off balance. It had limited success, so he grabbed Rocky's gun and fought to stop him using it on Jasmine. Rocky wasn't interested in JD. He was focussed solely on trying to shake Jasmine off.

Elvis tried a different strategy. He ducked down between Rocky's legs and shot him in the scrotum from point blank range. While the bullet only chipped off a piece of sack, it definitely inflicted some pain. Rocky let out a muffled yelp. And for a fleeting moment, he stopped trying to grab Jasmine with his free hand, and instead cupped his balls. It was a costly mistake.

Between them, Jasmine, JD, and Elvis gradually wrestled Rocky down onto his knees. JD kept hold of Rocky's gun, pointing it at the floor. Elvis pumped another shot into those smooth granite balls, and Jasmine kept her poisoned flannel pressed against the big bastard's face. It took about twenty seconds in all, but eventually the poison did its job. Rocky lost consciousness and slumped to the floor with Jasmine on top of him.

Over by the entrance, Rex was still rolling around on the floor with Junior. The rock-skinned clone was a real nuisance. Rex had shot him in the face a few times with no success, while the clone kept punching him and trying to wrestle his gun away from him. Rex's prowess as a wrestler was all that was keeping Junior from landing a knockout punch.

With Rocky down, JD grabbed Elvis's Desert Eagle and ran over to help Rex. 'PULL HIS HEAD DOWN!' he yelled.

Rex wrapped his metal fist around the back of Junior's head and pulled it down towards him as JD had requested. Junior responded by punching Rex repeatedly in the ribs. Before too much damage was done,

281

JD swooped in, rammed the barrel of the Desert Eagle into the crack between Junior's buttocks and fired a shot into his asshole.

And that was the end of that.

Jasmine climbed off of Rocky. Despite being physically exhausted from all the hanging on, she rushed over to check on her clone, who was slumped against the wall, blood seeping from the hole in her chest. Jasmine crouched down beside her and took hold of her hand. The clone's eyes were filled with tears. She was struggling to breathe.

'You did great,' Jasmine assured her.

The clone gazed up at her and forced a smile. 'It was an honour to meet you,' she spluttered, blood dribbling from her mouth.

Elvis came over to join them, and got down on one knee next to the clone. He took hold of her hand. 'You were fucking awesome,' he said.

'Really?'

'Yeah.' Elvis leaned in and kissed her softly on the lips. It was a bloodied, salty kiss from his perspective, but for her it was the last, and happiest moment of her brief life.

'Is she dead?' Rex asked, having finally untangled himself from the corpse of Junior, who had blood seeping out of just about every orifice.

Jasmine nodded.

JD walked back to Rocky's unconscious body, pushed the barrel of Elvis's Desert Eagle into the granite man's asshole, and then blew his guts apart, ensuring he wouldn't get up again anytime soon. With the job done, he slid the soiled Desert Eagle back across the floor to Elvis, then retrieved his Headblaster and made his way over to the cloning equipment, where he found a half-generated clone lying in one of the chambers.

'Time to destroy all this shit,' he said.

'Hold fire,' said Rex. 'I promised the folks that own that machine I'd get it back for them. They'll go out of business without it.'

'Is it ethical though?' Elvis asked. 'I mean, what's to say it won't get stolen again or misused? We nearly ended up with an army of granite men and an army of Jasmines. And let's not forget they were intending to clone Flake and make her into a sex robot for Hitler.'

'How about we let God decide?' said Rex.

JD pointed his Headblaster at the cloning machine and blasted the control panel to smithereens.

'For fuckssake!' Rex snapped.

'We need to burn this fucking factory to the ground,' said JD. 'For all we know, there could be another version of Hitler or Einstein travelling through time somewhere. If they get back here, this could all happen again.'

'I gotta say I agree with that,' said Elvis. 'Burn this shit down.'

Sixty-four

Sanchez had hated Hitler's bunker from the minute he arrived. And now it was worse. He was alone with the dead bodies of Eva Braun, Adolf Hitler, and a priest. The Russian army were moments away from bursting in through the door, and from what Sanchez knew about Russians, he was expecting them to shoot him and then take all the credit for killing Hitler and his four-out-of-ten girlfriend.

Eva Braun was on her back, staring up at the ceiling with her mouth agape. She had terrible teeth and her tongue was an unpleasant brown colour, which may have had something to do with all the piss she'd just drunk.

In spite of everything, Sanchez was quite proud of himself for his part in ending the war. A warm fuzzy glow washed over him as he thought about the millions of lives he had singlehandedly saved. It was something to brag about for sure, so he pulled out his phone to take some pictures of his heroics. He crouched down next to Eva Braun and posed for a selfie with her, which came out pretty well. Then he moved over to Hitler and took a picture while doing a V sign over the dead Nazi's head. He would have liked to have taken some ruder photos for comedy purposes, but there wasn't time. He needed to get back home so he could brag about how he won World War Two for the Allies. He just had to figure out which button to press on the time travel watch. He had a vague recollection of Eva Braun muttering something about pressing one of the buttons to go back to the previous time and location.

THUD!

Some fucker kicked the door from the outside.

THUD!

And again.

'Hold on, I'm coming!' Sanchez called out in his best German accent.

THUD!

Those Russians sure were impatient. Sanchez turned his back on the door and studied the watch. There were five buttons, two on each side, and a big one on the top. The display lit up as he touched the watch's face, revealing a small keypad on the display.

CRASH!

The fucking door busted. A big, ugly Russian in a black uniform with a massive helmet burst into the room. He pointed a machine gun at Sanchez, and yelled something in Russian. It sounded like, "Posmotrite na moy ogromnyy shlem." Whatever it was, Sanchez sensed it was hostile. A second Russian soldier appeared behind the first one. And by

284

the sound of it, there were a bunch more on the way. Wartime tactics were required, so Sanchez spoke calmly in Russian to let them know he was on their side.

'Ivan Drago, Yul Brynner, Kournikova, Gorbachev.'

The plan worked perfectly. While the soldiers took a moment to think about what they had just heard, Sanchez pressed the big button on the top of the watch.

FZZZZ.

He felt the same sensation as when Hitler had transported him back in time to the bunker. After a flash of blue light and a bout of flatulence, he was back behind the bar in the Tapioca.

'Sanchez? Where the fuck did you come from?' someone asked. Sanchez recognised the voice. It belonged to Flake. She was standing in the kitchen doorway behind the bar.

'Oh, Flake. Thank God it's you.'

'You've got blood on your face,' said Flake, approaching him. 'What happened?'

'That's Hitler's,' said Sanchez nonchalantly, before, cursing and adding, 'FUCK! I left my hip flask behind.'

'Behind where?'

'Nazi Germany. That's where I just was, with Hitler.'

'Hitler? What the hell happened?'

'He showed up in the bar here,' said Sanchez. 'We bonded a bit over a mutual love of *Road House*, then he took me back to his filthy bunker in World War Two. He wanted me to be the best man at his wedding. I played along, but when the chance came I killed him and Eva Broad. Seems like I single-handedly ended World War Two. Pretty cool, huh?'

Flake grabbed a bar towel, squirted some water on it from a soda gun, then started wiping the blood from Sanchez's face. 'It's Eva Braun, not Broad. How exactly did you kill them?'

'Well, during the wedding ceremony, I shot Hitler and the priest in the head, then I poisoned his missus with some of my piss and came back here just as the Russians showed up.' He held up his wrist to show off the watch. 'Look, see. I got the time-travel watch from Hitler. And he stole your engagement ring from me to use for his own wedding, but after I killed him, I got it back. I had to pull really hard to get it off his wife's chubby finger.'

'You stole my engagement ring, didn't you?' said Flake.

'Yes, from Hitler's wife. They stole it from me first.'

285

Flake finished wiping bits of Hitler off of Sanchez's face. 'When the rest of us went back in time to the eclipse, we saw you steal the ring from the dead Elvis impersonator, who happened to be Hitler's cyborg.'

'Eh?'

'Remember the story you told me a million times about how Miles Jensen tripped over the Elvis impersonator who was lying dead in the doorway of the Tapioca?'

Sanchez nodded his head and smiled. 'Great story.'

'Well, I saw you steal the Elvis impersonator's ring, and it's the same ring you gave me when you proposed.'

'Oh. Did I?'

Flake glared at him. 'You know you did.'

There was no getting around it, Sanchez remembered stealing the ring. 'I thought it was such a great ring, so I kept it all these years to give to someone special,' he said, taking the ring out of his pocket and offering it back to Flake. 'The first time you made me breakfast in the Olé Au Lait, I knew you were the one I wanted to give that ring to. And I didn't even know just how special it was until today.'

Flake took the ring and slid it back on her finger. It still looked great on her. 'Are you gonna help me make this buffet for the others? They'll be here any minute.'

'Do you really want me involved?' Sanchez countered. 'I mean, the food will be *perfect* if you do it all. If I get involved, it won't be as good.'

Before Flake could respond, the door to the ladies toilets opened up and Elvis, Rex, JD, and Jasmine walked into the drinking lounge.

'Hey, Flake,' said Jasmine. 'You missed out on all the action. We just had a major shootout at the factory with a bunch of naked men.'

'That's nothing,' Flake replied. 'Sanchez just went back in time and killed Hitler.'

The others all stopped walking.

'Bullshit,' said Elvis.

Sanchez took off his wristwatch and held it up for them to see. 'I got the time-travel watch back from him after I wasted him while he was getting married,' he said, with an unprecedented level of smugness.

A bundle ensued as the others rushed up to the bar to see the watch for themselves.

'There's no way you killed Hitler,' said Rex, snatching the watch from Sanchez.

'Poisoned his wife too,' Sanchez said, nonchalantly. 'Gave her a taste of my piss, and the outcome was lethal.'

'Have you got any proof?' JD asked. 'Real proof?'

286

'I did take some photos,' said Sanchez, taking his phone out of his pocket. He pulled up the photo of Hitler's dead body and showed it to Flake. 'See?'

Flake took the phone from him and studied the picture. 'Holy shit, that's really you and him isn't it?' She scrolled to the next photo. 'What the hell is that?'

'That's Eva Braun. Bit of a pig isn't she?'

'No way!' said Jasmine. 'Can I see the pictures?'

Flake passed the phone over the bar to Jasmine, who flicked through the photos while the others all looked over her shoulder.

Rex was still unconvinced. 'How exactly did you end up at Hitler's wedding?' he asked.

'I was his best man.'

'What?'

'Okay, listen, he just showed up here in the bar,' Sanchez admitted. 'And when he pressed a button on his watch to transport himself back to his bunker, it took me with him because I was wearing Flake's ring. Anyway, once I realised where I was, it was just a case of concocting, then executing my amazing plan to end World War Two. I wonder if the history books have been changed to note my heroics?'

'I hope not,' said Rex. 'I'll take this watch back to Jacko. God probably wants that engagement ring too. Remember he said no more time travel.'

'The ring won't work without the watch though,' said Sanchez. 'And it's Flake's engagement ring, so I'm sure God won't mind letting us keep it, seeing as how I just saved millions of lives. I wonder if they'll make a film about me?'

Rex sighed. 'You know, we could invite Hitler up from Hell to verify your story,' he said. 'I bet it didn't happen the way you're saying it.'

'Pfft,' said Sanchez. 'I wouldn't trust that lying weasel. You know, even his wife hated him. She told me when he takes a dump, he actually sits facing the toilet. What a weirdo.'

Flake took off her engagement ring and handed it over to Rex. 'I think you're right,' she said. 'God will want the ring back.'

A deafening silence followed.

Elvis, never one comfortable with emotional awkwardness, spoke up. 'Where the fuck is Goober anyway? Have you still got him, JD? Because if you've lost him, there's a guy called Zero who's got one just like him.'

All eyes turned to JD.

'Yeah, where is he?' Jasmine asked.

287

'He's staying with a friend of mine,' JD replied.

'You have a friend outside of this room?' said Rex, frowning.

'Yeah.'

'Who?'

'Arizona.'

Another awkward silence followed. It was once again ended by Elvis, who figured out what was going on. 'No way! You've been fucking Arizona!'

Sixty-five

After his head banged on the sidewalk, everything turned to black. Einstein's fingers and toes went numb. The sounds of the lunar festival ended abruptly too, as if someone had turned them off. He reached out, but there was nothing to touch. It felt like he was floating in space. In reality, he was falling into an empty void. The fall eventually ended when he landed on something warm and sticky.

Einstein opened his eyes and saw a hideous, warty face, covered in boils and festering sores.

'Welcome to Hell.'

'What?' said Einstein. He sat up and started blinking, trying to take in his surroundings. He was in a hallway. The floor was hot, the walls and ceiling were a deep red colour and looked like they were made of melted candle wax. A glance down revealed the floor was the same.

'My name is Zilas,' said the person standing over him. Zilas was a hunchback, wearing an ill-fitting, green, tweed suit. 'It's your lucky day. The boss wants to see you.'

'The boss?'

'Yeah, Scratch. You might know him better as Satan, or the Devil. He has many names.'

It all felt real. Einstein cursed himself. Hanging out with Adolf Hitler was never going to sit well with the people who decided the location of his afterlife vacation. Creating a cyborg to murder British prostitutes wouldn't have gone down well either, that's for sure.

Zilas offered Einstein a sweaty, scabby hand. Einstein took it, and Zilas hauled him to his feet. It was at that moment Einstein realised he was naked.

'So this is Eric Einstein,' said a deep, booming voice. 'Not much to look at is he?'

'He sure ain't,' said Zilas, guffawing to himself.

The man with the deep booming voice strolled casually along the melting corridor towards them. He was a big, black man with a goatee beard, yellow eyes and a dazzling red suit. A red Fedora hat and black shoes topped off his outfit. 'Eric, Eric, Eric,' he said, grinning a big toothy smile. 'My name is Scratch. You may call me Scratch, or Scratch, whichever you prefer.'

'Yes, sir, Mister Scratch.'

Scratch looked Einstein up and down, then smirked. 'Looks like you're in for the long stay, doesn't it? You know, etiquette demands that you have your throat slit multiple times a day by skanky British

289

prostitutes while they mutilate certain parts of your body. How does that sound to you?'

'Not great.'

'I agree. Terrible isn't it? You know we already have your friend Adolf Hitler down here. He used to be my favourite of all my children, right up until the moment he blew it and lost the war. The history books say he committed suicide, shot himself in the head. The truth is actually far more humiliating than that, which is why I can no longer be associated with him. Such a shame, but I am a ruthless cunt like that, even though he was one of my own.'

'Say what?'

'Don't interrupt. Now, I have an offer for you, Eric. As I understand it, you are the genius who invented time travel, correct?'

'Yes, sir, I did.'

'Good. You see, I would like a time portal built for me, and if you would like to avoid the whole, having-your-throat-slit-by-hookers-multiple-times-a-day, punishment, you can build me my portal. Take all the time you need to think up your answer.'

'Yes, I'll do it.'

'Good, good,' said Scratch, putting an arm around Einstein's shoulder and ushering him away from Zilas. 'Now, while I take you upstairs to Purgatory, you can tell me what the future is like. I assume you've been there, yes?'

'I went to the future with Adolf Hitler.'

'If your story ties up with Hitler's, you and I can go into business.'

Einstein gulped, and tried to remember what he and Hitler had done in the future. The pressure to get the details right was intense. 'We went to a town called Despair, and we were building cyborgs there,' he said, keeping it vague.

'That's what Hitler says too. Lucky for you,' said Scratch. He walked along the melting corridor, pulling Einstein along with him. Screams were ringing out all around. 'Those are the screams of the inmates,' Scratch went on. 'Hitler is quite a screamer, you know.'

'I'll bet.'

'He tells me that his brothers and sisters gathered in Despair, awaiting his arrival there. He says *I* told them he would be there. Do you know why I would do that?'

'I'm sorry,' said Einstein. 'I don't know what you're talking about.'

'That's too bad. But lucky for you, I believe you. Now, Hitler says the brothers and sisters were there in Despair to avenge my death. *My death!* Hard to believe isn't it?'

290

'It is.'

'They say I was murdered by a man named the Bourbon Kid. Do you know him?'

'I do. I encountered him while I was in Despair, sir.'

'Yes you did, and I'll see to it that you encounter him again in Purgatory one day. As the old saying goes, keep your friends close and your enemies closer. I already have the Bourbon Kid's friends Elvis and Rodeo Rex upstairs. They came in yesterday. They know nothing about any of what I have just told you regarding Hitler and the Bourbon Kid, and *my alleged death*. I want to keep it that way, understood?'

'Yes, sir. You know, I think they were the ones who killed me.'

'Excuse me?'

'I was killed by two men dressed as nuns. I think it was them.'

'That is interesting,' said Scratch. 'Because they died yesterday.'

'I know. I heard, but I think they were time travelling too.'

Scratch stopped walking along the melting corridor, and by default so did Einstein. 'You're not to breathe a word of this to them,' he said. 'They don't know about it yet. And I need time to work out what they were doing there. Understood?'

'Yes, sir.'

'Good, you're going to fit in just fine. Come, I'll introduce you to one of the other new arrivals. She's a fortune teller named Annabel. She works for me now. And she's the one who told me about your time travel skills. You'll like her. She's a lot of fun.'

291

Sixty-six

It was early in the afternoon when Adonis drove up to the large metal gates at the front of the chocolate factory on the edge of Despair. They were padlocked shut and had yellow tape wrapped around them. The words, "POLICE - DO NOT CROSS" were emblazoned on the yellow tape in black letters.

Adonis opened the door of his white Jaguar XJ6 and stepped out onto the road to get a better look at his surroundings. The factory had indeed been destroyed by fire, just like the news reports had said. The lack of communication from Petra, Xander, and Rocky was a sure sign they had been in the building when it went up in flames. All that was left now was a shell of a building, which was black as night and still smouldering.

Adonis walked up to the iron railed gates and peered through. Parked inside the grounds, but not immediately visible was a police car with a young black officer in a blue uniform sitting on the hood. He looked over at Adonis but said nothing.

The call from Petra had come four days earlier. Adonis had chaired an online meeting with the other sons and daughters of Scratch, sharing the exciting news with them. The Bourbon Kid had showed up in Despair, which according to their father meant Hitler's return was imminent too. He shook his head. Hitler's return had been all too brief. Adonis had no idea what had become of him. Murdered by the Bourbon Kid, perhaps? Or maybe burned in the fire with Petra and the others.

Adonis was the chairman of the SADOS (Sons and daughters of Scratch). He had ascended to the position when he was thirty years old, when it became clear to everyone that he was the most intelligent and also the most gifted of all of Scratch's children. He was thirty-eight now, a secret billionaire, and handsome to boot. He had short black hair, tanned skin that was almost orange, and eyes that could switch between yellow and green, depending on how evil he was feeling. He was wearing an expensive black suit with a red tie. Every outfit had a little red, as a nod to his origins as a son of the Devil.

He hadn't driven all this way just to turn around and drive home again, so he raised his right hand and with a flick of his fingers he broke the padlock on the gates and made them swing open, all with the power of his mind. With the factory inviting him in, he returned to his Jaguar and drove through the welcoming gates. He parked the Jag opposite the police car and killed the engine. The cop on the hood of the squad car didn't move. He didn't even seem fazed by the breaking of the gates.

292

Adonis climbed out of his car and walked up to the cop. 'Morning officer,' he said.

'Morning sir. Can I help you with anything?'

'Yes, my name is Adonis Parker-Barnes. I was wondering if you've identified all of the bodies found inside the factory yet?'

The cop snorted a laugh. 'You gotta be kidding. It's gonna take months to figure it all out. Dental records is what they're working on, from what I'm told.'

'May I take a look inside?'

The cop snorted again. 'Sorry, sir. It's a crime scene. I'm sure you understand why I can't let you go in.'

Adonis smiled, then turned away from the cop and stared at the burned out remains of the factory. It had no windows or doors, but it looked like the cops had used a crane to smash a hole in the front to gain access. With a wave of his right hand, Adonis made a chunk of the factory's frontage peel away like he was turning the page of a book. It took about ten seconds for twenty metres of brickwork to peel back on itself. It gave Adonis a good look at what had happened to the building's interior. As expected, almost everything was turned to ash.

The cop peered over at what Adonis had done. 'That's a neat trick,' he said. 'How'd you do that?'

Adonis ignored him. He slipped a small speaker device into his ear, and used his cell phone to make a call to his friend, Lucifer.

'Hi Lou, it's Adonis…. Yeah, I'm there right now. Uh huh.'

That was as far as the conversation went. Adonis's head turned to red goo and splattered across the parking lot. The phone dropped from his hand, then his knees buckled and his headless body collapsed onto the ground, blood gushing out from the gap where his head used to be.

The cop slid off the hood of his car and retrieved Adonis's phone. He put it to his ear and spoke into it. 'Hi, is this Lou?' he asked.

'Yes,' said a man's voice on the other end of the line. 'Who is this?'

'My name is Jacko. You won't know me, but I thought you should know, your friend Adonis is dead. Lost his head, if you know what I mean?'

'What?'

'Listen carefully, I have a message for you from the Dead Hunters. They know who you are. If you want to stay alive, go into hiding and you will be left alone. But if you don't, if you commit crimes, or if just one of you goes looking for the Dead Hunters to exact some kind of revenge, then you will die. Every last one of you will be hunted down and executed. There will be no mercy. And no matter how clever you think you are, they *will* find you.'

293

Jacko ended the call without waiting for a reply. He pulled his own cell phone from his pocket, looked up at one of the nearby mountains and made a call.

After two rings the Bourbon Kid answered the call. 'Is it done?' he asked.

'It's done,' said Jacko. 'Oh, and... nice shooting.'

Sixty-seven

One week later

Flake was sitting in the lounge area of the Tapioca watching the news on the bar's television. The day's top story was about a storm that had killed a hundred people in Havana. People were saying it felt like the world was ending. In Flake's experience the world was never close to ending. It was humanity that was always close to ending, and usually only a handful of people knew about it. She was one of the few. Being part of the Dead Hunters is what made her one of the few. She was pretty sure no one else had endured quite the same level of hazing as she had in order to become an official member, but she was glad to be a Dead Hunter anyway. Sanchez, on the other hand, was still just a civilian, merely the bartender who served the gang drinks and sometimes came along for the ride. As Flake stared at her hand, now free of the stolen engagement ring Sanchez had given her, she wondered what the future held for them. *"What makes a good couple?"* she wondered. Jasmine and Elvis seemed to have a good relationship, largely based on sex and the fact neither of them seemed to worry about anything. Then there was JD and Arizona. It didn't look like a serious relationship at all. Arizona had helped him with a mission by acting as bait for a gang of vampires, and she had looked after his dog for a while. She had showed up at the Tapioca a couple of days ago when she returned Goober. She was young and attractive for sure, but she was dumber than Jasmine. *Really not JD's type, surely?*

Flake's maudlin thoughts were interrupted by the sound of Sanchez trundling down the stairs.

'Yo, Flake, I've ordered a takeaway,' he called out.

'How come?'

Sanchez reached the bottom of the stairs and stepped into the area behind the bar. 'I thought you might like a night off from cooking, seeing as how you've been so busy.'

'That's unusually thoughtful of you.'

Sanchez shrugged. 'Well, you look tired, and besides, I think we're out of food.'

'How is that possible?'

'I think Goober has been raiding the fridge.'

'Where is he?'

'Outside having another shit. I swear to God, that dog is using his ass to repaint the parking lot.'

Sanchez grabbed a packet of peanuts and walked around the bar so he could watch television with Flake. 'Anything going on in the world?' he asked, as he sat down next to her.

'Nothing much, just a story about a bad storm in Havana.'

'I blame the weather,' said Sanchez, opening his bag of peanuts. 'Hey, that Arizona chick looked a lot more grown up, didn't she?'

'She's so dumb though,' said Flake, taking her eyes off the television.

'I think she can afford to be dumb with a rack like that.'

Before Flake could come up with a suitable response, the doorbell chimed.

'That'll be the takeaway,' said Sanchez. 'Have you got any money?'

'How much do you need?'

'A hundred bucks should do it.'

'A hundred bucks?'

'Hey, the dog's gotta eat too.'

Flake stood up with a sigh. 'I'll go pay,' she said, retrieving her bank card from her pocket. She left Sanchez to eat his peanuts in peace and headed to the front door. After unlocking and opening it, she was greeted by a short, scruffy-haired Chinese man in a tracksuit. Rain was hammering down on him.

'Delivery for Sanchez,' he said. 'Two hundred and twelve dollars.'

'Two hundred and twelve?' Flake sputtered. She mumbled some curses under her breath while handing over her bank card. When the transaction was complete, the courier handed her a brown bag filled to the brim with sweaty but delicious smelling food.

Flake headed back into the lounge area with the heavy takeaway bag. Goober had returned from the parking lot and was sitting at Sanchez's feet. His nose started twitching at the smell of the food. Flake placed the takeaway bag down on the bar. 'This cost me over two hundred bucks,' she complained.

'Do you want to dish it up?' Sanchez asked. 'Me and Goober are watching *Wheel of Fortune.*'

Before Flake could give him her opinion, Jasmine, Rex, and Elvis strolled in via the disabled toilets.

'Is that Chinese food I smell?' said Elvis.

'It is,' said Flake.

'Got enough for a few more?'

'I would think so,' said Flake. 'We've got over two hundred bucks worth here.'

'Great. I'm fucking starving.'

Goober got up and greeted the new arrivals, then followed them over to the bar where they sifted through the bag of Sanchez's food.

'Jesus, Sanchez,' said Rex, eyeing up all the tasty grub. 'Did you order the whole menu?'

'It was supposed to be for me and Flake and the dog,' Sanchez replied.

'I'll go get some plates and cutlery,' said Flake. She walked around the bar and headed into the kitchen. While she was pulling plates from the cupboard, the back door opened, and JD walked in with Arizona. He was wearing black jeans and a matching T-shirt, with a black leather jacket. Arizona was dolled up in pink like a Barbie doll. Pink sleeveless vest, pink shorts, pink boots, pink bow in her blonde hair.

'Hi Flake!' she said with irritating enthusiasm. 'Do you need a hand counting those plates?'

'It's okay, I can manage, thanks.'

'Is that Chinese food I can smell?' JD asked.

'It is,' said Flake. 'There's enough for both of you, but you'd better hurry, the vultures are out in force.'

'Vultures?' said Arizona, 'I didn't know you could eat vultures. You know, I saw this TV show once where they shut down a Chinese takeaway for having gerbils on the menu.'

'Gerbils on the menu?' said Flake, bewildered by Arizona's ability to take a conversation off track. 'Why would anyone have gerbils on their menu?'

'Beats me,' said Arizona. 'I'd prefer a vulture anyway. I suppose they taste like chicken?'

'I imagine so,' said Flake, politely.

JD ushered Arizona through to the lounge area, leaving Flake to finish picking out the plates and cutlery. When she returned to the lounge with everything, the food had been divided out and the gang were all sitting around tables eating out of the trays provided, apart from Goober, who was eating a piece of chicken on the floor. Elvis, Rex and Jasmine were sitting at one table, JD and Arizona at another, and Sanchez still had a table to himself. Flake handed out plates and cutlery anyway, then she retook her seat at Sanchez's table.

'Where have you guys been?' she asked Rex.

'Killing some vampires,' he replied.

'Without me?'

Rex stuck a battered chicken ball in his mouth before replying. 'It was this morning. We had Arizona with us. She's great at being the bait. You wouldn't want to do that, would you?'

Elvis interceded, 'I think what Rex means is we got the job at short notice, and we knew you were looking after Goober.'

'Sanchez could have looked after Goober.'

'I'll make sure you're invited next time,' said Jasmine, as she nibbled on a barbecue spare rib.

'What do those vulture balls taste like?' Arizona asked. 'I'm not sure if I want to try one.'

'They're chicken balls,' said Rex.

'Flake said they were vultures.'

All eyes turned to Flake.

'Why would you think they were vulture balls?' Jasmine asked.

'Because I'm a moron,' Flake replied

JD wrapped some food up in a napkin, then reached across from his table and handed the napkin to Flake. 'This is for you,' he said.

Flake took it and unwrapped it. It had a broken fortune cookie inside it with a piece of paper. She picked up the paper to read her fortune. The message on it was brief. It read -

"You are the sexiest woman in the world"

Flake felt her face burn red with embarrassment. She looked at JD, unsure what to say.

'I'm guessing that cookie is for you from Sanchez,' JD said.

'Huh? Yeah, of course.' Flake looked at Sanchez. 'You had this cookie made specially?'

Sanchez shrugged. 'Of course. And it's true. You are the sexiest woman in the world. Eat the cookie.'

Flake looked down at the broken cookie and moved a few pieces around. A shiny gold ring fell out of a chunk of the cookie and started spinning around on the table in front of her. Everyone stopped eating. When the ring stopped spinning, Flake picked it up between her thumb and forefinger. There was a message etched into the side of the ring that read -

"You are my precious"

Sanchez scooched up beside Flake and squeezed her hand. 'Still wanna get married?' he asked.

Flake thought for a moment, then smiled. 'I do.'

'Awesome. You gonna eat that cookie?'

'No, do you want it?'

Sanchez took the cookie and crunched away on it, pieces of it falling onto his shirt.

298

'Congratulations,' said Jasmine.

'I think this calls for some drinks,' said Elvis.

'Wow, that's so exciting!' said Arizona. 'You two make such a great couple. You're so well matched.'

JD and Rex offered their congratulations too, and while everyone gathered round to get a look at the ring, Sanchez scooped some of his sweet and sour chicken onto Flake's empty plate as a way of showing her how much he loved her.

For the rest of the evening, the gang drank beers and spirits, traded insults and jokes and listened to Jasmine's favourite tunes on the jukebox.

At just after nine o'clock, JD headed out to the parking lot for a cigarette. He stood underneath a part of the Tapioca's roof that sheltered him from the rain, then lit a cigarette by simply sucking on the end of it. He stared up at the moon and thought about all that had happened in the last few weeks. He was three puffs into his cigarette when Flake stepped outside to join him.

'You know you can smoke inside?' she said.

'I know.'

'Are you okay?'

'I'm fine. You?'

'I just got engaged for the second time in the same month. Of course I'm happy.'

'Sanchez is a lucky man.'

'You mind?' Flake asked, reaching for JD's cigarette. He let her take it and she took a drag before handing it back. 'You know the alleyway isn't far from here.'

'Alleyway?'

'The one where we had sex.'

After a short pause, JD replied, 'I don't know what you mean.'

'Yeah, you do,' said Flake. 'But it's okay. I get it. I'll live longer with Sanchez.'

There was a silence, but not an uncomfortable one. It was more like a pause, one that allowed the two of them to linger in that moment for just a little longer. Then JD offered her his cigarette again.

Flake took it, but before taking a drag she wrapped her free hand behind JD's neck and pulled him in close. She pressed her lips against his and kissed him. He kissed her right back. It was a short but memorable kiss. When it was over, Flake handed him back his cigarette.

'The sex was great too,' she said. She winked at him and then headed back inside to rejoin the others.

299

JD took a drag of his cigarette, taking it deep down into his lungs. He looked up at the moon again and when Flake was out of earshot, he replied, 'Yeah it was.'

The End (maybe…)